THE FELLOWSHIP

WILLIAM TYREE

PRAISE

for William Tyree's Blake Carver Series

"The Fellowship is a smart and stunning brew of shadow operatives, double agents, renegade scientists, secret societies, historical precedent and globe-hopping action that is both immensely entertaining and startlingly plausible."
– *Ragazine*

"The Fellowship has enough twists and turns to keep even the most demanding thriller fan happy, but Tyree binds it all together with the sort of taut prose that keeps you turning the pages and makes it hard to put down."
- *Paul Harris, author of The Candidate*

"Superb second novel...Tyree's reimagination of The Black Order, an organization of pious assassins with some historical basis, is what makes this one of the year's best thrillers so far."
- *BestThrillers.com*

"An espionage thriller for our times."
-Amazon.com Breakthrough Novel Award review for Line of Succession

"Line of Succession clips along at an astonishing pace with verve and grace, giving us no choice but to root for the complicated characters at the book's core."
- Jerry Gabriel, author of Drowned Boy

"Believable in its particulars and chilling in its implications, Line of Succession will keep you up at night long after you've turned the final page."
- Keir Graff, author of The Price of Liberty

"*Line of Succession* is a gripper that won't let go."
- Book Boogie

THE FELLOWSHIP

Published worldwide by Massive Publishing.
ISBN: 978-0615830391
Library of Congress Control Number: 2013909551
Copyright © 2013 by William Tyree

All rights reserved.

This book is a work of fiction, as are all books in the Blake Carver Series. Names, characters, places and incidents are products of the author's imagination or are used fictitiously. Any semblance to actual events, locations, names or persons living or dead is entirely coincidental.

No part of this book may be reproduced or stored in a retrieval system, or transmitted in any form or by any means, electronic, mechanical, photocopying, recording or otherwise, without express written permission.

Story by William Tyree. Edited by Michelle Dalton Tyree. Proofed by Jacqueline Doucette. Cover design by Damon Za.

The scanning, uploading and distribution of this book via the Internet, mobile network or any other means without the permission of the publisher is illegal and punishable by law. Please purchase only authorized electronic editions, and do not participate in or encourage electronic piracy of copyrighted materials. Your support of the author's rights is appreciated.

For Michelle, Layla,
and my grandfather,
who served with the 70th Armored Infantry Battalion
when the world needed it most

PART I

Caracalla Baths
Rome

The second act of the Teatro dell'Opera's outdoor production of Attila was coming to a close. Performed in the ruins of the Caracalla Baths, the 1800-year-old carved stones were tinged in magnificent red light under a starry Italian sky. And the actress playing the warrior maiden was just bludgeoning the audience with her vocal chords.

Adrian Zhu looked up at the postcard-perfect scene before him, drinking it in, trying to preserve it within his memory. In less than two minutes, his world would change. And in less than 10 days, he would change the world.

As Verdi's music swelled in preparation for the climax, Zhu felt his business partner, Spencer, tense beside him. Hours earlier, they had capped off the third stop in a lecture tour that had showcased their latest achievement and set the tongues of the European biotech community wagging. Although Zhu had been the unqualified star of the show, Spencer's role as sideman had been the highlight of his career.

This was the happiest he had seen Spencer in the three years since they had moved their company, LifeEmberz, from Boston to Beijing. He was riding high on Italian beer, opera and unregulated hotel WiFi. They had been accompanied to Rome by two high-ranking government officials and a couple of their best lab assistants. Spencer loved traveling with an entourage.

But Zhu was all too aware that this joyride was about to end. His friend would soon be inundated with interrogations by detectives and bureaucrats. He would be subjected to unimaginable scrutiny. Their corporate offices, and even their apartments, would be torn apart by investigators. Spencer would certainly be banned from the government research lab. He might even be forced to go back to the U.S.

Onstage, the actress playing Odabella raised her knife to stab Foresto. Three conspirators cried out, and the stage went black. As expected, a brief intermission was announced. It was time.

Zhu rose from his chair. "Be right back."

His colleague rose and raced after him, nearly knocking over an old woman. "You getting more beer?"

Spencer and the others had gotten smashed in the VIP area before the play. Zhu had been there too, but he had only pretended to drink, finding opportunities to drain his beer in the restroom on multiple occasions. This was the biggest night of his life. He needed full control of his faculties.

"Just hitting the restroom," Zhu said.

Spencer glanced at his black sport watch. "I might as well join you. Gotta make room for more beer anyhow."

The crowd began to stream around them as they headed for the restrooms and concessions. Where was the exit his contact had told him to take? And even if he found it, how could he shake Spencer?

At six foot five, Spencer towered over the much smaller Zhu. He was usually a gentle giant, but when he was drinking, he could get carried away. One year back in Boston, after the Patriots had made it to the AFC championship game, Zhu had watched his inebriated friend pick up a plus-sized woman, lift her up onto his shoulders like a toddler, and do laps around the stadium.

"I never guessed Italy would be this great," Spencer said now. "We should open an office here, dude! Everyone is so friendly."

These feelings of alcohol-inspired world unity were the same ones Adrian Zhu had felt years before. One of his early LifeEmberz projects had sought to clone and grow human skin. He had then gone to a tissue-engineering conference in Paris where he had met a burn victim who had benefitted from his research. He had been greeted as a hero. Zhu felt like he was on top of the world. But everything had changed after they moved the business to China. The money had been fabulous, but the corruption and the politics had gradually left him feeling empty and immoral. But now he had perspective on it. China was just part of his journey. It had all led him to this moment.

Now he saw the sign for Exit 16. The one his contact, Lars, had told him to take.

"I think I'm gonna be sick," Zhu said, placing a hand over his mouth. He dry-heaved, hoping the performance would be enough to gross Spencer out and send him back to their seats.

"You still can't hold your liquor!" Spencer roared, pulling his phone out of his pocket. "Ha! Tell me when you're gonna hurl. I'm gonna get this on video!"

Zhu stooped slightly as they emerged into the autumn night. The scientist scanned a small grove of trees and stone benches. Spencer was still fidgeting with the camera on his phone. Zhu ran out and ducked behind the shortest, thickest tree he could find.

He had to think fast. He had virtually no fighting skills. Even as drunk as Spencer was, there was no way Zhu would be able to subdue his massive friend, nor could he outrun him.

"Hey pukester!" Spencer called as he stumbled closer.

Zhu stepped back, nearly falling as he slipped on an empty beer bottle.

A beer bottle. Of course. He picked it up and raised it high above his head. He waited for Spencer to duck underneath one of the lower branches. Then he brought the bottle down hard over his partner's skull.

To his amazement, the bottle didn't break over Spencer's head, but the blow dropped him to his knees.

"Ow! Okay, okay! I won't video, all right? Just calm down!"

Heart pounding within his chest, Zhu sprinted through the grove and toward Via Antonina, across which he saw a parking lot full of taxis and buses. Spencer gave chase, and it was only moments before his long strides nearly made up the distance between them.

Zhu barely noticed the headlights of the black Range Rover flash as he sprinted across the busy street. He was already on the other side when he heard the sickening thud of a body against the SUV's grill, followed by a screech of tires.

The bioengineer stopped, looked back and glimpsed the broken and bloodied body sprawled on the pavement before the headlights turned away. It was Spencer. He stood frozen as the Range Rover's motor gunned again and swerved in his direction. A group of taxi drivers was running toward the scene of the accident.

Zhu wandered back out into the street and knelt at Spencer's side. A smear of tire cut across his business partner's khaki pants. His eyes rolled backwards into his head as his body convulsed.

The vehicle pulled up alongside him. The driver pushed the passenger door open. He wore driving gloves and a tight leather jacket that was crisscrossed with gunmetal-colored zippers.

"Get in!" he shouted in German-accented English.

National Counterterrorism Center
McLean, Virginia

Blake Carver peered at his opponent through the black mesh of his fencing helmet, right foot forward, waiting for the telltale sign of an imminent lunge. At six feet tall, he was at a slight disadvantage over his lankier opponent. His counterpart held his foil out to the side, as if inviting Carver to attack. But his right foot betrayed his true intentions. He lifted his toes slightly, preparing for a *balestra* – a short forward hop that would end in a quick thrust. Anticipating the move, Carver responded with a deft parry riposte to the gut.

The sprawling intelligence complex had taken a page out of the Silicon Valley office model. The newly expanded gym provided spaces where employees could join pickup games of basketball, foosball, handball and even fencing, which was surprisingly popular among the agency's left-brained workforce.

Carver knew the agency's facilities investment was designed to keep him working harder and longer hours than were really good for a person. But Carver didn't mind hard work. Having been tied to a desk job these past few months, he found the gym a welcome refuge from the endless hours spent in front of a computer.

Carrying a bag full of pricey foils, the younger analyst had entered the gym bragging about his exploits fencing on a championship team at Princeton and, later, with the U.S. National Team. Carver had also come to fencing in college, although his experience was hardly Ivy League. After failing to make the swimming team at the University of Arizona, the swim coach had waved his hand at the bronzed hardbodies chatting each other up in tight speedos around the sun-drenched pool. "These aren't your people," the coach had told the future intelligence operative. "Go on over to the rec center. The fencers practice in the basement. You've got the wingspan for it."

It was true that Carver's arms were freakishly long in comparison with the rest of his body. "Orangutan Arms," his sisters had called him. So against his better judgment, Carver had followed the coach's advice. But upon seeing members of the fencing club, he instantly resented the notion that these were "his people." They had been, without exception, engineering students with bad skin and worse social skills. Nevertheless, it had taken him only one private lesson to get hooked. He found fencing simultaneously cerebral and physical, like chess with swords.

He had only recently had time to come back to the sport after a 15-year hiatus. One of the only positives to a situation that had found him tied to a desk. It wasn't going so badly today. He had now scored eight touches in a row on the younger man with the fancy pedigree, and the analyst's mounting frustration would only continue playing to Carver's advantage.

"Again," the analyst said wearily. He was stiff now, standing nearly straight up. He had a bad habit of moving his blade in a predictable semi-circular oval pattern while preparing an attack. Carver had knocked the foil out of his hand a few minutes earlier, and now the analyst clutched the grip hard, decreasing his flexibility.

Carver bided his time, waiting for the next offensive. When it came, Carver angled his body away from the lunge, pivoting with his rear foot while simultaneously bending down and thrusting. A well-executed *inquartata*.

The analyst went into a rage, ripping off his mask, hurling it across the room.

"Agent Carver?"

The voice belonged to Arunus Roth. The skinny kid in the secondhand suit standing in the doorway was the last person Carver expected to see in the gym. Roth was 100 percent geek. His idea of a workout was an all-night hackathon with friends.

Roth scurried over to him. "We need you in the NCC," he said. "It's Crossbow."

Carver removed his helmet, running his fingertips through his gentleman's haircut and down his sideburns, which had always been slightly too long for conservative Washington. He stuffed his blade into the oblong gray sports bag containing his work clothes and headed for the door. It was drizzling as they made their way, walking and talking, across the sprawling campus. The Office of the Director of National Intelligence, or ODNI, was located, along with the National Counterterrorism Center, in one of the most modern complexes in the agency system. Its lone downside was its physical location, which was far from downtown D.C. and even farther from CIA headquarters.

"What's happening?" Carver said.

"Zhu's team was attending the opera," Roth said.

"Was?" Carver said, checking his watch. "It shouldn't be over yet."

"I'm getting to that."

"Is Callahan there?" Their man on the ground in Rome, Thomas Callahan, had only last night managed to infect Zhu's phone with malware that would allow them to both intercept his communications and track his location.

"Yeah, Callahan was there. His seats were about 10 meters behind Zhu's. He'd just called in saying Zhu and his partner had stepped out for intermission. Then all of a sudden, I get an alert that Zhu's on the move."

Carver walked faster. "What do you mean, on the move?"

"He was suddenly moving at 60 miles per hour, or about 96 kph."

"Stop converting everything to metric."

"Sorry. Okay, so then Callahan calls in. He says there was just a hit and run outside the Caracalla Baths. He has no idea where Zhu is."

"Great."

"At least we can still track his location."

"Don't be so sure. You said Callahan didn't see where Zhu went. For all we know, he tossed the phone into the back of a truck, and it's zipping along the freeway right now while Zhu is busy watching the third act."

The two men entered the National Counterterrorism Center, a massive X-shaped structure. Carver stood for a moment on the concourse, looking down on the pods of analysts dutifully going about their business. Immense screens on the room's outer walls displayed feeds from websites, TV stations, satellites and cameras around the globe.

"Are we getting any data from Zhu's phone?"

"Already intercepting data," Roth said. "We have full touchpad monitoring on his device, so we can see anything he does, bro."

Had the kid really just called him "bro"? He took a deep breath, reminding himself that Arunus Roth was only 21 years old. Like many of the agency's newest geek recruits, he hadn't even finished college. The American university system wasn't producing nearly enough computer science degree holders these days, and venture capital-funded companies were out-recruiting the federal cybersecurity teams.

Last year, Roth had been expelled from an Albuquerque community college for playing an elaborate prank. Roth had used his burgeoning hacker skills to infiltrate the school's vocational aptitude software, which several thousand new students were required to take each year. During the college's busy enrollment week, the administration office had been flooded with complaints after the guidance software recommended that students pursue a variety of unusual occupations, including Alpaca husbandry, buffalo slaughter and gang thuggery.

Roth may not have been disciplined enough to stay in school, nor was he brilliant enough to head out on his own and create the next Facebook. But in this talent-starved environment, he was good enough to groom for cybersecurity work. As a first step, he was on track to spend one probationary year doing technical mission support, which meant doing pretty much anything Carver asked of him.

Now they proceeded down the stairs toward Roth's pod. "What about voice monitoring?" Carver asked. "I want a recording of everything he says."

"I'm trying to make that work. Should be able to get it done tonight."

Carver checked his watch. The timing of this couldn't have been worse. He was due to give a briefing on Crossbow in an hour.

Rome

The Range Rover's velocity took Adrian Zhu's breath away. He hung on as the vehicle weaved in and out of the rows of headlights racing toward the suburbs. Zhu cast a sideways glance at Lars. Although the two men had met numerous times during Lars' trips to China, he hardly recognized him tonight. The security specialist had dyed his hair black and styled it into a short, fashionable cut. He was clean-shaven now, and he had gotten some sun on his face. He could have easily passed for a local.

He didn't know what title Lars held in the organization, or how he had joined. He only knew that the Shepherd himself had entrusted Lars to deliver him safely.

A few minutes later, Lars swerved the Range Rover abruptly into the parking garage of a large hotel. His black shirtsleeves had receded, revealing a set of thick, veiny forearms.

"The Shepherd is here?" Zhu said.

Lars didn't answer. He took a ticket at the parking gate, then drove quickly up the second-floor ramp, then the third, and finally to the fourth, where there were no other cars. He pulled into the middle of the otherwise empty row and kept the vehicle idling.

He activated a small silver device about the size of a credit card and pointed it directly at Zhu. A blur of yellow numbers began flashing on the device screen. It seemed to be scanning frequencies. Some type of bug detector, Zhu figured. It seemed that Lars was a cautious man. He wanted to make sure Zhu wasn't wired.

The German's serious, black eyes rolled up at Zhu. "What's in your pocket?"

Zhu pulled out his phone. He turned it this way and that in his hand, as if to demonstrate its innocuousness.

"Not good," Lars said. "They can track our location with it. Pull the battery out."

"Okay, but can I keep the phone for later? All my pictures and stuff are on it."

"No." He pointed to a white handkerchief neatly folded into a cup holder. "And wipe your fingerprints off the door panel and anything else you touched."

Zhu wasn't used to being talked to like this. Even his customers within the Chinese government treated him like a prince. "What's the point?" he said. "Spencer's blood is already all over the grill."

"Just do as I say, and you will survive." He pulled a duffel bag from the back seat and tossed it into Zhu's lap. "Then change clothes. I have a motorcycle waiting on the other side of the garage."

Zhu unzipped the bag and found a pair of black jeans, a motorcycle helmet, a white V-neck T-shirt and blue Superga sneakers. He picked up the helmet and flipped down the visor. It was painted black.

"The Shepherd is in a secret location," Lars said, explaining the blackout visor. "Trust me. A helmet is more comfortable than a blindfold." Then Zhu saw them. Over Lars' shoulder, a black Mini Cooper with tinted windows pulled up abruptly. There would have been nothing particularly threatening about such a small car, except that the cockeyed parking job made it clear that they didn't intend to stay long. The passenger-side window lowered.

The bioengineer's eyes suddenly expanded into coin-size saucers. Before Lars could turn to see what had frightened his passenger, the Range Rover's driver side was taking automatic gunfire. The side windows were instantly crystallized. Zhu ducked for cover.

National Counterterrorism Center

Carver stood in a darkened conference room, pointing a laser dot at a magnified surveillance photo. His jet-black hair – a gentleman's cut that was closely cropped around the sides, but short on top – was still damp with perspiration. The speed with which Crossbow had spun out of control had stunned him. He rubbed his unshaven chin with the back of his hand and looked at the five agency suits sitting around the conference table. The briefing had been planned as a simple FYI describing the ground game in Rome. Now it was damage control.

"The objective of Operation Crossbow," he started, "is to gain visibility into what military projects this man is working on. His name is Adrian Zhu."

He drank from a water bottle as the bigwigs in the room got a good look. The snapshot Callahan had taken at the opera showed Zhu with longish black curly hair, a small, angular face and black plastic designer eyeglasses.

"Zhu is considered one of the world's most brilliant bioengineers," Carver said. "He was born in Boston to first-generation Chinese immigrants. After dropping out of MIT, he hooked up with a business partner, Spencer Griffin, and started a biotech firm in Boston called LifeEmberz. Who here has heard of them?"

None of the suits raised their hands.

"You wouldn't have. In the early years, they worked in the shadows using private funds. But let me ask another question. Who here has had their genome decoded in the last year?"

Three out of the five people in the room raised their hands.

"LifeEmberz had a hand in making that possible. Before they tackled it, this was something that only the super-rich could afford to do. It cost about a hundred thousand dollars per person, and even then, the evidence of whether you were really carrying a Parkinson's gene, or a cancer gene, was pretty iffy. Within four years, LifeEmberz and its partners advanced the technology so much that the basic testing kits were being sold in over the counter."

"Who funded them?" The voice belonged to Claire Shipmont, the agency's deputy director. Like most everyone in the room, this was her first exposure to Operation Crossbow. She was a highly regarded career fed who, it was rumored, would soon be tapped to run Homeland Security.

"Good question. They were funded by an anonymous group that was so protective of its privacy that they actually delivered the seed money in cash. God knows what kind of kickback they got when LifeEmberz got bored of the genome business."

Carver advanced to the next slide, which showed a silent video of Adrian Zhu standing over a mummified body. "This was taken in Egypt. After LifeEmberz sold their genome decoding technology to a medical testing company, they used the money to do whatever interested them. One project had them utilizing the mitochondrial DNA found within hair samples to do what Zhu called 'extreme paleo-DNA' work. He was interested in exhuming dead bodies, preferably of people who had been dead for more than 300 years, and using the DNA within hair samples to find out things about them. For example, eye color, skin pigment, even defects that might have caused their deaths."

"And people paid them for this?" Shipmont said.

"We don't know. LifeEmberz never filed another U.S. tax return."

"They closed down?"

"I'm getting to that." Carver clicked to the next video clip, which showed Adrian Zhu, wearing a biohazard suit, working in a spotless lab. "Zhu had an idea that if LifeEmberz could exhume the body of one of your ancestors – a grandparent, for example – and extract mitochondrial DNA from it, they might be able to then take your embryonic stem cells and in a lab environment, create fertilized eggs that were just like your ancestors, but genetically superior."

"And that freaked people out," another voice said. Julian Speers, the Director of National Intelligence, had slipped into the back of the room. Speers had been the White House chief of staff under the previous administration before current president Eva Hudson offered him the role as her intelligence czar.

The move had been a controversial one. Speers was a superb operational manager, but he had no prior intelligence experience. Although the appointment had raised a lot of eyebrows, Speers was only the latest in a line of White House chiefs to head up a federal agency. Ronald Reagan's chief of staff, James Baker, had gone on to become secretary of the treasury, and later, secretary of state. Bill Clinton's chief of staff, Leon Panetta, had been appointed CIA director and later, secretary of defense. The theory was that operational expertise, coupled with a lack of specialty knowledge, could actually be an advantage. They were, by nature, forced to make decisions based on the big picture.

But heading up the ODNI was an enormous job, and one that even Carver didn't know if his friend was up for. Speers was now a cabinet member with oversight of the entire intelligence community, including the CIA, FBI, NSA, Homeland Security and other agencies.

"Glad you could make it," Carver said. "And you're right, of course. LifeEmberz threw themselves into all kinds of controversy. At one point they were getting a couple hundred death threats a week. Mr. Zhu packed his company up and moved their offices to Beijing."

"Why China?" Shipmont said.

"Besides a hot economy? Forty-two percent of the population is agnostic or atheist, and about 30 percent subscribe to folk religions, like Taoism. That equated to a lot less moral judgment about his research."

Speers stood in the back of the room, churning his right hand in a circular motion to get Carver to hurry up.

"Fast forward a couple of years," Carver continued. "The company's assets in the U.S. were frozen due to tax delinquency, and they needed money. So they accepted a commission from the Chinese government to improve child nutrition in rural areas. They got way more than they bargained for. LifeEmberz created a new breed of supercattle, achieved by leveraging a blend of mitochondrial DNA and nuclear DNA, and using what Zhu calls extreme cloning techniques. In the past week, they've told audiences at Oxford, University of Edinburgh and Sapienza University that they've reduced the per-animal cloning process to less than a week."

"Impressive," Shipmont remarked without enthusiasm. "But from a security standpoint, I still don't know why we care about this guy."

Carver dropped his laser pointer. "We think the Chinese government commissioned LifeEmberz to work on military programs. We fear at least one might be a bioweapon. And we think another involves cloning, uh, supersoldiers."

The room got quiet. The DD chuckled. "As in *Attack of the Clones*?" she said, referencing the Star Wars storyline.

Speers stepped forward. "That's right. Supersoldiers. A clone army. Go ahead and laugh, but I know people here in Washington who have discussed it with a straight face."

"But it's been difficult to get to Zhu," Carver said. "So when we heard that LifeEmberz was going on the lecture circuit, we decided to use the opportunity to get close to him."

The DD leaned forward. "Get close to him?" she said. "Why didn't we just hack in and plant the malware remotely?"

Oh yeah, Carver thought. For that matter, why didn't they just take him out with a drone strike? He was so tired of questions like this. Any operation that required an actual human on the ground was automatically questioned, and anything that could be handled via remote control from a secret government facility in the states was automatically applauded. Nobody understood that espionage was still a high-touch business. It was as much about psychology and relationships as it was technology.

Speers scratched his salt-and-pepper goatee. "Blake, I think Claire's question is a reasonable one. Why did we need an operative on the ground to hack into a phone?"

"Stealth," Carver said quickly. "Every LifeEmberz employee, including Zhu, now uses a device that's issued by the Chinese government. If we hacked into their network to get control on one or more specific mobile accounts, it's only a matter of minutes or hours before they detect the intrusion and start looking for us. Our solution is completely local, and allows us to reach one user at a time without the risk of getting past numerous gatekeepers. This way, the malware could theoretically go undetected for as long as he used the phone."

"Smart," the DD admitted. "But expensive."

"We just got some footage of Zhu's lecture from our contact in Rome," Carver said. "I think you'll find one part of the presentation very illuminating."

The door to the back of the room opened. It was Arunus Roth, and he looked even paler than usual. He drew an imaginary line across his neck.

"Sorry, everyone," Carver said. "We've gotta cut this short. Thanks for coming. I'll reach out to each of you to reschedule."

As the suits filed out of the room, Arunus Roth made his way to the front. "The hit and run victim is Spencer Griffin," he said.

Carver sat down. "And Zhu?"

Roth shook his head. "Callahan overheard the other LifeEmberz employees saying they can't get hold of him. They think he might have been kidnapped."

Carver's blood ran cold. If Zhu really was working on some sort of supersoldier project, or even an advanced bioweapon, there could be any number of countries that might want the secrets he had locked up inside his head.

"Well, we know where he is, right? Maybe we should go in."

"Slow down, bro."

"Don't call me bro."

Carver looked up. Speers was standing behind the kid. He had heard the entire thing. "You're asking for the go ahead to extract Zhu?"

"Think about it. His employees are convinced he's been kidnapped. If we could find him, we could bring him back to the U.S. for his own safety. And in the process, of course, have a chat or two about the work he's been doing."

"I was trying to tell you," Roth said, "That's not possible now. The phone, as far as we can tell, traveled very quickly three kilometers away. Zhu either went underground, or into something like an elevator or parking facility, or he pulled the battery out. The GPS just stopped chirping."

"So we're completely blind," Carver snapped.

"Yes."

"Where the hell was Callahan?"

It wasn't that the field operative was at fault, Carver knew. He wasn't even supposed to tail him – the malware in his phone was supposed to keep tabs on him. It was just that Carver wished it had been him there in Rome. He was jealous. This remote operations consulting stuff wasn't him. He had been born to be out in the wild, not cooped up here, thousands of miles from the action.

Hotel Parking Garage
Rome

During his 15-year career in private security, Lars had purchased virtually every type of made-to-order armored vehicle imaginable. They had all been good. Mercedes Benz especially, which had created a protective car for Japan's Emperor Hirohito way back in 1930.

But nearly as soon as he had left private practice to follow the Shepherd, he had sensed that the Great Mission would require something special. The Range Rover he drove now had been custom-ordered from a private company in Johannesburg, where the city's troubled past had given the company plenty of real-world experience. The glass and door paneling had been built to his exact specifications, rated to stop up to four successive 7.62 NATO armor-piercing bullets within a three-inch radius. The tires were airless run-flats, with reinforced steel that would withstand just about anything except a bomb.

Fortunately, they didn't face such heavy firepower tonight. Lars recognized the typewriter-on-steroids rattle of MP5 submachine gun fire. It sounded like the assailants' weapons were set to fire in three-round bursts, which they were squeezing off about as fast as they could. They were using 9mm rounds, he thought, instead of the .40 Smith & Wesson rounds preferred by the Americans and Canadians. With those guns, the Range Rover could easily take several dozen 9mm rounds into the vehicle's glass and doors without any ballistic leakage.

He just couldn't let them reload.

"I can't die yet!" Zhu shouted.

Wolf had reminded Lars of that very fact just hours ago. Zhu was destined to survive. It was in the Living

Scriptures. *And when he has gathered all that is necessary to know to bring all that is dark into the light, the One from the East will use her to make me anew, just as I have made you anew.*

The way Lars saw it, they had three choices. The first was to try out-driving their attackers. So long as the run-flat tires held, they might have a chance, although the Mini would be faster and more agile in traffic. The second option was to fight back. Lars had a Glock ACP in his ankle holster and, under the seat, a TEK-9 machine pistol, which fired .45 caliber rounds and had been converted to fully automatic. The third option was to use the vehicle as a weapon. It was, after all, built like a tank.

He reached into the floorboard and grasped Zhu by the collar, pulling him up into the seat. "Buckle up." He put the vehicle in reverse and backed up slowly. He wanted to stay within range of the assailant's guns. He wanted them to stay where they were. "Brace for impact."

Now sightless, Zhu trembled as the vehicle took rounds to the right front fender, and then to the grill and windshield. He heard the sound of the brass shell casings bouncing on the cement around the Mini Cooper. The disturbing clamor of the windshield crystalizing into thousands of tiny cracks. The noise of an empty aluminum magazine clanging against the cement as the gunmen reloaded.

The German shifted the vehicle into drive and stepped hard on the accelerator. They'd gotten the drop on him, but they had made one mistake. They'd mounted their attack from within a car that was very fast, but also very small.

There was just enough clear glass left on the windshield to see the gunman's eyes get big as the SUV raced toward them. The Range Rover T-boned the Mini with a satisfying crunch. Lars' vision was filled with white nylon as the vehicle's airbags deployed, enveloping him and Zhu in a warm, if brief, hug. Even as the airbags deflated, he kept the vehicle's forward momentum. He hadn't gotten enough speed to completely demolish the car in one fell swoop, but he had enough weight and momentum to push the wreckage up against a cement column.

Lars threw the SUV in reverse. The Mini looked like a crumpled soda can. As he had hoped, the right front wheel was bent hopelessly inward, and the driver's-side door was crushed against the column. The assailant's left foot extended out from below the passenger's side door. He'd put down his weapon and was devoting all his energy to trying to free himself. Lars wasn't going to let that happen.

He backed the vehicle up further down the empty aisle this time, making sure that he could get enough ramming speed. He was astonished by how small the airbags had become after deployment. They simply rested against the steering wheel and dashboards, scarcely larger than deflated birthday balloons.

Up ahead, he saw that the second gunman was halfway out of the passenger side window. He was crawling out headfirst. "Oh my God," Lars said as he watched one of the assailants climb over the other one to escape. "Brace yourself. No air bags this time." Lars stepped on the gas for his second attack.

As the force of the impact breached the Mini's interior, Lars could have sworn that he heard the sound of the driver's head being crushed against the Range Rover's grill. Zhu's helmeted head was thrown against the side window in the collision, but his seatbelt held. When Lars tried to put the Range Rover in reverse, the engine stalled.

"Are you all right, Mr. Zhu?"

Zhu pulled his helmet off. He looked dazed. "No, I'm not all right. I just wet my pants."

"A minor inconvenience, all things considered. Let's go."

He found his own door jammed shut. Zhu's was sealed as well. He grabbed his TEK-9, crawled over the back seat and exited via the rear hatch. Then he went around front, getting his legs under him as he surveyed the crash scene.

The driver's grisly torso and the gunman's decapitated foot were visible in the hulk of twisted metal. But he could not see the gunman's head or hands. There was no sense in taking chances. He aimed his weapon at the driver's side door and pumped four rounds into it. One of the men groaned. Lars shot through the door again. This time, there was no sound.

"Hey!" Zhu called out. "I think I hear sirens!"

Before moving on, Lars needed to know who had attacked them. He stretched his driving gloves tight over his hands, and then gripped the arms of the mangled corpse, dragging it out of the car until it was flat on the cement. He inspected the man's pockets and found nothing. Moving on to the jacket, he unzipped a long pouch that went diagonally across the man's chest.

Inside, he found a piece of black fabric – about the size of a cocktail napkin – with red stripes. It was octagon-shaped, and it had obviously been made with high-quality silk. On the flip side, the octagon's edges were stitched in golden thread, with the phrase *ad majorem dei gloriam* beneath it. The other side read, *Paratus enim dolor et cruciatus, in Dei nomine*. He was fluent in German and English, but he had never studied Latin. Dei, he surmised, had to be something having to do with God. The rest was a mystery. He pocketed it. The Shepherd would be able to read it.

Then he slid the tip of the TEK-9 barrel underneath the man's ski mask. It lifted easily, revealing the face of a man in his late 20s. He was of Mediterranean complexion, possibly Italian.

The dead man's mouth was formed into an O-shape. As if his last words had been "Oh," or perhaps, "Wow." Why was it that the dead always looked so surprised? What was it that they saw as they passed to the other side?

Lars took comfort in this. The Shepherd had once told him that he was destined to martyr himself for the Great Mission. He looked forward to whatever surprises awaited him during his journey.

National Counterrorsm Center

Speers was waiting for Carver when he returned to his office. It was a shabby, tight little space. No windows, some particle board furniture that had been pilfered from an empty office over at the SBA building. A far cry from the luxe offices he had once occupied over on K Street.

This was supposed to be temporary, a fact he reminded himself of every day. He had avoided personalizing the space in any way for fear of cosmically elongating the time here in his own personal purgatory. Last month, he had finally brought in some lamps to replace the florescent lighting. Most of the pasty people who came into his office were much more attractive by lamplight.

"Cute kids," Speers said, pointing to the only photograph in the entire office. The picture, unframed and taped to the bottom of a monitor, showed Carver in an orange river raft with two cherub-like kids under his arms. "Whose are they?"

"My sister's," Carver smiled. They lived with Carver's sister in Flagstaff, Arizona, about 80 miles from his parents' cattle ranch in Joseph City.

After the Ulysses Coup, as the American media had taken to describing the mutiny that had nearly toppled the American government the previous year, Carver had spent two days recovering in Walter Reed Hospital. He had then attended the funeral of his late partner, Megan O' Keefe, before heading out to Arizona for some much-needed rest.

He avoided all news and let his messages go unanswered for days at a time. As always, the first couple of days had been hard. His parents and extended family thought he was a contracting specialist for the State Department. He had to make his life in Washington seem like the most boring, milquetoast existence possible so they wouldn't ask too many questions. And then there were the excuses. For all the weddings, anniversaries and birthdays he had missed while working abroad. He was so tired of being the bad son, the irresponsible uncle.

But he had gotten past that. He had been there for his father's birthday for the first time in years. And he had taken his niece and nephew fishing on Lake Mary, and they had caught their limit of Northern Pike. It had been good to reconnect. Just being around his own blood had been good for the soul. They were so normal. So happy.

He had grown tired of Washington. With the exception of Speers, everyone he knew was either single, or wanted to be single so they could spend more time on their careers. Carver hated it, but knew he was just as guilty. He had never married. Never been engaged. The manner in which he had chosen to serve his country required keeping the people he loved at a distance.

Now he stood in the hallway outside his own office. "How are the twins?"

"Sweet when I'm home," Speers said, "But all I hear about when I'm gone is how much they cry. How they won't nap at the right times. How she can't get anything done."

"Maybe she just wants you home more."

"We're not here to talk about my personal life. Come in and close the door."

Carver did so reluctantly. His office was about the size of a large walk-in closet.

Speers pulled a purple lollipop from his pocket and began unwrapping it. "You handled that briefing well today."

"What do you want, Julian?"

"To give you a compliment."

"You must want something. My target in Rome is missing, and you're dishing out compliments. Doesn't add up."

Speers slid the lollipop between his cheek and gum. "You say you're not good at case management, but you are."

Carver frowned. "So you want me to take on a larger role. We both know I'm not wired to sit behind a desk. You promised me this was temporary."

"And I meant it. Stop being so paranoid. I'm just stashing you here until the whole thing blows over."

It didn't feel temporary. By the time he had returned to Washington from Arizona, he'd found that Eva Hudson's enemies were already hard at work trying to find ways to invalidate her line of succession to the presidency. They were demanding investigations into every aspect of the operation that had discovered and ultimately suppressed the mutiny. That in itself hadn't been so shocking, until Carver found that he himself was the focus of a misguided witch hunt that threatened to blow the anonymity he had spent so many years cultivating.

"How much longer until I can get back into the field?"

"It's up to you," Speers said.

Carver looked up. He hadn't heard that one before. "Up to me?"

Speers nodded. "You have to appear before the committee tomorrow."

So that was it. The House Committee on Domestic Intelligence had been pressuring the president for months to make Carver testify. Then they had gone to Speers, who had bought him some time. Apparently there was very little sand left in the hourglass.

"The administration has," Speers said, "for the most part, satisfied the committee's appetite for bloodlust already. You're the last person on their list. And you can make this go away for all of us. Just tell them is where Nico Gold is."

They had been through all this before. The committee needed one person they could single out as a scapegoat. Nico Gold was one of world's most gifted cybersecurity experts. He was also considered a convicted felon who, in Carver's opinion, had earned a pardon for his good deeds.

"If it wasn't for Nico," Carver said, "there probably wouldn't be any committee. There might not be any congress either, for that matter."

"You've gotten too emotional," Speers said. "It's enough to save your country. You can't save everyone."

"That's your rationale for throwing a hero under a bus?"

"I disagree. One heroic act doesn't change the fact that Nico Gold is a criminal."

"It was actually a bunch of heroic acts that added up over a period of days."

Speers shook his head and opened the office door. "Give it some thought, Blake. They're not asking you to be the judge and jury. They just want to know where they can find him."

He didn't need to think about it. The committee could crucify him, for all he cared. There was no way he was selling out the greatest intelligence asset he had ever worked with. Besides, someday, they were going to need him.

Piazza del Popolo
Rome

Lars drove the motorcycle around the enormous piazza once, and then again, so that he could make sure he and Adrian Zhu had not been followed. At this time of night, only a handful of tourists were present, all of whom seemed to be photographing the 24-meter-high obelisk at the center of the square known as the Flaminio. Like most of the obelisks in Rome, the Flaminio had been taken from Egypt. After being brought to Italy in 10 B.C., the obelisk had stood at the Circus Maximus, where it witnessed countless chariot races before being moved to the Piazza del Popolo, where it had seen an equal number of public executions.

Although the sun had been down for nearly four hours, Lars kept the tinted visor of his helmet pulled all the way down, covering his entire face. The visor on Zhu's helmet was painted black. It wasn't that they didn't trust him. They had spent years vetting him. But at least if he were captured, he would not, under the pain of torture, lead them to the Shepherd.

Spotting only the tourists and a few parked taxis hoping for a fare, Lars gunned the motor. The bioengineer gripped the seat frame for balance as the bike shot through the Porta del Popolo, an elaborate archway leading to Via Flaminia. He drove east for two and a half blocks, and then made a sharp left into the courtyard of an enormous villa that had originally belonged to a Venetian bishop. The mechanized iron gate closed behind them as Lars shut off the engine and dismounted the bike. He then led Zhu through the private courtyard to the immense double front doors, where two guards stood, brandishing TEK-9s like the one Lars had under his jacket.

Inside at last, Zhu was finally allowed to remove his helmet. *"Bellissima,"* he said, trying on one of the few Italian words he knew as he looked around the enormous foyer. The walls were painted crimson. Portraits of the Venetian bishop in various poses hung on opposing walls. An enormous Murano glass chandelier hung overhead.

The living area was hardly as pristine, resembling a war zone more than a historic villa. Enormous piles of earth and debris occupied most of the black-and-white checkerboard floor. Perhaps they had been tunneling, he thought. How else to explain this much dirt? It was a preposterous sight.

Now Lars led him up a creaky mahogany staircase. The entrances to the second and third floors had been sealed off with razor wire. On the fourth floor landing, a carpenter appeared to be engaged in some sort of construction project in the middle of the hallway. Several floorboards were pulled up and stacked in a row. Lars and Zhu stepped around him and proceeded to the end of the hall, where another pair of plain-clothed bodyguards stood.

"Is he awake?" Lars asked one of the guards.

"Very. He's been expecting you."

Lars opened the door, revealing a spacious study with dark wood paneling and a high ceiling. Another magnificent glass chandelier provided flattering overhead lighting. Several steamer trunks were lined up against the east wall.

An Alsatian sat vigilantly in the middle of the room. He wagged at the sight of Lars, but growled menacingly when Zhu stepped into the room.

"Off," a wizened voice called from the far corner of the room. The Alsatian instantly curbed his aggression.

Sebastian Wolf – known to his flock as the Shepherd – stood at a workstation that was easily the most modern piece of furniture in the place. The old man wrote long, looping cursive in a large leather-bound book. He wore a dark suit with a white silk tie, and a white shirt with French cuffs and black marble cufflinks. Aside from his full head of perfectly groomed white hair, he looked far more youthful than Zhu had imagined. The skin of his face was somewhat smooth, but he had none of the grotesque signs of excessive plastic surgery. Nobody knew exactly how old the Shepherd was, but even if he didn't look like an octogenarian, he had to be at least in his mid-80s, if not older.

At the sight of the old man, Zhu was suddenly overcome with emotion. *And there will be a Shepherd who walks among you who has seen into the heart of the tyrants, because he was born among them and has lived among them. And his name will be Sebastian.*

He dropped to one knee and bowed his head, sobbing. Wolf's Alsatian, Magi, growled and bared his teeth. This time the Shepherd did not correct the animal.

"Mr. Zhu," The Shepherd said as he put down his pen and smiled in a fatherly manner, "this is no way to rejoice after such a harrowing adventure."

He walked to Zhu and reached out to help him up, but the bioengineer grasped the Shepherd's left hand and kissed his ring. Wolf pulled back violently, his face suddenly red. Magi barked.

"Stand up!" he commanded. Zhu did so, disoriented as he was by the Shepherd's rage. "I am not the pope. Quite the opposite. I am a tool, just as you are a tool."

The bioengineer instinctively bowed his head again. "Sorry," he said. "Forgive me."

"You may ask God directly for that." The Shepherd turned his gaze to Lars, who had been watching the episode with amusement. "Considering the security situation, I had the staff seal off the lower floors."

"And we should redouble the guards," Lars said.

"No. Now that Mr. Zhu has arrived, security must be shifted to protect his work." The old man motioned to a round table and chairs. "Now then. Please sit."

He walked around to the other side. Only now, as his joints creaked as he slowly sat down, did Zhu see signs of the Shepherd's advanced age. Behind them, the double doors opened. A physician entered with a black case. The Shepherd motioned him inside.

"Hurry," the old man said as the doctor removed the cufflink of his left sleeve and rolled up the French cuff, revealing a surprisingly muscular forearm. He swabbed a vein with alcohol. Then he opened the case, removed a small electronic device and pressed it to the old man's flesh just above his wrist. It beeped briefly before the physician pulled it away and rebuttoned Wolf's shirt.

Something as innocuous as insulin injections, Zhu wondered? Or something more radical meant to reverse aging, such as human growth hormones?

The carpenter's hammering echoed loudly as the physician opened and closed the doors to leave.

"Termites?" Zhu inquired, recalling the man they had passed pulling up floorboards in the corridor.

"No," the old man responded. "Nightingales."

"A bird infestation?"

"No, Mr. Zhu. As you are no doubt intimately aware, our people are under attack. Many are dead, and I'm afraid there will be many more before we are on the other side of this. After realizing the lengths to which the enemy will go to preserve their stranglehold on power, I made a call to a friend in Japan and had him find the caretaker for Nijo Castle. Do you know it?"

"No sir. Can't say that I do."

"Oh, it's a remarkable ancient fortress in Kyoto. During the Edo period, the floors were designed so that the nails in the floor would rub against clamps when people walked on it. To prevent against sneak attacks, you understand. It sounds remarkably like nightingale chirping.

Hence the name, nightingale floors. An ancient but effective security measure."

The doors opened again. Two servants entered bearing trays of food and drink. They set them upon the table and backed out of the room. Magi crawled under it, lying obediently at his master's feet. The old man plucked a piece of meat from one of the trays, reached down, and fed the dog his reward.

The sight of the animal chewing made Zhu's mouth water. The old man gestured at the covered platters on the desk. "I was unaware of your preferences," he told his disciple, "so I had the kitchen make up suckling pig, and some rosemary lamb, and some *pasta alla carbonara* done in the traditional Roman style. I hope something will please you."

Lars and Zhu ate heartily without speaking. The old man nibbled on nuts and sipped *aqua con gas* while his guests ate. When at last he saw Zhu's pace slowing, he spoke.

"Now then, I know you will have many questions, but first I must ask a few of my own. Do you, Mr. Zhu, believe the conventional wisdom that we are to sit passively by through the ages and await the second coming of our savior?"

The bioengineer swallowed a mouthful of pork and, with some gristle protruding from his front teeth, said, "No, your…" Zhu almost said 'your Holiness,' but stopped himself. "No sir."

"Oh, and why is that?"

"I have read the Living Scriptures. I searched my heart and believe they are true."

The Shepherd grew impatient. "Use your own words! Speak from your heart!"

"Why else," Zhu tried again, "would God give us the smarts to invent space travel, or split the atom? Not to kill each other! We're supposed to use our brains and our technology to know all about Him, and truly become one with Him."

The old man smiled. "Spoken like a true believer. And what responsibility do you take for this belief?"

"I take full responsibility. I'm ready to apply the scientific knowledge God has granted me to fulfill our destiny."

The old man stood. Zhu found the Shepherd's mannerisms, and even his voice, completely mesmerizing. "Humanity has been led in the wrong direction. We must be the ones to reveal the great lies and wake humanity from its daydream of spiritual passiveness."

Zhu watched as the old man took the *spumante* in his hands and filled Lars' and Zhu's goblets, and then his own. He raised his glass in a toast.

"Tomorrow you will see that we have acquired all that you asked for. Tonight, let us pray that the martyrs in Washington and London who have passed may now be one with God's great unconditional love."

Blake Carver Residence
Washington D.C.

Carver woke with the feeling that something wasn't right. He reached for his phone. Sure enough, it was 4 a.m. An hour earlier than his usual wakeup time. Since he'd been on assignment out in McLean, he'd gotten up every day at 5 a.m. for a run. Except for Thursdays, which was when the ODNI fencing club met in the gym. Although none of the analysts had managed to beat him yet, he enjoyed the challenge of keeping them scoreless.

He never thought his exile from fieldwork would last this long, and he had to be disciplined to stay in shape. There was so much sitting around. So much waiting for things to happen.

Carver had spent most of the night in McLean with Arunus Roth, monitoring intelligence channels, Italian police radio scanners and the GPS for any sign of Adrian Zhu. He had finally gone home at 1 a.m. to grab a little sleep. He'd been dreaming about Zhu, he remembered. Carver's mind tended to gnaw on problems while he slept, and he found that he often rose with a number of possible solutions.

Not this time. He was still mystified. Had Zhu really been kidnapped? If so, by whom? Or did he run? But that made even less sense. He was not a prisoner in China. He did not have to defect. After all, he had gone to China to escape ethics questions that were uniquely American.

In five hours, he would have to appear before the committee. He cursed, pulled the covers back, and got to his feet.

It was too early to go for a run. Too early to eat. But not too early to hydrate. Carver walked into the kitchen of the one-bedroom duplex and drew a warm glass of water from his water ionizer. He had no doubt that one day the machine's health benefits would be outed as a sham, but until science proved it wrong, he was going to chug this stuff.

Then, as was his daily custom, he grated about a teaspoon of ginger root directly into the water, and drank it. His mother's recipe for healthy digestion still did a body good.

Then he took the potted pipe organ cactus that rested in the kitchen window – the only living thing in Carver's one-bedroom condo – and dribbled some tap water into the soil.

On his sister's insistence, he'd brought Marty – he had named the cactus after the country music star Marty Robbins, one of his father's favorites – back from Arizona on his last trip. Marty reminded him of home. And best of all, he could neglect Marty for weeks on end without killing him.

Carver decided to see if there was anything of interest on the video from Adrian Zhu's Sapienza University lecture, which he still had not seen in its entirety. He went to his living room, switched on his computer, and began watching the opening segment. Petro Parisi, the head of Sapienza University's Faculty of Mathematical, Physical and Natural Studies, stepped onstage holding a microphone. The 63-year-old professor, who wore a slim-cut gray suit complete with a pocket square, made a show of giving Zhu's hipster outfit a long look.

"I must admit," Parisi said in English over the microphone. "When I first saw you, and realized how young you are in relation to your scientific achievements, I became rather depressed at my own life."

Zhu smiled wryly. "Actually, I've always wished I'd been born a few decades earlier. Everything was so wide open. For example, sometimes I think about how free it would feel to live in the age before mobile phones. The thought of leaving the house, and having no way for people to contact you. It must have been so liberating."

"You must be joking," the professor said. "Imagine you make a date with someone to meet at a restaurant. You show up. They are running very late because of traffic, or the flu, or a tyrannical boss. Meanwhile, you are sitting there drinking wine in anger, thinking they forgot about you. Eventually you leave, having no way of knowing that they are about to arrive. Believe me, this was no golden age."

Carver fast-forwarded through the rest of the banter and most of the regular presentation, which he had seen from footage of previous appearances at Oxford and Zurich. The Q & A period was what he was interested in.

Now he watched as a queue of journalists lined up at a microphone in the center aisle. The first reporter began her question in Italian before Professor Parisi admonished her for straying from English, the official language of the conference. "Mr. Zhu," she began again in English, "Are the nutritional benefits from the milk of your cloned cows really superior to those of existing milk substitutes?"

"Without question," Zhu replied. "But to be honest, the challenge of cloning cattle from hair samples, rather than frozen embryos, was a lot more interesting to me than the public benefits of the project."

A writer from *La Repubblica* had the honor of asking the next question. "Mr. Zhu, you mentioned something about the milk of the cloned cattle called lysozyme. What is that exactly?"

"A good bacterium," Zhu said. "It contains proteins and vitamins and other things that help fight off infections and promote growth."

"Have there been any negative side effects in the children?"

"Nope. Next question, please."

The journalist remained at the mic, fending off the writer behind her with an elbow. "It's been rumored that LifeEmberz has actually cloned a human being that has matured beyond the embryo stage. Is there any truth to that rumor?"

The audience let out a collective gasp as they waited to see if Zhu would answer the question. Carver wondered if the journalist had heard the same rumors he had. An American asset in China had reported – without any proof whatsoever – that Zhu had already successfully cloned a child for the most senior officer of the People's Liberation Army, using mitochondrial DNA from the exhumed corpse of the official's great-grandfather. The same asset had produced a dubious-looking set of emails in which a senior Communist Party official appeared to ask Zhu to clone Chairman Mao, the grand patriarch of the Communist Revolution, whose body lay perfectly preserved in a Tiananmen Square mausoleum. He implored Zhu to apply his considerable skills to the cause, explaining that his wife would give anything to have children with Mao's DNA.

Nothing gave Carver the creeps more than the idea of making fertilized eggs from the DNA of a totalitarian who had been on ice for decades. Still, a small part of Carver could understand it. How many Americans mothers would love to carry a baby made from the DNA of Abe Lincoln, John F. Kennedy, Ronald Reagan or Bill Clinton?

Zhu licked his thin lips before speaking. "I'm not at liberty to comment on any research in progress."

Carver replayed the sound bite and played it again. And again. He called Arunus Roth, who was monitoring the situation from McLean. "Did you watch this Zhu video?" He didn't wait for Roth's answer. "Maybe I'm crazy, but I think Zhu just admitted to cloning a human."

U.S. Capitol Building
Washington D.C.

The hearing room had been fashioned in the style of a classic tribunal. Blake Carver and his attorney sat at a simple table on the hearing room floor. A panel of congressional representatives sat on an elevated panel in front of them. The height differential was designed to make the person testifying feel small and to exaggerate the power and influence of the committee members.

Bolstering the committee members were two additional rows of junior congressmen and their staffers. As Carver surveyed the tired, stressed-out bunch of public servants, he envisioned an equal number of medicine cabinets stocked with Adderall, Ambien and antacid tablets.

Luis Gonzalez, (D-New Mexico), Chairman of the House Permanent Select Committee on Intelligence, peered down from his seat in the front row. Although he sat scarcely 20 feet from his subjects, he switched on his microphone. "Glad to have you with us this morning, Agent Carver."

Carver, who was dressed in a shark-colored suit with no tie, leaned into the microphone situated on the table. "The feeling is not mutual," he said to polite laughter.

"It was a battle getting you in here," Rep. Gonzalez remarked, "So forgive me if we waste little time in getting down to business. This committee is concerned with events taking place 13 months ago. Can you please characterize your professional activities during that time period?"

He looked over his shoulder. Where was Julian? He had promised he would be here. It wasn't just that Carver wanted him for moral support. Speers had been a district attorney prior to joining the Hatch administration as general counsel, and later as chief of staff. He was imminently more qualified than the rental lawyer he'd sent in his place.

"Agent Carver?"

"The answer is no. I won't characterize last August."

Judging by the look on the committee members' faces, nobody had ever refused to answer a question before. "Excuse me?"

"It's nothing personal, Congressman. My activities at that time were highly classified in nature, and frankly, above your security clearance."

The attorney leaned into Carver's ear and whispered, "There's no reason to piss these guys off. The administration has your back, but if you create enemies here, God help you."

Carver turned his head and covered his mouth before whispering – just in case there were any lip readers on the panel. "We just met. You don't even know me. If you have sound advice of a legal nature, I'll take it. Otherwise, please let me do the talking."

Gonzalez cut in. "Agent Carver, we aren't here to uncover intelligence secrets. To be frank, we're primarily interested in the release of a federal prisoner named Nico Gold into your custody on August 21 of last year."

So Julian was right. Of all the ethical lines that had been crossed that day in the name of national security, it figured that the committee would waste Carver's time with this.

Personally, Carver found Nico Gold obnoxious, manipulative and arrogant. But there was no denying that he had an unparalleled mind. For years nobody knew his real name. He had been the Banksy of the hacking community. He had started as a teenager, lifting tiny sums out of millions of bank accounts in western countries. He would then redistribute the money into the accounts of NGOs in poor African countries. Modern-age Robin Hood stuff. But then he took a big score from the International Monetary Fund, and got a little carried away in flaunting his success.

As Nico would discover later, when he found himself serving 20 years, he had messed with the wrong lady. Eva Hudson had been the head of the IMF in those days. And once she learned the identity of the person who had stolen from their coffers, she was relentless in her pursuit.

"August 21 is widely considered to be the first day of the Ulysses Coup," Gonzales continued. "You saw Mr. Gold that day, didn't you?"

The Ulysses Coup. Carver shuddered at the name, which missed the point completely. It had only taken a few days with a TV network using the catchphrase before it had become a modern-day Watergate.

In what appeared at first to be coordinated terror attacks by religious extremists, a group of conspirators had succeeded in decapitating the presidential line of succession, an act of congress that had last been amended in 1947. President Hatch, his vice-president, the president pro tempore and the secretary of state were all killed. Of those in the immediate line, only treasury secretary Eva Hudson had escaped. Ulysses USA Inc., a security multinational that had grown to dwarf the once-mighty Blackwater Corporation, had only been the tool of the crime, not the cause of it. The complete information about the perpetrators and how they had infiltrated the president's inner circle was still known only to a small group of Washington insiders, and, by executive order of the president, those names would likely be sealed for many years to come.

It sickened Carver to think about the countless history teachers who would no doubt build curricula around the crisis in the coming years, only to get its most fundamental elements completely wrong. But that was neither here nor there. Ulysses USA Inc. was done for, even if all its puppet masters weren't. And the official line of succession had been reinstated, making

Eva Hudson, the fifth in line, the unlikely Commander-in-Chief.

One thing was for sure: For Carver, the memories of those six days in August were still too raw for his liking. The horizontal scar on his neck – he'd been grazed by a bullet while defending the White House – was a daily reminder.

The rent-a-lawyer was whispering something in his ear, but Carver wasn't listening. He sat forward again. "About all I can tell you, Congressman, is that Nico Gold was critical in helping us with the national security crisis we faced that day."

"Our records indicate that on August 21 last year, you arrived at Lee Federal Correctional Facility at 10: 30 a.m., with the intention of recruiting Mr. Gold."

"It was 10:41 a.m. when I signed in."

"You remember that precisely?"

He did indeed. What Carver's small-town doctor had once diagnosed in Carver as a photographic memory, was now known in the medical community as super-autobiographical memory, or hyperthymesia.

In short, it was the ability to recall an unusually high number of experiential moments in his life. He could point to most any day on the calendar and recall what he had for lunch, what the people he was with had been wearing, and what had been on the news that day.

Hyperthymesia was often regarded as a problematic condition more than a gift. Some people found the constant recall of archived memories emotionally crippling. Others found that the constant influx of the past impaired their ability to experience new things.

Carver was lucky. Although he occasionally had problems with focus, he was mostly able to wield the extreme amounts of data located within his brain to his advantage. His was a medical condition with benefits.

"Yes," he continued. "My partner and I signed in at 10:41. We were with Nico for approximately 17 minutes, during which time we were able to convince him to serve the very country that had incarcerated him."

Cindy Blick (R-Wyoming), a 55-year-old woman with a red beehive haircut, spoke into the microphone mounted before her. "Agent Carver, what I'm trying to understand is why you would enlist the help of a convicted felon when you had access to more than 20 qualified government and private cryptologists, including some from the NSA."

The attorney covered the microphone with his right hand and leaned in to offer advice. Carver nudged him away.

"They may have been qualified," Carver stated, "But they were ineffective. The cryptologists at my disposal had been working on the case for weeks without any progress. We're living in an age where one truly gifted person with a computer can do more in a day than a roomful of PhDs could in a year."

"I'm not disputing that Nico Gold is a smart person. But in this case, when you chose to enlist the help of a felon, you made a mistake."

He hated them. He hated *this*. His thoughts drifted to Operation Crossbow, which had only just gotten interesting. One of the world's most powerful bioengineers had said that he had the capability to clone a human being, and then had gone missing. Whatever country or organization had nabbed him now had a tremendous intellectual asset at their disposal, and you could bet they weren't going to use it for a good cause.

"Agent Carver?" Blick said. "We're waiting."

Carver quickly rediscovered his train of thought. "My only mistake was bringing Nico in too late. If it hadn't been for him, you might not be sitting up there today."

Gonzales leaned forward. "Save the speeches, Agent Carver. The committee will determine, upon learning more details, whether those choices were justified."

"No it won't. The committee is incapable of making that determination without all the facts, and those facts are sealed."

"Is that so? Then I'd like to hear Mr. Gold's heroics from his own mouth."

"I bet you would."

"Do you know where we can find him?"

"I really couldn't say."

Blick took off her glasses and peered down at Carver, her eyes darting back and forth between the federal agent and his attorney. "To be blunt, Agent Carver, we have evidence that you forged a judicial order to arrange for Mr. Gold's unlawful release. Out of respect for your service, the White House has strongly recommended that we look the other way on this transgression, which we are inclined to do despite the fact that nobody will tell us why you're such a value to our intelligence community, or even what agency you currently answer to. Despite this, we might be persuaded to comply with this request providing you help us return Mr. Gold into federal custody."

The double doors at the back of the room opened. Julian Speers blew in, nodding at Carver as he walked past the table and made a beeline for Rep. Gonzalez. The congressman leaned over the wood paneling to get a quiet but spirited earful from the DNI.

Gonzalez' face turned a shade of pink before he abruptly spoke into the microphone. "The director has just advised me the president has suspended these hearings in the interest of national security. Naturally, we will use every feasible legal and constitutional option to reverse this decision."

As the committee erupted into chaos, Speers motioned for Carver and started for the door.

Carver waited until they were in the hallway before speaking. "Took you long enough," he grumbled as they speed-walked. "Things were getting pretty heated in there."

"I didn't bail you out for your benefit," Speers said. "If you knew what was good for you, you'd have told them how to find Nico Gold."

"Then why are you here?"

"The president asked for you personally. We have a mess on our hands."

5th Street Northeast Washington D.C.

The inside of Speers' black Highlander was just as Carver had remembered it. It smelled like a candy store and was littered with chewed lollipop sticks and fast-food wrappers. The only new wrinkle was the pair of child car seats in the vehicle's second row. The babies were the result of a torrid relationship Speers had with a DOJ analyst named Lydia. Within four months of dating, Speers had gotten her pregnant with twins. Before he knew it, he needed a wedding planner, a financial planner and a real estate agent.

Speers pulled the SUV up to the address FBI Director Chad Fordham had given him on 5th Street Northeast. The home was inconspicuous among the row of three-story brownstones. "This is it?" Carver said incredulously. They were only a few blocks from the Capitol Building where Carver's hearing had been. "We could have walked faster."

They got out of the vehicle and walked into the tiny yard. The front door opened and he spotted Fordham inside, beckoning them up the stairs. What was going on here? Carver couldn't fathom anything happening at a residential address that would require the heads of both the FBI and the ODNI to make a personal visit. Nothing short of a major breech in national security.

Carver liked Fordham, who was a rare holdover from the previous administration. Last year Fordham had helped put an end to the Ulysses Coup. Sixteen FBI agents sacrificed their lives that week – a huge loss by any measure, especially considering that, until that day in August, only 26 agents had been killed in the agency's entire history.

After assuming the presidency, Eva Hudson had set about cleaning house from top to bottom. No one was safe. Of the 17 agency heads making up the intelligence community, only Fordham had been retained. He had proven himself to be an ally.

As they entered, Fordham greeted Julian and reached out to Carver with a latex-gloved hand. The presence of latex suggested a crime scene. And yet there was no police tape, no guys in FBI jackets swarming the yard.

"If you two will suit up, please," one of Fordham's men told them. He pointed to a box of aqua latex gloves and shoe prophylactics, which the two men quickly put on. As Fordham led them through the home, Carver heard the sound of a woman in hysterics. He poked his head into the living room, seeking the source of the commotion. He didn't spot the crier, but the calfskin rugs and original Eames lounge chairs told him that the occupants were people of means with western taste.

"Who knows about this?" Speers asked.

"As of now," Fordham said, "There are only seven people in the circle of trust, including you two and the POTUS."

The president? Whatever was going on here, it was huge. Either someone high-profile is dead in this house, Carver thought, or they've found a nuke in the basement.

Carver lingered in the doorway of a small study, where he found the source of the noise. A woman, mid-20s, sporting a blonde boy-cut and a sharp but conservative red dress. Her black flats danced on the floor as the rest of her convulsed in manic weeping. A plainclothes special agent with her back to the door was trying to calm the woman down and conduct an interview. Carver's eyes scanned the gray pantsuit that revealed a runner's haunches and slender, smallish shoulders. He knew those gams.

"Haley?"

Haley Ellis turned. The skin of her angular face was tanned and framed by wispy, shoulder-length hair. It was her, all right. The last time Carver had seen her, she had been a senior liaison for Pentagon-White House Affairs.

"Forgot you two knew each other," Speers said.

Carver hadn't seen Ellis in 13 months. And that had been on purpose.

"This way," Fordham urged, motioning for Carver to come to the end of the hallway. He held an old rectangular-shaped flashlight that looked large enough to light up FedExField.

"Who's that woman Haley's talking to?" Carver said.

"Mary Borst. She's the executive assistant to Senator Preston."

Carver got tense just thinking about what her days must be like. The executive assistant for anyone on the Hill was never paid enough in relation to the stress they endured. They had to manage huge egos, scheduling and even menial tasks for the Senator, like picking up dry-cleaning and babysitting.

They came to the basement staircase. "No lights down there," Fordham commented as he switched on his flashlight, which was less powerful than it looked, and led them down 15 steps.

The subject of interest was in the middle of the basement, which was unfurnished except for a row of tools and a wooden workbench along the far wall. A body clothed in a dark suit was crumpled in a fetal position, surrounded by a great deal of blood. The victim's red-stained shirt was unbuttoned, revealing several dozen small slashes across the stomach and chest.

"Who's the..." Carver didn't need to finish his sentence, as he quickly recognized the dead man's face as that of Senator Rand Preston.

This was huge. Preston was a third-term Republican from Texas. Over the past year or so, pundits had been touting him as a possible contender for the GOP nomination.

The furnishings upstairs made sense now. Preston was from a Texas oil family, and he was often seen wearing pricey cowboy hats and boots.

While some members of congress were forced to share apartments while congress was in session, many of those with means kept second homes in Washington D.C., while their families continued to reside in their home states. The location was perfect. They were just a few blocks' walking distance not only to Congress, but also to the Senate offices and Union Station.

Carver heard a scream from upstairs, which was followed by another bout of intense weeping. "What time did she find her boss down here?"

"She didn't," Fordham said, pointing to a solidly built man in a gray suit. "This is Hank Bowers. Section Chief with us for 15 years now. He and the senator were in the same fraternity at UT Austin. He was first on the scene."

Carver noted the silver TKE ring on the man's left hand. "You guys were still tight, huh?"

"Not so much. We see each other maybe a couple times a year these days. But Rand called me last night, said he wanted to get together. Something had him spooked. Wanted some advice on how to hire personal security."

"And he couldn't get Secret Service protection?"

"Didn't qualify," Bowers said. "As a senator, the only way to get protection is if you're the majority or minority leader, or if you run for president, and even for that, it has to be within 120 days of the general election."

"What was he scared of?"

"He didn't give any specifics."

"What else did he say?"

"Nada. We were supposed to meet up for coffee this morning. When he didn't show, I came here. Front door was wide open."

"We got lucky," Fordham said. "If Mary had found him first, this place would be crawling with reporters right now."

"Who called her?"

"Said the senator was a no-show for another meeting, and she got worried. Arrived just a few minutes before you two."

"I don't think he was down here long," Carver observed as he crouched alongside the body. Judging by the stains all over the workbench and covered pieces of furniture – not to mention several traps deployed along the far wall – the house had a major rat infestation. Yet there were only a handful of rodent bites on the senator's face and hands. "Not more than three or four hours. Much longer and the rats would've given him a full facelift."

"Are you in forensics?" Bowers said.

Carver shook his head. "I just watch a lot of TV. You guys find a murder weapon?"

"No," Fordham said. "We found his phone and his computer over there." He shone his light into the corner, where Carver saw the notebook computer wedged in a vise on a workbench. "The SIM card is missing from the phone and the computer's been gutted. My guess is they took the hard drive. Maybe we can pull some prints off the hardware."

Returning his attention to the body, it appeared to Carver that the senator's jugular had been slit with an extremely sharp blade. There was a great deal of congealed blood directly in front of the neck, but the incision was fine. Nothing to suggest the sort of tearing you might get with a domestic weapon of convenience, like a steak knife. They were going to need to get a blood spatter expert out there. He didn't want to be the one to tell Fordham how to do his job, but he couldn't fathom why there wasn't already a forensics team on site.

Suddenly Carver rose and looked around the room. "Hey, you guys find any ropes around the place?" Fordham shook his head. Carver crouched down again and used a gloved finger to expose the senator's right wrist. "See this?"

He pointed to an inch-long laceration cutting through the skin and muscle, down to the bone. The flesh around the left wrist was identically damaged. Speers stepped back and held his palm over his mouth. He hadn't been exposed to many dead bodies in his life.

"What could cause that?" Fordham said. "Handcuffs?"

"Doubtful. Look at the color of the skin on the back of his hands. He was bound with something thick and rough to the touch. I think Senator Rand was suspended in the air, somehow." He got to his feet and pointed at the ceiling. "Shine your light up there."

Fordham pointed his light overhead. The basement ceiling was about 14 feet high, with several exposed cross beams and pipes. "You should check out those beams," Carver said. "Look for rope fiber."

"What, you think he was hanged before his throat was cut?"

"Hanged, yes. But not by the neck. Check out his shoulders."

Fordham returned the spotlight to the body. "I don't see anything." Carver put his hand on Speers' shoulder and guided him to a more advantageous position. "Oh." The FBI director said. "Oh yeah, they don't look right."

"I'd bet his arms are popped out of his shoulder sockets."

Speers scratched his salt-and-pepper Van Dyke goatee. "Sweet Jesus. You're right."

"Don't take *my* word for it. Where is forensics?"

"Like I said, the president wanted you to see this first."

It was an odd request, but he appreciated the vote of confidence. Late last year, the president had offered Carver a role as a national security advisor. He had turned her down flat, insisting that he didn't belong behind a desk. Not long after that, he found himself behind one anyhow, although the desk he was assigned was far less prestigious than the one he'd been offered in the first place. During Carver's more paranoid moments, he wondered if the president still resented him for it. If he'd taken the job, would he still have the House Committee on Domestic Intelligence breathing down his neck?

"The way I see this," Carver continued, "the senator's wrists were probably tied behind his back. The same rope was used to hoist him up in the air. Judging by the damage to his wrists, a weight might have been attached to his feet. Then, at the right moment, they dropped him halfway, dislocating the extremities."

Fordham's face wrinkled in disgust. "That's medieval."

"Quite literally," Carver nodded. "It's called rope torture, or if you prefer, the *strappado*. It was a favorite interrogation technique used by certain European organizations over the centuries. That's not to say it's gone completely out of style. A few people in our own military were said to have revived it at Abu Ghraib in the early 2000s. I believe they called it a Palestinian Hanging. Their words, not mine."

"Could one person have done this?"

"Maybe with a hand winch or a pulley. But the senator's a big guy. It would normally be a two-person job."

Then he noticed something red edging out of the senator's mouth. He had seen it earlier and mistaken it for his tongue. Now he bent down, grabbed it with the tips of his gloved fingers, and pulled it out slowly. It was an octagon-shaped piece of fabric. Black, with two red stripes. On one side, a phrase was written in elaborate calligraphy: *Paratus enim dolor et cruciatus, in Dei nomine.*

He recognized the phrase. The Latin could be roughly translated as 'Prepared for pain and torment, in God's name.' He didn't translate it aloud, or discuss where he recognized it. He had seen too many investigations go down the wrong path based on the misinterpretation of symbolism.

But he also recognized the shape and color patterns. It was an old calling card of sorts. The people who had done this had gone to great lengths to mimic a methodology that the world had not seen in over 300 years.

"My God," Speers said, making eye contact with Fordham. "It's just like London."

The words shook Carver from deep thought. His eyes darted back and forth between the two Intelligence directors. "What's just like London?"

Independence Avenue SW
Washington D.C.

How strange life was, Carver thought. Just last night he had been feeling sorry for himself, pining to be back in the field, and dreading this morning's committee hearing. And now, only hours later, he was neck-deep into something that he couldn't even comprehend.

He sat in the third row of Speers' Highlander as they sped past Museum Row, near the National Air and Space Museum. The intelligence czar drove with one hand on the wheel and the fingers of his other hand in his black hair. He was pulling at it, as he always did when he was stressed. Chad Fordham rode shotgun. With the SUV's second row crowded with twin car seats, Carver and Ellis had piled into the third.

Ellis stared into a compact, touching up her makeup. Carver didn't blame her. They were headed to the White House for an unscheduled meeting with the President. Only a moron wouldn't want to make a good impression.

"That piece of fabric that was stuffed in the senator's mouth," Speers said. Carver looked up, meeting his boss' gaze in the vehicle's rear view mirror. "You mentioned it had some historical significance. Have you seen something like that before?"

"Nobody has," Carver said of the octagon-shaped fabric. "At least not in a few hundred years."

"But you recognized it."

He nodded. "From books. In Renaissance Europe, a certain assassination squad carried similar fabric with the same text written on it."

"A calling card? Like the Beltway Snipers?"

The Beltway Snipers, who had shot 13 people in the Washington metro area over a period of weeks in 2002, had left Tarot cards at some of the crime scenes, presumably to taunt police.

"Sort of. The organization was called the Black Order. They assassinated enemies of the Vatican, and sometimes left pieces of striped cloth in their victims' mouths."

Ellis raised her eyebrows. "Hector always said you were like a walking Wikipedia."

"Is that supposed to be a compliment?"

Hector Rios was Carver's best friend and had, once upon a time, been Ellis' boyfriend. After a steamy few months, she had shocked Hector by dumping him to focus on her career.

Carver knew that Hector still had feelings for her, and he could see why. Ellis was tough, sexy and surprisingly worldly for someone in her late 20s. She had been born into a Catholic military family in Virginia. Thanks to her father's frequent military transfers, she had scarcely gone to any school for longer than two years. After high school, she had enrolled in a 16-week training course in Fort Sam Houston in San Antonio, Texas, that would make her a combat medic. Within days of completing her course, she was deployed to Iraq.

Six months into her mission, the lead truck in Ellis' convoy hit an IED. The bomb was a prelude to a small-arms assault that left three dead. Ellis managed to gun down one of the insurgents before pulling a pair of wounded soldiers from a burning truck, earning her Combat Medical Badge. Not long afterwards, her own vehicle hit a roadside bomb that took her out of the war for good. After a couple of reconstructive hip surgeries, she was offered a desk job in Washington, which she took after some arm-twisting by her sister, Jill. Life after that had been a blur of administrative jobs at the DIA, NIC and the FBI.

Typical Ellis. She never let the grass grow under her feet.

She and Carver had first met by phone during the fight for Washington, and he had immediately been drawn to the sound of her warm Richmond dialect in his earpiece. Armed with an M4 carbine and a pair of binoculars, Ellis had taken up a position atop the Eisenhower Building, acting as the eyes and ears of the disparate forces fighting to ensure the president's safety. Like Carver, she had later been awarded the National Intelligence Distinguished Service Medal in a private White House ceremony.

A few weeks after she dumped Hector, Carver ran into her at the half-marathon up in Baltimore. Ellis had been decked out in blue and white running shorts and socks, quipping that she was "100% made in the USA." Her tone and body language had been unmistakably flirtatious. He felt sparks when they chatted, and they had run the first few minutes of the race side-by-side. Carver felt an undeniable attraction to her. But he didn't have many friends in Washington like Hector Rios, who was still licking his wounds. Ellis had tried to contact Carver after the marathon, but he had never responded. He could only hope that she had forgotten about the snub by now.

Carver felt the vehicle slow as Speers pulled into a private parking garage near the White House. The security staff waved him through, and he promptly pulled the oversized vehicle into a parking spot labeled COS, for chief of staff. Speers hadn't held that title since last year.

"That's ballsy," Carver said as they got out of the vehicle.

"The spot is still mine."

"What?" Carver said. "Shut up."

"I'm serious," Speers insisted as they walked across 17th Avenue toward the White House. "Eva's new chief of staff parks a few blocks away. When they offered me the job out in McLean, I told them I needed the spot. I knew I'd be going back and forth between D.C. and McLean constantly."

"You're offered the top intelligence job in the country, and the thing you want to negotiate is parking?"

Speers unwrapped a grape lollipop and slid it between his cheek and gum. "That's right," he said, talking out of the left side of his mouth. "My next move is getting my old office back."

The White House Washington D.C.

Carver hadn't seen the president's private study since before Eva Hudson's inauguration. During the previous administration, aside from the lavish molding on the walls and ceiling, the room hadn't looked much different from any home office. Now the small sitting area, phone, desk and printer were all gone, having been replaced with a sleek conference table that seated five and an enormous TV on the wall.

Carver, Ellis, Speers and Fordham sat around the sides of the table, leaving the head of the table for the president. Carol Lam, the 69-year-old grandmother of eight and the president's private secretary, walked in with a tray of drinks.

"Mr. Carver," Carol said with a huge smile. "It's been far too long since you've visited us."

Carver stood. "You look amazing." He meant it. Carol looked younger now than she had when she'd arrived at the White House seven years earlier. Maybe Eva wasn't really as high maintenance as Speers had led him to believe.

"There was a rumor last winter that we might be seeing more of you," Carol said, an obvious reference to Carver's turning down the national security advisor role. "I was disappointed."

Carol removed a cappuccino from the tray and placed it on the coffee table before Ellis. She set two more in front of Speers and Fordham.

"No thanks," Carver said when he saw her reaching for a fourth cup. "I don't –"

"Drink coffee. I'm well aware of your aversion to artificial stimulants. The cappuccino is for the president."

She left the room without offering him anything. He turned to Speers. "I think she just snubbed me."

"It's about time someone put you in your place," Speers said.

"What are you saying?"

"That your dietary requirements are obnoxious. Like time we went out to dinner and you wanted the venison, but you asked the waiter to find out where the deer had been raised."

"There's nothing wrong with wanting to know where my meat came from."

"If it's that important to you, kill your own deer."

They all stood as President Hudson entered. The bottle-blonde wore a slimming pantsuit with a matching pearl necklace and earrings. She was sporting a graduated bob cut that looked as if it had been shorn with a straight razor.

"I appreciate you coming in person," she said as they all sat down. "Chad gave me the basics by phone. I'll ask you all the same question I asked him. Was this a state-sponsored action?"

Speers shook his head. "No reason to believe that right now."

"What else do we know?"

Speers gave her the short version, explaining that it had looked as if the senator had been tortured, that it had probably been the work of two or more people, and that the killers had left a calling card with religious overtones.

The president rotated the bracelet on her wrist three times in a clockwise motion, as if winding herself up. "This morning I spent the better part of an hour on the phone with the British prime minister."

Carver sat forward. Based on how locked down the crime scene had been, he had hardly expected the president to discuss Preston's murder with anyone outside the circle of trust, not to mention the British PM. "What was his reaction to the news?"

"Actually, he called with news of his own. There was another octagon-shaped piece of fabric found this morning. This one was in London."

"London?"

Speers nodded. "Inside the mouth of Nils Gish."

The name didn't register with Ellis. "Who?"

Carver's fists clenched as he considered the implications of what he'd just heard. "Sir Nils Gish," he said just loud enough to be heard. "Member of parliament, leader of the Labour Party and possibly the next British prime minister."

Ellis made the sign of the cross – quick touches on the forehead and both shoulders.

The president leaned back, resting her elbows on the armrests of her chair in a classic power pose. "High ranking members of Congress and Parliament were assassinated on the same night, within approximately three hours of each other."

"Two killers," Carver deduced. "Or two *sets* of killers." Only a handful of military jets could get from London to D.C. in just three hours, and even that didn't allow for ground travel, to say nothing of the prep time that went into any professional assassination.

The treatment of the D.C. crime scene made more sense now. FBI chief Fordham had kept the late Senator Rand's D.C. residence locked down tight. This was much bigger than a lover's quarrel gone wrong, or the wrath of a vengeful loan shark.

"No group has claimed responsibility," Speers added. "In both cases, black-and-red striped fabric was left in the victim's mouth. Someone is clearly sending a message here. Agent Carver felt there might be a connection to some ancient European group."

"Not so fast," Carver objected. "What I said was that a piece of fabric like it was used by a certain assassination squad in Renaissance Europe. Since nobody alive has ever seen one, obviously this is an organization who's read about it, as I did, and decided to co-opt the symbol for their own purposes."

The president raised an open hand. "Work out the details on your own time. How are we going to handle this publicly?"

Speers' jaw tightened. "Whatever the spin, it's going to be a circus."

"All the progress we've made calming security jitters will vanish. It's not like these men were simply shot. They were brutally tortured. Forget the fact that we were under no obligation to provide secret service protection to the senator. People will look at this as a huge security failure. And since Preston was a presidential hopeful, the media is only going to fan the flames."

"And once people start speculating about whether these assassinations were state-sponsored, there won't be enough oxygen left in the room for anyone to think straight. It'll make it that much tougher to catch these monsters."

Every head in the room reluctantly nodded. Carver checked his watch. It had been at least four hours since the senator's death. The fact that no group had yet claimed responsibility for the murders was highly unusual. It was also deeply disturbing.

Fordham licked his lips before speaking. "We may need to practice misdirection as a strategy."

"With all due respect," Ellis said, "What are you going to tell people? That Senator Preston went to live on a big farm in the country?"

"Let me worry about that," the president said.

"If the truth gets out, the scandal would be bigger than the missing WMDs in Iraq. Bigger than Benghazi by a mile."

"Just do your job," the president put forth in a tone that officially sealed the discussion on that topic. She leveled her gaze at Carver and Ellis. "Starting now, this case is your entire world."

As much as Carver had wanted to get out from behind the desk in McLean, this wasn't the way he wanted to do it. After months of boredom, Operation Crossbow had only just started to get interesting, only to be wrenched out of his hands.

"What about support?" Ellis said.

"I want as few people knowing the details as possible," the president cut in. "Julian here, and Chad Fordham, will oversee this operation personally."

Speers' protest came immediately, but the president cut him off. "You both have competent deputy directors. Let them run things for a few days. I want your full and undivided attention on this."

"This is a mistake," Carver said. "We should have dozens, if not hundreds, of people on this."

"I think I've made myself clear. We can't afford a leak."

She had a point. As the business of keeping secrets went, this was about as big and juicy as they came. "When can I see the London crime scene photos?"

Speers sucked his teeth, as he always did when he was about to say something disappointing. "You can't. MI6 won't chance transmitting anything electronically."

Carver's face felt suddenly hot. "We have a pact to share intelligence data that is mutually beneficial to international security."

"Oh, they're fully willing to cooperate. It's just that they insist on doing it in person."

"What is this, 1985?"

"The hactivists have them spooked," the president explained. Earlier that year, a group claiming to be former WikiLeaks members had risen from the organization's ashes to release sensitive video that MI6 had shared with the CIA. Before either side could deploy its forces to shut the video down, the Allied Jihad had used the material to identify a

British double agent within the Iranian government. He had never been heard from again. Similar moves by hacker activists – who believed that governments had no right to withhold even sensitive information from the public – had so terrorized governments across the globe that even diplomats had been transported back to the industrial age, at times refusing to communicate even benign correspondence by email.

"Fine," Carver conceded. "I'll go to London if that's what you want. But I suggest that Ellis stays here." He deliberately avoided eye contact with his new partner. "We can't afford to let the trail in Washington get any colder."

"Noted," Speers said, "But denied. Chad and I will supervise the domestic end of this. You are both to go to London and anywhere else necessary to find out who did this."

The president stood up. "Until we know who's behind this, and why, we are fully exposed."

Speers glanced at his phone, reading an incoming text message. He looked up, apparently horrified by what he had read. "Madam President...Senator Preston's house just went up in flames."

Before anyone could react, Fordham also received a text. "It's Bowers," he said, gazing into his screen. "He's all right."

"Thank God," Speers gushed in relief. "And the senator's assistant?"

Fordham shook his head grimly. "Doesn't look good. She was inside."

Carver felt sick. It wasn't just that Mary Borst was likely dead. All forensic evidence had just burned up in the senator's brownstone.

Eisenhower Building
Washington D.C.

Speers ran his fingers over the oak surface of the partners desk that he had used during his seven years as White House Chief of Staff. Despite finding a few new nicks in the wood, he smiled, knowing that he wouldn't be headed back to McLean tonight. After his debrief with the president and the others, he had stayed behind and formally requested permission to reclaim his old office in the adjacent Eisenhower Building.

The president was visibly irritated, but granted the request nonetheless. Speers didn't mind a bit of social tension. That was part of the game. And timing was everything. As he had hoped, his audacity was trumped by the president's desire to stay in the loop during the investigation into Senator Preston's assassination.

The office's current occupant, a GS-14 from the Office of Management & Budget, had been out when Speers arrived. His startled assistant, who sat in the neighboring office, was trying to get hold of him at this very moment. Speers couldn't wait for the guy to get back here and take his horrendous photos down. A few beach pics from Guam, a random picture out the window of an airplane, and one of an old dog with an old woman that, for some reason he couldn't put his finger on, depressed him.

He sat in his old chair and adjusted the lumbar support and height to suit him. Then he set his computer on the desk, fired it up, and logged into the secure network. Per the president's directive, he dialed Claire Shipmont to temporarily delegate oversight of the ODNI daily operations to her so that he could focus on the crisis at hand. "Don't ask," he said before Claire could get the first question out of her mouth.

"Just know this is temporary, so don't go making changes that can't be undone a few days from now."

"Yeah, I was thinking Mondays should be wear your pajamas to work day from now on."

He liked Claire. He had, after all, plucked her from a Bay Area data analysis company to be his second in command. "Just one thing. There's a technical support analyst named Arunus Roth. He works under Blake Carver in the NCC. Give him access to my office. He'll be working in there."

"I know who he is. He's like a G-8 or something. He's always hitting on my assistant."

"Roth might be a little rough around the edges, but he won't trash the place. He needs complete privacy for the next few days, and we won't be seeing much of Carver, either."

As Speers signed off, a file request notification appeared in the corner of his screen. Someone was requesting access to a file that Speers owned. He didn't receive many these days, since he almost never had time to create any, much less administrate them. In the time that he had been heading up the ODNI, he spent more than 70 percent of his time in meetings, and the rest problem solving, reviewing reports and news. He scarcely had time to create anything of his own. Even his news releases and quotes were written for him.

He clicked on the file share request. It was from Chad Fordham. He was requesting access to Blake Carver's official dossier.

Speers called Fordham, knowing that the FBI Director would be startled to hear his voice. Making a file share request outside of one's own agency was a completely blind process. You couldn't see who owned them.

The FBI Director answered on the first ring. "Anything you want to know about Carver," Speers declared, "You can ask me right now."

It took Fordham a moment to form a response. "Sorry, Julian. I never guessed this would go through you personally."

"Just tell me what you're looking for."

"Well, everything, frankly. The president requested Carver's involvement, not me. I want to know more about who I'm working with."

Speers wasn't about to lay everything on the table. Besides, Carver's most interesting work had been deliberately omitted from the record. "You called me last year asking who the hell he was. You remember what I told you?"

He heard Fordham take a sip of something hot before speaking. "You said if I needed someone to parachute into a mountain fortress in the middle of the night to get somebody important, then Carver would be the guy."

"That's right. And here's what I should have said – if you needed someone to figure out that the target was there in the first place, then Carver would also be the guy. You remember two years ago when the CIA foiled an Allied Jihad plot to kidnap that drone pilot out in Nevada?"

"Don't tell me that – "

"Yes, that was Carver's operation. What else?"

"There's a rumor that he's in trouble with the House Committee on Domestic Intelligence."

"Then you already know he's protecting Nico Gold. It's not what I'd do, but at least Carver's loyal, which is more than I can say for most people."

"And that's all there is to it?"

"That's right. He's protecting an asset. That's it."

Fordham thanked Speers for his time and hung up. Speers had a hunch that Fordham wasn't the type to be satisfied that quickly, though. He'd find a way into Carver's file with or without permission. Speers unwrapped a grape lollipop and decided he better see if anything needed editing.

He navigated to Carver's dossier and began browsing through it, not quite sure what he was looking for. He cracked the lollipop between his molars, chewing it as casually as gum although it sounded like he was crushing rocks.

After college, Carver applied for the CIA's clandestine service. But the evaluating psychiatrist recommended him for the Joint Strike Operations Command (JSOC) – a paramilitary spy, capture and kill force rolled into one.

Pulling up the results of Carver's initial background check, he saw a handful of unpaid parking tickets that had shown up on his initial federal background check. Other than that, it looked like he had never broken the law. The polygraph hadn't budged when he'd claimed that he had never had drugs or alcohol. Heck, he'd never even had coffee. He had grown up in a small Mormon town in northern Arizona. When the examiner asked if he was religious, he answered no. When asked if he believed in God, he'd said yes.

Back then he had listed his primary hobby as "hunting." That figured. He had 5,000 square miles of Arizona's White Mountains as his backyard. His father had taught him how to stalk game in the woods and be stealthy enough to kill an antelope with a bow & arrow. The psychiatrist asked him how many of his kills he had eaten over the years. The point of the question had been to discover whether Carver valued animal life, or whether he felt entitled to kill for sheer enjoyment. A typical response would have been, "We eat everything we kill." Carver's response was off the charts: "Fourteen deer, 12 elk, 151 ducks, 3 antelope, 29 geese." He remembered *every single one* from the time he was nine years old. That was the super-autobiographical memory at work.

Aside from being an expert marksman, he had a high tolerance for risk, did not suffer from nightmares, and was just athletic enough to be dangerous.

Within five years of Carver's joining JSOC, his unit became extremely active in Afghanistan as the war on terror switched into high gear. His unit would go out after a bad guy virtually every night. As the months and years went on, they had filled secret prisons and cemeteries with their trophies.

Eventually JSOC created an intelligence support branch, which was initially staffed by CIA. Carver's commander reassigned him. They needed a mind like his in the command center. By all accounts he was great in his new role, but he hated it. He wanted to be out where the action was.

During the Hatch administration, when Speers had begun to suspect that something fishy was going on with the Pentagon's relationship with Ulysses USA, he had gone to the CIA Director and asked him who their best guy was. Someone that was as strong in intelligence as he was in execution. Blake Carver's name had been the first out of his mouth.

What followed was deliberately absent from the file. He had resigned from the CIA so that he would be accountable only to Speers. There was no more history.

Speers scrolled back up through the dossier. He stopped at the description of Carver's cognitive disorder. It concerned him. In the wrong hands, it could leave Carver vulnerable. *Due to enhanced episodic memory, most people with hyperthymesia spend an inordinate amount of time thinking about their past. They also have an amazing capacity to recall personal events or trivial details, including sensory details such as smells, tastes and sounds. Mr. Carver appears to have the rare ability to turn off "retrieval mode" so that he can focus on the present. He should, however, have regular neurological examinations to monitor the functions in his frontal cortex. Should he experience highly violent scenarios in the line of duty, for example, losing the ability to control his recall abilities could be far more crippling than a person with a normal prefrontal cortex.*

Speers highlighted the entire diagnosis. Then he deleted it.

Somewhere Over the Atlantic

With a phone call, Speers had arranged a private charter leaving immediately from Reagan National Airport. If they had to go to London, at least they were aboard a fast plane. The Gulfstream IV was capable of speeds just short of Mach 1, shortening the flight time to a little over five hours. That was way better than the winged whales Carver was accustomed to flying. With a few rare exceptions, his modus operandi had been hitching rides on military transport planes that happened to be heading his way. But in this case, he felt the cost of the charter – a couple hundred thousand dollars – was worth it. The trail was growing colder by the second.

As the Gulfstream cruised at 28,000 feet, Haley Ellis sat in a cream-colored leather chair facing his. She and Carver had said little to each other since taking off. They were both busy digesting a steady feed of public and classified information about the victims.

There was nothing obvious to suggest that Preston or Gish had ever met. The fact that they were both publicly elected officials from Western countries seemed to be just about the only thing they had in common. Carver was confident they would find a common link, but how long would that take? More than anything, it was the ensuing fire that puzzled him. How and why had it been started? The killers had placed a calling card in Preston's mouth. Obviously some sort of message. Why would they then burn the place up?

He composed a text message and fired it off to Julian: *anyone claimed responsibility?* Speers' reply: *nope. Playing hard to get.*

Now he received a stream of information from Arunus Roth about the senator's executive assistant, Mary Borst. She was 26 years old. She held a Dutch passport, having been born in Amsterdam to a prominent politician named Vera Borst. Graduated with honors from NYU, where she had studied political science. Immediately after graduation she had worked as a volunteer on Preston's reelection campaign, and had subsequently landed a job as a staff assistant in his D.C. office, where she had answered phones and staffed the front desk. In three years, she had worked her way up to an aide position, and then officer manager, before becoming Preston's executive assistant.

In an interview with a local newspaper, Vera Borst claimed to have raised Mary herself while working her way up through various positions in local and national government. By the time Mary had entered high school, her mother had taken a prominent position with UNICEF, and more recently, had been appointed an under secretary-general of the United Nations. She now lived in Seattle with her life partner, an American scientist.

"Mary Borst's mother is kind of a big deal," Carver remarked.

Ellis looked up. "Why focus on Preston's assistant right now?"

Carver switched off his tablet. "Say more about that."

"We have two high-ranking politicians ritually murdered on the same night. We should be looking for connection points. If we can find out what they had in common, and which relationships they may have shared, maybe we can find out who wanted them dead."

"Ever spend any time with the executive assistant to a senator?"

"Can't say that I have."

Ellis lowered her tablet, reached into the small bag she'd packed and pulled out a can of Venom energy drink. Carver's right eyebrow went up independently of the left.

"Venom? You'd actually buy something called Venom and put it into your body?"

Ellis shrugged. "It's just caffeine, guarana and sugar."

"More sugar? I couldn't help but notice that you added some to your coffee earlier."

"Could we stop talking about my nutritional habits for a moment? You were explaining why you think we should burn effort on the senator's assistant."

"Executive assistants on the Hill play a role that is simultaneously powerful and menial. They have a hand in everything from daily scheduling to the senator's personal life and what he wears. And still, they pick up dry-cleaning, get coffee, and act as a gatekeeper, which means dealing with a lot of irate friends and constituents who can never get enough time with him."

"What's your point?"

"That Mary Borst probably knew the senator better than his own wife did. If there's anyone who could tell us what the relationship was between Preston and Gish, it was her."

"You seem to be forgetting the fact that she's dead."

"No. I'm making the reasonable assumption that she had a confidant. Someone she told about her fears and anxieties. That person might be her roommate, or it might be her mother, but we need to talk to them, see if they know anything."

"And I suppose you'd like me to board the next plane back to Washington to do that?"

Carver held his hands up in surrender. "Whoa. This isn't personal. We're just talking strategy here."

Ellis chuckled the way people sometimes do when they are trying hard to remain civil. "Isn't it personal? Within 60 seconds of Speers assigning the two of us to this mission, you suggested I remain stateside while you go to London alone."

"I was trying to be practical."

"Were you being practical when you didn't get back to me after the Baltimore Marathon?"

So that was it. "You're right," he said. "I owe you an apology. You contacted me four times, and it was inexcusable of me not to get back to you."

"Four times?" Now you're making me sound like some kind of stalker. I left you one voice message, maybe two."

It had definitely been four, Carver knew. Her memory was average, but Carver's was extraordinary. The Monday after the marathon, Ellis had texted him at 11:48 a.m., saying it had been great to see him. She had then called and left a voice message at 2:10 pm the following day. She had called and left no messages at 7:54 pm on Thursday and again at 8:14 pm on Friday.

But Carver had learned long ago not to quibble over details in social situations, or reveal the freakish accuracy with which he could recall dates and events. His condition helped his work, but did little to improve his interpersonal relations. He had learned over time that insisting on the correctness of his recollections only led to needless arguments. And disclosing his hyperthymesia inevitably generated countless questions, in the form of pop quizzes. What did you have for lunch on March 2? What is the fourth paragraph on page 27 of *War and Peace*?

Better not to go there. He could never change the fact that the entire world suffered from mild amnesia, nor did it do any good to rub people's noses in it. It was easier just to change the subject.

"Haley," he said, "I'm trying to apologize. The reason I didn't call you was because of Hector. When we ran into each other, you'd just broken it off with him. He was crushed. I was trying to be sensitive."

"How is not calling me being sensitive?"

"If I'd contacted you, it would have led to dinner, drinks, etcetera. I couldn't do that to my friend."

Ellis leaned forward, looking him dead in the eye. "*Etcetera*? I wasn't calling you for a hook up, jerk. I was calling to ask about Hector." She unbuckled her seatbelt, stood, and stomped off to the plane's lavatory.

Well that was awkward, Carver thought. Had he really misread the situation that badly? Ellis hadn't been interested in him at all, and the four contacts within five days – none of which had mentioned Hector at all – were really just out of compassion for the guy she'd unceremoniously dumped? He thought not.

The buzz of Carver's phone broke his concentration. It was a message from Roth with a link to a live video feed. He clicked it.

The video showed FBI Director Chad Fordham standing at a podium. The ticket beneath the video read *BREAKING NEWS: Senator Rand Preston confirmed dead after tragic home fire.*

"We have very few details," Fordham began. *"The preliminary investigation into this tragedy indicates that the fire began within the senator's D.C. residence. I repeat that we have no reason at this time to suspect that the fire was arson. I can tell you that the senator's immediately family was safely in their home in Texas at the time of the fire. We are still investigating whether anyone else might have been home."*

Carver closed his eyes and leaned back against the headrest. It was only a matter of time before the conspiracy theorists were out in force on this one. The quicker he could find the killers, the better chance they would have of containing it. If they could solve this in a matter of days, there might even be time to set the record straight.

Their objective was clear. Discover who killed Senator Preston and Sir Gish. Find out why they killed him. And obliterate them before they can act again.

SIS Building
London

Their contact was waiting for them in the lobby of the building Carver knew as Legoland. MI6 headquarters had been built along the Thames River, and from afar, resembled something that had been constructed with toy-like building blocks. Others knew it as Babylon, due to its ziggurat-like shape.

Their man in London introduced himself as Sam Prichard. He wore a wrinkled blue suit that looked far too big for him. He quickly handed them visitor badges gestured toward the elevators. "Come on, then. You were expected upstairs a half-hour ago."

Carver waited to speak until the elevator doors closed. "Has anyone claimed responsibility?"

"Ten bloody hours, and still nothing."

When they reached the building's top floor, Prichard was the first off the elevator. He breezed them past a reception area and through two enormous white doors. "These are the Americans," he announced as he showed them into the next room. The office was a large cube constructed of white steel and glass, with an unusually high ceiling and an unobstructed view of the Thames. Despite the breathtaking grandeur of the architecture, Carver couldn't help but feel let down. This was his first time in Legoland, and despite its modern exterior, he was hoping that the inside would be more in line with his lifelong fantasy of the place. Walnut paneling, Chesterfield sofas, decanters of good whiskey.

SIS Chief Brice Carlisle stepped out from behind a semi-transparent standing desk. Unlike Prichard's frumpy attire, Carlisle's suit was downright crisp. He wore a somber black tie as if he himself were in mourning over the high-profile murders. He held his hands behind his back as his eyes darted back and forth between the Americans.

"Mr. Carlisle," Ellis said, holding out her hand. "It's an honor."

"I believe the proper salutation is Sir Brice," Carver corrected.

Carlisle shook Ellis' hand before turning to Carver. "Your reputation precedes you."

"Likewise," Carver said, but in truth, he knew little about Carlisle other than what was in his official biography. He had attended Cambridge and served as a diplomat in both Jordan and Saudi Arabia. He had since changed jobs like clockwork every two to three years, mostly in government posts relating to foreign affairs, with his last role as an intelligence advisor to the prime minister. He was thought to be an extremely bright man, but one with no apparent field experience.

The double doors through which they had come opened again. The bare legs attached to the exotic-looking brunette with the boy-cut were the first Carver had seen in London. "This is Seven Mansfield," Carlisle said. "She's working the case under Prichard here."

Carver held out his hand and tried not to stare at the legs underneath the houndstooth-patterned skirt-suit. "Ms. Mansfield."

"Call me Seven," she said. Her accent reminded Carver of the voices on the BBC World Service. Her look was decidedly sub-continental. The brown-skinned intelligence agent with the short-cropped hair was the first thing to bring a smile to Carver's lips all day.

Carlisle gestured to a sitting area furnished with four white leather Eames lounge chairs. "We watched the presser on Senator Preston. It was very convincing, don't you think?"

Carver shrugged. "If you say so. We've traveled a long way to get information that could have been transmitted by other means. I suggest we get into it."

Seven remained standing as she began walking them through the case. "Nils Gish was found in a storage room underneath the House of Parliament approximately 28 hours ago. The room was near an underground passage that's not open to the public."

"Who else had access?" Ellis said.

"There are several tunnels linking Parliament to the Westminster Tube station. They're used by government workers, mostly. The doors are locked from the Tube station side, but they come open with a swipe of a security badge or phone."

"Did Sir Gish often use these tunnels?"

"Unfortunately, yes," Carlisle cut in. "In my opinion, he was far too well-known to take public transport, and we understand his colleagues had discussed this with him. But he relished one-on-one conversations with his public. He boarded promptly at 5:30 most mornings, when it was possible to ride without being mobbed."

Carlisle cleared his throat. "That wasn't the case yesterday, however. For reasons unknown, he arrived to the office in the evening, when most workers had already left for the day. Let's see the footage from the station security camera."

Seven walked up to a massive monitor, nearly as tall as she was, built into the wall. It lit up instantly, displaying a number of folders containing media and findings from the crime scene. It flickered to life with a swipe of her fingertips, displaying a still image from a security camera. Sir Gish was shown entering the door in one frame. The next image was of two men wearing long raincoats. Their backs were to the camera, making it impossible to see their faces. They could be seen rushing to catch the door before it closed behind the MP.

"So he was followed," Ellis said.

"Yes. I regret to tell you that many of the station's other security cameras had not been recently maintained due to budget cuts. We did, however, manage to find a single image of one of their faces." She swiped the screen again, revealing a grainy image of a man with a Mediterranean complexion, perhaps in his late 20s, wearing wire frame glasses. He had a wide nose, with flared nostrils, and his eyes were set wide across his face.

"Ring any bells?" Carver said.

She shook her head. "We are, of course, running a facial recognition match through every database imaginable. And incidentally, we've also been pouring over the communications logs from Sir Gish's phone. Nothing unusual so far."

Before Carver and Ellis could ask additional questions, Seven displayed a high-resolution image of an octagon-shaped piece of black-and-red striped fabric that looked identical to the one he had found in Senator Preston's pocket.

"This is all we have linking the murders," she said, pointing to the handwritten text in the center of the handmade cloth. "The Latin stitched in gold thread here reads *Paratus enim dolor et cruciatus, in Dei nomine*. 'Prepared for pain and torment, in God's name.'"

Carver nodded. "Identical to the fabric stuffed in Senator Preston's mouth."

"Obviously the work of religious extremists," Prichard said. "We've had our boys working around the clock to find that language on sites operated by known groups. Come up with zero so far."

"You're headed in the wrong direction," Carver said. "Whoever is behind this, they aren't paying homage to any modern terrorist organization."

"And you know this how?"

"By reading your history."

Prichard crossed his arms, then his legs. "What history is that?"

"British. Ever heard of the Holy Alliance?"

"Allied Jihad splinter group, isn't it?"

"Wrong religion entirely," Carlisle cut in, glaring at Prichard as the man shrank into his chair. He then turned his gaze to the Americans. "If I follow you, Agent Carver, you're saying that these symbols are linked to Christianity, not Islam."

"Correct. The Holy Alliance was the common name for the Vatican's intelligence service, although the Vatican itself never acknowledged its existence. We refer to it simply as Vatican Intelligence."

"Don't see what that has to do with British history," Prichard quipped.

"Vatican Intelligence was thought to have come into existence in the 1560s as a reaction to the Tudor dynasty's rejection of the pope's moral authority over England. When Queen Elizabeth formed the English Protestant Church, it was clear that they would carry on the defiant tradition of her father, Henry VIII."

"We've all passed basic history, thank you."

"Shut up," Carlisle admonished Prichard. "Go on, Agent Carver. Obviously we could all use a refresher on the subject."

"Pope Pius V didn't take kindly to losing England to the Protestant movement. The most logical thing to do was conspire to assassinate Queen Elizabeth and pass the throne to Mary Queen of Scots, who was a devout Catholic. So he formed the Holy Alliance. Jesuits, mostly, since they swore their personal oath of allegiance to the pope."

Prichard smirked. "As I recall, Elizabeth survived until 1603, and she did not meet her end at the hands of Jesuits."

"True. They failed that time, but they evolved. Over the next century, two special ops units were created. The first was known as the Octagon. It was discovered when an operative named François Ravaillac stepped aboard the running boards of Henry IV's carriage and stabbed the king through his Protestant heart. When they caught Ravaillac, they found rosary beads and an octagon in his pocket. It was made out of parchment, not fabric, but it also contained a handwritten phrase that was roughly identical the one on our octagons. *'Prepared for pain and torment, in God's name.'*"

"I imagine pain and torment was exactly what he got," Seven said.

Carver nodded. "They brought four horses in, harnessed one to each of his limbs, and sent them running in different directions."

Carlisle winced. "Ouch. But you said there were two related organizations."

"The second was known as the Black Order. It was created in 1644 by Pope Innocent X's sister-in-law, Olimpia Maidalchini."

"A woman?"

"She was one of the world's first real intelligence chiefs. And she was merciless. The Black Order specialized in lethal operations against the church's enemies. Its victims were found with the striped fabric stuffed in their orifices."

Prichard folded his arms across his chest. "Are you implying the Vatican is still capable of this sort of thing?"

"No. The Black Order was formally dissolved. But it continued on as a separate and rogue defender of the church. The last trace of the organization was in the 1800s, after Napoleon's invasion of Rome. Some believe that they embarked on a failed mission to free the pope, and that was the end of them."

Prichard stood. "I say the killers plucked these tidbits out of a history book. They're copycat killers."

"Maybe," Carver conceded. "The only thing I know for sure is that there's more to come."

Carlisle sat forward, giving Carver his full attention. "What are you getting at?"

"We all know how this works. An organization commits a horrific act for shock value, and then claims responsibility. Sometimes they make demands. But our killers…"

"Have yet to make any demands." Carlisle slumped back in the chair, looking as deflated as an uncorked air mattress.

"Right. And that's what worries me."

Eisenhower Building
Washington D.C.

Pangs of envy grew within Chad Fordham as he made his way to Speers' office. The 1888 federal building, affectionately known as Old Executive, stood adjacent to the West Wing of the White House. One of the city's most stately buildings, it was adorned by an impressive 900 classical exterior columns.

In stark contrast, Fordham's FBI headquarters – The J. Edgar Hoover Building, located several blocks away on Pennsylvania Avenue – had been described by Reuters not only as a "dreary 1970s behemoth," but also as one of the world's ugliest buildings.

Fordham exited the third floor elevator and started down a well-lit corridor that was full of ambitious, clean-cut feds in conservative suits. Down at the end of the hallway, at the building's corner, he found Speers' office. The previous resident – a GS-14 from OMB – was carting his last box out of the place.

The FBI director closed the door behind him and glared at Speers, who was working behind a 19th century oak partner's desk that looked like it weighed more than his car.

"I'll say this for you, Julian. You've got cajones."

With Eva's blessing, Speers had just reclaimed the same office he'd had during the Hatch Administration. It was an insanely good space. A corner office complete with a view of historic 17th Street NW, a fireplace and a dumb waiter.

"It was the only sensible solution," Speers said. "I need to be in close proximity to you and the president during this crisis. McLean's just too far."

Fordham sat down in the chair before him. "When you hear what I've got to say, you're going to wish you were a lot farther away than McLean."

"Try me."

"The preliminary report on the Preston fire points to arson."

Speers nodded. "I assume the target was first responders. What did they use as a detonator?"

"You're thinking way too sophisticated. I'm talking pedestrian, no frills, old school arson. You might remember a stack of paint cans in the basement?"

Speers' face lost some of its color. "You're telling me someone just lit a match and set fire to the house?"

Fordham folded his hands in his lap. "And left the gas stove on, which caused the ensuing explosion."

Speers leaned forward. "When we left, the only two people in the house were Mary Borst and your guy, what's his name?"

"Hank Bowers. According to him, he stepped into the front yard to take a confidential phone call a few minutes after we left, leaving Mary in the home alone."

"I know Bowers is a trusted member of your team, but did you check out his story?"

Fordham nodded. "Phone records match up. But the other thing is…" Fordham leaned forward, resting his elbows on his knees. "They only pulled one body from the ashes."

"Which one?"

"Preston's. And that can only mean one thing. Mary Borst is alive."

SIS Building

Seven went back to the enormous monitor and touched one of the folder icons. A set of grisly crime scene photos appeared onscreen. Finally, Carver thought. This was what they had flown all the way across the Atlantic to see.

"Severe trauma around the wrists?" Carver asked.

Seven touched one of the thumbnail autopsy photos and dragged it to the middle of the screen, then zoomed in until Gish's wrists were visible. Deep flesh wounds, an inch wide, ground down to the bone. Much like Preston's.

"And were Sir Gish's shoulders dislocated?" Carver said.

"Two for two," Seven replied with some amazement.

Carver turned to Ellis. "Ropes again."

Prichard popped out of his seat. "Pardon?"

"The D.C. crime scene burned down before we could do a proper forensic examination, but I was reasonably sure the senator was subjected to rope torture."

Carlisle grimaced at the thought of Nils Gish strung up by a rope. "I suppose that is consistent with the predilections of this Black Order group you told us about?"

Carver nodded. "The *strappado*. They would tie the victim's hands together behind his or her back, loop the rope over a high point in the room, and hoist them up. At a certain point, the body would be suddenly dropped. The shoulders and wrists were the first things to break, but it also put pressure on the lungs, making it increasingly difficult to breathe."

"Bloody hell."

"But the strappado has made a comeback of sorts in recent years. It would be impossible to tie it to any particular group."

Seven touched the screen and opened another photograph. It was far more grisly, a photograph of Gish's legs, which were severely lacerated. "Poor man was cut to ribbons. They started with the balls of his feet and made their way up his ankles and legs. The first few dozen were shallow enough so that he might not have bled to death, but eventually, they punctured a main artery in the left leg."

Carver stood. "I don't think these were ritual killings at all. The rope is far from the quickest or cleanest assassination method, and if they really wanted to be sadistic, they would've cut genitals, ears or faces."

"Agreed," Carlisle concluded. "The killers were after information."

Government Flat
London

By the time they left MI6 headquarters for their flat, it had been approximately 14 hours since the killings of Nils Gish and Rand Preston. No group had yet claimed responsibility.

Or had they? It occurred to Carver that the entire point of placing the octagon-shaped fabric inside the mouths of the victims was to claim credit. Only the message wasn't for them. It was for someone who already knew who the killers were.

The St. James-area flat Speers had retained for traveling intelligence operatives was on the sixth floor of a building that had the old-world charm that Carver had missed at the ultra-modern MI6 headquarters. Carver and Ellis opened the door with the security code Speers had given them, and wordlessly set about sweeping the two-bedroom apartment for bugs. Ellis was done with her part in six minutes. It took Carver a few minutes longer to feel secure. After both electronic and manual inspections, he finally sat on the couch and switched on his computer.

"It's actually charming," Ellis remarked as she took in the hardwood floors in the living room, and the windows that, if she stood at just the right angle, had a view of Green Park. "Why would the ODNI spring for a place like this?"

"London hotel rates, obviously," Carver shrugged. "At 300 pounds a night, a place this close to Parliament probably paid for itself within the first eight or nine years."

Ellis scratched her underarm and caught a whiff of her own odor. "Mind if I shower?"

"Ladies first." The gesture was pure chivalry, as he himself had not had so much as a sink shower in the past 24 hours.

As he heard Ellis turn the shower on, Carver powered up his tablet, linked to the secure DNI satellite feed, and logged into the mission cloud. He was eager to see what, if anything, had been accomplished since they had stepped off the plane.

Arunus Roth had been tasked with mashing up all public information about Preston and Gish and looking for common links. He cringed when he read the kid's summary statement: *No obvious connections.*

Roth had prepared a grid with key information in categories, summarizing everything from education to public perceptions about each man's political positions. It was unlikely that either man would have been paired through an online matchmaking algorithm. Although both were politicians, Gish was socialist-leaning in his beliefs, and Preston was so far right that he was even considered a hardline conservative in his home state of Texas. Preston was so religious that he had led prayer circles on the campaign trail, whereas the only times Gish attended church were for weddings and funerals.

Neither man had any known relatives in the other man's country. They did not appear to be connected through any social networks. Gish had studied in D.C. for one year of college, but he was older than Preston, who would have been in high school in Texas at the time.

There were no known photos of Gish and Preston together.

There were no news articles in which they appeared at the same time.

Nothing to go on.

The trail was getting colder every minute, and yet no one had yet analyzed the two men's social networks for common connections. No one had yet cross-indexed the two men's standard contacts for first and second-degree connections. No one had yet analyzed their travel itineraries for common destinations.

As Carver stared at the depressing report, a new entry came onto the screen:

> Mary Borst's body NOT FOUND on arson site. Subject is now considered a person of interest in both the arson and the death of Senator Preston. POI has been added to federal NO FLY LIST. TSA is to notify Hank Bowers immediately should she book tickets or attempt to board any aircraft. Attempts being made to contact mother and stepfather. No classified information will be offered. As far as the public is concerned, she will be considered a missing person.

Carver got up, went down the hall and found that Ellis had left the bathroom door slightly ajar.

"She's alive," Carver shouted through the opening in the door.

"What?"

"Mary Borst is alive!"

He heard the water shut off and trickle to a halt. "Oh my God."

"This is getting very deep, very fast," Carver said, still standing in the hallway, trying not to be distracted by the fact that Ellis was stark naked on the other side of the door. "Even if they manage to catch her, she couldn't have done this alone. She'd had to have help in D.C., to say nothing of London."

"We need to tell MI6."

"What we need is some decent support. It's been eight hours since we left Washington, and our guys haven't been able to find a single connection point between Gish and Preston, other than the bizarre way they were killed."

"You heard the president. We can't put 50 analysts on this without raising huge red flags."

"We don't need 50 analysts, Haley. All we need is one incredible geek in front of a computer."

He heard the steel O-rings slide across the shower bar, then the smack of Ellis' wet feet on the bathroom tile. The door opened. Elis stood in a towel before him, her wet hair slicked back on her head.

"What do you suggest?" she said.

Eastern Cape
South Africa

Carver drove through scattered rain over twisting one-lane mountain roads. The rental car's GPS was useless, and his phone hadn't gotten a signal since leaving Johannesburg early that morning. He stopped for directions often. This was not only because there were so few road signs in the rural Eastern Cape. It was also because most of the people he asked for directions had never been more than 20 miles from home.

As night fell he listened to African pop music to stay awake. The highway became a series of mesmerizing canyon switchbacks that hugged steep cliffs without so much as a single guardrail. Ten hours after leaving Johannesburg International Airport, he got petrol in Stutterheim, a sleepy little town in the heart of farm country, and went on through the hilly, golden boondocks toward the backwater village of Kei Mouth on the eastern shore.

The last terrestrial radio station fizzled out as he entered the former Transkei, land of the Xhosa tribe. The Transkei region had been part of a wider homeland for the Xhosa tribe. Some of South Africa's greatest leaders had emerged from these hills. Nelson Mandela, Thabo Mbeki, and Govan Mbeki. But the rural areas were still virtually lawless, diplomatically isolated, and legally recognized only by the country of South Africa. Unification with the Eastern Cape had brought few tangible benefits over the past couple of decades. There were a few businesses, to be sure, and a few beach homes owned by white ranchers. But it was still so poor that many of the native Xhosas were still without basic plumbing. It was the perfect place to hide.

Xhosa children bartered beaded necklaces for candy bars as he waited 20 minutes for a single-car ferry to take him across the Kei River.

Carver entered the village two hours later. There were few services in town, and the few that existed had posted signs saying CLOSED FOR WINTER in English and Afrikaans. Business windows – all of them – were dark. Finally he spotted the sign that read BED AND BREAKFAST. He turned down a spooky-looking street that led to a gray cement building. This was supposed to be the place. It had better be, Carver thought. He had come a very long way from London under completely unreasonable time constraints.

He shut off the car engine and opened the car door. A pack of dogs raced out from under the front steps. Skinny, tenacious mutts. All bones and teeth. In the face of a hard drizzle, Carver fended off these hounds of hell with the car door, bonking their bony heads with it as they bit and tugged at his left ankle. He felt the familiar warm trickle of blood dampen his sock. Barking in the distance spared him further bloodshed as the pack suddenly broke away, howling at breakneck speed down the street he had driven in on.

"We're closed!" yelled a woman's voice from the motel office. She spoke from behind a screen. She sounded American. Good. This was definitely the place.

He unfurled himself from the car, smoothed the wrinkles in his gray suit and approached the building with his hands in the air.

"I'll shoot," the voice warned.

"I'd rather you didn't," Carver said as he measured his approach. He stood several feet from the door and could only make out a shadow in the dense screen door. "It's Madge, right?"

More silence. Then the voice said, "I suggest you get back in the car."

"Tell your husband Blake Carver is here to see him."

He heard her step away from the door. She returned moments later and opened it wide for Agent Carver to enter.

He stepped inside. The house smelled of barbecue. Aside from an expensive-looking entertainment console at the living room's far wall, the place was sparsely furnished. There were few books and no pictures on the wall except for a print of DaVinci's *The Last Supper*.

Nico's girlfriend, Madge, held a sawed-off shotgun. She looked unhappy. She had gained a great deal of weight since the CIA had last photographed her. Her long brown locks were graying around the temples and had been clipped into a short, unflattering cut. Judging by the jagged pattern of her bangs, Madge had done it herself using shearing scissors.

"Nice dogs," Carver said. "Yours?"

Madge didn't smile. "The kitchen." She pointed to the next room.

Carver found Nico Gold sitting at the kitchen table with three kinds of meat on a plate before him. He looked much as he had when Carver had first met him in the Lee Federal Penitentiary the previous year. The African sun had added little color to his pale skin, and the meat-centered African diet had hardly fleshed out his lanky frame. He had, however, dispensed with his eyeglasses and had dyed his hair blonde. The tattoos that had read "EVA" on both forearms were gone. He wore a t-shirt that said OBEY in stylized font.

"Close the door," Nico told him.

Carver sat in the chair where Madge had no doubt been eating across from her husband minutes before. The ex-con's face was full of dread. He had the sweet smell of alcohol on his breath. There was an empty pinotage bottle on the table and another that was half-full.

"Dreamed the grim reaper was coming for me last night," Nico said. "Couldn't shake the feeling all day. Never had a dream like that before. So bad."

Carver said nothing. He watched Nico's hand shake as he held his wine glass.

"I need to know how you found me," Nico continued. "I don't use credit cards. I've taken nobody into confidence. My only bank accounts in this country are in a town 200 miles away under a different name. They draw their funds from banks abroad that have no idea who I am."

"Don't blame yourself," Carver consoled him. "You were good. The best."

"So how in God's name did you find me?"

"Your eyes gave you away," Carver said, referring to the corrective vision procedure Nico underwent in Durban earlier that year. "Organ theft is a bit of a problem here. The government requires that doctors document every eye that gets the surgery. The images are uploaded into a national database. Naturally, we have a script running that scans every image of every retina and matches them up with profiles on our list."

Nico pounded the table with his fists, bouncing the dinner plates.

"Everything okay?" Madge yelled from the other room.

"Fine, dear," Nico yelled back through the door. He steadied his gaze on Carver and lowered his voice.

Nico reached for the open bottle of pinotage on the table and poured himself a full glass. He offered some to Carver, who politely declined. "I'd forgotten what a teetotaler you are. Probably made it all the way to Africa without so much as a wink of sleep or a drop of caffeine."

"I'm not here to talk about me."

"I read about O'Keefe," Nico said. "I'm sorry. I could tell you two were close."

Meagan O'Keefe, a young cryptologist from NSA whom Speers had turned into a field operative, had been Carver's partner. The auburn-haired firecracker was untrained in combat, but her grounded, pragmatic procedural style had proved to be the perfect match for Carver's aggressive energy. The two had worked together just long enough to get close when they were thrust into what would later be known as the Ulysses Coup. O'Keefe had died serving her country during the six-day siege. Carver missed her like crazy.

Carver got up, pulled a cup from the cupboard and helped himself to some tap water. He drank eight ounces and put the cup down. "I don't discuss Agent O'Keefe with anyone."

Nico finished his glass. "So. I guess Eva sent you?"

"Careful. Nobody calls her by her first name now. Not even me. It's Madam President."

"She's going to hand me over to the Saudis, isn't she?"

"She was thinking about it. Then she read Haley Ellis' report detailing the miraculous way that five Ulysses Bradleys disappeared from the South Lawn just in time for the motorcade to come through."

Nico folded his arms across his chest, looking partially validated. "Well, if you're packing a presidential pardon, I'd say it's high time you whip it out."

"The way the president sees it, you owe her one more favor."

Carver, of course, was taking liberties with the truth. The president had no idea he was there, and neither did Speers, yet. The way he saw it, if his mission status was deniable, then the methods and resources he used to complete it were up to him.

"I'm retired," Nico said. "Don't even own a computer. I've spent the last year learning Afrikaans and Xhosa. Madge tends to the guests during fishing season and cooks. I make repairs to the place, read books. We're not hurting anybody."

Carver pulled two newly issued passports from his jacket pocket. "We have an issue that needs tending to. Your services are required."

Then he pulled three South African Airways tickets from his pocket and laid them on the table. The flight was to leave from Johannesburg International Airport and land in Washington some 17 hours later.

"This flight is tomorrow morning!" Nico raved. "We'd have to drive all night to get to Johannesburg in time."

Carver gripped Nico's spindly right arm and pulled him from the table. "Good point. You've got one minute to convince Madge that it's a good idea. I'll give you ten to pack."

SIS Building

The first tangible connection between Rand Preston and Nils Gish was an address: 9002 River Road, Rockville, Maryland.

The murdered MP's official college records had been delivered to the Legoland war room where Ellis and Seven Mansfield conducted their investigation. The large paper file – Gish's college career had begun prior to the computerization of Oxford's administrative operations – had been delivered by the same assistant that kept their teakettle full all day. Ellis appreciated the constant influx of Earl Gray, as she still hadn't been able to locate a can of Venom in London.

With Carver off to Africa, and Prichard out gumshoeing Gish's old haunts, Ellis and Seven had focused their efforts on finding any link that Roth's semantic search exercise might have missed. While they had already discovered that Gish had studied abroad at the University of Maryland for one year, they had ruled out any connection to Preston, as it had occurred 12 years prior to the Senator's arrival in Washington.

Ellis had grown up in Richmond, but she knew the Washington area well enough by now to know that Rockville was an affluent area northwest of D.C., and 19 miles from the University of Maryland campus. It struck her as odd that Gish, then a young exchange student from London, would live so far from campus. The only reason she could think of was if Gish had chosen to live with a relative or friend.

She looked up the address, which corresponded to an enormous estate a half-hour from Washington D.C. She pulled up Street View. This definitely wasn't student housing. The term estate did not quite do it justice. The high ivory-covered walls and mounted cameras in the surrounding trees gave the place the feel of a compound. A sign above the gated entrance read "Eden."

On a lark, Ellis had VPN'd into McLean's dual-search tool, which allowed her to simultaneously run queries against both the intelligence community database – which included all declassified and classified data at her security clearance level – as well as public search engines. The record match on the residential address where Gish had lived during his study-abroad year postdated his era by nearly three decades.

Twenty-seven years after Gish's study-abroad year, Mary Borst had listed the same residential address on her collegiate records.

Kei Mouth South Africa

Carver pressed the RFID gun to Nico's bicep and pressed the trigger. The hacker yelped as the tiny tracking chip became embedded beneath the skin, extending tiny tentacles that would make it nearly impossible to remove without prior deactivation.

"Get a move on," Carver said as he unfurled his grip. "We're on a tight schedule."

He watched the fugitive leave the kitchen with his tail between his legs. A flurry of whispers, like steam hissing from a boiling kettle, floated in from the next room as Nico explained the situation to Madge. Carver almost felt sorry for him. He had never emasculated another man in the presence of his woman.

Most of the people Carver had taken into custody over the years had been loners by virtue of their professions. From Carver's perspective, the main thing that assassins, mercenaries and hackers had in common was that their sources of companionship tended to come through artificial means, satisfied either in the deep digital recesses of some massive multiplayer video game, or via anonymous encounters with sex workers. In this respect, Nico was an outlier. During his time in Lee Federal Penitentiary, Madge had written him more than 70 letters. As a middling programmer herself, Madge looked up to him as a superstar activist geek. She even bought into his manufactured Robin Hood mystique, although his lack of spiritual faith disturbed her. During the course of their courtship – during which she would drive up to his Virginia prison from her home in the Carolinas – she set out to reform him.

During the 12-hour drive here from Johannesburg, Carver had deliberated whether to tell Nico how hard the committee had pressed him to give up his location. Carver didn't expect or want a thank-you. He only wanted to impress upon Nico how his past deeds had fostered some goodwill.

A crash emanated from the next room, followed by shouting. Good Lord. Were they actually fighting? Madge was screaming at the top of her lungs. "They're going to have to go through me! They're just going to hand you over to the Saudis! Is that what you want?"

Carver peeked into the living room. Madge was sprawled over Nico, struggling for control of the shotgun. He slipped back into the kitchen, cursing himself for not being more careful. Why hadn't he disarmed her upon entering? He had actually believed that Madge, of all people, would want to go back to her life in the U.S.

He had clearly miscalculated. She and Nico had come here together and established a life far from the reach of the Americans or Saudis. A bond had formed, and in the process, it seemed that Madge was wearing the pants now. Carver had shown up out of the blue, a hostile force from another time and dimension.

Something made of glass smashed against the wall and shattered. Carver hadn't come all this way only to lose Nico in a lover's spat. He had to intervene.

He hoped the bullet-resistant vest he wore under his suit would be enough against Madge's sawed-off shotgun. By reducing the length of the barrel, she had effectively removed the gun's choke, giving the weapon a substantially wider spray pattern.

Carver reached inside his jacket and drew the SIG Sauer P226 from his shoulder holster. God help me, he thought. He had never lifted a hand against a woman, and he had no intention of shooting her. He decided to leave the weapon on top of the refrigerator. If he so much as grazed Madge, his working relationship with Nico would be over.

He grabbed a broad iron skillet from the stovetop. It was greasy and it smelled like sausage, but it was a reasonable substitute for riot gear.

Wielding the skillet, Carver rolled into the living room, then sprung forth like an undersized defensive tackle, keeping low as he powered toward Madge, who now stood with one foot atop Nico's chest and the gun pointed straight down at him. He caught sight of her bare knee, round and moon-like, exposed through slacks that had been torn in the scuffle.

She swung the barrel toward Carver, who charged like a kitchen knight with the skillet covering his face and neck. A blast of pellets strafed his midsection and the bottom of the skillet.

Forward momentum propelled him ahead regardless. He chipped Madge at the knees, their collective mass hurling into the wall, which caved like cardboard. Particle dust mushroomed in the air as Carver wrestled Madge for the shotgun. She managed to fire the right barrel. The heat of the shortened barrel burned Carver's hands and blasted a soccer ball-sized section out of what was left of the wall.

Carver felt another pair of hands tugging at his shoulders. He threw a donkey kick that landed in Nico's groin, sending him once again to a useless heap upon the living room carpet. He then bore his knee into Madge's chest, throwing an open-handed blow to Madge's forehead. The back of her skull cracked against a wall stud.

She fell limp under him. *Don't be dead,* Carver thought. *Don't even be brain-damaged.*

Despite the sting of welts rising under his vest, he reached out, feeling her wrist. Thankfully, her pulse was strong. And looking across her chest, he could see that she was breathing. She was just going to have a humongous knot on her head when she woke up.

He got to his feet, grabbed her ankles, and dragged her out of the wall crevice. Then he collapsed onto the sofa, lifted his shirt –which was riddled with dozens of tiny holes – and grappled with the straps of his under armor until the vest could be peeled away from his body. He let out an audible groan as he separated it from his body, letting his skin breathe.

Carver watched as Nico got to his hands and knees and crawled to Madge's side. He lifted the hand of the crazed lover who had attacked him and kissed it tenderly. Wonders never ceased. The man who had once been considered the world's most notorious cybercriminal was, emotionally speaking, stripped to the core.

He rubbed his rib cage with his fingertips, checking to see if anything felt out of place. "When did Madge start going to fight club?"

Nico's eyes rolled slowly upwards. Carver expected to see hostility in them, but Nico simply shook his head, as if to imply that Carver hadn't the vaguest understanding of human temperament. He drew his legs under his body and sat cross-legged.

"Madge is one of the gentlest people I've ever met."

"Could've fooled me."

"The Xhosa have a saying: There is no beast that does not roar in its den."

SIS Building

Finding out who owned the massive estate known as Eden, at 9002 River Road, was no easy task. Despite the address matching the collegiate mailing address of both Mary Borst and Nils Gish, there were virtually no public records on the property. Ellis finally had to get Speers to phone a friend at the IRS. Twenty minutes later, he came back with the name of the owner: The Fellowship World Initiative, a 5013C.

The nonprofit organization had no website, no social media presence and no listing on sites that rated charities. Not even a Wikipedia page.

After a lot of searching, Ellis finally unearthed an article that had been published way back in the early 2000s. The website it appeared on was at an obscure web address with spammy ads all over the place. It looked like an abandoned personal site that had been taken over by an ad network.

The article was called "The Country Club Cult that Runs Washington." Ellis scanned the 300 or so words on the first page.

It appeared to be a firsthand account of power meetings among several high-ranking congressmen at the estate known as Eden. Her eyes grew wide when she saw one of the names mentioned in the article intro: Senator Rand Preston.

It was easy to see how Arunus Roth had missed it. The article was a scanned image of a page out of a defunct print magazine called Inside Washington. Ellis' hands were starting to sweat. She clicked through to read the rest of the story. To her dismay, the link to the next page was broken.

She hit the back button and found the name of the writer, Nathan Drucker, on the scanned image. His bio read:

Nathan Drucker is a writer for Capitol Herald, covering congressional news and events.

Ellis navigated immediately to the Capitol Herald site, and then to its staff page. Nathan Drucker's photo was near the top of the page under the title Senior Editor. He was a curious-looking fellow, with small eyes, a monobrow and a flamboyant, waxed, handlebar mustache.

She wasted no time in dialing the Capitol Herald newsroom, selecting Drucker's extension from the phone tree.

"Nate Drucker," a man's voice answered.

"Hi," Ellis said. "I'm calling in regards to an article you wrote several years ago, called the Country Club Cult that Runs Washington."

The journalist didn't immediately respond. The silence was filled by the dull roar of newsroom chatter.

"Are you there?" she said.

She heard a door shut. Drucker had apparently gone somewhere private to talk.

"Who is this?" His tone had changed completely. Whether it was paranoia or anger, Ellis wasn't sure.

"My name is Haley Ellis," she said, immediately regretting that she had given him her real name. "Do you have a few minutes to chat?'"

Drucker exhaled deeply and loudly, as if merely mentioning the old article had touched a nerve.

"That piece was published a long time ago," he said. "Are you from the Bureau?"

The Bureau? Ellis had found smoke. She was betting that she would find fire, too.

Eisenhower Building

Speers cringed when a video chat invitation from Chad Fordham appeared on his screen. He accepted grudgingly. Although he himself had been an early adopter of video chat way back in the day, a part of him wished it had never been invented. He missed the freedom of multitasking during audio-only calls. He was constantly looking off-camera as he monitored his neverending feed of incoming messages.

"You've got lunch in your beard," the FBI director said as soon as the connection was established.

Speers moved a reasonable distance from the camera while he combed his salt-and-pepper goatee with his fingers.

"Better?"

"Yup," Fordham observed. "How's it going?"

"Just another day in paradise," Speers said, leaning back in his chair with his hands clasped behind his head. "I just spoke with the operatives whom we've entrusted with restoring global security."

"Something wrong?"

"It seems that Carver has enlisted the help of Nico Gold."

Fordham smirked the way people do when they hear about little boys getting up to mischief. "The president's not going to like that one bit."

"Better that she not know," Speers said. "We need to shield her for her own protection."

"Risky."

The two men didn't always agree with each other, but Speers respected him. That hadn't always been the case. They had knocked heads a few times during the Hatch Administration over funding and, more recently, issues relating to the DNI's increasing control over strategic intelligence operations. But when it counted, during the

Ulysses Coup, Fordham had made the gutsy call to deploy an improvised force of special agents to help defend the Capitol. Speers would never forget that.

"What choice do we have?" Speers said. "So far, the intel our people have turned up has been garbage, and Carver is the one out in the field, shouldering all the responsibility without even a guarantee that we would extract him if he got into trouble."

"What about the committee?"

"Screw the committee. Carver should get the job done any way he sees fit, as far as I'm concerned."

"All righty then. And what about Ellis?"

"She's on her way back to D.C. to interview some journalist that might know something. What about you?"

"It's 24 hours after Mary Borst disappeared, and we have no idea where she is. Her roommate says she didn't come home, and Hank has been unable to reach the mother."

"She's in Europe, right?"

"Relocated to Seattle, but she's constantly traveling on business. She's one of the UN's most senior people."

"But she must have seen the news about Preston. Weird that she wouldn't have come to Washington out of concern for her daughter by now." As soon as Speers said it, he thought of his own schedule. He hadn't even been home since the crisis began, and home was just a few miles away. "Did we triangulate Mary's phone?"

"Obviously. Zero activity. The phone either went up in the fire, or the battery's been removed. In the meantime, we've contacted her carrier and we have complete access to all her communications. The inbound calls are just piling up, one after another. Concerned friends, distant relatives who knew she worked for the senator keep dialing in, leaving messages of support."

"Outbound?"

Fordham shook his head. "Nothing."

Speers rested his elbows on the oak desk. "The simplest explanation is usually the right one."

"Meaning…"

"Our people made a mistake. Maybe she really did go up in the fire, and we just missed her. Let's get a second set of eyes onsite."

Johannesburg, South Africa

It had been a hard drive from Nico's hideout in Kei Mouth, through the winding roads of the Eastern Cape, and into the grassy golden flatlands of the Transvaal. Carver had let Nico drive while he kept a careful watch from the passenger seat. If they were going to work together again, he had to re-establish the trust Nico had destroyed when he fled the country. That meant giving him a job to do.

Nico had driven without incident, asking only that the radio remain off so that he could process all that had happened. Apart from lunch orders and bathroom breaks, there was very little talking between the two men. That was fine by Carver. He too had plenty to mull over. Chiefly, how the president was going to react when she found out that he had dug Nico Gold out of hiding for this. With luck, Nico would easily earn his way out of the president's doghouse. If he didn't show results, and fast, Carver himself might be looking for a hideout.

As they approached the airport, Carver pulled a battery out of the glove compartment and inserted it into his phone.

"Either you really needed some quiet time," Nico observed, "or you didn't want anyone to know where you were."

Carver nodded. "More like I didn't want people to know where *you* were."

"Houses built close together also burn together."

"What's that supposed to mean?"

"It means our wagons are hitched together, Agent Carver. The way I see it, The House Committee on Domestic Intelligence would have given you a pass if you'd disclosed my location. I want you to know I appreciate it. It's the only reason I haven't run this car into a ditch."

Carver turned in his seat. "That committee hearing was closed to the public."

"That sort of thing has never deterred me."

"You said you'd given up computers."

"What I said was that I didn't own a computer. And that was the truth. I did that to honor a promise to Madge. But I might have mosied down to the hotel every once in a while. The night desk manager was very accommodating."

As they pulled into the car rental return lot, Carver powered up an IP-anonymous browser on his phone, then logged onto the mission cloud. Arunus Roth had just uploaded a message he'd titled URGENT – FOR REAL – CALL ME!!! There were no other details.

He did so. Roth answered on the first ring.

"Where have you been?" he said breathlessly. "I've been calling you for hours. There's a break in the Adrian Zhu disa—"

Carver cut the kid off before he could say another word. "Per Julian, Crossbow is on hold. I thought he'd made that clear."

"This isn't about Crossbow per se," Roth clarified. "But it may be related. Just hear me out, bro."

"You've got 60 seconds. And don't call me bro."

"Zhu's last known location was at a hotel parking garage in the Rome suburbs. After that, the GPS stopped chirping. Tom Callahan called last night. It seems the morgue contains a couple of bodies that were found in the garage that night."

Carver's hopes for resuming the operation suddenly faded. "Did Callahan ID the bodies?"

"Neither one is Adrian Zhu, if that's what you're wondering. But here's the part that's relevant to us. One of them was carrying an octagon-shaped piece of fabric."

Carver signed off as Nico put the car in Park.

"Change of plans," Carver said. "Your homecoming will have to wait. We're headed to Italy."

For the first time all day, Nico cracked a smile.

The Villa
Rome

Adrian Zhu had no idea how far they had already descended. A hundred meters? Two hundred? Looking up through the center of the coiling iron staircase, the light from the villa, where they had left the Shepherd in a state of prayerful meditation, was rapidly shrinking away. The helix-shaped staircase seemed to plunge endlessly into the blackness below.

Lars was at his side now, leading him behind a small group of armed guards. The tuff rock surrounding the staircase had been recently excavated. The ironwork vibrated beneath his feet. Somewhere in the distance, a group of generators hummed, no doubt powering a series of small lights strung along the vertical passage.

In a few minutes, he would finally see the lab that he had so meticulously designed from the other side of the world. Creating a world-class paleo-DNA lab was difficult under the best of circumstances, but Zhu had done so in complete secrecy. The power that had come with the Chinese government contracts had been offset by a great deal of oversight. It was assumed that his phones, email and all other forms of communication were compromised, if not by the Chinese, then by the prying eyes of American intelligence. He had therefore conducted his work in person, in the rear of a Beijing mahjong parlor owned by a local Fellowship elder. Over the past three years, Lars had made 22 trips in and out of the country to meet with him, going over the exact equipment, procedures and staffing necessary to make the project possible. What they were attempting to do would surpass anything accomplished in world history. There was zero room for error.

His anxiety was coupled by a nervousness that he had never known. Maybe the assault in the hotel parking garage had rattled him more than he had thought. Each time he looked down, the movie began again in his head. His attempts to break away during the opera's intermission. His pathetic assault on his business partner, Spencer. The sight and smell of Spencer's flesh on the grill of the Range Rover. The relentless pounding of machine gun fire against the vehicle. The fear that he would be killed, and everything he had worked for, everything he had put at risk, would be lost. *Yea, though I walk through the valley of the shadow of death, I will fear no evil.*

But wow, he did fear evil. He couldn't help it.

"Watch your step," Lars said as their feet finally touched earth. They entered a cavern that was 20 feet tall and more than 60 feet wide. Above a particularly magnificent archway, Zhu gasped as he saw an enormous relief of Mithra slaughtering a bull.

"What is this place?"

"As far as we can tell, this is a branch of the underground Caracalla baths complex. An excavation just like it was unearthed a few years ago in another part of Rome." He allowed Zhu only a moment to take in the majesty of the relief before nudging him forward. "Come. We have work to do."

The next chamber was filled with more security personnel. Lars spoke to each of them as they passed, alternating between German, Italian and English. Zhu couldn't understand much of what they said, but the immediacy of their responses suggested complete obedience.

"The One from the East," someone said in English. The guards, all of them, removed their caps as Zhu passed with his entourage.

He was taken through a full-body scanner like the ones they had in airports. Beyond it was a narrow tunnel filled with floorboards.

"There's going to be a little noise now," Lars said. "Step lightly, please."

The boards squeaked, like chirping birds, as they walked. The nightingale floors the Shepherd had spoken of. The sounds echoed in the symmetrical cavern, and the effect was that of a massive flock of birds raising hell.

They came to a spacious open-air lift that appeared large and sturdy enough to support a commercial truck. It moved slowly up and down at regular intervals. There were no doors or buttons, and only a single rail prevented occupants from falling from the platform and into the chasm below.

"I see you didn't invest much in infrastructure," Zhu said.

Lars nodded. "The Shepherd insisted that the construction be minimally invasive of the ruins."

The descent was mercifully short. The air was suddenly much cooler. When they exited, he stood before a spotless glass-encased laboratory. At least a dozen people were working inside, making preparations for the Great Mission. Just as Zhu had specified in his instructions, the lab workers were wearing full body suits, with two layers of booties, and additional hoods, sleeves and gloves over the initial layer of outerwear.

Zhu was clearly pleased. "It's just like we talked about. How do we go in?"

Lars pointed to an exterior chamber at the far end of the room. "You and your assistants change there. Then you enter a secondary chamber equipped with an air shower. Per your requirements, each working area is in a self-contained chamber with its own individual climate control. All the equipment you requested was sterilized in a dedicated room before its introduction to the environment."

Across the chasm was a vast chamber with algae-damaged walls that had once been frescoed. Still, there were elaborately carved fountains, and in one place, a pool covered with ivory veneers and containing beautiful blue water. A vaulted ceiling was adorned with a mosaic depicting a chariot race. And beyond the chamber, a throne room.

Lars pointed to the stone-carved throne. Hundreds of tiny craters lined the arms and edges where jewels had once bedazzled it. "We believe that Nero himself sat there."

The grin on Zhu's face grew even wider. Only the Shepherd could have had such a brilliant idea. The Great Mission would be consummated in the house of one of the most notorious persecutors of Christians, whose intolerance had quite literally driven the movement underground. Filled with renewed inspiration, Zhu turned back toward the lab.

"*And you shall use wisdom to create life*," Lars quoted the Living Scriptures. "*Just as I have, for I have made you in my likeness.*"

Zhu nodded. "Game on."

Washington D.C.

The drizzle started as Haley Ellis exited the Metro Center subway station. She wandered over to a street vendor who had several mismatched umbrellas laid out on the cement before him.

"Ten bucks for the small ones," the guy said. "Twenty for king size."

"You have any new umbrellas?" Ellis said, noting the various levels of grime and dirt across the entire collection.

"These are just gently used. No leaks, I promise."

It was the idea that they might be stolen that bothered Ellis most. She decided to suck it up and move on. The hotel lounge where she was meeting Nathan Drucker was maybe ten minutes if she walked fast.

It figured that she had brought the English weather home with her. Every bit of this investigation had been star-crossed so far. Much as she hated to admit it, Carver's first thought – that they should divide and conquer – had been right. The only lead so far was a journalist whose office was within three miles from the crime scene.

The lead was, on its surface, flimsy. But Nathan Drucker's agitation on the phone – not to mention his kooky question, *"Are you from the Bureau?"* – had intrigued her. Was Drucker just a paranoid conspiracy freak?

Ellis had confirmed that someone from the Bureau – a Special Agent Will Hollis – had contacted Drucker years earlier. Unfortunately, Hollis had since passed away, and the memo he had filed on Drucker had been merged into a separate case file that Ellis didn't have access to. Bowers said he would look into it.

The group Drucker had written about, the Fellowship World Initiative, was conspicuously absent from local and national news. All she had found were a few old newsgroup postings, from the days before private social networks, listing local meetups for "FWI Alums." Maybe it was some kind of fraternity, she thought. That would explain the college connection between Gish and Senator Preston's missing assistant, Mary Borst.

Ellis walked into P.O.V., the 11th floor hotel bar known for its spectacular views of the city. She paused after entering, giving her eyes a chance to adjust to the dark lighting before perusing the patrons sitting on zebra-hide bar stools and red leather couches. She had been here once, years ago. She and a friend had waited an hour to get past the velvet rope, only to wait another 20 minutes to get a drink. It was nothing like that tonight. Just pleasantly bustling with tourists, many of whom were hoping to get a bird's eye view of Washington.

Once her eyes adjusted to the darkness, she recognized Nathan Drucker's handlebar mustache from his bio photo on the Capitol Herald site. He sat at a table in the far corner of the lounge, drinking iced tea, with his back to the room.

"I'm Haley," Ellis said as she slid into the seat opposite him. She regretted having used her real first name with him on the phone, but what was done was done. There was no going back now.

She didn't extend her hand across the table, a habit she had picked up from her boss at NIC, who believed there was little good that would come from broadcasting to others that contact with a potential asset was taking place for the first time. You never knew who was watching.

The journalist nodded once and said, "Nathan Drucker." She noted the worry lines around his eyes and the creased forehead of a man in his early 50s. His tweed jacket fit snugly over an unfortunate plaid vest and a bow tie. He wore black plastic-framed eyeglasses under bushy eyebrows.

"Is the Tweed Ride this week?" Haley said, referring to the annual event that had tweed revivalists cycling around the city dressed like 19th century Ivy League professors.

"No. I always dress like this."

"Oh."

"Without further ado, Ms. Ellis, will you please prove you're who you say you are?"

Ellis plucked a business card from a small stainless steel cardholder and discretely placed it on the table close to Drucker.

He inspected it for a long moment. He held the card up to the light, as if looking for a watermark, and still didn't seem satisfied. "Let me see your badge," he said.

She took it out of her purse and held it out for him to inspect. "Would you like a urine sample?"

"You think this is easy for me? I had to take something for my nerves this morning. Nobody's contacted me about this for years. Then, out of the blue, wham!"

Ellis somehow managed a reassuring smile. "No reason to be nervous, Nate. Can I call you Nate?"

"I guess."

"Good. Rest assured, Nate, I'm just looking for information."

"I didn't realize the FBI was still interested. How did this case get revived?"

She couldn't let him know that the original memo wasn't even available to her. It was time to improvise. "To be honest," she said, "the handoff was poorly handled. I was hoping you could help by recapping the last contact you had with the Bureau."

Drucker's mustache twitched up and down. "Okay then. An Agent Hollis had contacted me the same day the article came out."

Ellis smiled and nodded. "To be clear, the article we're referring to was the one you wrote called 'The Country Club Cult that Runs Washington.'"

"That's right. As I told Agent Hollis, the article was beyond my editorial control. I'll tell you what I told him, which is that the stuff in the article pales in comparison to what Sebastian Wolf may be up to. But Agent Hollis lost interest fast. We talked once more by phone, and that was the last time I heard from him. I tried calling the Bureau, of course, but he never seemed to be in, so I eventually said screw it and forgot the whole thing."

"Let's take this one item at a time," Ellis suggested. "You threw out a name. Sebastian Wolf. Who is that?"

Drucker made a face. His head appeared to slide backward on his neck, as if on a rail, until he was looking down his nose at Ellis. "You didn't even read the article you called me about!"

"I read two pages," Ellis confessed. "That was all I could find online."

Drucker sighed and shook his head. "This is all very disappointing. I can't risk meeting with anyone who isn't serious."

The journalist put a ten dollar bill on the table – which wasn't quite enough to cover his iced tea, much less the tip – and began to slide out from the booth. Crap. There was a time and place to use her feminine wiles, and this was one of them. Ellis reached out and touched the journalist's left wrist.

"Nate," she said in a gentle voice, her fingertips touching him gently, her eyes looking into his. "I'm sorry this wasn't handled well internally, but I wouldn't be here if I wasn't serious." He paused, as if frozen by her touch. "This is important. Please stay and talk to me. *Please*."

Drucker's pupils dilated, the telltale sign that Ellis had connected the old-fashioned way. He sighed, smiled and resettled himself on the leather couch. "All right," he said.

"I'm a little testy, I guess. I took an oath of silence on this stuff. They made me swear not to talk."

"Who did?"

"Wolf's people."

"Let's start with you telling me exactly who Sebastian Wolf is."

"Wolf is..." Drucker struggled for words. "He's not just a person. He's a prophet."

Eisenhower Building

Speers clenched his fists as he stared at the video image of the young woman passing through security at Toronto's Pearson International Airport. Still sporting a blonde boy-cut, she had not dyed her hair or changed anything but her clothes since she had last been seen in Senator Preston's den, just minutes before the fire.

There was no use stating the obvious. The body of Mary Borst, daughter to a UN under-secretary-general and assistant to an American senator, would not be found among the ashes of Preston's home. She was alive and well.

"Tell me she's still in the air," Speers said into his speakerphone.

"Wish I could," Chad Fordham said. "This image was taken about 12 hours ago, and she landed in Rome approximately eight hours later. It's possible that she then boarded a connecting flight to Tel Aviv, Cairo, St. Petersburg or Munich. We're exploring all eventualities as quickly as possible."

As Speers began shouting into the phone, he had the odd sensation of standing outside himself. He had thus far borne the stress of the situation stoically. He suddenly felt a complete loss of control.

"She used her own passport, for God's sake! How could we not know about this?"

He was barely listening as Fordham blamed the Canadian border authorities for their slowness in responding to his request for cooperation. As he speculated that Mary Borst must have used cash to pay for her plane ticket, thus evading the monitor they had put on her credit cards and bank account. As he made excuses for Hank Bowers, who had, as Fordham put it, followed standard procedure to the letter. As if that mattered. There was nothing standard about this situation.

Too little, too late. The only person of interest in Senator Preston's murder had been right under their nose. And now she was gone.

W Hotel

Outside, night had fully enveloped Washington. The White House and the Treasury Building sparkled, and the Washington Monument rose up like a beacon in the distance. Drucker sipped from a dark 'n' stormy cocktail. The alcohol seemed to have calmed his nerves. Ellis sensed Drucker's defenses coming down further.

"You described Sebastian Wolf as a prophet. You also slammed his organization as a cult. So what is he, a visionary, or a cult leader?"

"Don't get hung up on labels." The journalist looked around to make sure he wasn't being watched. He lowered his voice before speaking again. "The Fellowship is, and I quote from the charter, dedicated to exposing hidden truths that will change the course of humanity."

"Like what?" Ellis said. "Government corruption?"

Drucker shook his head. "No. That's small ball."

"Religion?"

"Warmer, but to be honest, Wolf doesn't believe in religion. He thinks it gets in the way of following Jesus."

Ellis was growing impatient with Drucker's bombastic declarations. He was simultaneously provocative and vague. She needed concrete details that could tie Preston, Gish and Borst together. But she had to resist rushing him. She had to be patient.

"Looks like there's nothing small about Eden," she said. "The address on file with the IRS looks huge on Google Maps, like a compound."

Drucker confirmed with a nod. "That's not inaccurate."

"Can we go there now? You could explain the backstory on the way."

The journalist gave Ellis a look. "Lady, you have no idea what you're getting into. You don't just show up at Eden uninvited."

"And how does someone get invited?"

"First, you have to know somebody. Second, you pretty much have to be either a scientist or a politician."

Drucker was neither a scientist nor a politician, Ellis noted. But Gish and Preston were. "How does it work?"

Drucker sighed. "The Fellowship is a hierarchical society. You have to level up over time. There are roughly 21 levels. Near the top, you've got world leaders, notable scientists. In the middle tiers you've got up-and-comers. They call them soldiers. At the bottom are students."

"How'd you get in?"

"My college roommate went on to become a congressman. I wrote a book for him during his initial campaign, outlining his position on healthcare reform. It didn't sell anywhere except the campaign trail, and quickly went out of print. We lost touch after he moved to Washington. Then one day he calls me up and asks me if I'd be interested in writing the personal memoirs of someone truly visionary."

"Wolf?"

"I'm getting to that. I said yeah, maybe, but who? He said he couldn't tell me over the phone, but the pay was a hundred thousand dollars. I was living on a freelancer's salary in Chicago at the time. The next thing I know, he sent me all these confidentiality agreements to sign, and he had me on a flight out to D.C. He had arranged for me to stay at Eden."

"Had you ever heard of it before?"

"No, of course not. And after I signed all the legal docs, he told me that Sebastian Wolf was *the man*. That's how he put it. *The man*."

"Go on."

"My taxi dropped me outside the gates," Drucker went on, talking right past Ellis' question. "I rang the buzzer and announced my name into the speaker, looking right up at the camera. The big iron gates opened, and I walked in. These two guys ran down this massive sloping lawn to help me with my suitcase. They reminded me of big puppies. They were so friendly, my guard went up immediately."

"They were students?"

Drucker nodded and sipped his iced tea. "Political science majors. They were just Level 3s, which meant they were still doing menial things like cooking and cleaning and hauling luggage. So they walk me up to this beautiful portico, between these massive Roman columns, and through a set of enormous doors. Not like the ones you see here. Like the grand ones they have in Europe. So I walk in, and the first thing I see, in this amazing foyer, is a tall sheik in white robes. Maybe he was Saudi royalty. But I can tell by the big rings on his fingers and the fabric of his robes that he's got to be super rich and probably important. And the Saudi can't take his eyes off the guy in front of him."

"Wolf?"

"One and the same. Tall guy with a silver mane and an aura that is palpable. One look and you know he's the grand patriarch. His age is deceptive. He's just one of those people who looks like he has all the answers, you know? So he spots me and comes right over, leaving this rich sheik standing there! He takes one of my hands, puts another hand on my shoulder, and makes eye contact. I don't even remember exactly what he said to me. I was just enamored with his presence. I felt like we were the only two people in the world at that moment." Drucker was blushing, as if remembering a teenage crush, or an encounter with a rock star. "It was intense."

"And then what?"

"In those days, it was common to see brilliant people from MIT or Cal Tech show up, not to mention the occasional senator or foreign minister. Some people even said presidents used to come, but that was before my time."

"What about Nils Gish?"

Drucker swatted at a horse fly that had somehow found its way to the 11th floor lounge. "I got the impression that Gish brought donors in to fund the research projects."

Ellis leaned forward, her elbows on the table. "What kind of research?"

"Mostly biomedical, bioengineering and anthro."

A fuzzy prickle ran down Ellis' arms. In his will, Rand Preston had left an endowment to a biomedical research foundation in Austin, Texas, and she had seen Gish's name on the board of an English bioengineering ethics committee.

"For example," Drucker went on, "I met an anthro at Eden who had gotten back from studying mitochondrial DNA in a 2,000-year-old burial tomb in Israel. This particular guy had his own agenda, but Wolf funded his project to see if he could expedite the process of decoding genome sequences using previously unexposed bits of bone marrow inside these ancient ossuaries."

"Why would the Fellowship fund something like that? What does that have to do with exposing essential truth?"

The waitress set down a plate of calamari. Drucker wasted no time in digging into it. "It gets weirder. More recently, Wolf has been obsessed with cloning. Those researchers that cloned an extinct species of goat from cells in hair that had been preserved in permafrost? The Fellowship funded that. Rumor has it that they're behind the team trying to clone that frozen hunter they found in Greenland last year."

Ellis got chills. "It's like playing God."

"And the world's great minds will join his flock. And so too will the world's great leaders, so that they may be in place when the time comes to usher in the new age of light."

"Don't recognize it," Ellis said. "Is that Old Testament?"

Wolf shook his head. "Wolf claims he wrote that after being blessed with a vision. He's got a book full of them, called the Living Scriptures. But don't waste your time looking for a copy. You can't get a look at the Living Scriptures until you're at least a Level 15."

"But you've seen it?"

Drucker nodded. "He's got the original copy in a library at Eden. The Living Scriptures is the least interesting thing there by far. He's got an actual mummy in there. He's got Roman antiquities. I guess it's not surprising considering who his father was."

"Do I have to ask?"

Drucker licked a piece of calamari breading off his fingers. "Wolf's father was a Nazi anthropologist. He worked for Heinrich Himmler."

Now she had heard everything. She had indulged Drucker's tall tales long enough. Ellis had flown all the way from London only to realize that the Capitol Hill journalist had already been dismissed by the Bureau years ago, and that he was more than likely mad as a hatter. She had come to find a simple, logical connection between the three murder victims, and the journalist was blabbering on about secret societies, cloning and Nazis.

It was time to cut to the chase. "Did you ever see Senator Preston at Eden?"

Drucker set his drink down and looked Ellis straight in the eyes. "Is that why you called me? You think there's some connection between Eden and Preston's death?"

"It's just a question."

"Like hell it is." The horse fly was back again. Drucker swatted in the air again as it buzzed about his head. "If the feds thought Preston really died in a residential fire, you wouldn't be here."

She revealed nothing in her expression. "How can I get a list of all the Fellowship members?"

The journalist snickered. "You can't. These are very cautious people. We haven't even scratched the surface of what they're capable of."

Ellis sighed. Maybe it was wise to get a look at Agent Hollis' notes on Drucker before investing any more time with him. She grabbed her purse and began scooting out of the booth.

Drucker's face lost color and turned dead serious. "Wait. The information you're looking for is in the book."

The comment stopped Ellis in her tracks. In the midst of all of Drucker's bluster, she had almost forgotten that he had been hired to write Wolf's memoirs. "I'm listening."

"Wolf was worried about his legacy after his death. He talked a lot about how the historians had been left to determine the way every important religious leader was viewed, from Moses to Joseph Smith to L. Ron Hubbard. He wanted the chance to tell his own story, especially about how he came to have the vision."

"Why should I care?"

"For one thing, I've got information about Preston. I had access to information that you don't get until you're at least a Level 20."

Ellis set her purse back down onto the table. "If the material is so great, then why hasn't it been published?"

The peevish look on Drucker's face foretold the fiasco he was about to describe. "My agreement with Wolf was that the book's publication was contingent on two things. The first was his death. The second was completion of the Great Mission."

"Great Mission?"

Drucker nodded. "But I got greedy. Before the old man had even seen the first draft, I sent a few chapters to a book agent. But this material was so hot. I thought maybe if we could get a big advance, then Wolf might change his mind and let us publish it right away."

"And did you?"

"Yes, in fact. But my agent blew it for me. Somewhere deep in the representation agreement, I had apparently consented to let my agent place my work in short form for fair market value so long as it was for promotional purposes. The next thing I know, a portion of it had been edited and published as the article you found online."

"I take it that didn't go over so well."

The very thought of it seemed to sap Drucker's spirit. "Wolf's security team used me as a punching bag."

"They actually attacked you?"

"Broke my jaw and two ribs. Check the hospital records if you don't believe me."

Ellis was already planning on it. "And then what?"

"Like I said, they made me swear an oath that I'd keep quiet, or else. They took my computer, and I'm pretty sure they put a virus into the one I bought after that." A smile crept across his face. "But they didn't realize that I was such a paranoid son of a bitch."

"You kept a copy?"

The ends of his handlebar mustache rose as he grinned devilishly. "All these years later, I'm still working on it. I know they periodically hack into my computer, but they'll never find it. The best defense against cyberattacks is old-fashioned paper."

Suddenly, Drucker slapped his neck hard. Ellis watched the horse fly bounce off Drucker's shoulder and fall below. "Got the bastard."

"Nate, I'm going to need to see that book."

Drucker opened his mouth to reply, but words didn't come. He groaned and moved his neck slowly to the right, straining against some unseen force.

It was then that Ellis noticed the growing welt on his neck, near his jugular. "Nate," she said, "have you ever had an allergic reaction to an insect bite?"

He grunted. His lips and tongue seemed suddenly out of sync, and he was glassy-eyed.

The fly had fallen onto the table. Two of its legs were detached from the main body. When Ellis prodded it with her fingertips, she knew what Drucker never would. The fly was man-made.

Verona, Italy

The journey from South Africa to Italy had been a circuitous one. Their flight into Rome had been diverted to Munich due to thunderstorms across Italy. They had then been promised another flight the next afternoon, but Carver wasn't content to wait that long. He opted instead to catch a night train heading south through the Austrian Aps.

Five hours later they arrived in Verona, where a train strike had forced the cancellation of the second leg to Rome. They would be forced to stay in the northern Italian town for the night. Both men were famished and grumpy as they headed for a late-night pizzeria near the station.

Now, sitting outside under a string of yellow lights, the two men looked better than they felt. They wore Hugo Boss suits and had both been to a barber at the Munich train station.

"About that thing you put in my arm," Nico said, running his fingers over the welt where it had been inserted.

Carver nodded. "The tracking chip."

"Not that I'm planning on it, but what's to stop me from digging that out with a pocketknife?"

"It's hooked around your cephalic vein. That's the big one running down your bicep into your forearm."

"What? How?"

"These hooks expand from the chip after it's embedded. They start off as tiny, flaccid tentacles. But if you attempt to remove the chip after it's embedded, the tentacles swell, go rigid and curl, cutting off blood flow."

Nico was horrified. "And this thing is in me permanently?"

"I'm not *that* sadistic. It's just that you can't just get any quack to remove it. One of our people in the States will deactivate the hooks and remove the chip after the mission's done."

"That's just wrong."

"Not as wrong as handing you over to the CIA, which is what they wanted me to do. You'd be back in Lee Federal Penitentiary. Or worse, extradited to the Saudis, who would be willing to take your head in exchange for the money you stole from them." Nico shivered visibly. Carver instantly regretted the remarks, hoping they hadn't further hardened his asset. He softened his voice. "Look, Julian gave his personal assurances that this mission will pay your debt to America in full."

"And Eva?"

"For the last time, it's President Hudson now. And yes, I'm sure she's on board as well."

Carver wasn't sure. But there was always a way. If Nico's contribution to the investigation turned out to be half as valuable as Carver was expecting, a presidential pardon would be a moral imperative.

After dinner, they checked into a shabby motel with one bed, near the train station. Carver surveyed the dilapidated room, chewing on the end of a straw he had taken from the pizzeria. It wasn't much, but they were just here to sleep before catching a train to Rome the following morning.

Carver urinated with the restroom door open, and then washed his face and hands. Then he pulled the blankets off the bed and handed them to Nico. "It's all yours," he said, gesturing toward the restroom.

"Where am I supposed to sleep, the bathtub?"

Carver nodded and tossed him a feather pillow. "Just for tonight. That way I won't have to snooze with one eye open."

"It's not like I'm going to run."

"I know. But it was only 24 hours ago that your girlfriend tried to shoot me, and I punched her in the face."

"Ah. You're afraid I'll smother you with a pillow in the middle of the night."

"Something like that."

"Fair enough."

Carver pushed the dresser against the bathroom door, sealing Nico inside.

"What if there's a fire?" Nico yelled through the door. "I'll be trapped in here."

"Take a cold shower."

W Hotel

The room lights were on full, offering Ellis a level of illumination that only the hotel bar's cleaning crew usually witnessed. Men in white biohazard suits examined the booth where Ellis and Drucker had sat earlier in the evening. Two other crews probed every piece of furniture, glass and surface for electronic devices or cameras.

Drucker had died within 90 seconds of the insect bite. Ellis herself had frantically searched the 11th floor, as well as the P.O.V.'s rooftop terrace, for anyone suspicious. It had been a fruitless task. By then the lounge had been crowded with people, half of whom could have potentially utilized their phones as either cameras or remote control devices.

The object in question was in a sealed petri dish on the bar countertop. A federal robotics expert hunched over it, peering through a microscope, gently turning its tiny wings with delicate tweezers. Ellis and Speers stood behind him.

"Amazing nanotechnology," the expert said.

Speers had divulged nothing of the situation – other than the fact that a man appeared to have been attacked – to any of the crew on site. "Who could have done this?"

"Beats me. I'm no entomologist, but whoever did this made a pretty convincing female tabanid, otherwise known as a common horse fly. Right down to the proboscis, which is that needle-like snout that a horse fly uses to extract the blood meal it requires before reproduction."

"Only this one didn't suck his blood," someone behind them said. The voice belonged to Chad Fordham, who had just come in. "I just talked to my toxins specialist. Drucker was poisoned. We'll have to confirm this in the lab, but based on Ellis' description of facial paralysis followed by respiratory failure, taken together with an early blood sample, they're 90 percent sure that little robo-fly injected him with a botulinum toxin."

Ellis scratched her head. "Isn't that stuff in Botox?"

Fordham nodded. "In its purest form, this is the deadliest toxin on the planet. Couple bags of this stuff, and a smart delivery mechanism, and you've got a bioweapon capable of mass eradication."

Ellis tried to imagine the people standing around them and seated at the bar. Lots of little black dresses. Lots of men in conservative dark suits. Typical Washington crowd. Nobody stood out.

Her head was spinning. Maybe the FBI hadn't felt Drucker was worth following up with in the past 12 years, but someone else did. "We're going to need to look at all the hotel camera footage. Maybe we can catch somebody operating this from their mobile device."

Speers pulled Ellis aside. "We've been assuming Drucker was the target. We have to consider the possibility that the target was you."

She had been thinking the same thought all morning. "Drucker had a crazy vibe," she said. "But if half the stuff he told me was true, he could have been dangerous."

"Dangerous to whom?"

She sat on a barstool and summarized all the madness Drucker had spewed in regards to the Fellowship World Initiative and its headquarters, Eden. Then she told him what little Drucker had said about its enigmatic leader, Sebastian Wolf.

Speers nodded, recognizing the name. He had met Wolf, years ago, at the Council on Faith luncheon. "I can hear about that later. Right now we have to assume that someone saw you two together. You can work from McLean until we know more."

If there's anything that can protect you from a killer fly, Ellis thought, I'd like to see it. But she couldn't think about herself right now. Someone had killed Drucker, presumably because he had agreed to discuss an article he had published more than a decade ago. She had to get her hands on that book of his before someone else did.

"I've got to get to Drucker's condo," she said. "It's in Silver Springs."

Speers' glare could have wilted sunflowers. "Are you deaf? I just finished saying I want you out of the field until we know who did this."

"Who's going to go, you? This isn't something you can just delegate. The president said she wanted to keep the team small. Besides, I'm the only person that knows what we're looking for."

Speers reached into his pocket grudgingly. "I'll drive."

Nathan Drucker Residence
Silver Springs, Maryland

A curvy 20-something office manager wearing yoga pants and a hoodie staffed the leasing office where Nathan Drucker had lived. After agreeing to let Ellis and Speers into the deceased journalist's condo, she led them up the building's stairwell. "This isn't my career," she volunteered, although they had not even asked about her ambitions. "I've got a degree in communications from Duke. I had an internship last year, but it didn't pay. I'm just doing this until I can get into something more permanent."

"I'm sure something will turn up," Speers offered as they came to Drucker's third-floor condo.

"Getting a job must've been way easier in your day," the manager said as she fumbled through an enormous set of keys. Speers let the age comment go. He was just happy the girl didn't ask them to get a warrant.

The extent of Drucker's paranoia was evident by two bulky cameras mounted over the front door, holdovers from before the era of miniaturization. No less than four dead bolts secured the entrance.

"The building association must have loved those," Ellis said, motioning to the cameras. "Did Drucker live alone?"

"He's got two kids that visit every now and then, but they live with the ex-wife." The girl unlocked the second deadbolt, and then turned. "Hold on. Why are you talking about him in the past tense?"

Ellis shot her boss a glare before rolling her eyes.

"I'm afraid Mr. Drucker is deceased," Speers said with a note of awkward finality.

"Oh my God. Is his body in there? Are we about to see a corpse?"

"No," Speers said. "Look, I need to ask you to keep this under your hat. We haven't even notified family yet."

Rattled, the girl unlocked the last two deadbolts. The apartment was completely dark. Out of habit, Ellis held Speers at the entrance as the manager walked in to flip on the lights. She used the other hand to open her purse and grope for her SIG. In Iraq, her unit had a couple of nasty experiences during home invasions. It was amazing what naughty things people could do with a little trip wire and basic explosives.

All seemed to be quiet. Satisfied that the spacious condo was still secure, Ellis went in, noting that the place had not been ransacked. She counted them lucky. If someone had taken the time to kill Drucker in a public place, it was only a matter of time before they showed up here.

They went from room to room until they found Drucker's study. The converted bedroom would have scarcely been wide enough to hold a queen-size bed. The walls held Drucker's UCLA degree, as well as framed movie posters for 'All the President's Men,' 'State of Play' and the George Clooney movie about TV journalist Ed Murrow, 'Good Night, and Good Luck.' All movies about heroic journalists. That figures, Speers thought. Drucker probably thought they'd make a movie about him someday. But journalists never died in the movies.

There was a computer, a printer, and also an old-fashioned analog typewriter. "This would look cool in my office," Speers said, admiring the Smith Corona's sleek black curves.

"It might look like a museum piece, but I think Drucker was actually using it."

"I don't understand those analog sentimentalists. Like those people who play vinyl records. It's just backwards."

"In this case, it was a security measure. A typewriter is the literary equivalent of paying cash for everything. It's not digital, it's far less likely to be traced, found or stolen."

Speers unplugged Drucker's computer and began boxing up his papers for analysis back at the office. Ellis searched through two tall filing cabinets, discovering nothing. She then went back to the living room, where the office manager had her feet up on Drucker's coffee table and was peering into her phone. "How much longer?" she said without looking up.

"As long as it takes." Ellis went back to the study. She climbed atop the rickety desk while Speers steadied her legs, then pushed open one of the ceiling panels and, fearing a chance encounter with a rat trap, used a plastic back scratcher to poke around in the unseen darkness. Moments later she hit something. She reached in with her hands, pulled, and was soon holding a rectangular box filled with something heavy. Behind it, she found two more that were identical. She handed the boxes one by one to Speers, grunting a little with each heave.

Then she climbed down and opened the first box. It was filled with several legal pads, as well as a bunch of old mini-cassette tapes. "I'd venture a guess that these are…"

"Interview transcriptions," Speers confirmed after taking a quick look at the content.

He opened the second box. In it, he found a two-inch thick pile of typewritten paper. There was no cover sheet. The double-spaced type started on the first page, and it was crowded with handwritten annotations.

The third box contained a manuscript printed in bluish text, with margins that had tiny holes in it. "This came out of a dot matrix printer," Speers said. "We actually had one of these things when we were kids. They were really noisy."

"I think I saw one in the Smithsonian," Ellis said. Speers chuckled before realizing that his younger subordinate hadn't been joking.

Ellis opened the closet and found a large trail-grade backpack. She put the contents of the three boxes into it.

Glass exploded somewhere in the apartment. Stunned for only a moment, Ellis motioned for Speers to stay quiet.

She drew her Beretta and spun out into the hallway. The manager was in the living room about 20 feet in front of her, bending to inspect whatever had just been thrown through the living room window. Ellis didn't need to get any closer to know it was bad news.

"Run!" she shouted at the manager before ducking back into the study. There was no time to try to save her. "Cover up," she told Speers. They had only just gotten their hands over their ears when a blast rocked the entire floor.

If the size of the explosion hadn't made it obvious, the amount of plaster whizzing past the study confirmed that the office manager was toast.

Waves of regret coursed through Ellis. Not just for failing to instruct the office manager to leave the premises, but also for involving Julian. She should have come alone. Now both their lives were in danger.

In Iraq, Ellis had learned that explosions were sometimes just a prelude to armed entry. Ellis was willing to bet that at least two invaders would be inside as soon as the dust and smoke cleared. She stood and then pulled Speers to his feet. The paunchy intelligence director was unarmed, and would be of little value in a firefight. They had no choice but to try to escape.

"Take a deep breath and hold it," Ellis instructed. She shouldered the heavy backpack containing the manuscript and stepped out into the hallway, leading Speers by the hand. The air was filled with particles that made her eyes burn.

They went into the room opposite the study, heading straight for the window. She looked outside, hoping for a cable they could slide down, a rooftop close enough to jump to, or a fire escape. All she saw was a brick wall, with only enough clearance for a set of flowerpots.

She led Speers back into the hallway. Someone was shouting now. It could be anyone, she reminded herself. But as she looked back toward what had been Drucker's living room, the sight of three red laser dots squelched any hope of heading out the front entrance. Drucker's killers were already here.

She led Speers to the back bedroom and shut the door behind them. Next to the door was a tall maple wood wardrobe. With Speers' help, she toppled it so that it was blocking the door sideways. She didn't want to make a stand here, but at least it might stop someone from kicking down the door for a while.

Two windows looked out over a dimly lit courtyard. Once again, there were no tree branches or wires within reaching distance from the window, nor was there a fire escape. That, she realized, would have been outside the living room, which the invaders had no doubt utilized to their advantage.

"Look," Speers said, opening the window on the other side of the bedroom.

Three floors down was a community swimming pool, illuminated by a pair of lights at the bottom. There was nobody there at this time of night. Even from her angle at the other window, the water was clearly too far to jump.

"No," Speers said, pointing straight down. "Down there!"

Ellis' view was blocked. Before she could stop him, Speers already had one leg out the window. She lunged, grabbing for his other leg just as he let go. They both screamed as he jumped.

Several gunshots ripped through the top portion of the door, above the substantial protection that the heavy wardrobe offered. Rays of light emanated from each hole in the door.

She pulled off the backpack, knowing that it would inhibit her ability to break her fall, and tossed it out the window without looking. Ellis turned, firing three rounds through the door just before she leapt. There was no hope of killing three assassins equipped for night operations.

She crossed herself. Then she jumped.

Eurostar Express Train

The Eurostar running from Verona to Rome sped past a vast field of grapevines that were heavy with fruit and ready for harvest. On the right, a hill town came into view. A citadel-like village surrounded by ancient stone walls and topped with medieval architecture. Completely unblemished by billboards, high rises or neon signs, it had hardly been the first jaw-dropping scene they had passed so far. But unlike his fellow passengers, Nico was oblivious to the bucolic scenery. He was about to boot up a beautiful new machine.

He savored the feel of the round power button on the sleek computer Carver had purchased for him. He grazed his finger over the button several times before finally depressing it, savoring the satisfying whirr of the processor flickering to life.

During the 13 months spent hiding on South Africa's Eastern Cape, he had kept his vow to Madge. No computers in the house. No web-accessible phones. No temptations. Except for the occasional trip down to the hotel, where the night manager had obliged his indulgences.

It had been for his own good, he knew. After all, it had been his inability to control his urges that had put him in lockup in the first place. But in a world where bills were paid online, customers paid for access to entertainment rather than owning it, and paper maps were relics of the 20th century, going web-free had been a difficult promise to keep.

He had managed the inevitable inner conflict mostly by immersing himself in the Xhosa and Afrikaans languages. Becoming fluent in both languages, as well as taking on the challenge of teaching himself how to fish the Transkei riverways, had proven to be surprisingly rewarding. In recent months, the old impulses had nearly died off.

He had lapsed just once, after finding a discarded phone in a Transkei garbage dump. Rooting the phone to steal free web access had been more than the Internet-starved hacker could resist. For three nights in a row, he had pretended to fall asleep, only to get up in the dead of night to explore the ever-changing universe of net security on the phone's tiny screen. With Nico increasingly ragged and temperamental from his all-nighters, Madge finally recognized the warning signs and demanded that he hand over the contraband device.

Now the familiar rush of adrenalin returned to him as he logged onto the hotspot provided by Carver's satphone. The encryption key was impossibly long, which only intensified the pleasure when the first site appeared before his eyes. But once he got started, the download speed was blazingly fast. Incomprehensible compared to anything he had ever experienced before.

Carver placed a Limonata and a pastry on the tray before him. With the train worker strike apparently still on, Carver had bought ahead, making sure they wouldn't be hungry or thirsty on the trip to Rome. Nico set the food and drink aside and continued his bonding session with the new machine.

Before boarding in Verona, Carver had explained his immediate objective. Going on the presumption that a hidden relationship between Senator Rand Preston and Sir Nils Gish existed, he was to use any means necessary to expose any possible connections. For now, they would leave the mysterious case of Mary Borst's disappearance aside, although he could tell that whether he liked it or not, that some portion of Carver's brain was still working on it.

He would start by analyzing the two politicians' itineraries, both private and public, looking for any overlap in destinations or meeting places. He would then pull a full social graph for the two men, working up a full profile on any first and 2nd second-degree contacts that the two men had in common.

Virtually any tactic was fair game. They had already received Preston's personal email data from the FBI, and Carver was working on getting Gish's. That was about all the risk-free help they were going to get. They could not reach out directly to private companies for account access, for fear of exposing the investigation.

The quickest way to discover who these men were, and where they had been, was to follow their money. That meant breaking into their credit card accounts. Nico salivated at the thought of it. In the old days, he had favored bringing down financial networks through denial-of-service attacks. He had formed cyber gangs of users from different geolocations to overwhelm networks with the number of simultaneous requests needed to bring them to their knees.

Unfortunately, that type of offensive was no longer an option. He hadn't maintained his contacts in the hacker community during his exile. And even if he had, involving them would be too much of a risk. The sensitive nature of the operation required extreme discretion. As an alternative, he could enslave a great number of machines, masking the IP of each through a randomized spoofing process. In the past, his favorite targets had been large American state universities like Penn State. Any institution with a hefty on-campus population, where large numbers of students would create and eventually abandon accounts, was perfect. Nico would simply revive those accounts and use them for his own means.

He wasn't yet privy to the details of the case, but he figured that Carver wouldn't have come all the way to South Africa if the stakes were small. And that was just fine by him. High stakes suited him.

Now he felt alive in a way that he had not in ages.

He thought of Madge. Poor lonely Madge, who had left her good home and good job in America to hide from the law with him. Who had, even before that, written him dozens of letters in prison because she wanted to reform him.

And then, as quickly as he had felt high on adrenaline, a wave of guilt washed over him. *Damn,* he thought. I don't even miss her.

He shrugged and opened the can of Limonata.

Nathan Drucker Residence

Haley Ellis streamlined her body slightly as she sped toward the small patch of blue reflective water below. Less than a second later her three-story jump was broken by 39 inches of bubbling Jacuzzi water. She landed in a crouch, breaking the fall as much with the flexibility of her knees as with the water's bubbly buoyancy.

A hand gripped her arm and pulled her toward the steps. She looked up, expecting Speers, but was instead eye-to-eye with a frightened spa-goer in soggy swim trunks. She smelled vodka on him, and was immediately aware of three other spooked residents with cocktails in their hands.

Now Speers hobbled toward her. His suit was dripping wet and he was holding the pack.

"Are you guys okay?" someone asked as Ellis found dry land.

A ferocious blast ripped the wall away three stories up. Ellis acted before she thought, shoving the spa-goers out of the way just before the water was deluged with scorched wood, glass and insulation.

Speers was suddenly over her, pulling Ellis up from the cement walkway. Her forearms were scraped up and bleeding, but she barely felt them.

"Get out of here," Speers shouted at the residents as they scattered. "Call the police!"

The intelligence chief was hobbling now. Ellis grabbed the pack containing Drucker's work and steadied Speers as they made their way toward the parking lot. Now she knew these bastards wanted Drucker's book. She was willing to do just about anything to deprive them of it.

Speers opened the doors of his SUV and slid behind the wheel. "You are about to witness some serious psycho driving."

He pulled into the late-night traffic, then stepped on the gas and powered past several dozen cars. He took an abrupt right turn, then navigated down an alleyway and through to the next street, where he came dangerously close to mowing down some pedestrians while merging into more traffic. It was some pretty fancy driving for a government exec.

"I didn't expect you to jump out that window," Ellis said.

"What was I supposed to do, die there?"

He winced as he stepped on the brake. His ankle was badly twisted, if not broken.

"You need a doctor."

He nodded. "Later. First we need to get you somewhere safe."

Ellis tensed at the thought of being cooped up. At least she had Drucker's manuscript and notes to keep her busy. She couldn't remember the last time she had read a book, but this was different. They'd have to kill her to keep her from reading this one. Lord knew they were trying.

Mayflower Hotel
Washington D.C.

Ellis had often fantasized about staying in the historic Mayflower Hotel, but her fantasies had not been anything like this. Blackout shades had been applied to all the windows, and a security detail outside the 9th-floor room kept them confined. Overnight, Speers had grown increasingly concerned about the possibility that it had been Ellis, not Drucker, who had been the target of the attacks at the hotel bar and the condo. Ellis thought that theory was nonsense. Trouble just had a way of finding her.

At least the four-star accommodations were spacious, and the room came at no extra cost. The vacant suite was booked year-round for visiting dignitaries, and it was equipped with an exceptional workspace. Speers had felt it was best to keep Ellis' work away from the prying eyes at McLean.

Ellis' sister, Jenna, was curled up in an armchair, wearing a hotel robe and audio headphones that were as large as tennis balls. For Jenna, Speers' decision to move the Ellis sisters to a secured location was a *bona fide* staycation. If she had been spooked by the security in the hallway, or by the fact that her sister wasn't allowed to disclose the security threat that had forced them to come to the hotel, she wasn't letting on. After a grueling shift taking complex coffee orders at Starbucks, Jenna had already ordered room service twice and used the suite's Jacuzzi tub. This was as good as it got.

Ellis was significantly less content. Although she had hours of work ahead of her thanks to their raid on Drucker's apartment, and her body was sore from their near-death escape, she was no less antsy for freedom. Understanding that

Speers had placed her here for her own protection didn't help. Every part of her body was screaming to get back on the trail.

Unable to relax long enough to concentrate, she surrendered to the hotel mini-bar. She found tiny containers of Jack Daniels and two brands of rum that she had never heard of.

"Whoa," Jenna said as she watched her sister doing shots with the tiny bottles. She popped the enormous headphones away from her skull just enough to hear the sound of her own voice. "Can we order some room service?"

"Sure, Sis."

Jenna wasted no time in popping open the menu. "Can we order prime rib?"

The government per diem for employee meals while traveling was $71 per day in D.C. The prime rib was going to take half their food budget in one fell swoop.

"Please?" Jenna pressed.

She was too tired to negotiate. And besides, it wasn't every day she escaped death twice. "What the hell."

As Jenna dialed room service, Haley sat cross-legged on one of the beds. She emptied the contents of the backpack they had removed from Drucker's apartment and spread the manuscript, photographs and handwritten notes out before her.

Now she saw something that she hadn't seen in Drucker's condo: the infamous issue of Inside Washington magazine. The page was turned down to the article. A bold headline, 'The Country Club Cult That Runs Washington,' appeared across the top. Someone had drawn a red circle around the title and written SENSATIONALIST CRAP!!! The handwriting matched Drucker's scarcely legible scrawl.

She really hadn't bought Drucker's claim that it had been published without his consent, but now she saw he was probably telling the truth. Why else would he have been so critical of his own writing?

She flipped through the handwritten legal pads. Some were filled with quotes supposedly attributed to Sebastian Wolf. She was surprised to see pages and pages of scripture. What was it Drucker had said? *Wolf believes that religion gets in the way of following Jesus.* For a guy who disapproved of religion, Wolf sure liked to quote the Bible.

Go therefore and make disciples of all nations, baptizing them in the name of the Father and of the Son and of the Holy Spirit - Matthew 28:19

But you will receive power when the Holy Spirit has come upon you, and you will be my witnesses in Jerusalem and in all Judea and Samaria, and to the end of the earth." - Acts 1:8 ESV

And I will give you a new heart, and a new spirit I will put within you. And I will remove the heart of stone from your flesh and give you a heart of flesh. - Ezekiel 36:26, LS XXIV

And in turn, you will return my heart from stone to flesh, so that all men may share in the wisdom of the LORD. And the whole world shall rejoice. - LS XXXI

Ellis recognized some of the scriptures from her studies at Our Lady of Lourdes, the Catholic school she had attended during junior high and high school, as well as her adult Bible study classes. Others weren't familiar. The capitalized abbreviations at the ends of each passage typically referred to Bible versions. KJV stood for King James Version, ESV was English Standard Version, and so forth. She had never heard of LS. She could only guess that it referred to the Living Scriptures that Drucker had spoken of.

There were pages and pages of such odd scripture, many of which appeared to have been altered significantly from the versions she was familiar with. There was a strong emphasis on resurrection throughout all the passages, as well as many that seemed to validate the pursuit of science as a God-given directive.

Soon she came upon what looked like a series of hand-drawn org charts. Most were half-completed, a mixture of names and question marks. There were dozens of names, representing every ethnicity imaginable.

Written at the top of the chart on the first page was, S WOLF (SHEPHERD). Sebastian Wolf, she assumed, although the term "Shepherd" meant nothing to her. The level immediately below it had two spaces, both filled with question marks. The third and fourth tiers contained some names she recognized, among them N. GISH, and on the same level, R. PRESTON, among others.

She felt a rush of excitement. This was what she was looking for. A membership list. The fact that there were so many question marks, and no full names or titles, was unfortunate. But she had a written document that appeared to validate the victims' induction into a secret society. Now maybe she could connect the dots.

A knock at the door broke Ellis' focus. She paused a moment, orienting herself. There were supposed to be two guards outside. The knock came again, more insistent this time.

"Ms. Ellis?"

She got up from the bed and tightened the white robe around her waist.

"What is it?" Jenna said, pulling her headphones off. Her eyes got big as she watched her sister retrieve the handgun from the nightstand next to the bed.

Ellis shushed her sibling, then went to the door and looked through the peephole. It was Jack McClellan, a longtime secret service agent who had been assigned to lead the security team guarding the suite. Ellis figured Speers had put McClellan on the job because he was a familiar face, having worked with her to defend the capitol during the Ulysses Coup.

The rumor was that he had taken a bullet meant for George W. Bush that he would never get public credit for.

Why didn't he just retire? He had served five administrations. Surely he'd maxed out his pension by now.

She opened the door and found herself staring at the horrendousness of Jack's homemade dye job. He was obviously gray by now, and the jet black smear of thinning hair wasn't doing anything to conceal it.

"Major fail," he scolded. "As we discussed, you need to ask one of our qualifying questions before opening the door. What if someone was behind me, holding me at gunpoint? That might be my only way of signaling to you that there was danger."

Ellis sighed irritably. "Okay, Jack. You got me. Are we done?"

He turned to the side and waved his hand. A hotel staffer approached with a room service cart. "I think maybe I should have a bite of that prime rib," McClellan said as Ellis pulled the cart into the room. "Might be poisoned."

"Nice try."

As Jenna dug into her dinner, Ellis' focus returned to Drucker's list. She was sure now that Gish and Preston had known each other through the Fellowship World Initiative. Now she had to try to identify some other names on the list.

Throughout the chart, a Y-axis indicated numbers by each level on the org chart. *The Fellowship is a hierarchical society. You have to level up over time. Near the top, you've got world leaders, notable scientists.* Wolf's name had no numerical attribution, which appeared to place him as the big kahuna. The second level – where there were only question marks – was the number 21. The number 20 was written beside Gish, Preston and a few other names she didn't recognize. On the subsequent pages were a list of 19s and a few 18s and 17s.

The amount of diversity among the listed surnames was worrisome. While Ellis guessed that there were plenty of ethnic minorities in the House and Senate these days, as well as in British Parliament, there couldn't be this much diversity.

That meant this list contained people from all over the world. The Fellowship World Initiative appeared to be truly global. Could all these people be world leaders? And if so, did that mean they were all in danger?

The thought of the crisis spreading to additional nations was frightening. She had to talk to Carver.

She went to her bag, looking for her satphone, and remembered she no longer had one. Speers had confiscated it, fearing that it had been compromised. Carver's satphone number, as well as Arunus Roth's, had been programmed into it. She went to the desk, powered up her computer, and logged into the secure mission cloud. She posted a private message: *call me.*

She got up and paced, then flattened herself into the carpet and bent her legs into a pigeon pose, pondering next steps. Without first names, titles and associated nationalities, identifying these people would be hard. Ellis kicked herself for not keeping up more with international political and scientific news. Maybe then she would recognize some of these people.

She flipped to a back page and found a whole new slew of Level 20 names. One stood out among them: V. BORST.

Something shifted within Ellis. Vera Borst? Mother of Mary?

She did a web search for the name. It was evidently quite rare – there were virtually no other exact matches. United Nations Under-Secretary-General Borst. Like Carver said, a big shot.

Ellis quickly navigated to the woman's Wikipedia page, where Borst's headshot was pictured above an image of the United Nations flag. She realized she had never really considered the flag's design before. It had a blue background, with white laurel wreaths framing what could only be described as a bleached map of all the world's continents as seen through a rifle scope.

Borst's face was soft and round under a Peter Pan haircut that made her head appear to be remarkably orb-like. The 49-year-old UN leader hadn't worn any makeup, even in what was obviously a posed photograph. One of those ultra-organic types, Ellis thought.

According to her Wiki page, Borst had been born in Amsterdam and earned a Ph.D. in biomedical engineering before abruptly leaving science for politics. She had been elected to the Netherlands' lower house during her first try, and had served in the country's diplomatic corps for a decade before being appointed UNICEF director. She had subsequently been appointed an under-secretary-general of the United Nations.

If Drucker's claims were any measure, Borst's background in both science and politics made her a lock for Wolf's inner circle.

Ellis scrolled lower on the page, reading the text under "Personal Life":

> Borst is a frequent lecturer worldwide, discussing the need for enhanced global cooperation on the use of embryo stem-cell research to detect and prevent disease. She lives near Seattle, Washington with her life partner, Dr. Dane Mitchell, a professor of biology at the University of Washington.

"Feeling better, Sis?" Jenna said, spotting the triumphant look on Ellis' face.

"Thank you Jack Daniels, thank you Coke."

And thank you Drucker, she thought. May you rest in peace.

Dane Mitchell's number wasn't publicly listed. But she knew that the State Department kept contact information for UN leaders.

She used the hotel phone to dial a friend at State, allowing her typically suppressed southern accent to surface just long enough to charm the desperately single guy into looking up Borst's personal phone number. In exchange, she promised to go out on a date with him. It wouldn't be all that bad, she thought. He was kind of cute.

She hung up and dialed Borst's number. After four rings, a woman answered the phone. "This is Vera."

Via della Conciliazione
Rome

Rome's cobblestones felt good under Carver's feet. He had discovered years ago that this street, which stretched between the Tiber River and St. Peter's Square, was the only vantage point where it was possible to properly appreciate the Vatican's grandeur. High walls surrounded the majority of the tiny Vatican nation, making only the upper heights of its massive basilica and palaces visible. But from here, just blocks from the boundary between the Vatican and Rome, it was possible to see St. Peter's Square, St. Peter's Basilica, the Apostolic Palace and the many buildings occupied by various orders all at once.

"First time here?" he asked Nico, although he already knew the answer by the awestruck look on his face.

Nico pointed to the towering, four-sided monument with a pyramid-shaped cap. "Why is there an Egyptian obelisk in the center of St. Peter's Square?"

Carver smiled. Every time he saw the obelisk in St. Peter's Square, it was clear where L'Enfant, the architect that created the plans for the National Mall, had gotten his inspiration for the Washington Monument and the surrounding federal buildings. From a distance, it was uncanny how much the massive columns and basilica of St. Peter's resembled Capitol Hill. Washington D.C. was America's Rome.

"Rome has seven obelisks taken from Egypt," Carver said. "That one was originally installed in the Roman Forum. It's the only one without the original Egyptian hieroglyphics."

It seemed to Carver that the clergy were just as thick on the ground on Via della Conciliazione as they must have been when the four-story building had been erected in 1480.

The street was the Vatican's equivalent of Pennsylvania Avenue, and the Palazzo Della Rovere before them had been the home of countless cardinals, bishops, noblemen and nuns over the centuries until finally coming under the ownership of the ancient Order of the Holy Sepulchre, which answered to the Vatican, and still occupied the west side of the building.

"Our hotel," Carver said, pointing to the structure. The east side was a modern hotel called the Hotel Columbus, which was frequented by Vatican visitors and dignitaries.

"Dude!" Nico said. "Now this is the kind of place where I can get some serious work done."

As they entered the crowded lobby, Father Callahan was impossible to miss. In a city full of priests wearing black frocks, the Irish-born CIA operative's shock of short red hair separated him from the rest. At six foot two, Callahan should have appeared slightly taller than Carver, but his stooping posture put the two men at eye level.

Carver submitted to Callahan's crippling handshake. Then he introduced Nico.

"Your reputation precedes you," Callahan said in his typically charming Irish lilt. "Welcome to my second home, as it were. You are in luck. My favorite suite on the second floor is available. Two bedrooms. Space to work, a view of the courtyard, and best of all, the ceiling frescoes are all originals, painted by a Renaissance master."

As the priest-cum-intelligence operative turned, Carver noted the folds of soft fat at the base of his neck. Callahan had always been a big boy, but it was clear that he'd put on 20 or 30 more pounds since they had last seen each other.

Carver could hardly believe his eyes when they exited the elevator onto the second floor. A section of wall had been intentionally exposed. He touched the 1500-year-old brickwork with his fingers as he passed, admiring the finishing on the corners and artwork on the ceiling and the stucco finishing work on the walls. The entrance to their room was encased in a beautiful marble frame. Callahan beamed as he unlocked the door and let his guests into the spacious suite.

"A Salviati?" Nico exclaimed as he saw the artwork. "Seriously?"

Callahan looked at Carver. "You didn't tell me Nico was also an expert on Renaissance art."

Carver wasn't paying much attention. He was too busy admiring an elaborate iron candelabra that hung over the dining table in their suite. It was a magnificent work of art, with the sign of the Vatican – the crossed keys of St. Peter beneath the triple crown – masterfully replicated at its center. "I hope you didn't lay down your personal credit card for this room," Carver said, "Because this candelabra is going to look great in my condo in D.C."

He led Callahan to the master bedroom and shut the door, leaving Nico to salivate over the furnishings. Then the American began scanning the room for bugs.

The priest looked nervous. "You think your friend will be, uh, okay out there on his own?"

Carver nodded. "That chip in his arm is a strong deterrent against flight. Plus, I think he likes this place."

The priest smiled, taking in Carver's ripped form. "Still running several miles a day, obviously."

"I try."

The priest paused for a moment. "And now, a person with normal social skills would return the compliment by telling me how great I look."

"To be honest, you look like you've seen some hard miles, Father. I thought Rome was supposed to be a cushy post."

"*To whom much is given, much will be expected,*" Callahan said, quoting Luke. A brilliant student in his youth, Callahan had been recruited by the CIA almost as soon as he had entered the priesthood in Dublin, Ireland. Under the agreement, he was encouraged to fully pursue his ambitions in the Catholic Church in order to rise in the church hierarchy and broaden his intelligence-gathering capabilities. Over the years he had become a highly paid messenger, delivering information, technology and occasional surveillance services while still managing to keep his day job.

Four years ago he had been offered a role in Vatican Intelligence. With the organization having maintained close ties with the CIA, Callahan had become the primary linchpin in joint operations between the Vatican and American intelligence, as well as other organizations such as MI6 and the Mossad. He was officially a double agent. But the CIA hoped they would remain his true master.

Carver had finished his electronic sweep of the room, and now stood on the bed as he examined the light fixtures for bugs. "I think we're okay. Let's get on with business."

Callahan opened his satchel. He unpacked a SIG P226 wrapped in cloth, along with several spare clips. It smelled freshly oiled. It looked every bit as good as the one he had been forced to leave in Johannesburg when airport police presented him with an 11-page declaration form that he had failed to fill out upon entering the country. As much as he hated to leave a weapon behind, it was better than missing his flight.

"No serial numbers," the priest added.

Carver wrapped his fingers around the grip, then popped the clip into the handle and chambered a round into the barrel, testing the action.

"Perfect," he said. "I assume you'll take cash?"

The priest smiled. "It's on me. My monthly stipend from the CIA more than covers little popguns like this. You should see the stuff my Israeli friends ask for."

Callahan reached into his satchel again. This time, he produced a new satphone and handed it to Carver. He had gotten into the habit of switching phones every few days as a security precaution. Until recently, he had been content to simply switch SIM cards out of the same phone on a regular basis. That was no longer enough. It had simply gotten too easy to infiltrate other parts of the handset.

"There now," the priest said. "You can communicate and you can defend yourself. Now can you tell me why you're here?"

Carver sat down in a small, elegantly crafted chair made of wood and leather. Father Thomas Callahan had been a valued operative for years, and he had been the eyes and ears of Operation Crossbow for a handful of days. Still, Carver didn't yet feel comfortable disclosing the ins and outs of the Gish and Preston assassinations.

"You contacted us, Father. Something about two bodies in the morgue?"

"Quite right. It seems there was a gunfight in the hotel parking garage where we last had a location on Adrian Zhu. Nothing I couldn't have sussed out on my own."

"Who are they?"

"They're still John Does, as you say in America."

"I need to see them immediately. Care to come along and offer last rites?"

"Since when did you care about the souls of strangers?"

"I've saved lots of strangers. Millions, even. They just don't know it."

Callahan's eyes twinkled. "Aye, but you've also sent a few to meet their maker. And ever so humbly, I might add."

Mayflower Hotel

"I have a message for Mary," Ellis told Vera Borst. It was not what she had imagined saying to the sitting under-secretary-general of the United Nations. It was far from anything Speers would have approved. But it felt right.

As far as Ms. Borst was concerned, the government still considered her daughter missing. Ellis had decided not to let on that they had discovered her name on the passenger manifest of the Toronto-Rome flight the previous day. After Hank Bowers had been unable to secure a meeting with Vera, McLean had tapped her communications. So far, the log on the mission cloud showed absolutely no activity between mother and daughter.

"My daughter?" Borst said in Dutch-accented English.

"Yes," Ellis confirmed.

"Who is this? How did you get this number?"

"My name is Haley Ellis. I was with Mary before the fire at Senator Preston's house." All true. All verifiable.

"I see. You two knew each other?"

"I have to tell her something important. Something Senator Preston was supposed to tell her."

"I can't tell you where she is," Borst said without missing a beat. It wasn't a denial. Just a statement.

"The messenger is a Level 19," Ellis said. She was completely improvising now. There was very little to lose.

Borst was quiet for several seconds. Ellis thought she heard running water. "We shouldn't discuss this by phone," Borst said finally. "We should meet. Are you still in D.C.?"

"Yes."

"Then you have to come now. I'm leaving for Europe tomorrow."

Now? Not ideal. But a chance to question the mother of the only person of interest they had? She had to act. And her chances of finding the killers from a hotel room? Zero.

"I'll have to check flights," Ellis said. In her excitement, she had almost forgotten that she was confined to the hotel. How would she get past Jack?

"There's an Alaska Airlines flight at 7:10 every night from Reagan National. With the time difference it puts you at Sea-Tac at about nine. If you miss that, there's a Virgin flight a half-hour later."

Given Borst's role in world government, Ellis wasn't surprised the under-secretary would have memorized the Washington to Seattle flight schedule. She imagined Borst was also fairly familiar with flights into and out of New York.

She checked her watch. It was already a few minutes past four. There might be enough time to get to the airport and get on a standby list for the 7:10. There was no time to ask Speers for permission.

Rockville, Maryland

Speers and Fordham watched from the back seat of a black sedan as the city gave way to suburbs and eventually, to a hilly, verdant Rockville neighborhood populated by expensive cars and enormous mansions. "This is the address," Fordham said into his earpiece as they rolled up outside the massive estate known as Eden. "Let us take the lead. Everyone else stay back until we give the signal."

The property's 15-foot walls were covered in ivy, except at the top, where loops of razor wire glimmered in the sun. Tiny cameras were mounted around the entire perimeter.

Speers got out of the car. Wincing at the pain from his ankle, he propped himself up on a cane that the nurses at Walter Reed had given him. The MRI had shown no broken bones, thankfully. They had given him something for the inflammation, wrapped the ankle, and discharged him. As he put weight on it, he regretted not getting a prescription for the pain.

He looked down the hill, noting no less than eight black sedans parked about 50 yards away. Their passengers had been instructed to stay put for now. Per the president's request, none of Fordham's agents except Hank Bowers were privy to the case details. They had been told only to seize all files, computers, strongboxes and weapons from the premises.

"Are those chemical toilets ours?" he said, noticing an outhouse trailer at the end of the caravan.

"Damn right," Fordham said. "I took one look at the size of this place on the map and figured we'd be out here all day. I've also got a craft services truck coming at noon."

Fordham pulled the federal warrant out of his pocket. Speers didn't want to know how the FBI director had gotten it so quickly.

Suddenly, a grinding sound emanated from the front gate, which looked as if it was made of solid iron. The gate opened slowly. The FBI agents backed off, some of them ducking behind cars. Speers held his ground, mesmerized by the emerging view.

A long, winding driveway snaked up a sloping hill. It was covered with autumn leaves. A flock of ducks flew in perfect V-formation overhead and began to circle over the main house. Speers imagined a pond deeper on the property, or perhaps a gigantic swimming pool.

A real estate agent in black stockings and a conservative red dress stepped out to the street. Apparently oblivious to the G-men on the street, she began pounding a sign into the dirt with a rubber mallet. It read PRIVATE SHOWINGS BY APPOINTMENT ONLY.

Speers hobbled across the street with Fordham beside him, and called out to the woman so as not to scare her. "Excuse me."

The woman turned. Her face was cragged with wrinkles and was much older than her shapely figure and blonde mane had conveyed from the rear. "Yes?" the woman responded.

"Just saw the sign going up." Speers hoped to gain entrance without using Fordham's warrant. "We'd like to see the property."

The woman sized the two men up. Although they had stepped out of a new black Lincoln Continental, neither was wearing a luxury watch and their shoes were worth less than the bottle of wine she had bought for dinner last night. "I'm afraid there is a prequalification process in order to secure an appointment. With a property like this, one does have to screen out the looky loos."

With the gates now fully open, Speers could see the white columns leading up to the enormous residence. Nobody seemed to be around, but it was easy to imagine world leaders being driven in and out of the property and squads of young students mowing the lawn and raking leaves.

"Happy to oblige," Fordham said. "Can you tell me how long it's been vacant?"

"Maybe a week?" she replied, seeming somewhat baffled by her own answer.

"You're not sure?" Speers said.

She set the mallet down beside her and wiped her forehead. "I must admit," she sighed. "This place has been a mystery for 43 years. I grew up in this neighborhood. I was a teenager when the new owners moved in one night and started putting up these big walls. Even though there always seemed to be big parties here, nobody really knew who lived here. You can imagine my shock when their attorney called me to sell the place."

Speers nodded. "Leaving in such a hurry, they must have left some things behind."

She shook her head. "The place is in cherry condition. Absolutely cherry. They didn't leave so much as a box in a bedroom or a crumb in the kitchen. With a place this gigantic? That's something you don't see every day."

Speers' spirits sank. The odds of finding anything useful on the premises had just decreased dramatically.

"We'd like to look around," Fordham suggested.

She folded her arms across her chest. "About all I can tell you without an application are the specs. Twenty-three bedrooms, 20 bathrooms and 16 fireplaces." She paused, noticing Fordham surveying the cameras over the gate. "Now then. May I ask what business you and your friend are in?"

Fordham raised his left hand above his head and snapped his fingers. The woman's jaw sagged as she watched 32 FBI field agents step out of their cars.

City Morgue
Rome

Detective Antonio Tesla was a distinguished-looking fellow, perhaps in his mid-50s, clean-shaven, with the short, curly hair that was seen on the busts of ancient Roman noblemen. He wore brown suit pants and a white button-down shirt under an unstructured jacket.

Carver let Callahan handle the introductions between him, Tesla and Nico. Tesla shook hands without a word, turned, and led them past the administrative offices and down some stairs, where the air was markedly colder. It seemed that morgues all over the world looked the same. Unflattering lighting. A series of gurneys with unclothed bodies in various levels of assembly. Rows and rows of drawers.

Tesla began talking in Italian at a steady clip as they entered a second, and much larger, room. Father Callahan began translating as he received the information. "He says the two victims were found four nights ago in the parking garage of the Hotel Angelico."

"How did they die, exactly?"

Callahan started to answer, but it was all he could do to keep up with the detective's quick tongue. "There was a shootout. The victims were found in and around the Mini Cooper, which was apparently rammed several times by a Range Rover with stolen plates. It was left on the premises."

"Did you say, *in and around* the Mini Cooper? I thought there were only two of them."

The priest clarified the point with Tesla. His revulsion was evident before he began translating. "It appeared that the men might have been attempting to escape the vehicle. Their extremities were smashed in the process, rendering certain, em, pieces of them outside the wreckage."

"A regular demolition derby," Carver remarked.

Tesla resumed talking.

"Yesterday," Callahan translated from Italian, "He discovered that the car had been registered to a young couple in Florence who had driven it for four years before donating it to a local Monastery. It's currently unclear how it ended up in the hands of the victims."

A morgue employee in a hooded white uniform took note of Detective Tesla's entrance and, apparently expecting his arrival, motioned in the general direction of a wall of drawers. He walked to one such drawer and opened it about three feet, revealing a black body bag.

"He says it's going to be unpleasant," the priest explained.

Nico looked away as Tesla unzipped the bag, revealing the decapitated cadaver. What remained above the neck was a twisted, ravaged lower jawbone covered in jerky-like flesh.

Tesla spoke rapidly. He went on nonstop for a minute, gesticulating with his hands. At last Callahan said, "He thinks the people in the Range Rover might have just walked away. There's no accounting for their departure in the hotel security cameras. But he said it looked like they tried to blow up their own ride before they went."

"Tried?" Carver said. "Was it armored?"

The priest nodded. "He says the Range Rover had a serious anti-terror package. The driver's side glass alone took 20 rounds without giving. They managed to set the gas tank on fire, and the outside was scorched, but the interior withstood the blast."

"There can't be many vehicles that tricked out in the world."

"Tesla's squad already looked up the plates. Stolen from a Fiat."

The plates might have been untraceable, Carver thought, but surely there were only a handful of security companies in the world that could have outfitted the Range Rover to take more than 70 rounds of gunfire and also be resistant to self-sabotage.

They probably just changed vehicles, Carver thought. He was going to need to review the garage security footage for himself.

"Ask the detective if we can see their phones," Carver said and then waited for the translation.

"He said you're welcome to see them, but that the SIM cards had been removed by the time police arrived at the scene."

SIM cards stolen from dead men? This was both strange and disappointing. Even if these men had used disposable handsets, the call logs could have exposed anyone they had communicated with recently. Carver could only conclude that whoever had kill these men wanted the data for the same purpose. Killing them wasn't enough. They wanted their friends, too.

Meanwhile, Tesla was still talking. "They appeared to be firing MP5 submachine guns," Callahan translated. "And they had plenty of time to shoot, apparently. They found 72 shell casings on the cement around them."

By the time Callahan was finished translating for Carver, Tesla had already opened up a second drawer. He unzipped the body bag and turned the cadaver on its side. This one had a face, but was missing a foot. Carver crouched to see the man's face. He looked no older than 25, with olive-tinted skin.

Tesla waved his hand, motioning Carver to the other side. As Carver came around, he pointed to a tattoo on the man's back, just below the collar. It was a circular sun, with the block letters IHS in the center. A cross was above the abbreviation, with three nails below. Carver knew it well. It was the symbol of the Society of Jesus.

"Jesuits," Tesla said in English, tapping the inked skin.

"Whoa!" Nico exclaimed. "These were some badass priests!"

"Not all Jesuits are priests," Father Callahan cut in. "Some are lay brothers. And I'd venture to say that the presence of a tattoo is hardly proof that they were in the Society at all. Vandalization of the flesh is hardly standard. *You shall not make any cuttings in your flesh or tattoo any marks upon you: I am the Lord.* That's from Leviticus. It wouldn't be approved by Father General, I can tell you that much."

Carver understood the reference. Father General was the leader of the Jesuits worldwide. It was a powerful position within the Roman Catholic Church, officially known by insiders as Superior General, and to some outsiders by the mildly derogatory term, Black pope. Like the pontiff, superiors general were generally elected for life, their reign typically ending only as they drew their last waking breath. Ignatius of Loyola had been the first leader of the Jesuits, in 1541.

"What were they wearing?" Carver said.

The answer came back quickly. "Track suits."

Carver looked up at Tesla. "There was some mention of an octagon found on one of the bodies?"

"Ah, *ottagono*," he nodded. Tesla zipped up the body bag and rolled the cadaver drawer back into the wall. Then he led them into an office with plastic bins on shelves. Most had a name. The employee went to a shelf that had several bins that were labeled by number only. He pulled #51, which corresponded to the cadaver drawer they had just seen.

The octagon-shaped piece of cloth was on top in a plastic Ziploc bag, resting atop the bloodied tracksuit and sneakers the dead man had been wearing. To Carver's eye, it looked exactly like the octagons at the Gish and Preston crime scenes. The inscription on the front was *Ad Majorem Dei*

Gloriam – for the greater glory of God. He flipped it over to read the inscription on the back, *Paratus Enim Dolor et Cruciatus, in Dei Nomine.* Prepared for pain and torment, in God's name.

"Where's the other one?" Carver said.

Tesla shook his head and held up one finger.

"Only one octagon?"

"Pocket," Tesla replied, opening his own jacket and pointing to an inside pouch.

"The octagon was in his pocket?" Carver said. "Not in his mouth?"

The priest translated. Carver understood Tesla's response before Callahan interpreted. "He wants to know why you would expect it to be in his mouth. And that goes double for me."

Carver could not say what he was thinking. An octagon in either dead man's mouth might have indicated that they were victims of the same organization that had killed Preston and Gish. But the presence of the fabric in their pocket could mean the opposite.

But these men had not killed Gish or Preston. Their deaths had in fact come several hours before the assassinations in D.C. and Rome.

That meant that the organization they were up against was large enough, and sophisticated enough, to operate in three time zones simultaneously.

Sea-Tac Airport

It was past 11 p.m. Pacific time when Ellis' plane touched down, waking her from a deep sleep. She was immediately self-conscious of her boozy breath. To calm her nerves, she had downed a couple of strong martinis in an airport bar prior to boarding. As soon as she disembarked, she would be searching for a can of Venom, coffee, anything. It was a vicious cycle.

She stretched as much as possible without encroaching upon the space of the elderly gentleman sitting next to her. Then she opened the window shade and peered out the dewy window. The thick airport fog reduced the airport buildings to hazy illuminations of yellow light.

She had no luggage except the backpack she had taken from Drucker's condo. In it she had packed her weapon, Drucker's manuscript and notes. The hotel situation had forced her to travel light. After her conversation with Vera Borst, Ellis had been left with the challenge of escaping Jack McClellan's watch. After hearing nothing through the door the adjoining suite for several hours, she took a chance and forced it open. One look at the room told her it was still occupied, but the guests had apparently stepped out. Ellis rifled through the closet, looking for anything that might pass for a disguise. She quickly located a stylish long black trenchcoat that fit to a tee, and a furry hat with long earflaps and poms. A pair of sheepskin boots were a half-size too large for her, but she decided she could manage it. She bolted out of the adjoining suite with her back to McClellan's position in the hallway, walking with purpose toward the elevators at the end of the hall. She never looked back.

Ellis had left the hotel before her new satphone had arrived from McLean. Traveling without a device made her feel both vulnerable and free. She was so accustomed to having the mapped world at her behest that the thought of finding Ms. Borst's address – which she had handwritten on a piece of hotel stationary – seemed daunting. At the same time, she was grateful to be spared the inevitable barrage of demanding messages from Julian Speers. That went double for having her location trackable. She checked her watch again. It was 2 a.m. in D.C. With luck, she would be on her returning flight by the time Speers woke up.

Despite her eighth row window seat, Ellis managed to be the first one off the plane when the doors opened, elbowing her way past even the first class passengers.

Ellis quickly made her way through the tidy airport toward the signs for ground transport. Once she reached the outside, she stood for a moment on the curb, breathing in her first taste of Northwest air. Wet. Crisp. Verdant.

She jumped into a cab.

"Evening," the driver said. "Just the pack? No other luggage?"

She handed the driver the Mayflower Hotel stationary on which she had written Borst's address. She remembered watching her mother do the same thing once, when she was a child, before the age of smartphones.

The cab driver let out a hearty laugh. "Miss," he chuckled. "Do you even know where this is?"

Ellis took it back. She saw nothing wrong with the address. "What's the problem?"

"The zip code. It's on Vashon Island."

Crap. Ellis was vaguely aware that the Northwest was partitioned by lots of inlets, lakes and rivers, but she had no concrete knowledge of its actual geography. She had already spent a ton of her own money on the plane ticket, without any guarantee that Speers would ever agree to reimburse her for it.

"Okay. How much?"

"I can't just drive there, if that's what you're asking. If it was Mercer Island, no problem. There's a bridge to Mercer. For Vashon, you have to take a ferry, and the ferries stopped for the night already. You'll have to wait until morning."

That was out of the question. Vera Borst had said she was flying to Europe in the morning, presumably on UN business, although she hadn't specified. She had said to come tonight.

"Are there water taxis?" Ellis said.

The cabbie chortled again. "There should be, right? Fact is that there's a lot of people that want water service privatized, which would mean more jobs and service all night and all day, right? But no, the county protected the union jobs like always."

"Is there someone else you can call? Someone with a boat?"

The driver shook his head.

Ellis reached into her pack, fished out one of the outdated NIC business cards she had shown Drucker, and handed it to the cabbie. "I'm not usually this pushy. It's just that I'm here on a matter of national security. It's important."

Rome

The sun fell behind St. Peter's Basilica just as Father Callahan turned his tiny Fiat onto Via della Conciliazione. Nico sat sideways in the car's tiny back seat, watching as a group of tourists posed for pictures in front of the Santa Maria della Transpontina church. The car passed the embassies of Brazil, Iraq and Egypt. How was it that over the past two thousand years the Vatican had shrunk from a vast geographical empire of papal states to a tiny sovereign nation wedged inside Rome, and yet it influenced more people worldwide than any other government?

At last, the Fiat pulled up to the Palazzo della Rovere. "Buy you a drink?" Carver asked the priest, who was shaken from seeing the mangled corpses.

"I could use it," he said. "I'll meet you in Le Colonne."

Carver and Nico unfolded themselves from the tiny car and watched as the priest pulled through the arched driveway in search of parking. The two hadn't talked since Detective Tesla had shown them the bodies and the personal effects found on the dead Jesuits down at the morgue.

"In your estimation," Carver said, "How accurate was Father Callahan's translation?"

Nico scratched behind his left ear and rolled his shoulders up and down, as if to work the tension out of them. "Mmmm," he said, "Detective Tesla talks a hundred miles an hour."

Carver smiled. "I have a hard time believing that you, of all people, couldn't understand him."

"Of course I could understand him," Nico quipped. "I'm just qualifying my answer first. The priest lives here, so naturally his comprehension is going to be a bit better than mine."

"I get it. Now answer the question."

Nico placed a hand flat against the wall and leaned into it, bringing his left leg up behind him as he spoke. "I didn't notice any glaring omissions, but I thought it was curious that Father Callahan kept referring to the bodies as victims. Tesla never used that word to describe them."

"What word did he use?"

"Gunmen."

"That's interesting."

"Mind if I go up and wire in? You didn't drag my ass all the way from Africa to hang around morgues."

That much was true. Carver needed Nico to find connections between two more famous stiffs – Preston and Gish. Maybe it was time to let the tracking chip in Nico's arm do the chaperoning for a bit. He took one of the room keys from his pocket and handed it over.

Carver held the door to the lobby open. "I want to know the moment you find anything."

Nico scampered upstairs. Carver made his way through the lobby to Le Colonne, the hotel bar where Father Callahan had already sidled up to a bar stool. The priest had ordered whiskey for himself, along with a plate of pizza, and unsweetened iced tea and salmon for his American colleague.

Carver pointed toward a booth at the back of the room. He had no intention of disclosing the full details of the operation to Callahan or anyone. But the conversation would undoubtedly veer into territory that would be far too sensitive for anyone else's ears.

"Now then," Callahan began as they settled into the booth. The priest was smiling, but he wasn't in a merry mood. "If you'll do me the courtesy of disclosing the real reason you're in Rome, perhaps I'll feel like less of a jackass."

"This isn't about Operation Crossbow per se."

"So I gathered."

"Some very important people are dead. I'm looking for the assassins."

"Plural?" Callahan asked.

"Yes. We believe this is the work of a sophisticated organization."

"Is this somehow related to Adrian Zhu or LifeEmberz?"

"A valid question, Father. I don't have the answer to that yet. But I have to find the organization behind these assassinations."

Without naming the dead, or detailing the exact circumstances, Carver explained how they had found identical octagons in Washington, London, Seattle and now Rome.

The bartender walked over with the drinks and set them on the table. Carver held his tongue until the man was back at his post. "That octagon we saw today. Have you ever seen something like that before?"

The priest took a slug of his whiskey. "As a matter of fact, yes. The moment my security clearance was accepted by the Holy See, I went to the archives and read everything I could about the history of Vatican Intelligence."

"I'm actually jealous."

"You should be. It's a cracking read. But yes, I saw a couple of preserved octagons like the one we saw today. Calling cards, apparently, for a group of nasties that went by the name Black Order."

"How recently?"

"Not very. 1700s, if memory serves."

That checked out. Carver knew that the Black Order had been officially dissolved by Pope Leo XIII in 1878. "What else can you tell me?"

"I'm not sure," the priest continued. "You've given me almost nothing to go on."

The American wasn't ready to show his hand yet. He still had more questions. "Who's your boss at Vatican Intelligence?"

"My direct boss is a nobody. When I really need something, I go to the very top."

"Heinz Lang?"

The priest nodded. Heinz Lang had served as the Superior General of the Society of Jesus for 12 distinguished years. Lang had made headlines by retiring several years earlier, despite appearing to be in excellent health. The rumor in Europe had been that Lang had quietly stepped down in order to direct Vatican Intelligence, which, officially speaking, did not exist.

"What's he like?"

"Very German. Good at delegation and leadership. Personally, quite cold. And like one of our former popes, Lang is a product of the Second World War."

"Hitler Youth?"

"Aye. And then some."

The bartender came with the pizza and salmon, some sparkling water and two sets of silverware. Carver waited until he was safely away. "Are you saying Lang was an actual Nazi?"

"Depends on your definition of a Nazi, doesn't it? As the war went on, they were drafting them right out of high school. They say he was only 15 when Vatican Intelligence caught him. Just a boy, really."

"Was he sent to a POW camp?" Carver cut a slice of salmon and chewed. It was undercooked. Just how he liked it.

"Father General needed no prodding to switch sides, apparently. He was from a closeted Catholic family living under an oppressive fascist regime. As the story goes, his information led directly to the capture of Heinrich Himmler."

Carver paused, sipping his water, wanting to word his next question delicately. "If the church was somehow threatened, would Lang have the authority to reconvene the Black Order?"

The priest laughed before answering. "For one thing, there is no such thing in this day and age."

"The Vatican has been denying the existence of its intelligence agency for hundreds of years, but you just told me that the director of this mythical organization is Heinz Lang."

"This is different. If the Black Order existed today, it would no more be controlled by the Vatican than an Illinois militia would be controlled by the White House."

It was a flimsy comparison that Carver wasn't about to be satisfied with. "I'm not asking whether the pope himself is running the Black Order. I'm talking about someone for whom espionage is the primary profession. Specifically, Heinz Lang."

The priest's jaw tightened. His eyebrows drew together. Carver had seen Callahan frustrated, but this was the first time he'd ever seen him ready to fight. Good. Now they were getting somewhere.

"You seem to be proposing that a person or persons in the Vatican are involved in something extremely sinister. That hits pretty close to home."

"Not to be crass, but we pay you more than the Vatican does. So I would think our interests would also hit close to home."

"I've always earned my keep. But this is more than just business to me. I deserve to know why you're suddenly so interested in the Vatican."

"The murder victims were people of considerable influence, Father. And they weren't just assassinated. They were tortured. They suffered the *strappado*."

"Suspended by a rope?"

Carver nodded. "The very method that made Venice's Palazzo Ducale synonymous with Jesuit-inflicted torture."

The priest massaged his wrist. "You do realize the likelihood of the Black Order having survived in complete secrecy all these years is…"

"Tiny, I know. But if this is a copycat killer, it's one hell of a trick. It would require at least two tribute killers working in the same style on different continents. There's no precedent for that."

Callahan sat straight up and ran his palm down the length of his face.

"You've ruled out state-sponsored terror?"

"For the most part."

"Look, all I can tell you is that if I had any knowledge of any such activities, you know full well that I would report it."

Carver used his fork to fish a lemon wedge out of his tea. Carver took a bite of the lemon, relishing the sourness for a moment. "I need to find out for sure. How high is your security clearance, Father?"

"Not nearly high enough." The priest began to sweat, knowing full well that he was being asked to spy on his own boss. "One doesn't poo where one eats, now does he?"

"You just told me that your allegiance is to the CIA." Carver leaned in. "I'm telling you that there's smoke at the Vatican, Father. I need you to find out where the fire is."

Harbor Island Marina
Seattle, Washington

It was after midnight by the time the taxi dropped Ellis at the 80-slip moor between the main city and West Seattle. The water in Puget Sound tonight was as still as it had been on the Virginia lakes Ellis had waterskied on as a teenager. The smell was something else, though. An unpleasant mix of salt and decomposing shellfish from an adjacent mud beach.

A ruddy-faced man who called himself Captain Zack stood before her in yellow rubber waders, a peacoat and a white cap. He slipped Ellis' $300 into his pocket and began leading her toward his vessel. "We'll be in a convertible," he whispered as they walked. "It's only about 14 nautical miles, but it'll be cold."

"How long will it take?" Ellis' voice seemed to boom throughout the stillness.

"Shhh," Captain Zack scolded. "Keep it down. Some of these boats are sleepers."

He pointed to a 19-foot Harbercraft boat with the name Scorpion Water Taxis along the running boards. "That one will run you about $300."

Ellis threw her hands up in exasperation. "Seriously? For that thing?"

"It's after midnight, lady. For an extra $200, I've got a boat with an aluminum top."

Ellis shook her head. She had already spent well beyond her means, and the odds that she would get to expense the plane ticket here were dim. "Nothing wrong with a little night air."

"Suit yourself."

Captain Zack took them out with an electric motor and then cranked up the diesel engine when they were a reasonable distance from the marina.

As they pulled out into Puget Sound, Ellis saw a vast industrial port where thousands of shipping containers were stacked like multicolored Legos. A row of enormous cranes reminded Ellis of Imperial Walkers from the Star Wars movies. The Seattle skyline was hazy as viewed through the fog, but nevertheless far more impressive than she had imagined.

"Must be gorgeous in the daytime."

Captain Zack shrugged. "Guess so. Hard to appreciate it when business is slow. Course, this is just my first year running water taxis. I was a commercial angler before that, up in Alaska."

"How slow is slow?"

"Over the summer, maybe three calls a day. After Labor Day I'm lucky if I get one."

"Ever thought about changing the business name?"

Captain Zack took his eyes off their course for the first time and looked at Ellis. "Why would I do that? What's wrong with the name?"

Ellis already regretted saying anything. "The irony doesn't work for me. Just my opinion."

"What irony? Me and my wife and our daughter all have November birthdays. We're all Scorpios. And there you have it. Scorpion Water Taxis."

It was hard to believe nobody had brought this up before now. "Nobody's ever mentioned the fable of the frog and the scorpion?"

The captain shook his head again. "Can't say that they have. What is it?"

Ellis sighed. "The story goes like this. A frog made his money taking animals across the river. He had never turned down a customer. Then one day, here came a scorpion. The frog was afraid, and said he couldn't take him. The scorpion said, 'Mr. Frog, I would never sting you. If I did, then we would both drown.' That seemed rational, so he let the scorpion climb onto his back, and they went out into the river. When they had almost reached the other side, the scorpion stung him. As they started to sink toward what was certain death for both of them, the frog wanted to know why. The scorpion just told him, 'Sorry, buddy, but you just can't fight nature.'"

She watched Captain Zack's face as he absorbed the moral of the story. He was quiet for nearly a minute. "So you're saying that everyone who's ever heard that fable thinks about drowning when they hear the name of my water taxi business."

"Not everyone. But hey, every customer counts, right?"

"The way I see it, the dangerous one in that story is the insect, not the frog. And as the water taxi driver, I'm the frog."

"True. Well, I'm a Scorpio. And I promise not to sting you."

He was silent for a few minutes. Finally he cleared his throat and said, "Here's one. How about Titanic Taxis?"

Ellis laughed. At least he was thinking big.

The Apostolic Palace
Vatican City

Father Callahan donned a new white collar for his audience with Heinz Lang. In his years of services to the CIA and the Vatican, the priest had used his cover to gather sensitive information from a litany of powerful people throughout Europe. He had trafficked stolen data and weapons for some of the world's most lethal operatives. He had eliminated a fanatic who planned to detonate a dirty bomb in St. Peter's Square. Yet today, in preparation for a meeting with the 85-year-old head of Vatican Intelligence, his forehead was slick with sweat.

He climbed the stairs toward the third floor of the Apostolic Palace, rubbing a dollop of hand sanitizer between his palms and over his lips. After his tense evening with Agent Carver at *Le Colonne*, he had been up much of the night praying for guidance. Of his vow of poverty, he was sure to be in good standing with God. The entirety of his salary from the CIA and various other clients was piling up in a Swiss bank account, and would be tapped only in retirement, with more than half the funds slated for charity. Regarding his vow of chastity, he also presented a nearly flawless record, with his only slip a heated embrace and brief kiss with a widow he consoled early in his career as a priest. It was his vow of obedience that he had failed in. There was nothing he could do. Obedience to the CIA and obedience to God seemed, at the moment, like conflicting actions.

Although the Jesuits maintained a fortified headquarters nearby known as the Jesuit Curia – which was, coincidentally, less than a city block from Carver's hotel room at the Palazzo della Rovere – Lang preferred to office in the Apostolic Palace. Citing security concerns, as well as a desire to be as close as possible to serve His Holiness, he had requested an office on the third floor and moved in less than a month after his election.

In a maze of offices, reception rooms and tiny chapels, Callahan spotted Lang's office by the hallmark Greek IHT letters that were displayed in bronze above the door. The society explained this acronym – which the priest had also seen etched in ink on the bodies of the gunmen in the Rome morgue – as an abbreviation of the Greek spelling of Jesus, *iota-eta-sigma*. Rumors of alternate meanings had dogged the Jesuits for centuries. Some said that Constantine – the ancient master of the Roman Empire who had first declared Rome to be a Christian city – had created the acronym himself from the phrase *In hoc signo vinces*, meaning, "In this sign you shall conquer."

Lang was behind his desk when the priest entered. Wood paneling behind it depicted painted images of the first three superiors general from the 1500s, Ignatius of Loyola, Francis Borgia and Everard Mercurian. Lang's hair looked whiter than when Callahan had last met him, but his frame looked just as fit underneath his black ankle-length cassock. A simple wooden cross dangled from a necklace made of simple leather.

"Your Excellency," Callahan said with his hands folded before him.

The corners of Lang's lips curled up. He stood and walked around his desk, held out his right hand and watched as Callahan knelt and kissed the brass ring that bore the Jesuit symbol. It was said that superiors general in recent times had dispensed with this custom among their own kind, deeming it too demeaning for those within Vatican Intelligence.

But Lang was a classicist. During his reign as Jesuit Chief, he had openly yearned for the formal era of his youth, when the church's exclusive use of Latin in Mass, elaborate liturgical rituals and formal attire added an aura of mystery to the Holy See.

He had been as active a superior general as the church had ever seen. Few before him had attempted to manage the entirety of the Jesuit mission. The society's schools and orphanages and other groups operated in every corner of the world. Lang, having made a commitment to visit each and every one of the provinces during his first two years in the post, possessed an itinerary that would have been aggressive for anyone, let alone a man in his 70s and 80s. He appeared to have a limitless well of energy.

Since stepping down, he had brought the same level of devotion to Vatican Intelligence. Now Lang raised the hem of his cassock slightly and walked to a sitting area at the far end of the room, an intimate array of chairs where visitors could enjoy the priceless view afforded them from the Apostolic Palace.

"So," Lang began. "When we last chatted, you were to inform me of any inroads we made as to the investigation. I assume by your insistence about this meeting that you have something to report that was too sensitive to be handled by telephone."

"In a matter of speaking, Your Excellency," Callahan replied before breaking out into a coughing fit.

"Is it that troubling?"

"Forgive me. The hours I've been keeping of late have not been good for my health."

"Then I would thank you to cover your mouth with your sleeve when coughing. At my age, I can't afford to get sick."

"Naturally," Callahan replied. "In regards to the matter at hand, I regret to report that the two young lads you asked me to find are in the city morgue."

Lang's face flattened. "Did they die violently?"

The priest nodded. "In a most brutal fashion, I'm afraid."

Three days prior to Carver's arrival in Rome, Callahan had received a surprise call from Lang, who had been visiting a Jesuit province in Brazil, where it was said that the church was losing ground to a groundswell of Mormon missionaries. But Lang's call had nothing to do with evangelism. His request was cryptic, and he had given the priest almost no information to go on, other than to ask him to find two operatives who had disappeared in Rome after what he had described as a critical operation. He had mentioned only their names and nationalities. Lazlo Cruz, from Argentina, and Cesar Macchione, who was from Florence.

The superior general stood, clasped his hands behind his back, and went to the window, looking out over Rome. Callahan hoped that he would not be asked how he had discovered the young Jesuits' bodies. Although Lang was fully aware of Callahan's working relationship with the CIA and other intelligence organizations, revealing that the information had come to him via the Americans would only incite Lang's legendary paranoia.

"I trust you did not claim the bodies."

"Correct," Callahan answered. "And as you asked, I instructed Venice to deny any knowledge of the men if police are somehow able to trace them there."

Venice had been the birthplace of the Society in 1540, when Pope Paul III established the Jesuits as a formal religious order at the Palazzo San Marco. But the Jesuits had never been well received in the city of endless canals, and it had been abandoned as an outpost for centuries. Unbeknownst to most even within the Holy See, Lang had reclaimed it shortly after his election, transforming a shuttered church into a private barracks where future Vatican Intelligence agents were trained. When he had first learned of the Venice unit, and heard of the rumored 24 new recruits in training there,

Callahan had wondered why intelligence services had been inflated at such a rapid rate. In recent years, they had fielded no more than 20 operatives in total. In light of recent events, Callahan was willing to entertain the notion that Agent Carver's suspicions might be correct. Perhaps the Black Order had been resurrected after all.

"Your Excellency, there must be some other way that I can serve you. Perhaps I can somehow complete the mission you had set out for the lads."

Only a slight turning of Lang's head gave the priest any indication that his offer had been heard. The head of Vatican Intelligence stood at the window for half a minute longer, then returned to the seating area, sitting directly opposite his subject. The thin eyelids retracted themselves over Lang's substantial eyeballs, and his lips pulled back at the edges, baring both teeth and gums. "Their chance is over," he said. "We must be more aggressive, if that is even possible."

"To what end, your Excellency?"

"Nothing less than the continuation of the one true Apostolic Church is at stake. The world criticized us for standing in the way of science," Lang went on. "Yes, we persecuted heretics. Yes, we demanded repentance when scientific advancements contradicted church dogma. For centuries they said we were wrong. But now what will they say? What will the world say? How will God judge us if this comes to pass?"

The priest smiled, but only because he was genuinely afraid. Nobody in the Vatican talked like this. Those popes and cardinals who had tortured and killed men of science were long dead. The mistakes of the past were, as a rule, either ignored or chalked up to the imperfection of man. Callahan had never in his life heard anyone in the Vatican suggest that the torment of Galileo, for example, had actually been justified.

"I'm not sure what you mean," Callahan said. "What will come to pass?"

The head of Vatican Intelligence stood. He went to the grand desk, slid open the middle drawer and retrieved a tattered black and white photograph. A medium close-up of three boys who looked to be in their early teens. All three wore button-down military field shirts with black ties and long shorts. Each wore oversized swastika armbands. Despite the several decades that had passed since the photo had been taken, Callahan instantly recognized the boy on the left. He was the tallest, with white-blond hair and some sort of merit head pinned to his shirt. It was Heinz Lang.

Then Lang pointed to the boy in the middle, tapping the boy's head repeatedly. He was the best looking of the three, with chiseled, serious features.

"This man," Lang said. "His name is Sebastian Wolf. Find him for me, and you will have done a lifetime of good deeds."

Julian Speers Residence
Arlington, Virginia

It was nearly 3 a.m. when Speers, having left McLean a short time earlier, pulled up to the four-bedroom colonial house. Despite having moved in several months earlier, he still felt like a stranger here. There was just so little time now. Somehow, Speers had fooled himself into believing that no job could have been more demanding than his former role as White House Chief of Staff. Nothing could have been farther from the truth. He routinely worked over 100 hours per week now. Some nights it didn't even make sense to come home. The cushions of his office couch were nearly as familiar to him as the mattress in his bedroom.

The ankle he had twisted was still swollen and weak. He stepped out of the Highlander and used an aluminum crutch to limp toward the house. The moment he unlocked the door and heard the twins' cries, he knew the injury wouldn't earn him any sympathy points. His wife met him at the door, kissed him tersely and handed him one of the swaddled infants.

"I had to go to the ER," he said, but his exhausted wife did not hear him over the twins' wailing. She took the other child upstairs without looking back.

He kissed the baby on the forehead and hobbled to the kitchen pantry. He reached onto the highest shelf and searched blindly with his fingers for a Tupperware container. A wave of relief washed over him as he located it, pulling down the secret stash of pink pacifiers. His wife had banned them several weeks ago, fearing that the children weren't learning – how had she put it? – "self-soothing techniques."

The baby's response to the sight of the pacifier was decidedly Pavlovian, the mouth opening and puckering instantly. Speers rinsed it under the kitchen sink faucet and promptly put it into the child's mouth. She was asleep in seconds.

She felt good in his arms. He held her with one hand, retrieved an ice pack from the freezer and went into the living room. He sat in an easy chair and removed his shoes, socks and the ankle wrap without setting the child down. Then he rested the bag of ice on the ottoman, nestled his swollen ankle into it, and reclined.

The little darling was swaddled and asleep in his arms. Speers felt himself drifting, too. He didn't fight it. He rather enjoyed the sensation of letting go for the first time all day.

His phone buzzed. And just like that, his state of bliss was gone. Speers sometimes fantasized about having the kind of job where you could turn off your phone.

He glanced at the screen. It was Blake Carver. He answered.

"Blake?" he whispered.

"I can barely hear you," Carver said.

"I'm holding Isabella." He looked at his watch. It was nearly two in the morning.

"Must be nice," Carver said. "I'm visiting morgues, and you're playing house."

The DNI didn't need Carver's judgment right now. The Eden search had turned up nothing. He had three bodies on his hands, a tiny team stretched across the globe and a president that needed results right away.

"You called for a reason?" Speers said.

"I'm trying to get hold of Ellis. She left a weird message saying she was at the Mayflower Hotel. Is it just me, or are you guys just living it up over there while I'm busting my butt?"

Speers swore and told Carver to hold on. He used his crutch to get to his feet, gently setting the baby down onto the soft leather where he had been sitting, balancing her in the cradle of the seat cushion so she could not roll out. Then he hobbled into the next room.

"Had you bothered to read Ellis' update on the mission cloud," he barked, "You'd know that we almost got killed last night!"

He provided Carver with a brief summary and, once he had cooled down, told him about the notes and manuscript they had fished out of Drucker's now-incinerated apartment. "That's why she's locked down at the hotel," he added. "I've got Jack McClellan leading security there."

"That's weird," Carver said. "I just talked to her sister, Jenna. Apparently Haley left the hotel a couple hours ago."

Puget Sound

The boat traced the contours of the West Seattle coastline. Its stern finally pointed southwest. It was getting colder. Ellis was losing the feeling in her hands. The dampness was seeping into her bones. It wasn't too cold – about 40 degrees – but on the water, it felt frosty. She envied Captain Zack's coat.

"There's a fuzzy blanket under your seat," he said. "No charge."

No charge for the business advice either, Ellis thought. She got to her feet, lifted the seat cushion and found a silver and blue stadium blanket emblazoned with the Seattle Seahawks logo. She wrapped it around her shoulders and stood next to the captain.

"I reckon this must be pretty important," Captain Zack said. "Anything you can talk about?"

"Missing person," she said, and there was some truth to it. Her original objective had been to connect the dots between Preston and Gish and, if possible, find out who their common enemy was. Now that Mary Borst had gone missing, however, she was more intrigued by the role the Borsts themselves played in all of this. According to Drucker's notes, Vera Borst, Gish and Preston were all high-ranking Fellowship members. What, if anything, was Mary's role? Had she simply witnessed a murder and freaked out, or had she had a role in either Preston's death or the fire?

The fog seemed to lift some. The boat picked up speed. Captain Zack pointed to a black silhouette in the distance that was peppered by a few residential lights.

"That's Vashon. Which side of the island we headed to?"

Ellis reached into her pack, retrieved the piece of hotel stationary with the address written on it, and handed it to him. "Don't guess that's of any help."

He held it under the light for a moment "Sure is."

"Seriously?"

"Yeah, that's Dane Mitchell's place. One of the big gated homes on the west side of the island. Dane's got his own little dock out there. We can motor right up to it."

Bingo. Mitchell had been listed as Borst's life partner on her Wikipedia page. Ellis asked the captain if he knew Mitchell, raising her voice above the grinding drone of the Harbercraft's 90-horsepower Yamaha engine.

"It's not like everyone's got their own boat out here. And it's a pretty tight community among those that do."

"Have you met his partner?"

"Oh, yeah. She's got a funny name. Is it Worst?"

"Borst. Vera Borst."

"Ah yeah. Met her just once or twice. Nice lady, seems like. Said Seattle reminded her of her hometown. Oslo, ain't it?"

"Amsterdam, I think."

"Ah yeah. Amsterdam. Dane used to be a lot more chatty before she came along. He'd stop and talk boating. For a while he was into crabbin', and he'd pick my brain on it. Other times he might come and share what he caught. But he's kept more to himself since she came here."

"Why is that?"

He shrugged. "People change. And a lot of times, they get changed by other people."

"You think she changed him?"

Captain Zack nodded certainly. "I got the impression from someone on the island that Vera is a real religious lady. And a politician too. That surprises me, you know, with him being a man of science an' that."

Just like Drucker said, Ellis thought. Scientists and politicians. A match made only at Eden.

They went faster now, making good time across the still waters. As they came nearer, Ellis saw that the island was much larger than she had imagined. The shoreline did not appear to be heavily developed. Captain Zack took them to the north side, and then slowed, pointing to a three-story Cape Cod-style home built into a densely foliated hillside.

"That big'un there. They've pretty much got this stretch of shoreline to themselves. Real private."

The Borst place was fully aglow with orange light. Windows on every floor were lit up. Ellis had the unnerving feeling that she was being watched.

The Harbercraft crawled toward a jetty that extended about 40 feet out from the shore. There were already boats on either side of it. "That's a little peculiar," Captain Zack said.

"What?"

"That one there is Dane's boat." He pointed to a 22-foot boat of the type Ellis associated with recreational sea fishing. He motioned at the other, which was nothing but an aluminum skiff. "Don't recognize that other'n. That registration sticker on the front is about rubbed off. It's not like Dane to be out of compliance."

He piloted the boat to the end of the jetty, cut the motor and lassoed a rope around one of the boat anchors.

Ellis stowed the Seahawks blanket in its storage compartment. "I appreciate you coming out here. I know most people wouldn't have gotten out of bed for this."

"I needed the money." He climbed out onto the jetty and offered Ellis a hand. "All the same, I'd feel much better if I could see you to the door."

Me too, Ellis thought.

Vera Borst Residence
Vashon Island

The front door of the three-story home was ajar. A heavy coat rack was overturned in the foyer. Captain Zack extended his hands to both sides of his body as he stepped back, as if to shield his high-paying customer from harm. "We should call the cops and get out of here," he suggested quietly.

Ellis pulled her Beretta M9 from her shoulder holster. She had become competent with the weapon during her service in the Army. Although Glocks were favored among her coworkers in the intelligence community, Ellis had stuck with the Beretta for familiarity's sake. The sight of the weapon startled Captain Zack. He took a step back, as if deferring the situation to her.

Ellis' mind filled with Speers' inevitable scorn. She had come here without permission, and without backup, less than 24 hours after Drucker had been killed right under her nose. At times like this Ellis took comfort in a mantra put forth by one of her old yoga teachers: *The Zen master acts from the heart, not the mind.*

She turned to Captain Zack, knowing she could not risk another civilian dying on her watch. "I have to ask you to get back in that boat."

"Lady, there is zero chance of me doing that. I am not leaving."

"Fine. But at least leave the boat motor idling. If anyone comes out of the house without me, get away as fast as you can."

She watched Captain Zack retreat down the path. Hopeful that he would keep his distance, she went in through the open door, staying low, clearing the first room with her back against the wall. Pieces of broken figurines were crushed around the stairwell. Every light in the house seemed to be switched on. Someone was evidently searching for something.

She crept into the living room, keeping her back to the only windowless wall, and then regrouped for a moment behind an armchair that was covered entirely in cowhide. The house smelled like apple wood and was furnished with cozy sitting chairs arranged around a fireplace that was European in size, reaching nearly up to Ellis' sternum. Art depicting various biblical scenes hung on the wall.

The home's back porch floodlights were on, illuminating a manicured, sloping hillside dominated by a life-size sculpture of Jesus that had been erected within a fountain. Jesus' eyes gazed downward, and his hands were outstretched, palms facing the heavens, as if he were imparting wisdom on followers gathered around his feet. Water poured through holes in either palm.

A tortured wail drifted throughout the house. It sounded more canine than human. Ellis couldn't be sure, but she thought it was coming from the ground floor.

Having cleared the living room, she got to her feet and crept to the dining room. There she got down on her hands and knees and crawled under a long stainless steel table large enough to seat 12 guests. She peered through the doorway to the kitchen, where a man's feet – barefoot and sprawled – jutted out from behind a food prep island. A broad streak of red blood painted the floor, extending around the corner. The body had been dragged there from another room.

Keeping low, Ellis crawled toward the body until she was only inches away from the man's head. She recognized Dane Mitchell from the profile picture on his University of Washington faculty page. Vacant eyes peered through wire frame glasses. His bare arms and shoulders were etched with several inch-long lacerations. His hands were blue and the meat around his wrists looked more like ground beef than human flesh.

Another excruciating cry crackled through the air, remaining more or less constant. A woman, for sure. Borst, probably. They had tortured Mitchell to death first, and had dragged the body upstairs to make room for her.

Ellis followed the blood-streaked path through the house while still maintaining the careful clearing posture – back to the wall, pistol outstretched in front – that she had first learned in the Army. The training was all wrong for this, she knew. This situation was completely off-script. Her training had always been working in teams or in pairs. This was the type of situation where she was supposed to retreat to a surveillance position and request backup.

And yet she had the opportunity to save at least one high-ranking Fellowship member with solid ties to Preston and Gish. Stop thinking, she told herself. If she wanted to save Borst, she had to act now. She followed the blood path, and the noise, to an open door and descending stairs.

A basement. Of course. It followed the pattern. The killers in London and D.C. had chosen windowless places where the cries of their victims wouldn't be heard. Here on Vashon, there seemed little chance of that. The home was huge and the dense foliage and gentle white noise of Puget Sound would have obscured virtually any disturbance from even the closest neighbors.

Ellis removed her shoes. She stepped lightly down the stairs until the most horrifying image of her career came into focus.

Rome

Trusting that the tracking chip embedded within Nico's arm would keep him tethered to the palazzo, Carver set out on foot across the Tiber River. He had accepted Father Callahan's invitation to meet at Caffé Sant'Eustachio, a legendary coffee house in Old Rome. The priest said he had some information for Carver, but wasn't willing to be more specific over the phone. Some nuggets about the identities of the assassins in the Rome morgue, perhaps? When they had talked at *Le Colonne*, Carver had given the priest plenty to chew on, but had stopped short of divulging the identities of the deceased politicians, Sir Nils Gish and Senator Rand Preston.

Despite the fact that Rome was eight time zones away, the events of the past 24 hours told him that caution was justified. In D.C., a seemingly insignificant journalist had been assassinated right under Ellis' nose. Someone had then ambushed Ellis and Speers in Nathan Drucker's apartment, nearly killing both. Now Ellis herself had gone missing.

The café was located in a tiny neighborhood square just two blocks from the Pantheon. The labyrinthine design of the neighborhood hid it from casual foot traffic, and kept the crowds down to a tolerable level. Carver stopped at the square's edge, scanning the patrons sitting at outside tables. Seeing that none of them fit suspicious profiles, he then took a moment to admire the stag's head that seemed to watch over the square from atop the church named after the saint, antlers framing the simple iron cross. Two columns on one side of the church's exterior were said to be remnants of Nero's baths.

He found a place inside at the coffee bar, with his back to the wall. The café was abuzz with a cacophony of conversation and the intense aroma of premium coffee and dark chocolate. He ordered fresh-squeezed orange juice, keeping his eyes squarely on the door. As he eyed each and every customer with suspicion, he reminded himself that meeting in public had hardly provided safety for Nathan Drucker. Not only would Carver have to be on the lookout for the usual eavesdroppers and hit men, he would now have to watch out for deadly horseflies.

Callahan loped into view a few minutes late, at 10:36. This time the priest did not try to hug him, and that was fine with Carver. He leaned on the counter with his back to the door. The barista, a thin, leathery man, approached Callahan from behind the counter. "*Café Americano?*" he asked.

The priest shook his head. "*Doppio,*" he replied, then turned to Carver. "Four years in Rome, and my face is still so pale, they still offer me the watered-down stuff. You want one?"

"No thanks," Carver said. "You have some information for me?"

The barista set Callahan's coffee before him. The priest's eyes followed her movements until she was out of earshot. "Unfortunately, I've hit a dead end on the two lads in the morgue. I trust Detective Tesla will find out who they are."

"We don't have the luxury of time," Carver said. "We can't just leave this to some local cop."

"Tesla is quite tenacious," Callahan said. "In the meantime, I do have a name for you. Sebastian Wolf."

The priest brought the small white cup to his lips and sipped the double shot of espresso, never breaking eye contact with his American counterpart.

Bells rang in Carver's head. Ellis had uploaded a recording of her conversation with Nathan Drucker to the mission cloud a few hours earlier. Carver had listened to it quickly, but was sure the name Sebastian Wolf was mentioned in association with something called the Fellowship World Initiative. In the audio transcript, Ellis had tagged Wolf's name as meriting follow up.

Still, Carver managed to maintain perfect control over his facial features. "Who is he?"

"Well well," Callahan said, "I thought you knew everyone worth knowing in D.C. I understand Wolf is quite the swinging dick over there."

"Influential?"

"Important enough that some very bad people are looking for him. I got the strong sense that he might be connected to this nasty business you alluded to."

"And you know this how? Vatican Intelligence?"

The priest ignored the question. "This is his last known address." Callahan handed Carver a slip of paper with a Rockland, Maryland, address on it. Eden. The one in Ellis' case notes. "He moved without leaving a forwarding address. Perhaps you can get one of your people on it?"

The American slipped the paper into his pocket and smiled. He had been around long enough to know how double agents played their employers. One side would ask for information. They would then go to the other side, framing the request itself as a golden nugget. When the subsequent investigation then yielded fruit, they would take it back to the original source.

But Carver didn't like being played.

"I'll do that," he said. And then he told his second lie of the evening: "I'll let you know what we find out."

Vera Borst Residence

Vera Borst was suspended in mid-air by a rope that was attached to a pulley and a hand winch. Her hands were tied behind her back, her torso arched forward. Her blouse was torn open, revealing sagging white breasts and a bulging stomach, which was already bloodied by several open incisions. Carver had been right. It was just like he had predicted. Rope torture.

Borst's mouth was fixed in an "O" shape. Her eyes were closed. Her chin bobbed wearily against her chest. Her vocalizing was less constant now, breaking up into great spastic bursts of guttural release.

A man in dark coveralls stood at her feet. He seemed to be attaching some sort of weight to her ankles, which Ellis imagined might be enough to actually break Borst's wrists and sever them from her body. Ellis judged the distance between her and the tormentor to be about 30 feet. As much as he might deserve to die, she wanted to take him alive. He had to be questioned.

He didn't look like the most overpowering physical specimen. Perhaps five foot ten, with a trim, but not especially muscular, build. Ellis was no dojo master, but she had studied a variety of hand-to-hand combat techniques in the Army.

The man had his back to the staircase. He seemed to be preoccupied with affixing the weights to Borst's ankles. There was no telling whether he was alone. Ellis did not have a full view of the basement, nor was it well lit. However small, there was a chance that another perpetrator could be behind the row of canoes, kayaks and oars to the right of where Borst hung, or lurking in a dark corner of the space, perhaps behind the crates of Christmas ornaments or behind the air hockey table at the far end.

Nevertheless, there was no time for deliberation. Borst's life was quickly slipping away.

Ellis crossed herself before leaping down the stairwell. Although she had perfected her flying kick several years earlier en route to earning a brown belt in karate, she had been skeptical about its effectiveness in an actual combat situation. That had changed while watching a cage match on TV the previous year, when a 230-pound bruiser was dropped senseless by a much smaller man using such a move. It was time to find out for herself.

Borst's cries masked Ellis' footfall, but the perp sensed the reverberations an instant before she took to the air. He turned his shoulders and neck just as the edge of Ellis' right foot plowed into his neck. The blow knocked him into Borst's suspended torso, snapping his neck back violently. The undersecretary-general swung grotesquely back and forth like a bloody piñata.

The perp collapsed at her feet, legs and arms twitching violently. Ellis was shocked by the effectiveness of the maneuver, fearing that she had killed him after all. "You better not die," she growled.

Another. Another. The words seemed to pop into her head, as if whispered from angels. *Another.* She looked up. The words were Borst's. A warning.

A canoe paddle struck Ellis' back, felling her head-first into a column of crates filled with tree ornaments. The Beretta flew from her hand. Two dozen silver balls popped loose, breaking into hundreds of tiny shards against the concrete flooring. Ellis tumbled over them, instinctively rolling on her right shoulder so to as avoid eating glass. She rose slowly, just enough to see that the first perp was still where she had left him, twitching beneath Borst, who continued to swing like a freshly butchered hog.

The second perp stood several feet away. He wore a black plastic smock that was hooded at the top. A prickly black beard protruded from his face.

He threw down the oar, reached into his pocket and removed a small Taser. Oh hell. The Beard was going to Tase her.

Ellis had once been told that the best defense against a Taser was a firearm. That advice was now of little help, as her Beretta was nowhere in sight. She rolled right across the bed of broken Christmas ornaments, heading for the foosball table. She heard a burst of compressed nitrogen. Two electrical probes crackled toward her at 135 feet per second. They struck her left side, right in the ribs, piercing her shirt and skin. Ellis' momentum sent her rolling, the wires wrapping around her midsection as her body was flooded by 50,000 volts. Her hands clenched involuntarily. Every muscle in her body seemed to seize and cramp. Her sinuses seemed to actually screech.

As her mind traversed the edge of consciousness, she tried to roll over. Her extremities were unresponsive. She could do nothing but observe as the Beard appeared over her, like some reaper from a dark fairy tale. He tightened the cooling probe wires around her, turned her on her stomach, and began tying her wrists together with some sort of elaborate knot. And now the Beard was talking in some foreign language. The same phrases over and over. *Benedictus Dominus Deus meus qui docet manus meas ad proelium digitos meos ad bellum. Deus, refugium meum salvator meus scutum meum et in ipso sperávi. Benedictus Dominus Deus meus qui docet manus meas ad proelium digitos meos ad bellum...*

Ellis tried to block out the pain and think. Why was the Beard praying? Was he asking God for forgiveness, or was he giving thanks for the latest prey that had fallen into his trap?

She managed to raise her head and get her bearings. She must have been dragged from the place where she had fallen. She was underneath Borst now, right next to the Beard's fallen companion. The Beard would probably finish Borst off and drag her upstairs, like he had done to her boyfriend. Then it's my turn, she thought. The *strappado*.

Carver and Speers would eventually find their way here, she realized. They would find her in a heap on the floor, her body scarred by the telltale signs of the rope torture. And slipped inside her shirt would be an octagon. Just like the one they found on the others. And they would look at the number of wounds on her body and based on that, they would try to deduce how much information she had given up. It was the last thing she could control, she realized. Her life was over, but she could decide to stay strong, to keep her mouth shut until the end.

She spotted the twitching man's Taser gun, perhaps four feet away now. If only she could get to it.

Mary. Mary. Mary. The voice again. Ghostly, as if blown in from the Puget Sound. *Mary.* She looked up to see if angels might be hovering overhead. It was the opposite. The motion of Vera Borst's body had slowed, but the rope still carried her back and forth over the twitching man. She had stopped wailing. Her eyes were open now. She couldn't seem to move her head, but her eyes were tracking, and they looked deep into Ellis'. Her lips moved, more of a whispering wind than a human voice. *They want Mary.*

Why did they want Mary?

My daughter. The virgin. They know. It's her that they want.

A boot struck the back of Ellis' head. Someone was using her brain as a soccer ball. Roman candles showered her eyelids as the pain flowed through her skull and neck. A sick wetness oozed from her scalp.

She did not fully lose consciousness. The fading electrical shock seemed to have numbed her senses somewhat, but the texture of the rope fiber was unpleasant against the delicate skin of her wrists. A knot rose on the back of her head.

Blinding light suddenly filled the room. She squeezed her eyes shut and still saw nothing but white. A passage to the other side.

But something was burning. Her ears were filled with a screeching that all but drowned out Borst's soft moans. Ellis flipped onto her side and saw her tormentor. The Beard. Hair and hood alight in flame, pawing at his flaming face.

Rome

With night fallen, Carver's return walk along the Tiber River was a luxurious indulgence. The Tiber snaked directly through the heart of the city, running under one historic bridge after another. He followed it, peering down narrow streets, admiring the medieval architecture

Ellis still had not returned his call. Don't think about it, he told himself. She's fine. She can take care of herself.

As the city geared up for another frenetic evening, the quiet reflection of the moon against the gently flowing river was the perfect antidote to the chaos of the mission. Soon, Castel Sant'Angelo came into view. It had been there all along – perhaps two football fields from the palazzo where they stayed – and yet he found himself truly seeing it for the first time.

What a glorious visual disaster Castel Sant'Angelo was, especially in a city that valued symmetry and architectural integrity. He considered the dome of the Pantheon, masterfully engineered into a near-perfect sphere. And the elliptical balance that Bernini had achieved in designing St. Peter's Square, complete with the Egyptian obelisk providing a hub for the four rows of Doric columns on its outer perimeter.

And yet here was Sant'Angelo, a monstrosity of ancient architecture, reimagined in multiple phases over nearly two thousand years, having slowly evolved from Hadrian's tomb into a fortress that was the site of both battles and executions. Even now it remained linked from the Papal Apartments by an elevated passage where popes had sought refuge over the millennia. Sant'Angelo seemed to embody, more than any other structure, everything that Rome was to Carver.

He turned onto Via della Conciliazione, slowing his pace and checking both sides of the streets. The meeting with Callahan had raised his anxiety levels. During Operation Crossbow, the priest had been the perfect contact, having provided both the malware and the means to infiltrate Adrian Zhu's network. But as much as Callahan's information had proven that he was a valuable contact, Carver worried that the priest might alert Vatican Intelligence to his presence in the city.

Nothing seemed to be stirring, not even at the street's lone café. The palazzo was up on the left. St Peter's Cathedral glowed imposingly at the far end of the street, beyond St. Peter's Square.

The American scanned the lobby before heading inside. He stepped inside slowly as a group of drunken tourists emerged from Le Colonne. He followed them into the elevator and headed up to his floor.

The smell of eggs and coffee greeted Carver as he entered the suite. Clothed in a hotel bathrobe, Nico sat on a barstool with a plate full of food and his computer before him.

Carver lifted the top off of a second breakfast plate. He frowned at the sight of the sausage, eggs and coffee.

"Brinner is served," Nico said.

"What happened to 'When in Rome'? This is like an All-American So-and-So Slam at Denny's."

"Mmmm. Denny's. Never thought I'd say this, but I'm homesick for American food."

Carver played an imaginary tiny violin. "Any progress?"

"As a matter of fact," Nico said, "I'm going to show you something. And afterwards, I'd like you to say, 'Thank you, Nico. Great work.'"

"Never expect a 'thank you.' Life is less disappointing that way."

Nico turned his laptop so that Carver could see it. The screen was a table of airlines and hotel names cross-indexed with locations and dates. "Ever hear of the Advocate Committee for Small Island Developing States? Or maybe the Investment Council for Landlocked Developing Countries?"

Carver shook his head. "Nope."

"Neither has anyone else. An exact match for those names won't even come up in a plain old web search. But both Senator Preston and Sir Gish traveled to properties where hotel meeting rooms were reserved in those names numerous times over the last five years." He pointed to his grid. "Over those five years, the two men took a combined 68 trips outside their home countries per year on a combination of official and unofficial business. I was able to find evidence that they were in the same place, at the same time, at least 19 of those times."

Carver sat down. "So what?"

"So…I'm not even sure that these committees really exist. I think they made them up just in case somebody started asking questions."

"How'd you find this stuff? Did you break into their frequent flier accounts?"

"If only it was that easy. These guys were fairly well-heeled. They took a lot of private charters. So I had to mash up credit card purchase history with frequent flier accounts, hotel points accounts, hotel POS systems and, of course, their personal communications. Preston was clearly less careful with privacy than his British counterpart. He even sent emails to his wife a couple of times disclosing the actual location and the committee name."

Carver grinned. "Not bad. I knew that trip to South Africa would pay off."

Nico folded his arms across his chest. "That statement is entirely self-congratulatory."

"It's as close to a 'thank you' as you're going to get right now. We have more work to do. I need to know who else attended those meetings. I need to know what they were working on."

His phone rang. Speers' face lit up on the Caller ID.

Carver answered. And he could tell by the darkness in Speers' tone that he should sit down for whatever news was coming next.

Harborview Trauma Center Seattle

Speers stood outside Ellis' hospital room, watching through the glass as a physician bent over her bed, holding a tiny flashlight between his thumb and forefinger. He tilted it up, left, and then right, watching as Ellis' pupils followed the light. He straightened up, smiled and listened as she spoke. He was Asian, about five foot nine, with a clean-shaven, kind face.

Ellis did not look nearly as shiny and new. Her entire body was bruised. Her arms and legs were nicked up, as if she had walked through a sandstorm. The back of her head was swollen and bandaged, having received a number of stitches. Her bottom lip was busted, and the expression on her face could only be described as bewilderment.

It was nearly noon. Speers had just arrived. When the call had come that Ellis was in a Seattle trauma center, he had been sure it was a mistake. He would have gladly wagered a month's salary that Ellis and her sister were over at the Mayflower under the protection of Jack McClellan's security detail.

Speers could not remember the last time he had traveled alone. He had not just one federal agency at his disposal, but all of those in the American intelligence community. He typically traveled with staffers that coordinated his meetings, accommodations and transportation. Nearly any of the DNI's employees would take his call at any time, and do virtually anything he asked of them. But when it came to this case – which now counted victims on both American coasts as well as Europe – he could count the number of confidents with full operational clearance on one hand. His own deputy director, Claire Shipmont, had zero visibility into the operation. President Eva Hudson was keenly aware, but was being purposely kept ignorant of the details for her own protection. Arunus Roth, who at this moment was probably drinking his 12th Red Bull of the day in the McLean office. Blake Carver, who was still half a world away. And the Brits, who had still shared very little intelligence despite Carver and Ellis' in-person visit to London.

FBI Director Chad Fordham, the only other agency director with knowledge of the case, was scheduled to arrive shortly.

Local police had found the heinous Vashon Island crime scene in which three people had been murdered, and another in critical condition. Ellis had apparently been electrocuted and beaten. Thank God for Fordham. With one call, he had ordered a pair of local bureau agents to seal the crime scene. It had been far too late to contain the situation, of course. The mess Ellis had stumbled into was already the talk of the local police department.

Now the doctor emerged from Ellis' room and closed the door behind him

"You can see her," the doctor said, "but you have to go easy. She doesn't even know who she is right now."

"By that you mean…"

"Exactly what I said. She can't remember her own name. It's a pretty bad concussion. The good news is that the chance of permanent brain damage is minimal. In cases like this, amnesia is usually temporary."

Speers was beside himself. "Usually?"

"Usually there's no memory of the blunt trauma that caused the concussion, and sometimes there's a blackout window that spans a few hours or days before it happened."

"You don't know Ellis," Speers said. "She's a combat vet."

"Iraq?"

And D.C. too, Speers thought but didn't say. He had managed to keep quiet the names of most the combatants that defended the capital in the Ulysses Coup. They were heroes, for sure, but they had also been forced to kill Americans to save the nation's soul. The families of those Ulysses USA fighters weren't about to forget so easily. Even now, the FBI had planted moles within a militia in South Carolina that was plotting revenge.

"Don't underestimate this," the doc warned. "It looks like she was in one hell of a fight." The doctor opened the door to Ellis' room. "Shall we?"

With the help of his cane, Speers got to his feet and entered the room with the doctor close behind. "Look who's here," the doc said. "You recognize this guy, Haley?" Ellis said nothing. The doc turned back to Speers. "Five minutes, and not a minute more."

He shut the door on his way out. Speers pulled up a plastic orange chair and sat, leaning forward with his elbows resting on his legs. He didn't know what to say.

"This is really weird for me, okay? I'm Julian Speers. I'm your boss."

"I don't like it here," Ellis replied. "I need to go outside. Can we go outside? Right now?"

"Later," he said. "Haley, do you know why you came to Seattle? I need you to try to remember."

She shrugged, clearly too exhausted to even try.

There was so much he needed to know. Had Ellis known Mary Borst's mother would be in danger? Was she operating on a hunch, or had she seen something in Nathan Drucker's work that led her to that conclusion? How did Sebastian Wolf fit into the picture? The answers were locked away in the rafters of Ellis' mind.

He reached into his pocket, removed his phone, and pulled up a photo of Jenna Ellis that he had taken at the Mayflower Hotel just before heading to the airport. He handed the phone to Ellis and waited a moment as she looked at the photo.

"You know her?"

Ellis peered at it uncertainly. "Maybe. I'm not sure."

"That's your sister," Speers pressed. "Her name is Jenna."

Haley handed the phone back. "I want to go outside."

Now tears streamed down her cheeks. She clutched the sheets, pulling them to her chin, then up over her face. Speers sat on the edge of the mattress. He wiped the tears away with the cuff of his shirt, turning it so that his cuff links wouldn't scratch her face.

He thought of his elderly neighbor back in Georgetown, Mrs. Tenningclaus, and her late husband who had suffered from dementia in the months before he died. In the early days, before he had to be confined to a facility that was skilled at keeping forgetful patients safe, Speers had seen him get so frustrated over his lack of memory that he was verbally abusive. Sometimes he would cry. Other times he would throw things. Once, he had hit his wife in the forehead with an ashtray.

Until he had seen Mr. Tenningclaus' slow, cruel deterioration, death by fire had been Speers' biggest fear. Now it wasn't even close. His fear was not knowing who he was anymore. The thought was terrifying. It seemed worse than death. Like not existing at all. Seeing Ellis like this was unbearable. Was she still in there?

Speers went to a print shop near the University of Washington, where he personally scanned every page of the Nathan Drucker manuscript, as well as a set of handwritten notes he had retrieved from Ellis' backpack. He then uploaded them to the mission cloud and ordered Carver to read them right away. Ellis couldn't tell him what had led her to hop on a plane bound for Seattle to visit Ms. Borst, but he had a feeling that it had something to do with Drucker's research.

Now he sat in a corner of the hospital cafeteria with his ailing ankle propped up on an opposing chair. He ate from two heaping plates of Jello while reviewing the Vashon crime scene photographs that he had downloaded to his tablet computer.

He clipped a facial photograph of the dead perp who had been found underneath Borst's suspended body. Then he uploaded it to a secure site where Arunus Roth could access it, tapping out a short message: *Give this creep a facial.*

"Facial" was short for 3D Facial Recognition System, an invaluable intelligence tool that had first been developed by researchers at Technion, the oldest technology university in Israel, and had since been improved with the help of certain companies in Silicon Valley. He followed with photographic copies of the passports belonging to the two perps', which he assumed were false. Finishing the image gallery was a pic of the tattoo on the perp's shoulder, as the IC possessed a separate database that cross-indexed profiles with tattoos and birthmarks.

The most important image – those of two octagons that looked, to Speers' eyes, identical to those found in the D.C., Rome and London murders – he uploaded for Carver's eyes only. Gory as it was, he also sent Carver a video clip of Ms. Borst suspended by her wrists.

Carver continued to amaze him. Within the first two minutes of studying Senator Preston's wounds – the ruined wrists, the dislocated shoulders, the gashes across his front – Carver had correctly surmised the precise method of torture. And here, in full color, was absolute proof.

He did not have time to send Carver a qualifying statement. His phone announced the arrival of Chad Fordham, who was, at this very moment, waiting for him in the lobby. Having eaten every morsel of the Mediterranean pizza he had ordered, Speers left the tray on the table and made his way toward the lobby.

The FBI director looked cold and pale and his head was drenched from drizzle. Fordham was only in his mid- 50s, but he maintained a "natural bald" look – the sides and back of his head were unshaven – that pegged him as a man from a different era.

Speers extended his hand. "Appreciate you coming."

"How is she?" Fordham asked.

"Too banged up to tell me what led her here in the first place."

"Are these the a-holes that did the senator?"

Speers spoke in an elevated whisper. "We don't know. But even if they are, they can't also be the people who killed Gish. There are more bad guys out there."

"Still can't rule out Mary Borst as a person of interest."

"It's looking more and more like she was running scared. Her boss and her mother were on these animals' hit list. She probably thought she was next."

"Agreed. I just wish we could find her."

The intelligence czar consulted his facility map, then motioned toward a hallway that would lead them to the central tower. "The surviving perp should be out of surgery by now."

They came to an elevator and went inside. Speers used the butt of his cane to push the button for the 11th floor. He waited for the doors to close and then said, "Ellis doesn't even recognize me. If she had listened to me in the first place, she would've never ended up here."

"You think someone is targeting her?"

"All I know is she met with Nathan Drucker, and he ended up dead. Then Ellis comes out here, and we've got three more bodies on our hands. A water taxi captain with a goofy name claims that he charged her 300 bucks to take her out to

Vashon, then saved her life with the only weapon he had on the boat, a freaking flare gun."

Fordham's face lit up. "Flare gun? I've always wondered what one of those would do to a person. Seems like they could burn a hole right through somebody."

"No such luck. It hit the a-hole right in the face, though. Caught his beard and hair on fire. Captain Zack said the guy looked like an asteroid with legs when he ran out of the house."

They took the elevator to the 11th floor. Fordham's special agents were stationed outside the room. Two thick-necked studs in their mid-20s. They eyed Speers and Fordham warily.

"Can I help you?" the elder of the two agents said.

"I can see why you wouldn't recognize me, but my friend here?" Speers motioned toward Fordham. "Seriously?"

Both men shook their head. "Some ID might make this go faster."

"How about you go back to the Seattle field office and look at the picture of the guy plastered on the wall next to the president?"

By then Fordham already had his FBI badge out of his jacket. A light went on in the talker's eyes as he stood a little straighter. "Mr. Director, sir. I apologize."

"That's not necessary. The FBI has 35,000 employees and at the end of the day, I'm just one of 'em."

The double doors opened. The talker stepped aside so that the surgeon could pass. Speers flashed his ID. "Director of National Intelligence." Then he took out the passport belonging to the assailant, Roberto Melfi. The man was balding and bearded, with a stocky-looking neck and face.

"Ah," the surgeon said. "You're here about the burn victim?"

"It's the other way around, doc. He's not the victim. He's the bad guy."

"Well I hope force was really justified, because in addition to the burned face, fractured vertebrae and broken ribs, I had to remove what was left of his right eye."

"We need to talk to him. Is he awake?"

The doc stiffened. "Did you hear what I just said? Your people really jacked him up. He'll be lucky to make it through the day."

Speers' phone rang. He pulled up Eva's mobile profile on his phone and showed it to the doctor. It was Eva's official presidential portrait. "Okay, doc. You tell the president we can't talk to a suspected terrorist."

"Wait, that's really her calling? Right now?" The doc put up his hands in surrender. "Okay, okay. Talking is going to be tough, though. His lips are burned off."

Speers answered the phone as Fordham ushered the doctor out of earshot. "Madam President."

"It's been four hours since I had a progress report," she said. "That's too long relative to the heat I'm feeling."

"I'm sorry, Madam President."

"The prime minister is having second thoughts about keeping this under wraps. I need some good news."

Speers understood. The longer this crisis went unresolved, the more likely that it would become an international scandal.

"We identified two suspects," Speers said. "One deceased. The other one's in bad shape."

He heard the tension in Eva's voice ease a bit. "That's encouraging. So what's the bad news?"

Speers told her about Vera Borst and Dane Mitchell.

There was a long silence before the president spoke again. "So let me get this straight. Three international leaders, representing three separate bodies of government, have been brutally tortured and killed, thousands of miles apart from each other."

"Plus the professor," Speers reminded her. "I understand Dr. Mitchell was a rising name in the bioengineering world."

He did not tell her the truly terrible news. Captain Zack had called 911, and the local police and paramedics had been on the scene within minutes. The FBI had, of course, asked the first responders to keep the story out of the press, but with this kind of a horror show, these embargoes never lasted long on the local level. There was little they could do short of sequestering everyone involved. Sooner or later, details about the heinous crime were going to hit the press. He would be worried enough about that part for both of them.

*

No one – not even his brothers in Venice – would have recognized Brother Roberto Melfi. Bandages covered his entire face. Two small holes had been carved into the bandages. One, over his nostrils, enabled him to breathe. The other permitted him to see out of his remaining eye.

The monk could only stare up helplessly as a man positioned himself over the eyehole, looking down as if peering into a deep, dark well. He heard the man take the Lord's name in vain. Melfi forgave him for that. Anyone would have been horrified by his appearance.

"Hello," he said. "My name is Julian Speers. Blink twice if you understand English."

Melfi knew English all too well. He also knew that he would not be alive much longer. Even now, his pain had receded, and he felt a certain lightness of being, as if his spirit was separating itself from his flesh. The Lord would take him soon. He felt obligated to use his final moments meaningfully. If only he knew how.

"You are under arrest for the murders of Dane Mitchell and Vera Borst," Speers said. "Understand?"

He blinked twice.

"Good. Can you tell us anything about the death of Rand Preston?"

Melfi blinked only once.

Speers' face was suddenly tense. He did not believe him. "Are you telling me that you did not visit the home of Rand Preston in Washington D.C.? Blink twice if you were there."

Melfi blinked only once.

Speers disappeared from view. Melfi heard him swearing again. He was chatting with someone. Yes, there was someone else in the room. They talked for a moment before Speers appeared again in his tunnel-like field of vision.

"I'll be honest with you. You killed a Swedish citizen on American soil. The Swedes are going to want you. You know what their prisons are like? It'll be like being in a hotel. If you tell me what I need to know about the senator, I'll consider releasing you into their custody."

Brother Melfi was not motivated by promises of light punishment. He would soon get his reward in heaven. Nevertheless, he blinked twice to show that he understood. Then he focused all his energy on his right hand. With considerable effort, he managed to lift it. He curled his fingers together and moved them slowly up and down, as if he were writing.

Speers said something to the other man in the room. He disappeared from view. Melfi felt someone open his hand and place a pen between his fingers. Then he saw a note pad appear overhead. Speers must have been holding it. It seemed impossibly far away, but with the other man's help, his writing hand was lifted toward it until the inky tip was pressed against the pad.

He jotted a quick note.

You must stop them.

Speers flipped the notepad over and read it. His face broke into an icy grin. "Stop them? You did a pretty good job of that yourself. Those people are dead."

Melfi pressed the pen to the paper again.

The others. The world is in danger.

He felt his arm fall to his side. He heard the pen clatter on the linoleum floor. His right eye closed and he felt himself drift. He began to feel inner warmth. Someone lifted up his arm again, placed the pen within his grasp, and guided the hand toward the notepad. He opened his eyes.

"Tell me how," Speers commanded. "Concentrate. How is the world in danger?"

He wrote again.

False prophets. A global war. Without state. Without end.

He rested his arm for a moment as Speers digested this. His body was depleted. He could scarcely focus. How could he make them understand, when the words did not come to him?

"Why did you kill Vera Borst?" Speers pushed.

Melfi felt a burst of energy. A burst of inspiration. His hand shot back to the paper and he began writing:

> They said, "Come, let us build a tower whose top will reach into heaven, and let us make for ourselves a name." The Lord came down to see the city and the tower which the sons of men had built. The Lord said, Behold, they are one people, and they all have the same language. And this is what they began to do, and now nothing which they try to do will be impossible for them. So the Lord scattered them abroad from there over the face of the whole earth, and they stopped building the city.

His arm once again fell to his side. The pen once again clattered on the floor. But now Melfi could see Speers with both eyes. How was this possible? He had heard the surgeon say that his right eye had been burned, and he was certain that it was covered with bandages.

He saw Speers flip the pad and devour its contents. "Damn. I think he's just writing random scripture."

The machine next to the bed emitted a loud noise. Suddenly Speers was over him. "Hello? Hey! Chad, Get that doctor in here!"

Rome

Carver struggled to keep his emotions in check as he viewed the grisly Seattle crime scene photos. There was a lot of blood. No doubt that some of it belonged to Ellis. What had she been doing there? It was just like her, getting on a plane without telling anyone.

He took a deep breath, flooding his body with fresh oxygen. The truth was that he blamed himself. Maybe if he hadn't jetted off to South Africa to get Nico, leaving her to fend for herself in London. Maybe if he hadn't been so vocal about the fact that the team was so thin.

He refocused on the images. Speers had annotated the snap of Vera Borst strung up with her hands tied behind her back: "You were right about the method."

He felt no pride in knowing that he had been able to deduce the killers' technique upon observing Senator Preston's body. What good had it done? It hadn't stopped the murders from happening again. No one had been saved. It only told him that the killers were an unusually disciplined and cruel organization. What remained to be seen was whether they used torture to punish their victims, or whether they were actually extracting information.

This thing was spreading like the flu. D.C., London, Rome and now Seattle. Four time zones. *Four*! How many assassins could there be? He understood Speers' desire to keep the team size small for security reasons, but it was a gamble that was already blowing up in their faces. They needed more people on this.

And to that end, how many more victims were targeted? Five? A hundred? And from what countries? The presence of a United Nations leader from the Netherlands among the casualty list only further clouded things.

Nico was in the other room expanding his search. He was now focused on data-matching Borst's purchase and travel histories with those of Preston and Gish. He hoped Arunus Roth was looking into Mary Borst's background, because they had their hands full here.

Carver opened a bottle of Pellegrino, settled onto the suite's leather sofa and opened the document Speers had uploaded. He had scrawled, in all caps, a directive on the first page:

DIGEST THOROUGHLY – DO NOT SKIM!!!

Did Speers really expect him to read this entire thing? The document Nathan Drucker had made his life's work was an unwieldy collection of typed and handwritten passages that had been worked and reworked countless times. What a mess. There were attributions and qualifications and scrawled illustrations all over the place. There were even sticky notes in Ellis' handwriting that had been photocopied right onto the page, at times obscuring the original text. Some of the document wasn't even edited, but rather looked like straight transcriptions from interviews.

Carver focused on the first page of Drucker's typewritten document and began to read.

The Memoirs of Sebastian Wolf
as told to Mr. Nathan Drucker

I should start by telling you that the man who will try to stop us – all of us, from the very thing humanity has sought for these past two millennia – was once my best friend. I do not say this to be sentimental. I mean only to demonstrate that the harmonic echoes of the spiritual war we are now waging have sounded time and again throughout history, and I am but one conduit through which they are transmitted. Heinz Lang and I share a destiny. Every man has his Judas and Heinz Lang is mine.

By the time you have read my story, my purpose in this epic will have been completed. This has been foretold. Sadly, Lang's purpose, which is to preserve the empire of lies that he serves at all costs, and along with it a legacy of deceit, may still be underway. But know that what we have been waiting for shall come to pass, and know, too, that this is precisely what the Great Architect requires from us. Soon we will, all of us, I promise you, receive our heavenly reward.

How shall I tell you how we arrived at this moment in history? There are so many possible starting points. Shall I describe the first time the stigmata flowed through my hands and feet?

Without context, it could seem like some sort of cheap parlor trick. Or shall I tell you about The Fellowship, and how this great organization was created? Alas, it is possible that at the time this work is shared with the wider world, our senior brothers and sisters in the movement may yet need to remain hidden for several more years (Know that they both walk among you and look upon you from high, waiting for the right moment to reveal themselves to the world).

Each of us experiences a pivotal moment in time when we are suddenly propelled at high speed toward our destiny. This is not the same as an awakening. It is rather a triggering moment, when we realize painful inconsistencies between our beliefs and reality. It is a moment when we realize that we are being led by God's will toward Total Awareness.

My moment occurred in Feldafing, Germany, on November 6, 1942. I was fifteen years old.

This is my story.

PART II

The Reich School
Feldafing, Germany
November 6, 1942

Cadet Sebastian Wolf woke moments before the merciless clang of the steel triangle echoed throughout the yellow mansion. The cadets had 15 minutes to relieve themselves, dress and assemble outside for morning calisthenics. As he did every morning, Wolf sat up and groped for the box of matches next to the bed. He broke the first match by striking it against the wrong side of the box. He turned the box and sparked the second, touching the ensuing flame to the wick of the gas lantern on the nightstand.

    He spat into his palm and swept the moisture over the wild tuft of white blonde hair at his widow's peak until it lay flat. As usual, Heinz Lang stirred in the bunk beside him. And as usual, a shoe flew from Lang's hand, striking the still-sleeping Albert Hoppe in the bunk across the room. Albert was a heavy sleeper.

    The boys donned white exercise shorts, white tank tops and brown lace-up saddle shoes with steel toes. They trickled downstairs like white blood cells into an artery, speaking little as they joined other cadets in the cold morning air. Nearly 200 other cadets exited the other mansions, which, they had been told, had been owned by Jewish bankers who had decided to emigrate in the 1930s.

    The grass was tipped with the first frost of the season, glowing faintly in the purple pre-dawn light. Although it was still too dark to see clearly, they formed remarkably symmetrical callisthenic lines. The previous months and years of drilling had instilled a sense of automated navigation in the boys. They moved as a single organism, powerful in their unity.

Obersturmführer Beck– a veteran of the first war with France whose fingers were calloused and bent, like tree roots – led more than 200 students in jumping jacks, pushups, sit-ups and various stretching exercises. Beck's voice exuded unforgiving authority, and yet somehow, managed to be encouraging rather than punishing. A full year after his arrival at the Reich School, the boys were fully synchronized, bending, stretching and pushing in perfect harmony.

As the purple morning light faded to bluish yellow, Wolf noticed that the bleachers, which were typically free of spectators, were full. Two men sat front row center, surrounded by a large number of aides. Soon whispers began, blowing softly across the field from one column of students to the next.

"Vogel," Lang whispered just after he had heard it from another boy. A visit from Otto Vogel, Hitler's private secretary, was not so unusual. The Reich School was the most prestigious of all Germany's political leadership institutions, and it was only natural that Hitler, through Vogel, wanted regular progress reports on his country's future leaders. But Vogel had another reason for coming to the school so often. His son, Adolf Otto Vogel Jr. – named after his godfather, Adolf Hitler – was enrolled in one of the lower grades. The concept of royalty was anathema to National Socialism, but there was no denying that the Vogel boy, by virtue of his relationship to the *führer*, was regarded as a prince.

Wolf imagined the solid-looking Vogel, a man with a square jaw and no neck to speak of. The red lapels of his uniform – adorned with the party eagle surrounded by gold laurels – marked him as one of the party elite.

As the boys launched into jumping jacks, Lang whispered, "Himmler!"

This was truly a name worthy of gossip. Heinrich Himmler was head of the *Schutzstaffel*, or the SS. Following the assassination of Reinhard Heydrich months earlier, Himmler had firmly established himself as the second-most powerful man in Germany. The very name prompted Wolf to step up his workout. Himmler was a man to be feared.

*

After calisthenics, the boys were split into their units and marched toward the lake. They marched everywhere, and always in neat columns. Despite the frigid water, Wolf looked forward to these morning swims. Upon his first visit to the Reich School, he had been stunned to see the picturesque community of yellow mansions situated on the verdant shore of Lake Starnberg. Although it was an easy train trip from his hometown, Munich, the campus felt refreshingly isolated from the political tension he had grown up with in the city. As far back as he could remember Munich had been a place of endless party rallies, political speeches, military parades and ethnic violence.

Now the lakefront glistened orange as the sun rose over the surrounding hills. Wolf removed his clothes and leapt over a half-meter patch of semi-solid ice around the lake's perimeter. None of the boys complained about the temperature as they swam the four laps between the shore and Rose Island. That was typical of the Reich School attitude. But with the high command watching, there were no pranks today. No boy dunked any other boy, and no boy pretended to be taken under by the ghost of Ludwig II, the Bavarian King who had drowned in the lake in 1886.

A breeze had picked up by the time Wolf and Lang returned to shore and began dressing. As usual, Albert was still swimming his last lap. Albert was a slow swimmer, and Beck usually waited for him before moving the unit to their next activity. Not today. As Beck began marching the shivering unit across a wheat field that the cadets had harvested themselves in July, Albert was alone in the water.

Wolf looked over his shoulder as they rounded the first hilltop. There was still no sign of Albert.

"He better catch up," Lang muttered. "Himmler will bring the dogs."

Stories of Himmler's cruelty were legendary. One tale had him picking out a straggler from a line of boys and, after giving the student a 20-second head start toward a grove of trees, setting a pack of vicious dogs on his trail.

"Nonsense. Maybe at the NAPOLA schools. But not here. They have invested too much in us."

It was true that the Reich School had the highest admissions standards of all schools in Germany. Exemplary achievement in either athletics or academics was mandatory. Another hurdle was racial qualification. A person born in Eastern Europe was not eligible for enrollment at the Reich School. Neither was a person whose family had been in Germany for less than 140 years. The bloodline, it was thought, needed at least that much time to be purified of other races. In addition, students were eligible for admittance only if they could prove that their family had been of pure German descent since the year 1800.

Wolf's mother, Gertrude, had hired a certified genealogist to create an extensive family tree showing that the family had been of Germanic descent since at least the 1500s. And even with all the right paperwork in place, doctors from the SS came to the family apartment in Munich to measure Wolf's cranium. It was believed that the skull should be of a certain size as proof of intellectual aptitude and, of course, there were certain undesirable curvatures that were supposedly telltale signs of an ethnic minority. To Wolf, these requirements had seemed more ludicrous than sinister. After placing a set of very cold calipers against Wolf's head, the doctor declared, "Your skull is not overly round." Within two months, he had received his admission letter.

*

The unit did not catch sight of Himmler and Vogel until they neared a barn in a neighboring field. There was still no sign of Albert. Wolf offered a stiff-arm salute as he passed wordlessly, feeling the inspecting eyes of the German high command upon him.

Moments later, Wolf spotted the longcoats. They were standing at the end of a barn with stone siding and a gambrel roof. They were setting up a movie camera.

A movie camera could mean only one thing. They were going to jump today.

Trust jumps. That is what Beck called them. In Wolf's two years at the Reich School, he had leapt from a guard tower, several school and government buildings and, once, a gorge in the Austrian Alps. Trust jumps were always unannounced and, more often than not, they were also filmed. The footage of boy after boy leaping from great heights made terrific propaganda footage. It was nothing less than proof that the country's next generation of leaders had already coalesced into a formidable, unified socialist machine. Germany's future was bright indeed.

What awaited the boys on the ground was always a mystery. Sometimes they landed on a sort of trampoline held by older boys. At other times, a safety net had been tied in place ahead of time. In the Alps they had landed in a deep river. There was no choice but to have faith in Beck's preparation. That, of course, had been the point. To follow orders without hesitation.

But Wolf had no faith in Beck's oversight of this activity. His stomach filled with dread with each new ascent. His mind exploded with questions. When had Beck prepared the landing? Had he scouted the landing himself, or had he delegated the task to a junior instructor? What if the conditions had changed in the hours since the landing had been prepared? Could a trampoline tie not break? Could a tree or an animal or a boulder not fall into their path?

Now they were led inside a barn cavernous enough to hold at least 100 cattle. Beck instructed them to climb a wooden ladder to the hayloft, and then to ascend to the rooftop. Wolf measured his pacing as they made their way toward the rickety wooden ladder. He slackened his pace deliberately, falling back in line.

Don't be the first, he told himself. Be second, or tenth. Anything but first. To see a boy jump before him and land safely was marvelous for Wolf's courage.

By the time he reached the ladder, he was third in line. He climbed behind two other boys into a spacious loft that slanted sharply to accommodate snow drainage. A prominent steeple at the apex allowed for heat ventilation as well as an exit onto the rooftop for occasional repairs.

Looking down, he saw that Albert had finally caught up. He had no shoes or shirt on, and he looked rattled, wet and out of breath as he stood at the bottom of the ladder.

He soon found himself in the sunlight, standing near the steeple. He paused to admire the vast expanse of golden farmland. Hundreds of majestic acres bristled in the gentle morning breeze.

Suddenly he was jostled forward. He found himself at the head of the line. Beck's voice cut through the morning, urging them to jump. Wolf looked left, down the eastern slope of the roof. He saw Beck, his finger pointed toward the far edge of the roof. Himmler, Vogel and the two longcoats were by his side. All waiting for Wolf to leap.

A flip of white-blond hair tottered back and forth on his forehead. Goose pimples rose over his legs as the breeze picked up. His peripheral vision was suddenly rimmed with darkness, as if looking through a pair of old binoculars. He stood on his tiptoes, but he could not see the landing zone.

As each succeeding student exited the steeple, Wolf found himself bumped further down the rooftop. He felt Lang behind him, hands pressed against the small of his back, pushing him. He heard Lang's breath in his ear. "Go on, Sebastian! Jump!"

Suddenly Albert ran past him. Wolf was thrown off balance. He teetered, then felt Lang's grip on his bicep. He recovered his footing just in time to glimpse Albert's body disappear over the horizon.

The boys held their collective breath, waiting for the sound of Albert's inevitable war cry. It did not come. Only a crunching thud and a chorus of worried noises erupted from Himmler's entourage. One of the longcoats rushed to the film camera and switched it off.

Forgetting his fears, Wolf walked to the edge and peered over the side. Albert was a broken smear of skin and bones and flesh over a parked threshing machine. A large piece of torn netting was pinned between the body and the machine's cylinder. The truncated ends were tied to nearby trees, flapping like windsocks in the morning breeze.

Now there was no sound except that of the wind and the breathing of the other boys and their footsteps as they took turns walking to the edge to see Albert's body. They had all, of course, seen other dead children. Outbreaks of flu, tuberculosis, whooping cough and smallpox routinely thinned the ranks. But to see a cadet die in this way was truly novel. But Wolf detected no evidence of pity in the other boys. The boys' overriding emotion seemed to be fascination. Except Lang, of course. He had always been a sensitive boy. Even now, his body convulsed as he tried to suppress his tears.

The sharp report of a pistol broke the silence. Wolf's eyes snapped toward the ground in time to see Beck's breath cloud the chilly air. Then Beck fell face-first onto the field. The trigger man stood over the body. It was Heinrich Himmler.

*

The unit was relieved of duties until lunchtime. Lang held himself together until he and Wolf returned to their room. The sight of Albert's bed and footlocker set him off. Wolf stood by idly as Lang came unglued, unsure whether he was more upset by the force of his friend's emotion, or by the lack of his own.

When Lang finally gathered himself, he said, "I'll go first."

Wolf went to the door, leaning against it and holding the doorknob tightly with both fists. With the door secured, Lang kneeled before Albert's bed and began to recite a psalm.

This act – standing guard for each other during prayer – was a daily ritual. The two boys shared a secret. They were practicing Catholics.

Being Catholic was not yet an official crime, but Wolf knew that someday soon, it would be. He had not seen a priest since 1939, when the government had closed the Catholic school he and Lang had attended in Munich, and along with it, every parochial school in the country. Their parish church had been closed later in the year and converted into a government building. And yet priests still presided over the weddings of high-ranking German officials, a fact he knew only because of occasional photographs in the newspaper. It was all very confusing.

When Lang was done, Wolf took his turn kneeling at the foot of Albert's bed. He clasped his hands before him, but when he closed his eyes, he did not see Albert, and he certainly did not see God. He instead saw Himmler, eyes peering through wireframe glasses, standing over Beck's body. Resting his boot on the man's chest as if he were a hunting trophy. He then looked up at the barn and saluted the boys on the rooftop. *I punished this man for his negligence*, the gesture had seemed to say. *I did this for you, boys. This is how much you mean to the Fatherland.*

*

Later that morning, the cadets washed and dressed in brown shirts, brown pants and black ties. Although they were too upset to feel hungry, the daily rituals of the Reich School remained unbroken. When Wolf and Lang made their way to the dining hall, however, they quickly found their appetites as they sat down to a lunch of smoked trout, potatoes and milk.

"Something's up," Lang said as he regarded the meal before him with suspicion. Although the students at the Reich School had the best of everything, to see fresh fish was unheard of. The whole of Germany had been on rationed food portions for some time. The Minister of Propaganda, Joseph Goebbels, had recently set civilian rations of meat at one-tenth of one pound per day and had also downgraded portions for bread. Vegetables were impossible to find, especially in the cities.

"Putting on a show for Himmler," Wolf speculated.

"No," Lang said. "Himmler's been here before. He's impressed by performance, not nutrition."

Wolf bumped Lang with his elbow and motioned across the dining hall. Two soldiers were erecting a poster depicting a proud cadet brandishing a dagger. The slogan read:

THE SONS OF GERMANY GIVE THEMSELVES FREELY FOR FÜHRER AND FATHERLAND

"You're right," Wolf said. "Something is up."

*

In mathematics, Wolf and Lang sat before a slab of varnished pine that was angled at 15 degrees. There were 39 other students in the class. Albert's chair was empty.

The math instructor had written this word problem on the chalkboard:

> German armor enjoys vast superiority over Soviet ground defenses. At an average loss rate of just three German tanks in exchange for the destruction of 35 Soviet pillboxes, how many tanks would be required to break through a front line consisting of 607 pillboxes?

Wolf opened a black leather-bound notebook and began to work out the problem with a deftly sharpened pencil. Academically, Wolf took after his scholarly father, who had, before the war, been a professor of Indo-Germanic studies at the University of Munich. Wolf was far above average in all subjects, but especially in biology, math and foreign languages. He credited his early education for this, having studied under a handful of strict, but scholarly, Jesuit teachers, all of whom had been excellent linguists and mathematicians.

But the Reich School curriculum had dulled Wolf's passion for numbers. The mathematics problems were always war-centric. He found these exercises disturbing. When party leaders spoke about the French threat, or the Russian threat, Wolf felt anxious, like all Germans. But he did not possess the bloodlust of the other cadets. He had no desire to kill. He wanted to teach in a university, like his father.

Lang edged closer to Wolf's elbow, sneaking peeks at the equation. He was not a particularly gifted student. He had gained admittance to the school primarily through his strength as a sprinter. Until the war had broken out, he had been considered a lock for the track and field team in the 1944 Olympics, which were to be held in London. The war threatened to ruin all of that. They spent hours each week discussing it. What if Churchill was beaten by 1944? If London could be occupied and secured by then, couldn't the Olympics then go on as scheduled?

Confident that his calculations were correct, Wolf left his notebook open for Lang's wandering eyes.

Minutes later, the math instructor stood, his walrus-like torso filling the space between his desk and the chalkboard. "Stand up!" the instructor barked. "Leave your tests where they are! We will march in an orderly fashion to the gymnasium."

A confused silence fell over the room. The cadets were scheduled to be in class for another 40 minutes. "What's going on?" Wolf whispered.

"Told you," Lang said quietly. "Something's up."

They filed out of class and crossed the athletic field en route to the gymnasium. It was already crowded with students. Red tapestries featuring enormous swastikas hung from either side of a stage. A pianist manhandled an upright piano, playing a Wagner-esque march that Wolf recognized as one of Puzzi Hanfstängel's compositions for Hitler. He had last heard it at the annual midnight rally in Munich's *Odeonsplatz* – a large outdoor plaza just outside Munich's urban palace – where thousands of newly minted SS officers pledged their loyalty to the führer.

Lang, the taller of the two boys at six foot three, stood on tiptoe and peered over the crowd. "I see Himmler," he said. "Vogel is there too."

They were suddenly pushed by a wave of students arriving behind them. Older boys who lived in one of the other school houses. The crowd surged forward, then sideways. Wolf was swept toward the far wall. He had lost Lang. In an institution that did everything in an orderly fashion, this was an unusual moment of mayhem.

The music suddenly stopped. A voice came over the public address system. It was Himmler's.

"In war," he said, "Possessions are destroyed. Entire families may die. There is but one thing that survives, and that is the glory of a boy's deeds for his country. Today Albert Hoppe demonstrated his courage in front of my own eyes. Albert Hoppe is an inspiration for all of us!"

Wolf was suddenly filled with pride. It was true that he feared Himmler. Every rational German did, and Wolf did more than most. But there was no denying that he was a natural-born leader. Hearing Albert's name spoken by such a man was exquisite.

The *reichsführer* then read from the *Oera Linda* book, a text written in Old Frisian that the cadets had read in their Germanic studies classes. Himmler's interest in ancient Germanic religions was well known. Wolf's own father, who had once worked under Himmler, claimed that the reichsführer not only believed in reincarnation, but also believed that he was the re-embodiment of King Henry the Fowler.

Some said that Himmler was in fact a warlock. They talked of his magical ability to motivate people to do things that were against everything they had ever been taught. Wolf did not find this so difficult to believe. The regime had come into power when he was only a toddler, but when people spoke of the transformation of Germany since the Treaty of Versailles, the poverty they described was unfathomable today. He had only ever known Germany as a strong, spirited and seemingly invincible force. And all he had known since the age of 11 was victory. Since 1938, war announcements had rolled through school like sporting news. Victory in Poland. Victory in France. Victory in the Netherlands, Luxemburg and Norway. Alliance with Romania. It was assumed that each new invasion would automatically be followed by a victory within days or weeks.

Wolf refocused on the stage, where Himmler was still talking. "We must find a new set of values for our people," he said. "We must once again be rooted in our ancestors and grandchildren, the eternal sequence of our destinies. Let us follow the example of this brave boy who cared nothing for the physical world, and gave everything for society."

Wolf felt a hand on his arm and looked up. It belonged to a black-uniformed SS soldier with two parallel silver stripes and two silver pips on his lapel. A *scharführer*. Not quite an officer, but nevertheless, someone deserving of wide berth.

"Sebastian Wolf?" the soldier said even though the reichsführer was not yet finished with his speech. "How would you like to meet Himmler?"

Wolf did not hear himself say yes. Nevertheless he found himself following the scharführer outside, where the sun had given way to a cold drizzle. He was escorted across campus to the third floor of the yellow mansion, where he was seated on a bench in the hallway outside the headmaster's office.

✱

He sat alone for nearly an hour. His legs felt rubbery. He was thirsty. He had not been filled with this much anxiety and dread since his father's funeral, when Gertrude had asked him to go to the coffin and kiss his father's corpse on the forehead. He had not wanted to feel the coolness of the skin. Had not wanted to face the unbearable stillness of the hands folded across his chest. And yet he could not disappoint her. She pleaded with him. It was somehow important. As if to prove his devotion. Or perhaps just to verify that it was real.

Now sweat ran down Wolf's arms, slickening the insides of his elbows. His tongue seemed to thicken. Himmler was said to have personally ordered the executions of 85 SA leaders in order to eliminate political rivals. The dreaded *Gestapo* ultimately answered to him. Nevertheless, he was going to face this man. His mother had sold her soul to position him for this moment. He would not disappoint her now.

Gradually, several older boys joined him in the hall. Although Wolf had been the first boy seated, several were called into the headmaster's office before him. At times he heard shouting. That was not so peculiar at the Reich School, as the instructors were passionate about their work. Each preceding boy spent several minutes in the office, and then was escorted down the hall by the scharführer, who would then return to escort the next boy in.

When Wolf's name was finally called, he entered in a hurry, clicking the heels of his shoes together in an emphatic "*Heil* Hitler!"

The room smelled like oak furniture. The office walls were painted the same shade of yellow as the building's exterior. The window provided a clear view of the lake, the surface of which was peppered with hard rain.

Himmler was not there. The man standing behind the headmaster's desk was much older. His cap was pulled low over his brown eyes. He held his chin elevated, so that he literally looked down his nose at the young cadet. He wore a thick but narrow mustache that, in subsequent eras, would be regarded as a staple of Hitler parodies. In this era, it was nothing less than an homage to the führer.

Wolf had noticed him that morning from the roof of the barn. He had been in Himmler's entourage. Had he helped carry Albert's body back to campus? He wore jackboots and black pants that were tight in the knees and bloomed around the thighs. An Iron Cross – a highly coveted black and silver combat medal – hung just over the knot on his tie. He wore a forest-green shirt with a black tie under his coat. His lapels showed the double-thunderbolt runes of the SS, and were decorated with three diamonds and two double-stripes, making him a *hauptsturmführer,* a captain.

"This is Obergruppenführer Nagel," the scharführer said as he shut the door behind him. Wolf jumped, having forgotten that anyone else was in the room.

Nagel walked around the desk until he was standing directly in front of the cadet. He touched Wolf's face with his right hand, holding the boy's chin between the oversized thumb and forefinger of his left hand.

"Strong jaw," he observed, inspecting him as a farmer might appraise a prize goat. With the calloused thumb of his other hand, he stretched open Wolf's eyelids and peered straight into them. "Blue eyes."

The scharführer held out a half-inch thick file with Wolf's name on it. Nagel removed his hands from the cadet's face and took it, walking back around the desk to the window. With his back to Wolf, the officer licked his fingertips and began flipping through documents detailing Wolf's Hitler Youth activity, school history, examination results and Reich School enrollment materials, including documentation proving his Germanic bloodline. A separate section contained information about his parents, brother and extended family.

"Competent student," he said without turning from the window. "How is your French?"

"*Bon.* And I also speak English."

Nagel nodded and read on. "A seven-generation German?" He grunted with approval and read silently for a minute more, then snapped the folder shut. "You may relax." He turned toward the window, watching a flock of ducks in V-formation circle the lake. "What do you imagine you'll do when you graduate from this place?"

"Become a scientist and one day teach. Like my father."

The officer laughed, but the expression on his face was dark. "Who do you think you are going to teach? If the war goes on for another year or two, every man between 16 and 60 will be fighting the Russians."

The remark had been made almost casually, yet Wolf felt stung by it. What did that mean? Were the Russians so strong that it might really take two years to defeat them?

"My brother is in Stalingrad," Wolf said. "His latest letter said the Soviet army is larger than he expected, but that Germany weaponry was more sophisticated. He wrote that the *Wehrmacht* was already in control of 90 percent of the city."

"We could control the entire city," Nagel replied, "But what good does that do if the Soviets control all that surround it?"

Wolf didn't know how to take this. Was the obergruppenführer speaking hypothetically or factually?

Nagel walked around the desk again, studying Wolf's face. He gestured to the scharführer to leave. The squad leader did so quickly, exiting through a side door that Wolf assumed lead to another office.

"Most of the cadets I meet don't want to teach," Nagel said with an edge to his voice. "They don't want to fulfill the political leadership roles we are grooming them for. They just want to kill Russians."

True, Wolf was not like the others. He did not even care for hunting. When he had first arrived at the Reich School, he noticed how often his fellow cadets had talked longingly of fighting the French, drinking their wine and taking their women. But with German occupation in France and Belgium, the nation's longstanding grudge against the French seemed to have been avenged, and the focus was now on the Russians. Meanwhile, his own fantasies were still centered on academics.

Now Nagel searched Wolf's face. "Don't you want to defeat Bolshevism?" he said.

"I will serve the Fatherland in any way the führer sees fit," he said, dodging the question without lying.

Nagel's eyes returned to the massive file in his hands. "Your father served in the *Deutsches Ahnenerbe*," he said.

The Ahnenerbe, as it was commonly known, was the Society of German Ancestral Heritage. It had been founded by Heinrich Himmler as a government initiative to research the anthropological and cultural history of the Aryan race. A singular preoccupation with rediscovering not only the accomplishments of the Fatherland's Aryan ancestors, but also the origin of the race. Although the Ahnenerbe was a division of the SS, which was itself a paramilitary organization, it took a fact-finding approach to the war of propaganda, publishing its research in newspapers and books.

The country's museums were filling up with artifacts from Ahnenerbe expeditions to far-flung places such as Persia and Antarctica. Reich School textbooks were peppered with exotic photographs of strange-looking beasts, alien terrain and savage tribes that looked as if they had been summoned from a prehistoric era.

"Yes," Wolf answered. "My father died after returning from an Ahnenerbe expedition to Tibet. Some disease he caught from the locals."

Nagel nodded, but his face was devoid of sympathy. "By all accounts, your father served the Ahnenerbe admirably. Once he was convinced to join, that is."

"Sir?"

"Your father did not join the party until there was virtually no other choice."

This was also true. Wolf wondered what else was in the file. Did Nagel also know that his mother, Gertrude, had herself only joined the Nazi party in order to get work? For the past three years, she had toiled as a nurse in the *Lebensborn* birth program in Munich. Lebensborn was a government organization that helped families with racially desirable blood to meet and have children. Joining the party had been a non-negotiable requirement.

"Himmler is looking for an elite, handpicked group of boys to help him carry out special operations," Nagel said.

The phrase "special operations" made his blood run cold. He imagined a troop of young saboteurs working behind enemy lines to poison food supplies or explode weapons factories. It sounded dangerous. Regardless of how well-designed the propaganda posters put up around the school, no matter how moving Himmler's speeches, Wolf did not want to give his life for the Nazi movement.

"He wants young recruits from respectable German families. In the strictest political sense, you are not ideal. There are cadets here whose parents joined the party as far back as 1921. True loyalists. But there are other things more important than the date of one's party registration. The ability to speak foreign languages, for example."

The temptation to name other students that had superior translation skills came and went in a hot flash. He managed to resist, sensing that overt displays of cowardice would not be tolerated. He focused on the window as it rattled with intense wind and rain.

"And your exemplary genealogical documentation is highly valued," Nagel went on. "Four centuries of church baptismal records as proof. Remarkable."

Wolf's voice quivered with nervousness. "Thank you, sir."

"Which brings me to one other requirement." Nagel rested his backside on the headmaster's desk. "The recruit must have an advanced knowledge of Christianity."

With that, Wolf's face reddened, and he could no longer contain himself. He smelled a trap. "Our family has disavowed Catholicism," he exclaimed with nearly as much conviction as when he had practiced the line with Lang. "We have not set foot in church for three years."

Nagel clucked his tongue. "Of course you haven't. But there is no need to be ashamed of what you know. My own father was a Lutheran pastor in Pomerania. As you know, Hitler himself was raised Catholic. And prior to attending the Reich School, you studied under some of the brightest Jesuits in Germany. Is this not so?"

"My studies were rigorous," Wolf conceded.

Nagel shouted for the scharführer, who must have been waiting in the next room, for he was back inside in an instant, holding a small wooden box. "As of this moment, this cadet, Sebastian Wolf, is a Reich School graduate."

Wolf felt certain he had misheard. He was not due to graduate for two more years.

"As a sign that you are a full member of our community, I present this weapon, which you have earned."

The scharführer set the box on the table, took a sheathed dagger from it, and passed it into Nagel's waiting hands. The officer then handed it to Wolf. Reality itself seemed to crumble. The presentation of the dagger was a rite of manhood that every student looked forward to. Wolf felt far from ready to receive it.

"Go on," Nagel said, sensing the cadet's anxiousness. Wolf unsheathed the blade and read the inscription: *Mehr Sein als Scheinen*. Be More Than What You Seem.

He studied the dagger, flipping it over and over in his hands, testing the sharpness of the point against the palm of his hand.

Meanwhile, Nagel resumed his position behind the desk and watched as the scharführer hunched over it, completing a government form. When it was finished, he pushed it across the wooden desktop to Nagel, who signed his name with angular, forceful strokes. Nagel picked up a purple stick of wax and heated it with a lighter until it dripped a coin-sized spot onto the document near his signature. He made a fist and pressed the skull ring from his left index finger into the hot wax.

The scharführer presented the document to Wolf. "Go to your room and gather your personal items," he said. "You are limited to one piece of luggage. You may leave your clothing here, as new uniforms and gear will be issued. Report downstairs in 20 minutes."

Wolf staggered into the hallway in total disbelief. Only five hours earlier, he had awakened believing that he, Albert and Heinz would be roommates for nearly two more years. He had believed that the war was winding toward its inevitable conclusion, with victory in Russia. He had envisioned himself earning an advanced degree at the University of Munich while enjoying the privileges of a Reich School pedigree. The entirety of his dreams seemed to be suddenly reduced to what he held in his arms. A knife and a notice of conscription.

Suddenly, Lang appeared beside him. "Did you see Himmler?" he asked breathlessly. Before Wolf could answer, he was surrounded by other boys, most of them seniors. Lang grabbed at the conscription order, running his fingers over the wax seal. Only then did Wolf observe the double thunderbolt runes on the document.

The reality of what had just happened seemed to hit him all at once. He had been drafted into the SS.

✻

Wolf descended the stairs of the yellow mansion for the final time, carrying a small brown suitcase containing the few personal effects he had managed to fit into it. A pair of athletic shoes made by a specialty shop in Munich. Assorted socks, briefs and a black peacoat. Two books of essays that he had composed in school. A green Duncan yo-yo that his father had brought back from a lecture series in America several years ago. Several family photographs. A framed photo of Lang, Albert and himself taken at a school festival the previous year.

He wished for a Bible, although he knew that even if he had one, he could not risk carrying it. Instead he brought a wilderness survival handbook and, with much regret, left all his other reading material behind. With the remaining space in his bag he had packed a deck of playing cards, a new leather-bound journal, pencil bag and, of course, his newest possession, the Reich School dagger.

He was shepherded through the pouring rain into the back of an Opel Blitz, a large green vehicle with a long wheelbase covered by wooden shingles on both sides of the truck bed. The top was covered with a brown canvas canopy and the back was left open.

Two more troop transports arrived. Over the course of the next 20 minutes the trucks were gradually filled with cadets. Wolf was joined by nine other boys, most of whom he knew only casually, as they were two years older. Regardless of age, all appeared to be in shock.

It was with great relief that, just as the truck motor started, Heinz Lang climbed into the back. The two boys grinned and shook hands, stopping just short of embracing. They grew silent as the vehicle began moving, watching out the open back as the yellow mansion they had called home gradually shrunk away.

"Where are we going?" one of the boys said.

Lang turned. "Isn't it obvious?" He held up his conscription notice and pointed to a mark in the upper left-hand corner. It was the symbol of an *Irminsul*, the Life Tree in the ancient Saxon religion. "We're not just in the SS. We're in the Ahnenerbe. We're headed to Berlin."

At this observation, a gloom settled over the boys. For cadets that wanted nothing more than to bayonet a Russian in the chest, the prospect of joining the Ahnenerbe was a fate only slightly preferable to death.

"I wish they had sent me to a NAPOLA," the boy said. The NAPOLA schools – or National Political Institutes of

Education – were, despite the name implying otherwise, primarily military in nature. The Third Reich needed a steady supply of well-trained young officers who were properly indoctrinated in National Socialism.

Wolf was just as shell-shocked as anyone. But if he was going to be drafted, he wasn't going to complain about the Ahnenerbe. The society's members were recruited from all walks of life. They were pathologists, poets, scientists, runologists and even anthropologists, such as his father.

And this was the part that confounded Wolf most. The boys had obviously not gone to university. They possessed no particular field of study. They had not really even properly graduated from the Reich School. What use would they be? What were these special operations Nagel had alluded to?

Central Train Station Munich

Unlike most of the other boys, Wolf had not been afflicted by homesickness during his time at the Reich School. Perhaps this was due to how drastically home had changed recently. His father was dead, his brother was off to war, and his mother was, for the first time in her life, working full-time to support the family. Despite its rigors, his time in Feldafing had seemed, at times, like a kind of extended vacation from life itself.

And yet as they stepped out of the trucks and were marched into the train station, Wolf was hit with a painful urge to see his mother. The *Lebensborn* clinic where she worked was scarcely five blocks south of the train station. He had not seen her since September, when parents were invited to watch the boys compete in a track and field competition.

Perhaps she was here, waiting for him? Surely the school had called to notify her of his graduation. The cadets were immediately marched inside the enormous glass and steel structure and toward their platform, where a short passenger train awaited them. None of the boys' families were on hand. The only familiar faces belonged to Nagel and his staff.

Near the first platform, a brass and wind ensemble was playing Wagner's Ride of the Valkyries for a group of *Wehrmacht* recruits boarding a train bound for the eastern front. Wolf did not envy the soldiers' destination, but he envied their company. The soldiers were, one and all, draped with women – girlfriends, sisters, mothers and wives.

Wolf and Lang sat next to each other as the train snaked away from Munich and into the outlying farmland. The boys from the Reich School were packed into a single coach car. There were more cadets than seats, so three of them sat on their luggage near the rear.

Shortly, Nagel stepped in from an adjoining car that Wolf imagined was far more comfortable than their own. Observing Nagel from a distance, Wolf noticed how heavily decorated his uniform was. In addition to the Iron Cross that hung from his collar, he also wore a Wound Badge and a War Merit Cross and many other medals that must have been from the Great War.

He was an intimidating figure, but there was also something paternal about him. The boys quieted, focusing their attention on Nagel in hopes that he would reveal details of their journey. To their surprise, he grinned broadly and began singing *a capella*:

Good-bye, my sweet darling,
good-bye, good-bye, good-bye.
It has, it has to be parted,
good-bye, good-bye, good-bye.
It is about Germany's Glory,
Glory, Glory,
Hail Victory! Hail Victory! Victory!

It was a song that the boys knew well. The previous year it had spread like wildfire to every NAPOLA, Reich School and Hitler Youth organization in Germany. And so they all sang the second verse:

Sight and target are adjusted,
good-bye, good-bye, good-bye,
To Stalin, Churchill, Roosevelt,
good-bye, good-bye, good-bye,
It is about Germany's Glory,
Glory, Glory,
Hail Victory! Hail Victory! Victory!

Even Wolf, who did not care for battle songs, felt a tingle of jubilance as they sang the third and fourth verses. At the song's end, the boys fell silent, once again eager for information. Nagel's gaze lingered on the cadets' faces, making eye contact with each before speaking.

"It is time that we were properly introduced," he said. "I am Siegfried Nagel. I joined the military before many of your fathers were even born. I stood shoulder to shoulder with the führer in the Odeonsplatz during the 1914 war rally."

Wolf had seen a now-famous photograph of the Odeonsplatz rally in government offices. On the eve of the 1932 presidential elections, the party had published the photograph of a man bearing Hitler's likeness among a crowd of thousands in the Odeonsplatz, a public square outside the *Residenz,* the formal royal palace of the Bavarian monarchs. When he was a child, Wolf had heard his father's university friends quietly arguing over whether the photograph had been faked. Nevertheless, it had been institutionalized as a symbol of Hitler's longstanding patriotism.

"Five years later," Nagel continued, "The Treaty of Versailles robbed us of our dignity. But I did not give up. Germany did not give up. Twelve years after leaving the army, Reichsführer Himmler called me to serve in the SS, and I embraced the opportunity with an open heart. I have watched proudly as our nation has pulled itself up from dereliction to take its rightful place as a world empire. Today I am commandant of Wewelsburg Castle. That is our destination."

An astonished silence settled over the boys, which was followed by an electric gush of cheer. Lang had been wrong about the destination. The cadets were not bound for Ahnenerbe headquarters in Berlin, as he had predicted.

Wewelsburg Castle had deep nostalgic significance for all young Germans. It had been mythologized in nearly every Indo-Germanic history course. Every boy at the Reich School knew that in the year 9 AD, on the very property where Wewelsburg Castle now stood, Germanic tribes had gloriously defeated three Roman legions in the Battle of Teutoburg Forest. At nearby Paderborn Cathedral, Charlemagne had been made the first emperor of the Holy Roman Empire in 799 AD. Hillside fortresses dated back to the ninth and tenth centuries and had been built and destroyed numerous times over the past millennium.

Wolf's worries seemed to fall away. He suddenly felt as if he were on a pilgrimage. Or in a fairy tale. He looked at Lang, whose face was filled with ecstasy.

Nagel allowed the cadets 30 seconds of jubilation, and then settled his index finger over his lips until they had quieted. "Each of you has been chosen for a special purpose," he said. "The Deutsches Ahnenerbe is the soul and conscience of the SS. The success of our research and operations is directly proportional to the strength of the German culture. We are therefore the guiding light for the entire Third Reich. As such, Reichsführer Himmler has brilliantly restored Wewelsburg Castle to be the beating heart of the Ahnenerbe. The Fatherland's spiritual epicenter for the next thousand years. Your journey, my boys, will begin there tonight."

Paderborn Station

By the time their train arrived at the station, it was nearly 10 o'clock. The cadets were hungry, but the SS soldiers were all business, ordering them into the backs of three Opel trucks identical to the ones that had ferried them from Feldafing to Munich that day.

The truck picked up speed as the city streets gave way to a country road. Wolf pulled his peacoat from his suitcase. Although it was cold in the open-air vehicle, it was nothing compared to the morning swims in frigid Lake Starnberg.

Thoughts of the lake triggered memories of Albert. The image of Albert's body slung over the thresher flashed in his mind. And then – proof that for every action in the world there was an equal reaction – there had been Beck, lying in the field on the other side of the barn. Wolf allowed himself to linger on the image of the bluish smoke wafting up from Himmler's sidearm. Maybe Beck deserved that, Wolf mused. The bastard's negligence had killed Albert.

Lang shook Wolf out of his daze, pointing out beautiful lamp-lit farmhouses and country manor homes as they drove in the woods outside Paderborn. He took in a deep breath for what seemed like the first time all day, noting the sweet scent of the conifer forest as the truck climbed a series of foothills. Soon, the branches of enormous beech and oak trees arched over the road. The night air grew several degrees cooler. Lang drew close, his teeth chattering.

When the truck finally stopped, Wolf leaned out the back and found himself face to face with an SS guard holding an MP-38 submachine gun in his left hand. A second guard appeared at his side with a flashlight. The guard peered into the truck bed, counting the 11 boys within.

"Welcome to Wewelsburg Castle," he said finally, and shouted for the guard to open the gate.

The truck motored across an arched stone bridge that was built over a moat. Torches were lit along the castle walls. An SS guard stood inside a sentry box, rubbing his gloved hands together to keep warm.

Nagel's voice cried "Attention! Out of the trucks!"

The boys climbed over each other to get a look at the castle at night. It was too dark to see much, but Wolf's Jesuit teachers had equipped him with enough knowledge to imagine what he could not see. It was constructed of yellow stone with three towers in a triangular pattern. Seen from an airplane, it was said to resemble the shape of the Holy Lance, the spear used by Longinus to pierce Christ's side during the Crucifixion. The triangular-shaped castle's north tower formed the spear's tip, with the two domed towers forming its sides, and the road leading up to it comprising the lance's shaft.

Nagel commanded the boys to line up. They did, standing in two neat rows in the crisp night air. "With radiant hearts," he said, "You will now enter Wewelsburg Castle, prepared to carry out what the nation, the National Socialist State and I expect of you."

They marched through an arched doorway decorated with stone-etched images of the Nordic gods Thor and Odin. The entrance hall was a great, oak-paneled room that, judging by the exposed wiring strung along one wall, had only recently been outfitted with electricity. The glow of several low-wattage lamps revealed suits of armor, medieval crossbows and immaculate tapestries. Wolf was awestruck by the size of the roaring fireplace, which was nearly tall enough to stand in.

Even at this hour, restoration efforts were underway. Two workers were busy hanging an oil painting. Crude cross-shaped patches were sewn to the chests of their striped shirts and pants.

Nagel halted the march. He went to the head of the line, sweeping his hand across the scene before them. "These are just two of hundreds of foreign workers living in a nearby camp for stonemasons, carpenters and electricians. They are Jehovah's Witnesses, and they are free to go at any time. We ask only that they renounce their religion, swear obedience to Hitler and join the German Army. Fortunately for my reconstruction project, they have so far been unwilling to do so."

Wolf did not know what a Jehovah's Witness believed. He had been told by his mother that they were not real Christians and would not be permitted into heaven. Then again, she had said the same thing about Lutherans, and Wolf had met plenty of very decent Lutherans.

The cadets followed Nagel down a narrow set of stone stairs, through two sets of iron gates, and into an enormous cavern that was stuffed with artifacts. The boys were surrounded on either side by portraits of Germany's leaders dating back to the Middle Ages. An enormous portrait of King Heinrich was suspended over the entrance by wires at an angle of 45 degrees, giving the stoic king the impression of one looking down from the heavens.

"You are now standing in Himmler's private museum," Nagel said in a tone that was gentle, almost fatherly. "As each of you will learn, ancestry is as fundamental to the war effort as the innovation of new weaponry. In light of these directives, Himmler has given his permission for you to experience your heritage firsthand."

Wolf disengaged from the pack, wandering, not knowing where to begin. Every corner seemed to be filled with priceless artifacts. He first gravitated toward several slabs of cut stone, each decorated with ancient runic etchings. They looked impossibly heavy. How many weeks had it taken to bring them here? How many mules or tractors had it taken to haul them to the nearest train?

Along the same wall, bronze urns, swords, ancient sculptures and jewel-encrusted daggers were showcased in shallow enclaves. A series of glass enclosures held piles of ancient Roman coins and rings with precious gemstones. So numerous were the artifacts that many seemed to be hastily thrown together, stacked in mismatched piles.

He examined a delicate lute that was estimated to be 600 years old. Next to it, a display of ancient battle gear used by Teutonic knights. A scarred triangular shield painted with a red cross. Thirteenth century chainmail, now rusted, as worn by mounted warriors. A breastplate bearing the Teutonic emblem. Axes, spurs and bonze bits for medieval warhorses.

The museum wasn't entirely devoted to Germanic heritage. A section of the cavern had been devoted to non-Germanic paintings imported from the occupied countries. There, straight out of Wolf's primary school art history textbook, was Hans Memling's painting *Madonna with Child*. It was surrounded by works by Rembrandt, Cezanne and Van Gogh.

The presence of French art was astonishing. The national schools taught only that the French could not be trusted, and that France was merely a territory to be exploited. Wolf owed his knowledge of French art to his mother, who had, before the war, taken Wolf and his brother to the finest exhibits in Berlin and Munich. He wished she were here to see this. Never had he seen so many riches packed into one place.

Now he edged toward a glass case holding a bedazzled ceremonial robe. He bent lower to study the garment. It was spectacular, though slightly tattered at the edges. The inscription read IMPERIAL REGALIA OF THE HOLY ROMAN EMPIRE – 10th CENTURY. In an adjacent glass case were the crown, scepter and the orb of the Holy Roman Empire.

The Imperial Crown was studded with more than 100 pearls, sapphires, emeralds and amethysts. The stones were polished into smooth, rounded shapes and appeared to emit light from within. The crown featured four plates, each depicting a biblical scene. He knelt down to read the inscription on the right front plate, where Christ was depicted enthroned between two childlike angels. *Per Me Reges Regnant.* By Me Kings Reign.

"I see you have a taste for Christian artifacts."

Wolf turned and found himself face to face with Nagel. Out of nerves, and habit, he stiffened.

"No need to mask your enthusiasm, boy. The führer was beside himself with joy when he laid eyes on the Crown Jewels in Vienna. His first act upon entering the country was ensuring their immediate return to their rightful place in Germany."

Wolf turned his attention back to the jewels. "They are," he nodded, allowing himself a small grin, "Quite amazing, actually."

"There is something else you should see." Nagel put a hand on Wolf's shoulder and guided him to the other side of the display. The gesture was paternal. Wolf felt oddly comforted by the old man's attention. A wave of guilt flashed over him as he remembered his mother's warning before his initial term at school: *They want you to believe that the party replaces your parents, and that Hitler replaces God. If they can convince you of that, then they can make you do anything.*

Nagel pointed to a display containing a bronze and gold spear, about 50 centimeters in length. "Do you know what this is?"

Wolf shook his head. Nagel pointed up at the painting hanging overhead. An authentic Lucas Cranach painting, *The Crucifixion with the Converted Centurion*. 1536. Wolf had actually seen it before. Berlin, he remembered, with his brother and father. And here it was. Locked away for the private pleasure of the high command.

What exactly was Nagel implying? That Himmler had found the Spear of Destiny? It looked old, all right. Old enough to have seen nearly 2,000 years of world history. But the Jesuits had taught him that it was in the Vatican, in St. Peter's Cathedral. He had seen photographs in a textbook.

"It's not real," Wolf objected. "It can't be."

"On the contrary. Our historians have determined that it is, without a doubt, the same lance that Constantine carried as his armies were victorious in battle. And if Constantine himself believed it to be the lance that pierced Jesus Christ on the cross, then Himmler is more than ready to do so."

Wolf grunted in wonderment. Of course he was familiar with the legend of the Holy Lance. Whoever possessed it was said to be rendered invincible. He considered the remarkable speed with which the German armies had rolled across Europe. Poland. Austria. Norway. France. Belgium. Denmark. Egypt. Romania. Yugoslavia. At times, it seemed as if the very presence of the Nazi armies collapsed the will to fight entirely.

"And what is the name of the centurion who lanced Jesus?" Nagel asked. He clearly knew the answer, but was probing.

"Longinus," Wolf answered quietly.

"So you have also studied the Apocrypha," Nagel said, clearly impressed.

Wolf nodded. Longinus' name did not appear in the canonical Bible. A centurion had been mentioned in the book of John, but had not been named specifically except in the somewhat esoteric Gospel of Nicodemus. According to these ancient writings, Longinus had been an old soldier with poor eyesight. Pontius Pilot had told him to go to Calvary and remove the bodies of those who had been crucified since it was forbidden to perform crucifixions on the Sabbath. As Jesus was not yet dead, Longinus pierced his side with the lance. Blood and water rushed out of Jesus' body, some of it splashing into Longinus' eyes, miraculously restoring his vision.

Nagel checked his watch, a black Omega Regulator with golden numerals. Time was up. "I look forward to continuing our discussions."

As the other cadets scrambled for the exit, Wolf lingered over the Holy Lance. He remembered Nagel's words on the train. "The spiritual epicenter for the next thousand years." But what kind of spiritualism was this? Hitler publicly decried the Vatican while Himmler embraced fairy tales about Odin and Asgard. The parochial schools had been shuttered. Priests had all but disappeared.

And yet here was the Spear of Destiny. And the crown jewels of the Holy Roman Empire. And the work of Cranach and Memling. Wolf had the sudden feeling that everything good in the world was being bottled up here in the castle.

Maybe Wolf's father had been right about Himmler all along. Maybe he really was some kind of sorcerer. Maybe it was through the power of these divine objects that he had managed to put Europe under his spell.

Nagel led the boys through a narrow stone portal to the basement level of the castle's north tower. By now Wolf was famished. He had not eaten in 16 hours.

Now they found themselves standing at the edge of a large circular room. A bluish-yellow pyre burned in the center. The room smelled like gas, and its walls of yellow stone were devoid of art or tapestries. Thousands of small copper canisters were arranged in a circular pattern along the room's far north edge. Beside them stood a wooden chest.

It was the first time any of the boys had seen a flame burn without wood or charcoal. Wolf edged closer to the fire sprouting from the tiny hole in the marble floor, wondering how it worked. Was this more evidence of Himmler's dark arts?

"This room is called The Vault." Nagel's voice was subdued and respectful. "A memorial to past, present and future SS officers. All of us, even those who are dead, commune here in an endless loop of honor and glory."

He extended his left hand and walked slowly in front of the boys, displaying the *Totenkopfring,* or skull ring, worn on his left index finger. A gleaming chunk of silver with skull and crossbones at the front. Sig and hagall runes were carved into the sides. "This ring," he continued, "was earned through blood and sweat. Himmler placed it on my finger himself. If you are very clever, and very brave, you will return to this room someday to receive your ring."

Nagel opened the wooden chest. "Come pay your respects to those who have made the ultimate sacrifice for the Fatherland."

Wolf was suddenly filled with dread. He stood his ground in the back of the room as the others went toward the open box. The castle commandant was staring at him now. He gestured for Wolf to come forward and witness what was inside.

But Wolf's mind was elsewhere. His thoughts flashed to his father's wake. Gertrude took him by the arm, pulling him toward the pine coffin. "Come look," she begged, gripping his arm and pulling him. "Why won't you pay your respects to your father?" Even from a distance, the sight of the expressionless face was too much to bear. He did not look at peace. He looked sullen, sickly. Wolf was suddenly dazed. He lost his balance and stumbled against the coffin, his mother's palm against his back, pressing him forward.

"Kiss him," his mother had demanded. "Kiss your father goodbye."

Now Nagel's hand was pressed firmly into Wolf's back, pressing him toward the open chest. "Bear witness to those who have served before you."

The other cadets parted before him, clearing a path. To Wolf's great relief, there was no body in the iron chest. It was instead filled with thousands of skull rings. The front of each ring bore the death skull and crossbones emblem of the SS.

"Closer," Nagel urged, pressing harder, and as Wolf bent down, he saw that the rings were far from identical. The type and number of Nordic runes engraved on the sides varied. The insides of the bands were personalized, with the surname of the soldier and the date of issue.

"Read the names," Nagel demanded.

Wolf knelt closer. "*Maier, 4-4-1939. Muller, 12-5-1941. Patzwall, 9-3-1937.*"

"When an SS officer dies, his ring is sent to the castle to rejoin the others in this chest." Nagel pointed to the copper containers. "His ashes are placed there, in view of the eternal pyre, which is never extinguished. My hope for you, my boys, is that you will have the privilege of revisiting this room exactly twice. Once in body, and once in spirit."

The sheer number of rings was staggering. So many dead. And these were only Germany's so-called elite, Wolf realized. SS soldiers were not multi-ethnic, as were the *Waffen-SS* and *Wehrmacht*, and so there were far fewer of them. They did not form regular combat divisions and so, he had assumed, they did not die in great numbers when compared to Germany's regular land or naval forces. And yet the chest was filled to the brim. So much sacrifice. So much wasted blood.

He straightened himself and backed up, stepping on the steel toes of his fellow cadets' shoes. He looked around, studying the boys' faces. He saw conviction. Earnestness in their tight-lipped expressions. Only this morning, any of them would have preferred to rush a line of Russian machine guns rather than join the Ahnenerbe. But that had all changed. Wolf could feel it. Now they were ready to be wedded to this ideal of eternal brotherhood. Nagel had presented the boys with an opportunity not just to join the SS, or the Ahnenerbe, but also to be eternally sealed in a family of modern-day Teutonic Knights.

*

They marched again. Up a twisting staircase, down a hall filled with deer taxidermy, and down again. Through a cold, unlit passageway that left Wolf disoriented and unaware of anything except the hunger pains in his stomach and the sound of the other boys' boots on the castle floor.

At last they approached a warm orange light. Squeezing through a tiny corridor, they did not walk into the castle's north wing so much as they were born into it. Like the Vault, it was circular with a high-domed ceiling and a marble floor and was illuminated by candlelight from four iron chandeliers. At its center was a black sun symbol with 12 jagged arms. Twelve stone pillars were arranged in a circular pattern, and between them hung six red floor-to-ceiling tapestries bearing the swastika emblem.

Over the center of the black sun was a modest wooden reclining chair, a stool and a tray full of sharp-looking knives and needles. A shiver coursed through Wolf's legs. His knees felt weak.

"Attention!" Nagel shouted. The boys lined up shoulder-to-shoulder and stiffened their posture. "This is the Hall of Supreme Generals. This room is the center of the Reich and, in fact, is the center of the universe. Here you will assume the mark of the Ahnenerbe and enter officially into the sacred brotherhood of the SS."

Wolf had been so entranced by Nagel's oratory that he had not noticed two men standing near one of the pillars. SS officers with silver physician's patches on the lapels of their uniform.

"You will now recite the oath of allegiance to the *Schutzstaffel*," Nagel stated. "Repeat after me. I vow to Adolf Hitler imperturbable loyalty."

The boys repeated in unison.

"I vow to him and to the leaders that he sets for me, absolute allegiance."

The recruits mimicked his tone, their voices stronger now.

"Adolf Hitler: *Sieg Heil!*"

The feeling of speaking as one, moving as one, was oddly comforting. He thought of Beck and the sensation of being led through synchronized calisthenics – at times in full darkness – with 200 of his fellow cadets, acting as one collective organism, was as essential as breathing. He dreaded the absence of his morning routine more than he feared the castle itself.

Sensing Wolf's wandering attention, Nagel placed a hand on his shoulder and pulled him out of line. "First initiate," he announced, guiding Wolf to the chair in the center of the room alongside the tray of knives and needles. "This is Sebastian Wolf," Nagel told the physicians. "Age 15. Blood type O."

He was ordered to remove his jacket and shirt. He obeyed quickly, hoping to disguise the trepidation coursing through his body. One of the physicians pressed him into a reclining position and raised his left arm over his head. The physician held a large, two-coil tattoo machine that had the letters MADE IN THE USA imprinted on the copper-colored metal. The needle was fat, tapering to form a point at the end. A wire covered by thick black insulation protruded from the bottom, snaking across the floor to some unseen power source.

"This will hurt," the attending physician said unapologetically. He took hold of Wolf's arm, pressing it alongside his head, flush with Wolf's left ear. The primary doctor touched the tattoo machine needle to the underside of

Wolf's bicep. Painful vibrations flashed through his body as the machine whined.

Nagel turned and spoke to the other boys. "The identification of blood types was innovated through the ingenuity of the German people," he said. "But SS officers alone have the privilege of wearing the blood type tattoo. In the event that you need a transfusion and are unconscious, this mark may save your life."

The physician was not gentle, but he was at least efficient. In less than a minute, a seven-millimeter 'O' was tattooed on the underside of Wolf's arm. Wolf allowed himself a tight smile as the physician wiped the blood away. He had no sooner let his guard down than the assisting physician gripped his right arm and pressed it back against his right ear.

The primary moved in with the needle and began the procedure again, boring into the soft, sensitive skin. Now Wolf was delirious with pain. He closed his eyes and tried to think of his mother. But he could not. He saw only his dead father, cold and sullen in the coffin.

At last the high-pitched grind ceased. Sensing a shadow over him, Wolf opened his eyes and found Nagel holding a small pocket mirror, angling it so that Wolf might see the new markings. He focused on the tiny smudge of newly inked skin. Not another "O." This was Tyr, the spear-shaped rune.

Nagel gave no explanation for this, and none was needed. Lessons about the meaning of ancient Nordic myths dominated Reich School literature classes. Tyr, the Nordic god of war. Tyr, the symbol that German runologists associated with energy and magic, connecting the heavens and earth with man. Tyr, the rune Himmler ordered carved into the steel of daggers, swords and even infantry rifles.

But to carve Tyr into one's flesh was overtly mystical. It was said to have been done by ancient Nordic warriors so that if a Valkyrie decided that they must die in battle, they might be recognized as a true warrior and brought to Valhalla, the magnificent hall of dead warriors ruled by the Norse god Odin.

The commandant helped Wolf to his feet, where he stood shirtless and bleeding from both arms. Nagel held a golden chalice before him, on which an eagle with eyes of garnet clutched a swastika-emblazoned world.

The newly marked recruit took the chalice in both hands. It was heavy, containing several semi-coagulated ounces of reddish-purple fluid. He did not know whether the blood in the chalice was human or animal. His stomach soured at both prospects, but it did not matter much. He would have to drink or die.

"Now you will share in the eternal bond of the Ahnenerbe," Nagel said.

Wolf brought the cup to his lips. As the metallic-tasting slime passed his teeth, tongue and throat, he tried to imagine that it was his mother's sausage gravy.

Central Train Station Frankfurt

The night train bound for Paris smelled of pipe smoke and boot polish. Wolf and Lang followed an elderly conductor through a coach car, occupied largely by *Wehrmacht* soldiers, en route to a separate car that consisted entirely of private cabins.

Other than the MP-40 submachine guns and their packs, they had no baggage. The conductor opened a door for them, and the boys stepped into what was easily the most spacious and elegant mode of travel they had ever seen. The private cabin was nearly as large as Wolf's bedroom in Munich. Opposing brown leather couches were accented with golden stitching. A small bar stocked with liquor and highball glasses was built into shelving just beneath the window.

The silver-haired conductor entered the room, shut the door behind him and pulled an overhead handle, revealing a fold-out bed. "Silk linens," he said smiling. "Imported from Istanbul."

"We won't be sleeping," Wolf assured him. "We're expecting a third."

In their first official assignment, they were to board this train, where they would meet Dr. Rudolph Seiler and accompany him on a mission to Paris. Dr. Seiler's security was their sole concern. They had been given no other details.

Seiler was a noted authority on Rome, ancient Nordic society and the Middle East. Wolf had, in fact, seen his work referenced in the official Ahnenerbe journal, *Germanien*. His new book, *The Mastery of Runes*, had quickly become a staple of the Reich School curriculum.

Wolf caught his reflection in a full-length mirror behind the door. It was the first time he had seen himself in uniform, as they had only been issued and tailored a few hours earlier. Brown shirt with black leather buttons, tied with a black tie. Black pants. Shiny black jackboots. Black tunic with the red, white and black swastika armband on the left sleeve. The Ahnenerbe Tree of Life stickpin in his lapel.

On his collar, sig runes on one side and a silver button pip on the other indicating his rank: *unterscharführer*, or junior squad leader. Several ranks more than he had deserved, to be sure. It seemed that graduates of the Reich School never started at the bottom, even when they had been recruited two years ahead of schedule.

The conductor opened a storage compartment and lifted Wolf's pack. He raised it to waist-level and then fell back against the door, apparently dizzy.

Wolf relieved him of the heavy pack as Lang guided him to one of the leather seats.

"My dear boy," the conductor said as he caught his breath. "I apologize."

"You shouldn't be lifting baggage at your age," Lang scolded.

"I retired in 1934, and not a moment too soon. Can you imagine my surprise when a minister from the *Reichsbahn* called me? Said they were desperate for labor. Obviously the tourist trains are no longer running, but it seems there are substantial military needs. He said they were running 40 times the number of routes that they had during peacetime. Forty times! Can you imagine?"

"Astonishing," Lang answered without enthusiasm.

"It seems the train crews have been decimated by Wehrmacht conscription, and also by saboteurs. You must have heard." He paused, waiting for further comment from the soldiers. When none came, the conductor seemed to backpedal, saying, "Not that I mind the risks, you understand. The Fatherland needs every man, woman and child right now. I am happy to serve."

With this, he stood, saluted and backed out of the room, shutting the door behind him.

Both boys laughed. After six of the most intense weeks of their lives, they could hardly believe their luck. Lang picked up a crystal decanter with a stag head on top. It was full of amber liquor. "Should we live a little?"

A knock at the door interrupted the celebration. With his submachine gun still slung over his left shoulder, Wolf opened the door.

He recognized Dr. Seiler from an official Ahnenerbe photograph that Nagel had given him. The professor's small blue eyes searched Wolf from behind wire-rim spectacles. Although he was a civilian, he nevertheless wore a red, white and black swastika band around the left arm of his black overcoat. Lang took his luggage – a small leather overnight bag – and showed him into the private compartment where they would spend the next five hours together.

Seiler was irritated, demanding to know why they had not left for Paris from Cologne. He explained in excited, verbose sentences that he taught at the University of Halle, in Mittenburg, and that Frankfurt was several hours out of the way, costing him a full day of extra travel.

"We are sorry for the inconvenience," Wolf said. "Cologne has suffered heavy air raids since May. I'm sure the obergruppenführer had only your safety in mind."

Wolf was merely speculating. He and Lang had in fact assumed that Frankfurt had been chosen to accommodate Dr. Seiler. Nevertheless, his explanation seemed to satisfy the professor, who removed his heavy coat and sat down just as the train began churning away from the platform.

"Please," he said, gesturing to the opposite couch. He removed a silver cigarette case from the inside pocket of his brown blazer and offered the boys a smoke. Lang demurred. Wolf took one, lit it, and puffed it in an exaggerated manner, not knowing whether to inhale or exhale. The government campaigns against smoking had been remarkably effective with the boys at the Reich School. This was his first cigarette.

"You must be hungry," Lang said.

Seiler shook his head, studying his young bodyguards. "Bavarian accents. Well-spoken. Are you from Munich?"

"Yes. But for the past two years we attended the Reich School in Feldafing."

Seiler's eyebrows danced. "So you're not just any SS brutes," Seiler said. "You must have a few brain cells between you."

He removed his black fedora. He was bald, and made no attempt to comb over what hair remained on the sides of his head. Wolf had originally taken him for a man in his 30s. Now it was clear that he was older, perhaps in his late 40s.

"Have you been to Paris?" Seiler asked. Wolf and Lang shook their heads. "I see. Well, the charms of Paris can be quite distracting, so be warned now that this is not a pleasure trip. We must be alert. Despite what you might hear Goebbels say on the radio, we are still very much at war in France. The resistance is always looking for opportunities to kill Germans. That goes double for those who are seen as threatening of its cultural heritage. I expect you to be vigilant so that I can focus on my work."

A polite knock interrupted Seiler's rant. The conductor had returned. He passed a yellow telegraph envelope to Dr. Seiler. The professor opened it immediately. His face tightened as he read, as if he had eaten something sour. "SS-1 will rendezvous and pickup at *Gare du Nord* upon arrival."

Wolf did not understand. "SS-1?"

"Himmler's personal car," Seiler said with distaste. "Unexpected. This was to be a quick fact-finding trip. I can only assume something new has come to light that will undoubtedly turn it into a circus. With Himmler it is always a circus."

Suddenly deflated, Seiler leaned against the train window, removed his eyeglasses and rested the fedora over his eyes. Within minutes, he was asleep.

Occupied Paris

The black BMW 335 bore the license plate SS-1. The car sped down the Quai de la Tournelle, tracing the southern edge of the Seine River. It seemed to Wolf that they were cornering too fast for such a drizzly night. From the vehicle's cramped rear row, he pressed a leather glove against the window and wiped away a layer of condensation. The silhouette of Notre Dame Cathedral's massive central spire appeared against the rainy Paris skyline.

The priests of Notre Dame were forbidden from illuminating the cathedral at night, so as to deprive Allied bombers from a valuable aerial landmark. With only the dimmed lights of Paris as a backdrop, the silhouette of gothic architecture cut a forbidding, jagged figure in the night sky.

Heinrich Himmler rode in the front passenger seat, peering at the Parisian skyline through round wire-frame glasses. "Turn right at the bridge," he instructed his driver. The BMW's tires squealed as it turned onto the bridge to Ile de la Cité, the oldest part of Paris.

Dr. Seiler rode in the middle of the rear row, between Wolf and Lang. He and Himmler had shared little conversation since the rendezvous at Gare du Nord.

Wolf gazed up in awe as the car crossed over the river and neared the cathedral's front façade. Notre Dame, a place he had only dreamed of. Except for the Sistine Chapel, it was the most revered cathedral in Europe. Wolf recalled from his history courses that Napoleon had been married here, as well as countless members of French royalty. It was even said that the Holy Crown of Thorns, forced upon Jesus' head before the Crucifixion, was kept within its walls.

The car crawled the last 20 meters over the cobblestone square, its headlights illuminating the cathedral's western entrance. Wolf and Lang were the first out, exiting the car before it came to a full stop. They knelt in defensive positions, MP-40 submachine guns tucked tightly against their shoulders as they scanned the rainy square.

On the far end of Rue de la Cité, Wolf spotted a figure watching them – a hooded man in a long robe on a bicycle. It was too dark to see his face. Wolf whistled and waved for the cyclist to move away. The figure turned the bike eastward and pedaled into a side alley.

Satisfied, he rapped twice on the BMW's roof, giving Himmler's driver, *Obersturmführer* Franz Hoffman, the all clear. Hoffman shut off the motor, but left the headlights fixed on the cathedral entrance. Himmler stepped out of the car, using the finger of his glove to smooth his narrow mustache. The reichsführer's five foot nine frame was dwarfed by the youthful, textbook Aryan physiques of his bodyguards. Seiler was out of the car next, walking slightly behind Himmler.

Himmler's eyes searched the plaza. "Where are the others?" he asked Hoffman.

"We're early. Perhaps we should wait in the car."

"No. The professor and I will keep the priest occupied upstairs while you begin."

Himmler turned, appreciating the first of three elaborate portals leading into Notre Dame. "Besides, I will be the first to admit that there is much to see and admire." His eyes danced excitedly at the statues engraved into the stone entranceway. A decapitated Saint Denis, holding his own head. A demon trying to extinguish the candle of Saint Genevieve. Mary on her deathbed, surrounded by Jesus and the 12 disciples. "Magnificent," Himmler muttered, and with his entourage following in line behind him, he wordlessly moved toward the center entrance, the Portal of the Last Judgment. The carvings surrounding the heavy wood doors were even more violent. A sculpted figure of Christ displaying his wounds. Warrior angels bearing spears and crosses. The

Virgin Mary and St. John kneeling at either side. Dozens of tormented souls writhing in hellish agony.

"Catholics," Himmler muttered to no one in particular, "have always understood the power of symbolism and fear."

"Precisely," Seiler said. "That's why the church has survived two thousand years."

Hoffman focused his attention on Wolf. "What are you waiting for? Check inside!"

Wolf pushed the front doors wide, revealing the most cavernous, grandiose structure he had ever laid eyes upon. Germany's own Trier Cathedral did not begin to compare. Only the majesty of Munich's urban palace even came close. Notre Dame's vaulted ceiling was impossibly high for a building created some 800 years earlier. How had mere mortals done this?

There was no mass at this time of night, but the rear pews were nevertheless occupied by a handful of worshippers in silent meditation. Behind and above him, eight thousand massive organ pipes clustered before a circular spectacle of stained glass that seemed, with every step deeper into the cathedral, to fan out like the feathers of a magic peacock. He was overcome with emotion. With his superiors still outside, he quickly dropped to one knee and crossed himself, mouthing a Hail Mary. Only then did he compose himself and return to the entrance to give the all clear.

The Nazi presence in the cathedral was felt before it was seen. The half-dozen worshippers in the rear pews broke from prayer to turn and regard the invaders. Although the red armband bearing the swastika on Himmler's sleeve was a well-known ancient Tibetan symbol, to the faithful in Notre Dame, the swastika was antagonistic – a twisted, deliberate perversion of the holy cross of Jesus.

Himmler removed his trench coat and handed it to Hoffman, revealing a new black dress uniform that Hugo Boss had personally designed for him. The uniform was both elegant and sinister, resurrecting the skull-and-crossbones imagery of the early 1920s German Worker's Party uniforms. Black tie with swastika tiepin, twin death's head patches on his cap, and a silver dagger on his belt. A fitting costume for the high priest of the Nazi religion.

Wolf noted a hooded figure on each side of the hall, lighting prayer candles. They were wearing the same style of brown robe he had seen on the cyclist on the street. Simple wooden crosses strung with strips of black leather hung from their necks. Perhaps they were monks.

He tightened the rifle against his shoulder and checked his weapon to ensure the safety was off. However confidential the nature of their mission, Wolf imagined that news of Himmler's presence in Paris would travel quickly.

With the professor at his heels, Himmler stomped down the long center nave, looking for the priest on duty. An elderly clergyman emerged near the main altar. He was dressed in a white collar and a simple black cloak that reached the tops of his shoes. As the Nazi entourage approached, he pressed his fingertips against his chest, outlining the four points of the cross. It seemed to Wolf that he was steeling himself for unpleasant business.

The priest lifted his arm in a perfunctory *sieg heil* as he greeted them. Such a gesture would have been unheard of a year earlier. But that had been before the disappearance of hundreds of thousands of French citizens over the summer and fall. "I am Father LeFevre," he said in passable German. "To what do we owe this pleasure?"

"Let's talk in private," Himmler said. He turned to Hoffman. "You have your orders."

Father LeFevre pulled a heavy gas lamp from its wall fixture and led the other four Nazis – Himmler, Seiler, Wolf and Lang – across the choir ambulatory to a doorway in the far south corner. They soon came to a tightly wound stone staircase leading up to the south tower. Before ascending, Wolf turned back and observed Hoffman lingering by the high altar. He seemed to be examining it. What were his orders? Wolf wondered. Who were the others Himmler had been expecting?

Each stair step bore the deep grooves of centuries of use. The ascent proved to be a remarkably steep climb. By the third-floor landing, Himmler was breathing heavily from his mouth. The more athletic priest stopped and looked down at him, grinning. "It's 387 steps to the tower," the priest remarked. "Lucky for you, my quarters are on the next landing."

They exited the staircase and came to a narrow hallway consisting of several closed doors. The priest's lamp shed dim light on a row of humbly framed portraits illustrating a long succession of French clergy. A cold draft swept through the hallway. Notre Dame seemed even colder than Wewelsburg Castle. Wolf could see his breath.

The priest went through the first doorway on his right. He took a wooden match from his pocket, struck it against the wall and lit a second gas lantern. The room was quite large, and the walls were jammed with bookshelves from floor to ceiling, each of them bowing under the weight of thick manuscripts. LeFevre walked behind a large desk that was bare except for a magnifying glass, a pen and an ink well. He gestured for Himmler and Seiler to sit in the chairs opposite him.

"Guard the hallway," Himmler told Lang. "Make sure no one gets past." Lang shot Wolf a jealous glare as he exited and shut the door behind him, leaving his friend privy to the reichsführer's private business with the Catholic Church.

The priest cleared his throat. "How can I be of help?"

"Let us get right to the point," Himmler replied. "We are here for the Holy Relics."

Father LeFevre managed a nervous smile. It was public knowledge that Notre Dame claimed to hold the true

Holy Crown – the crown of thorns worn by Jesus during the Crucifixion – as well as a nail from the True Cross, a fragment of the Holy Sponge, and other treasures.

"The Relics of the Passion are on display for believers on the first Friday of each month," he said. "But for you, of course, yes, we can arrange a private viewing. Tonight, if you wish."

"You misunderstand," Himmler said. "We are taking the relics, all of them, with us to Germany."

The priest's lips parted at the audacity of Himmler's request. "That is…that is quite impossible."

Had Wolf not seen the vast quantities of Christian antiquities Himmler had already acquired for his private museum at Wewelsburg Castle, he would not have believed the request himself. But now he knew what the priest did not. Himmler was not afraid of being labeled a heretic. He seemed to have no fear of God whatsoever.

Himmler smiled. "Was King Louis IX a heretic when he brought the Holy Relics to Paris from Constantinople?"

The priest could scarcely conceal his temper. "Saint Louis considered himself a lieutenant of God. Although he was King of France, when he delivered the relics he was but a humble servant. He wore no royal robes, no shoes even. He was a picture of humility."

"Is it not true that this saint you speak of was, in fact, a wealthy crusader responsible for the mass slaughter of countless Islamists?"

"With all due respect, Herr Himmler, you are many things, but you are not an expert in French history."

Seiler winced, seeming to brace himself for Himmler's response. Wolf too feared for the priest's life. On the morning Albert died, he had witnessed firsthand the speed with which Himmler solved his problems. If he would execute Beck in public for reckless negligence, he could only imagine what would be done to a belligerent French priest that did not want to hand over precious relics.

And yet Himmler remained calm. "We have nevertheless followed proper Vatican protocol." He reached inside his jacket pocket, produced a sealed envelope and tossed it unceremoniously onto Father LeFevre's desk.

The red wax seal was imprinted with the Fisherman's Ring. "The mark of His Holiness," LeFevre intoned as he ran his fingers over it slowly, as if cataloguing the moment in his mind.

Finally he broke the seal with a brass letter opener. Then he carefully unfolded the letter and read the concise note twice before resuming eye contact with his German adversary.

"Surely His Holiness did not know what he was signing."

Himmler's voice was calm, almost tranquil. "Is it really so unbelievable? As you must know, Pacelli is a longtime friend of the German people."

It was well known that Pacelli – who had taken the name Pius XII upon his election in 1939 – had seemingly done virtually everything in his power to establish friendly relations with Hitler. His submissive behavior had not been entirely unexpected, given that he had spent several years living in both Munich and Berlin as Papal Nuncio to Bavaria, and later, to all of Germany. Even after being called back to Rome to serve as Cardinal Secretary of State, he had helped broker the *Reichskonkordat*, the treaty that had supposedly guaranteed the rights of the Catholic Church in Germany. The pope had been widely criticized for not breaking the treaty despite widespread violations by the German government.

LeFevre leaned back in his chair. "What are you implying?"

"When Pacelli was ambassador, he hosted German leadership at his residence in Berlin on many occasions. And so, when the death of Pope XI was announced, we extended our influence within the Vatican to sway the conclave."

"No. God chooses Popes. Cardinals are merely his instruments."

"Believe what you wish," Himmler said. "But I assure you that the pontiff remains not only a steadfast friend and supporter of the German people, but also one that longs for the historical bond between the Vatican and the Holy Roman Empire. Even now the Crown Jewels and the Spear of Longinus have been returned to their rightful place at Wewelsburg Castle."

"Nobody has returned anything," the priest spat. "They were stolen when your armies occupied Austria."

Dr. Seiler sat forward. "Father LeFevre, as a civilian observer, I urge you to watch your tone. You speak as if you yourself are eager to become a martyr."

Himmler held his hand up and smiled. "Professor, relax. I actually enjoy intellectual banter with men of the cloth. And even I am too superstitious to kill a priest in Notre Dame Cathedral."

LeFevre's face flushed. "Forgive me. I do not wish to be uncivil. But regardless of what His Holiness has authorized, the removal of artifacts from Notre Dame would be regarded as a cardinal sin."

"Let those without sin be the first to cast stones, Father. When Napoleon sacked Rome, he brought the entirety of the Vatican archives with him to France. More than three thousand chests' worth."

"At least Napoleon was a Christian," LeFevre shot back. "He wanted nothing more than to be closer to Jesus Christ. Hitler's reputation is quite different."

Himmler crossed his left leg over his right before he spoke. "Had you read the führer's autobiography, you would know he was raised Catholic."

"Judging by the way he has treated the Jews of France, I sincerely doubt that he can truly love Jesus Christ, who was himself a Jew."

"Ah!" Himmler stood. "Yes. Precisely the problem. The matter of Jesus' alleged race."

LeFevre rose, wringing his hands. "There is no question of Jesus' background, which is why your interest in possession of the relics confounds me."

"I beg to differ. Scholars such as Dr. Seiler here have created new hope for Christianity in the Third Reich."

"By what means? Dare I ask?"

"If I may," Dr. Seiler interjected, clearing his throat. "Three years ago I embarked on an archeological expedition of the Middle East to discover whether Germanic people had served in the Roman army during biblical times. Significant evidence was found of Nordic influence, including a number of ancient sites where Germanic runes were present. And furthermore –"

"We've no time for lectures," Himmler interrupted. He removed his eyeglasses, and with a handkerchief from his pocket, leisurely wiped spots from the lenses. "To make a very long story short, our scholars at the Ahnenerbe have determined that Jesus of Nazareth is likely of Aryan descent."

LeFevre's eyes bulged. "Apparently your scholars have not even read the Bible!"

"Be honest," Himmler said. "Two thousand years of interpretations and translations. Substantial amounts of prophecy omitted or missing. Even you must admit scripture cannot be trusted word for word."

LeFevre paced the other side of the room. "Church doctrine is very clear. Jesus was borne of immaculate conception in Mary's womb."

Himmler reached inside his jacket pocket. Wolf saw a glint of metal and feared the worst. Alas, it was only a black-faced Doxa pocket watch with large white numerals. "The matter of Jesus' divinity is not in question. Those who know me realize that I am quite open to the paranormal."

"*Paranormal*? Divinity is hardly part of the occult!"

The reichsführer did not raise his voice as he spoke and wound the watch. "You will admit that the Bible never specifically identifies Mary's parents?" He gave the baffled priest only a moment to contemplate his question before continuing. "An expedition to Palestine revealed that German people were recruited into the Roman army a full century before Jesus' birth. These divisions with high concentrations of Aryan soldiers occupied Nazareth and Galilee. Further, there is ample evidence that the non-Aryan populations were moved out of Nazareth and Galilee well before Mary's birth. Do you follow me, priest?"

Father LeFevre's hands were trembling. He bore the look of a man pushed to the edge of sanity. "I am trying."

"The dissemination of genetic material, both willingly and by force, is an inevitable consequence of military occupation. Given the ethnic makeup of the Nazareth and Galilee, and the presence of young male soldiers in the vicinity, then Mary would be at least partially Aryan, if not fully Aryan."

The priest shook his head. "What is the point of this conversation?"

"The point is that this war cannot last forever. Europe cannot sustain a protracted conflict. But imagine if the führer could be persuaded to turn to Christ?"

Wolf felt dizzy. What was it that Nagel had said on the train? *The success of Ahnenerbe research and operations will be directly proportional to the cultural strength of the German people.*

"Consider it," Himmler said. "If the führer could embrace the notion of a Christian state, rooted in Germanic blood, the war could end tomorrow. Millions could be saved."

Wolf struggled to contain his emotions. Until now he he'd had trouble reconciling Himmler's passion for collecting

Christian artifacts. He wondered if it was nothing less than a desire to bottle up the entire religion and lock it away. But now he realized that he had been wrong about that. Christianity was, in fact, central to the war strategy.

The priest brushed past Wolf. Despite the frigid temperatures within the room, he reeked of nervous perspiration. "Your slim theories about the rape and resettlement of the ancient Jews will prove nothing."

"You underestimate German ambition. No one could have foreseen the invention of the V-2 rocket. A rocket that can reach London without a pilot! Just as our scientists have honed our powers of destruction, recent advancements in biological science may also expedite peace. For example, our researchers have studied nucleic acids called DNA for many decades. Are you familiar with the concept?"

"No."

"DNA is nothing less than the genetic code with which living organisms are constructed."

"Nonsense. God alone is the architect and creator."

"Perhaps. But I am told that one day soon, the concept of using cranial measurements to determine ethnicity will be replaced by DNA examination of each individual. In the meantime, blood research is an acceptable intermediary step. Already, German physicians can determine paternity from simple blood tests. Our forensic investigators can determine guilt in murder cases with a growing degree of accuracy based on dried bloodstains. Even as we speak, a racial studies team at the University of Leipzig is working to harness the ability to perform blood and DNA tests on ancient bone fragments."

Finally the priest could take no more. He opened a desk drawer and took a heavy set of keys from it. He took his lamp from the wall and opened the door. "You are wasting your time," he sighed. "I will prove it to you."

He went past Wolf and Lang toward a door at the far end of the landing.

"But the treasury is downstairs," Dr. Seiler objected.

LeFevre shook his head as he inserted a key in the door. "The occupation has left France impoverished. Even the most devout Parisians may be far too hungry to ignore the treasury's temptations."

He entered the room and lit two additional lanterns, illuminating a windowless chamber crowded with glass enclosures displaying robes, various reliquaries, crucifixes, ancient Bibles and more. The collection was every bit as crowded as Himmler's private museum – more so, in fact – but had clearly been hastily assembled.

LeFevre set his lamp to the side and unlocked a large cabinet. He pulled from it an elaborate shrine constructed of bronze and glass that, judging by the grimace on the priest's face, was quite heavy. It was 88 centimeters high, and the top was fashioned to resemble a royal crown encrusted with diamonds and other precious gems. The base was encircled by figurines, the most prominent of which was a likeness of St. Louis, sitting on a throne of lion's head armrests, holding the Holy Crown in his hands. Himmler stood behind LeFevre as the priest first donned white gloves and then removed the top, setting it carefully aside. He reached inside and removed the transparent circular reliquary that held the braided holy thrushes. The thrushes were tied together with golden thread.

He turned and held it under the lantern's illumination for Himmler and Seiler to examine. "As you can well see," LeFevre said, "There are no thorns in the crown. It is a forgery. You have wasted your time, professor."

Wolf and Lang shared a glance. The priest was clearly lying. The papal document that Himmler had brought with him, clearing the transfer of the relics to Germany, would not be enough to convince the priest to let them go without a fight.

And now a much darker fear came over Wolf. What if he was ordered to kill the priest? During his six-week training at Wewelsburg Castle, Wolf had been schooled in hand-to-hand combat, basic security, and to a lesser extent, marksmanship. He had come to the realization that he might be asked to kill an enemy spy or soldier, but he had never considered that the enemy would be a priest. That would be an unforgivable sin.

Seiler leaned forward. His small eyes seemed to dart around the relic for several moments. "If I may," he began, taking the precious circular glass into his gloved hands. Seiler's face displayed a look of mild satisfaction that worried the priest. "This *could* be authentic. Christian art traditionally portrays the crown as a thorned branch that has been twisted into a circle. But the Catholic Encyclopedia itself tells us that the crown was created from jujube reeds and the Roman soldiers plaited the thorns together into a sort of cap. It further says that the thorns themselves were distributed centuries ago, as Byzantine and French kings began the seemingly ill-advised practice of giving the thorns away as gifts. This crown would seem to be consistent with those findings."

"Even so," the priest protested, "Your scientists can learn nothing about Mary's ancestry from this."

Even as LeFevre continued to lodge protests, Seiler restored the glass containing the reeds to its home within the larger reliquary. Behind them, Himmler had located the reliquaries containing pieces of the True Cross and a nail used in the crucifixion. "Just look at the craftsmanship," he said admiringly.

LeFevre flung himself at the reichsführer, knocking Himmler off balance while wrestling the reliquary of the True Cross from his grasp. He hugged it to his chest and backed into a corner of the sacristy. The relic was pushed against his robe, revealing a set of bulging ribs, his torso having been wasted by malnourishment. His eyes darted between the five Nazis, daring them to act.

Himmler sighed. "Don't be a fool, priest. Yes, we will take the Holy Crown since it interests the professor. But these are not even the relics of the passion that we came for. They pale in comparison."

The priest gritted his teeth. "What are you talking about?"

"The Holy Ossuary, of course. The bones."

Confusion reigned in the priest's face. "Ossuary?" he repeated slowly, as if uttering the words for the first time.

Wolf had come across the term only once or twice in his ancient civilization studies. If memory served, he believed an ossuary was some sort of secondary burial crypt containing the bones of a person that had already decomposed.

Himmler's eyebrows arched. "Well well. It seems that our informant was correct. The relic is indeed a well-guarded secret. Not even the resident priest knows what riches lie within his own church."

A great crash was heard, followed by the unmistakable sound of something hard – marble, perhaps, or plaster – breaking into pieces.

Lang suddenly appeared at the doorway. "There's something going on downstairs!"

"The others must have arrived," Himmler said. "Let's go."

Dr. Seiler took the reliquary of the Holy Crown into his arms, seemingly surprised by its heft. LeFevre remained in the corner, muttering in Latin as he hugged the reliquary of the True Cross for dear life.

Wolf and Lang led the descent, followed closely by Himmler and Dr. Seiler. Wolf heard voices. German, French and – as unlikely as it seemed – Italian. As they neared the ground floor, he heard shouting, followed by the crackle of gunfire.

The foursome froze. With the others falling in line behind him, Wolf pressed his back against the stone wall, fumbling with the bolt handle of his MP-40 for a moment before managing to push it forward. The shooting went on uninterrupted for several seconds. It sounded as if at least three guns were at work, if not more. He imagined Hoffman fending off a group of French resistance fighters.

The young SS soldier was filled with insecurity. He was 15 years old. He was a child of the city. He had never so much as hunted a rabbit in his life. His rifle practice had been limited to a handful of sessions picking off stationary targets in the fields below Wewelsburg castle. More sessions had been scheduled, but a shortage of live ammunition had forced their cancellation.

"Back upstairs," Dr. Seiler urged.

"No," Himmler said. He pulled his Luger from its holster, switched it off safety, and chambered a round. "We aren't leaving without the ossuary."

"With all due respect, you are the second most powerful man in the Reich!" the professor hissed. "I am sure that the führer would agree that the bones are not worth your life."

Himmler considered this for several tense seconds. Downstairs, the gun battle continued, although it sounded as if there were now only two shooters.

"I saw a south exit at the bottom of the stairs," Wolf suggested.

Himmler nodded. "Then the professor and I will try to escape. You must go back into the cathedral and secure the ossuary."

The professor noted the blank looks on the soldiers' faces. "You are looking for a rectangular box made of chalk," he said, speaking at a rapid clip. "About 51 centimeters long and perhaps half as high. There may be inscriptions on the exterior. Hoffman was to look within or beneath the High Altar."

Seiler said more, but Wolf did not hear him. His senses heightened as the group descended the stairs. His nostrils were filled with the scent of extinguished prayer candles. The rattle of shell casings clanging against the floor tiles was so tangible that he could taste the brass in his mouth.

They reached the ground floor. Just as Wolf had remembered, the south exit to Rue Cloître Notre Dame was to their right. To their left was the entrance to the main cathedral.

"Good luck," Himmler muttered as he exited the south door with his Luger drawn. Seiler followed, his gait burdened by the heft of the reliquary of the Holy Crown.

Wolf and Lang shared a look. It was instantly understood that although they were both scared, they were going to fight. They crossed themselves. Then they crept through the doorway, the barrels of their submachine guns poking out like antennae.

They scampered into a row of pews near the Portal of the Last Judgment. The cathedral was smoky. The gunfire was sporadic now, but excruciatingly loud as it echoed in the vast acoustics of the cathedral.

It seemed to be coming from the sanctuary area. Confident that they had not yet been seen, the boys filed out into the aisle and, putting some distance between each other, crept toward the center of the church. Wolf was the first to spot the dead. Two figures dressed in thick hooded brown robes identical to those worn by the bicyclist.

Lang pointed toward the painted screen surrounding the choir. A third assailant who looked very much alive. He crouched, and then crawled, to the body of one of his fallen brethren. The assailant grabbed for the dead man's weapon. Either his own gun had jammed, Wolf figured, or he was out of ammunition.

A single shot was fired from somewhere in the church. Wolf heard it cut through the air near his head. He dropped to a knee as a second burst rang out. This time, Wolf felt a burning sensation rip through his left shoulder.

He dropped to the ground, rolled left in hopes of getting out of the line of fire, and looked at Lang. Good,

Catholic Lang. Devout Lang. He was hiding behind a pew, staring at Wolf's right shoulder, which was bleeding.

"Help me," Wolf said. But Lang did not move. For a moment, Wolf thought that he too had been hit. But then he saw the fear in his friend's eyes. He was not hurt. He was frozen in fear.

Now the assailant had moved back to the screen. He was firing again, but in the opposite direction. Wolf's shoulder was burning hot now. Letting his arm dangle to his side provided the only relief. He got to his feet and made his way down the row to the south side of the nave. The echo of gunfire in the massive structure covered the sound of his jackboots against the marble floor.

He moved into position behind the hooded figure. Forcing the pain from his mind, he knelt behind a pew, trying various firing positions without the assistance of his left arm. As he had found during training, the MP-40 was built for fighting in close proximity to one's enemy. It was practically made for rushing defensive positions. But its long vertical clip and practically nonexistent stock made it an awkward rifle to fire from a stationary position.

Wolf finally caught the assailant in his iron sights. Mother Mary of God, he thought. Forgive me for what I am about to do. And he pulled the trigger, ripping off a burst of 9mm rounds. The gun's blowback caught the inexperienced rifleman off guard. The weapon slipped, sending the bolt smashing against his forehead.

The swelling on his lower forehead was immediate and painful. But as he looked up, he saw that his shooting had been true. The robed man was slumped sideways, motionless.

All was silent. Wolf got to his feet and crept closer. Now he saw that a piece of the man's robe was caught on the woven screen surrounding the choir.

From his neck, a simple wooden cross hung from a strip of unrefined leather. Wolf crouched close to the body.

The face framed within the hood was olive-toned and sun-weathered and, judging by the length of beard, had not been shaved for a very long time. The brown eyes were open, but they saw nothing. At his side was a Beretta Model 38 machine gun. Italian made.

A faint groan came from the sanctuary. It sounded like Hoffman.

Wolf got to his feet and entered the choir area. As he neared the high altar, which was smashed into pieces, he counted three bodies in gray SS uniforms. He recognized all as former upperclassman at the Reich School. They had all received their initiation tattoos with him at Wewelsburg Castle.

He found Hoffman in a prone firing position behind a broken section of statue that had been atop the altar. A pool of blood had bloomed beneath his chest, where he had been shot.

Wolf rolled him onto his back.

"They took it," Hoffman said. The words were accompanied by a good deal of blood that seemed to have pooled in his mouth.

"Took what?" Wolf asked.

"The ossuary. The inscription…" He seemed at a loss for words.

Hoffman turned on his side, coughing up even more blood. He would be dead soon.

"Try harder," Wolf urged, keenly aware that he, too, was losing blood from his gunshot shoulder. "What did the inscription say? Tell me now!"

The obersturmführer's throat seemed to tighten. He clasped it with his right hand, as if being choked by some unseen force. He gurgled as he struggled for breath. He brought the fingers of his left hand to his lips and wetted them with blood. Then, with great difficulty, he began drawing on the white piece of broken statuary. A series of jagged, angular strokes. Wolf strained to make out the blood-streaked shapes.

Suddenly Hoffman's face turned purple, his expression one of shocked wonder. His eyes widened as he struggled for breath. Wolf grabbed the obersturmführer by his chalk-speckled tunic. "What was it?"

Wolf focused all his attention on the drawings. So many seemingly disconnected lines. He could not make out any letters at all. Could they be pictographs? His gaze intensified, as if looking through it. For one split second, his eyes crossed. And then he saw.

Hôtel-Dieu de Paris

Wolf woke in a clean hospital room with yellow walls. It was still dark outside, and he could hear rain beating against the window. His left arm rested in a sling at his side. The gunshot had passed through the muscle, narrowly missing the bone.

He rose up briefly before the pounding in his head forced him back into the pillow. His stomach gurgled, and then twitched. He turned on his side and promptly vomited over the edge of the bed. The foul-smelling goop stank of alcohol.

He wiped his mouth with his forearm, turned onto his back and tried to piece together how he had gotten here. He remembered being pulled away from Hoffman's body. He sat up despite the pain in his shoulder, trying to remove the cobwebs from his mind.

He recalled meeting an elderly French surgeon whose breath smelled of strong liquor. He had only looked at Wolf's shoulder for a moment before declaring that he would have to remove the bullet immediately.

"We're out of penicillin," he had warned. "And anesthetic. The Wehrmacht sent it to the eastern front."

The surgeon cleaned the wound from the same bottle of homemade grain alcohol from which he had been drinking moments before. He then passed the bottle to Wolf and encouraged him to take several long drinks. "For the pain," he said. That was the last thing Wolf remembered.

He had dreamt of Hoffman's bloody scrawl. Unlike his other memories, the formations were crisp and clear in his mind.

A nurse entered the room and opened the window opposite the bed. Pretty, and thin, but with a hateful look in her eyes. Wolf felt vulnerable here under the medical care of the occupied French. Where were his clothes? He remembered what Dr. Seiler had said the night before. *"The resistance is always looking for opportunities to kill Germans. That goes double for those that threaten its cultural heritage."* Where was Lang? Why had he left him all alone here?

The nurse went to him and felt his forehead. "Too hot." Then she removed the sling and the bandage to look at the wound. "Not infected."

Wolf somehow doubted she would tell him if it was.

He fell back into a fitful sleep. He relived the cathedral firefight over and over in his dreams. In one dream, Himmler had been gunned down in the streets outside the cathedral. Or had that really happened? He could not know for sure.

He woke himself as he cried out for his mother. Judging by the light coming in through the shades, it was afternoon. Nobody seemed to be around. Was he the only patient in this hospital? Although still unwashed, his clothes were folded and placed near the bed. He wanted to look around, but still felt too weak.

The old surgeon returned sometime after dark. He was anxious and spoke of unrest in the streets. Notre Dame had been desecrated by occupation forces, he said. Three monks had been murdered inside.

Those so-called monks had been carrying machine guns, Wolf thought. He was pretty sure that had really happened.

The surgeon rambled on. It seemed that there had already been reprisals. A nightclub frequented by German officers had been blown up in the nearby 6th arrondissement. At least ten Wehrmacht soldiers had been killed in separate street attacks across the city.

Wolf sat up and reached for his clothes. "No," the surgeon objected. "The wound has not been cleaned in hours! You could get an infection!"

Of course he would say that. *The resistance is always looking for opportunities to kill Germans.* Wolf pushed the doctor aside. He put on his pants. Then he put on his brown shirt, which was crisp with dried blood, and his tunic and overcoat. All three top layers had a hole in the left shoulder.

Waiving off the surgeon's protests, he went downstairs to the hospital's administration office. The dreary office was full of unhappy patients. When they saw Wolf's black SS uniform, they slowly slipped out of the room, carefully avoiding eye contact.

Wolf sat at an empty desk. He picked up the telephone, connected with the local operator, and asked to be connected with Ahnenerbe headquarters in Berlin.

"Who is speaking?" the operator asked.

Wolf declined to say. "I just want to know whether Reichsführer Himmler has returned safely from Paris," he replied.

The question was self-serving. If Himmler had made it home safely, Wolf might be credited with ensuring his safety. On the other hand, if Himmler had been gunned down in the streets of Paris, Wolf imagined he would be held responsible. It would be his death warrant.

His question was met by a moment of silence. Suddenly the voice on the other end turned hostile, demanding to know his name and rank. Wolf hung up immediately.

German Barracks
11th Arrondissement

After leaving the hospital, Wolf recuperated in a former French military barracks that had been taken over by the German army. His pain had gradually subsided, but the low-grade fever had remained. The French surgeon's claims had been true – all penicillin, and even the unit's medic, had been shipped to the eastern front.

When he had arrived, he had shared the room with two other patients, both of whom were the victims of attacks by the French resistance. While under the care of a big-boned farm girl from the Loire Valley who had been sent by the foreign ministry, the other two had died in their sleep. She went about her business of tending to wounded Nazis dutifully, if not joyfully. Wolf welcomed the cold compresses she placed on his head, but refused her pots of herbal tea. He decided to eat only from the hand of another German, even if it meant starving to death.

Now the radio alternated between cheerful chanson and anti-Semitic propaganda. The girl sat in a wooden chair while mending the bullet hole in Wolf's tunic. Suddenly the radio station broke for a message from Heinrich Himmler. At this, Wolf sat straight up in bed. Until now, he had not been certain whether Himmler was dead or alive.

The reichsführer began his radio address by describing glorious victories in North Africa. He did not mention Paris, nor did he mention Stalingrad. He ended the holiday message by encouraging all troops to celebrate the Winter Solstice.

At this, the nurse's face twisted in puzzlement. She had said little to Wolf until now. "Solstice?" she questioned. "Don't you Nazis celebrate Christmas?"

A simple question. The answer, colored by what he had seen in the past several weeks, was more complicated than Wolf cared to admit. He could no more share what he had learned with the farm girl than he could with his own mother.

"Well?"

The door at the far end of the room opened. To Wolf's astonishment, the soldier standing in the doorway was none other than his childhood friend.

Lang looked considerably thinner, as if he had been wandering the streets of Paris for days without food. He sprang more than walked to Wolf's bed. The farm girl stood and backed away.

"Where have you been?" Wolf demanded.

"Never mind that," Lang said. "Can you travel?"

"He's still running a fever," the farm girl protested.

Lang didn't look at her. "We are to report at Wewelsburg Castle in eight days. Eight days! If we leave now, we can go home for Christmas."

Gare du Nord

By chance, the train that Wolf and Lang boarded was the same that they had taken to Paris days earlier. The elderly conductor recognized them right away.

"Boys!" he exclaimed, noting Lang's frail disposition and Wolf's arm sling. "Let me show you to a private car. The least I can do. The very least!"

This time, Wolf helped himself to some schnapps in the bar. Lang tried to stop him. "What if the Gestapo sees you drinking?"

"I would call it medicine," Wolf told him, although he was the first to agree that puritanism seemed to be in vogue. The previous year, the Nazi Party was said to have authorized the sterilization of more than five thousand known alcoholics. Anti-smoking and -drinking campaigns featuring healthy Aryan babies were plastered all over public transportation.

They had spoken little until now, having been under armed chaperone en route to the train. "Not a word to my mother about this," Wolf said, gesturing with his arm sling.

"Sebastian," Lang began, speaking just loud enough to be heard over the grind of the train. It was the first time in ages that anyone had called Wolf by his first name. "When we were in the staircase at Notre Dame, Himmler had said something about an ossuary."

Wolf nodded. "I remember."

"He said the ossuary was important. Do you know what he meant?"

Wolf was not certain of what he was allowed to share with his friend. Himmler had ordered Lang to stand in the hallway outside the priest's quarters. Surely that had been a random security assignment, had it not? He and Lang were identical in rank, experience and education.

Even so, was he free to share what he had heard? Perhaps it was better not to take any chances, he decided. Besides, he knew next to nothing. Himmler had mentioned the ossuary only once, in the treasure room. He had called it a Holy Ossuary, although he had not specified the name of the saint whose bones supposedly resided in Notre Dame.

"I don't know," Wolf said at last.

"Those men in the robes," Lang pressed. "Did they look like French resistance to you?"

Wolf shook his head. The simple robes. The crosses. They had seemed more like monks than the freedom fighters he had imagined.

"I went back to Notre Dame that night," Lang continued. "After dropping you at to the hospital."

Wolf set his glass on the bar. "Are you crazy? What if they had returned?"

"By the time I went back, the police had arrived. They were loading the bodies into a truck. I identified Hoffman so they could take his body back to his family. Did you happen to notice what was in his mouth?"

"There was nothing in his mouth except blood," Wolf said. "He was trying to explain what he saw. I told him to write it instead."

"Then they put it there after we left."

"Put what there?"

"This." Lang reached into a tunic pocket. He held a piece of black-and-red striped fabric that had been cut into an octagon shape. "It was sticking out from between his lips."

On one side, a phrase was stitched in golden thread: *Ad majorem dei gloriam.* The other side read, *Paratus enim dolor et cruciatus, in Dei nomine.*

Wolf Residence Munich

Aside from any changes he had made during occasional visits home, Wolf's mother maintained his bedroom as it was when her son had left it before leaving for the Reich School in 1938. An oval-framed faculty photograph of his late father hung on the far wall. Atop the dresser, a chessboard with ivory pieces. A small statue of the Virgin Mary. A bowl containing a rosary.

On the far wall, a remarkable sketch signed by a young Dutch artist name Escher that his father had purchased for his 11th birthday. And hanging over the bed, an oversized silver crucifix. Even here in Munich, the very heart of National Socialism, he could not escape Christ's accusing glare.

He heard the strains of Richard Strauss through the wall. For as long as Wolf could remember, playing Strauss had been his mother's version of civil disobedience. Strauss, whom Goebbels had once appointed president of the *Reichsmusikkammer*, had been officially censored for a number of political infractions. Only the composer's popularity had kept him out of prison. Real Nazis, it was said, listened to Wagner, who had gone public with his anti-Semitism long before Hitler had even been born.

As he had done twice each day since arriving home, Wolf slipped out of bed, turned and knelt, resting his elbows – both of them – on the bed. As far as he was concerned, the pain shooting down his left shoulder during these prayer sessions was entirely deserved.

He had killed a man, and in a church, no less. He had contributed to the desecration of one of the most holy cathedrals in Europe. He had listened to Himmler speak blasphemously about the Holy Mother and yet had done nothing to stop him. He was both a coward and a murderer.

Making matters worse, he had lied to his mother, telling her that his gunshot had been a training accident. She already had one son in combat. There was no sense in having her worry about both of them.

His head ballooned with heretical notions. Curiosities seeded by Himmler, the very man his parents had warned him about. The infallibility of the pope. The authenticity of a Bible that had been edited and translated through the ages. The ethnicity of the Holy Mother.

Round and round his thoughts went like some sinister carousel. He prayed that these ideas would be vanquished from his mind. He prayed for his mother, who had still not heard any news about his brother, Hans, from the eastern front. He prayed for Lang, who had seemed like a stranger to him since the firefight in Notre Dame.

Wolf stopped short of praying for a German victory. How could he? In just four short days, he was to return to Wewelsburg Castle, where Himmler was stockpiling the world's great Christian artifacts. As he had learned in Paris, Himmler was no closeted Catholic, as Wolf had hoped when he had browsed the treasures in the castle museum. He was intent on co-opting Christianity for political and military gain. If Germany won the war, the Holy Roman Empire would be restored, and Christians worldwide would look not to Rome or Jerusalem, but to Wewelsburg Castle. Their Jesus would be recast with Aryan features and a Germanic bloodline.

The music in the other room stopped. Wolf heard the radio flicker on. The announcer's voice was muffled, but there was urgency in his tone.

Wolf rose, exited the bedroom and went to the living room, where his mother was sitting in a chair near the radio. She covered her face with her hands as she wept. That could only mean one thing – there had been news about his brother's outfit.

Wolf kissed her on the forehead and turned the volume on the radio back up and listened to the rest of the news bulletin. Although surrounded, the Sixth Army has vowed to fight to the last man, the announcer said. They would rather die than surrender to the atheist Bolsheviks.

Lang Residence
Suburban Munich
Christmas Day

The Lang country home sat on several acres of suburban Munich at the edge of the Perlacher Forest. Mrs. Lang – a tall, gregarious woman in a pretty green party blouse – met Sebastian Wolf and his mother, Gertrude, at the door.

Mrs. Lang had toted the party line well enough to maneuver her son into a position at the Reich School, and later, into the Ahnenerbe. But on this night, in the privacy of her own home, she wore makeup. She wore pants that had been imported from America. And she was smoking. Not exactly a candidate for the National Cross of Motherhood.

She showed them into the living room, where a square bench made of birch surrounded a magnificent fireplace. The extravagant size of the home was grounded by its rustic furnishings. In the far corner, someone played carols on a grand piano.

Mrs. Lang offered the Wolfs some cherry brandy from the bar. In addition to the Lang's four children, several dinner guests were already on hand. Most were familiar family friends, although with the exception of the Langs, Sebastian had seen none of them since leaving for school. Looking dapper in a simple gray suit and white arm sling, he listened politely as the other guests fawned over how much he had grown in the past four years.

Heinz Lang was all smiles as he bounced downstairs with his dog at his side. The sight of his black SS uniform immediately quieted the room. The piano faltered, and then trickled to a halt. Although the boys' recruitment into the Ahnenerbe was known to all, the presence of the uniform was jarring. The guest list consisted entirely of what Mrs. Lang called antisocial Nazis – those who had joined the party only to avoid suspicion.

Seeking to deflect the awkwardness, Mrs. Lang turned her attention to Wolf. "Sebastian dear. How is your shoulder?"

"On the mend. Even if Heinz did take me to a drunk French surgeon."

The guests laughed, the piano resumed, and the room crackled back to life. When asked about his war wound, Wolf repeated the same story that he and Lang had agreed to on the train back to Munich. They had been conducting research in Paris, he told them. A French policeman had tripped and fired his gun. Merely a random accident. There was nothing for anyone to worry about.

In truth, Wolf felt less confident about his recuperation than he let on. It was true that he was regaining range of motion and his mother, an experienced nurse, had dressed the wound the night before, proclaiming it free of infection. But the sweats he had experienced in Paris still came and went. At times they left him dizzy. And when he slept, he was haunted by demons. He saw the faces carved in the Portal of the Last Judgment. He saw the symbols that Hoffman had written in his own blood. He had left Notre Dame, but the cathedral had not yet left him.

Mrs. Lang took Gertrude aside and, with a hand on her shoulder, chatted in a corner of the room. Wolf did not have to read lips to know what they spoke of. Everyone had heard news of Stalingrad. Gertrude had been up all night crying.

The smell of roasted goose wafted in from the dining room, and the guests did not wait to be invited to the table. Wolf was astonished when he saw not just one bird, but two, on identical silver platters. The sight of so much meat was shocking.

"You must have been saving your food stamps for months," Gertrude said. Wolf knew otherwise. Mr. Lang, who was a high-ranking official in the Ministry of Education, had acquired the birds through a connection.

Mrs. Lang called out across the room. "Father Kruger! Come to the table!"

Had she said Kruger? Wolf had known a Father Kruger once. A Jesuit priest from his old parochial school. A formidable teacher who could recite countless texts on any number of subjects from memory.

The pianist maneuvered from the song's bridge into several closing chords. He pushed the bench out from behind him and made his way to the table. The Father Kruger that Wolf had known had been barrel-chested with thick, powerful forearms that were impressive even under the long sleeves of his black cassock.

This man was disturbingly thin. He wore a gray civilian sweater with a white oxford shirt and a black tie. He had thinning gray hair that was long and slicked back behind his ears. He avoided eye contact with the other guests.

Yet it *was* him. Remarkably transformed in just three years.

"Father Kruger," Wolf said. "It's Sebastian Wolf. Do you remember me?"

The priest sat down and placed his napkin in his lap before looking up. "Yes," he answered. "You were quite bright, as I remember. And quite ambitious, evidently."

Mrs. Lang tapped her wine glass. Conversation among the 12 guests stopped. "At the risk of being cruel, I should like to delay our meal for just a moment longer for a Christmas prayer. Father Kruger, would you give us the honor?"

The priest placed both hands flat on the table. "Although I trust we are all friends here," he said, his eyes glancing across Lang's uniform, "I have signed an oath that I will refrain from engaging in any type of religious ritual. I therefore must, with much regret, pass."

The table was quiet for several awkward moments. At last Gertrude raised her glass. "Well then, if we can't pray, then I will propose a toast."

At 36, Gertrude's good looks defied all that she had been through in the past four years: the death of her husband, the job she had taken at *Lebensborn*, and four months without letters from her oldest son. Her chin was still angular, her hips were reasonably trim, and most of her wavy hair was still golden.

"First," she said, "A toast to the Langs for bringing a bit of cheer into our lives today." The guests sounded murmurs of approval. "Second, I'm grateful for the sons that could be with us today, and I pray for those who are yet far afield that the Lord may watch over them and deliver them home safely. Finally, I express my gratitude for returning Father Kruger to us after so many years. This alone should give us all hope."

Arms crisscrossed as wine glasses clinked and lively chatter commenced. Plates were passed as Mrs. Lang carved the goose.

Wolf leaned into his mother's ear and whispered. "What happened to him?"

Gertrude smiled for show, as if she were about to whisper something amusing. She shielded her lips with her wine glass, and spoke. "The Dachau camp."

Wolf had a vague notion of the prison camp located in the suburb of Dachau, a 30-minute train ride from central Munich. It was rumored to be the principal destination for political prisoners, including a large number of Christian and Jewish clergy that refused to toe the party line. Lately he had heard rumors that captured Russian prisoners were taken there to make munitions.

As curious as Wolf was about the crime Father Kruger had committed, and in the punishment he had received, another agenda was rapidly forming in his mind. He resolved to find out where Father Kruger spent his days now. He had important questions that he wondered if his old schoolmaster could answer.

BMW Factory
Munich

Wolf stepped off the bus in front of the BMW factory. He heard a distant droning and peered skyward, scanning the skies for aircraft. Although Cologne had so far gotten the worst of the British air raids, Munich had not been entirely spared. It too had suffered a raid in September. The city's first taste of British bombardment had been relatively mild, but Wolf figured that sooner or later, the BMW factory – which had shifted most of its production toward aircraft engines and military motorcycles – would be on the Allied hit list.

"It's just the machines," a gravelly voice said.

Wolf turned. The voice belonged to a man in a brown jumpsuit with a circular BMW logo patch on the front. His hair was gray and wild atop his head, like a fox that had rubbed itself in the dirt.

"That sound," the man clarified. "It's not the RAF. It's just the machines inside the factory."

"You work here?"

"Yes. I have papers if you need to see them."

"Relax," Wolf said. He pointed at the insignia on the lapels of his black SS uniform. "I'm not Gestapo. I'm looking for a man named Leo Kruger."

"East wing, third floor. Kruger works on pistons."

Wolf tipped his hat and went on his way, striding through the front doors without pausing at reception. Although not yet an officer, nobody seemed to question the legitimacy of a black SS uniform. Besides, he did not want his visit documented. This was personal business.

He walked past rows of identically dressed workers assembling propellers. Each worker had a nameplate, a number and various tools and parts before him. The workers were, without exception, gray or silver-haired.

Wolf broke out into a sweat as he took the stairs to the third floor and surveyed another hundred or so workers. He easily spotted the supervisor, who was, judging by the amount of fat around his midsection, enjoying extra food rations.

"I'm looking for Kruger," Wolf whispered. The supervisor walked into the middle of the floor and plucked Kruger out of one of the rows of workers.

The former priest wore a greasy blue shirt and a black wool cap. Eyes cast downward, back bent. Sleeves were rolled up, revealing forearms streaked with scar tissue.

When Kruger had spoken of his employment at BMW, Wolf had imagined that the great Jesuit teacher was some sort of supervisor, perhaps leading a team of researchers. He imagined Kruger smartly dressed, drawing up development plans on a drafting board. Although the priest had said nothing to lead him to this conclusion, Wolf felt somehow beguiled by the man standing before him now.

The two exchanged perfunctory greetings. Virtually every single worker on the floor was watching them.

"Is there somewhere we can talk privately?"

Kruger leaned close, speaking into Wolf's ear. "Sebastian," he said, "you've managed to build something for yourself. You can't afford to be seen with someone like me."

"Nonsense," Wolf insisted. "I need to talk to you. Is there somewhere we can go?"

Kruger motioned to the wider room. "Obviously not."

"Then meet me after work. Please."

Kruger hesitated, feeling the eyes of his fellow workers on him. "Where?"

"Haufbrauhaus," Wolf whispered. It was one of the oldest and most popular beer halls in Munich. Although there was far less drunkenness on display in recent years, it was still lively.

"No. Too public."

"Then the *Ratskellar*," Wolf suggested, referring to the basement restaurant beneath the medieval town hall building with the famous *Glockenspiel* clock tower. It was cavernous, a bit darker than the other beer halls, and certainly less popular.

Kruger stepped back and spat on the cement floor. "Five thirty," he said. "Be punctual."

Marienplatz
Munich

At 5 pm, Wolf set out for the Ratskellar, leaving his arm sling behind for the first time since leaving the hospital in Paris. The shoulder still throbbed, but he thought it wise to toughen himself up before reporting for duty again. Nagel had questioned his suitability for service repeatedly during training, mocking his dream of a life in academia. By his third week at Wewelsburg Castle, Wolf decided that he would never again reveal any weakness, no matter how difficult those shortcomings were to mask. From then on, he resolved to live the motto that was inscribed on his dagger: *Be more than you seem.*

  He walked through his old neighborhood, noting with regret how quickly the architectural perfection of Marienplatz was being changed by the war. The façade of a bank had been reduced to brick during the September air raids. In response, two anti-aircraft batteries had been erected on opposite sides of the square. Several Hitler Youth patrols roamed the streets. The patrol leaders were younger and more aggressive than ever before. As dusk fell, a pack of boys went door to door, ordering shopkeepers to turn off their lights so as to deprive Allied planes of ground targets.

  On another corner, a pair of boys harassed a young woman for being too thin. Slim women were not good for childbearing, one of them told her. She should fatten up and find a husband.

  "And how is she supposed to do that?" Wolf shouted as he came up behind the youth patrol. The boys stood at attention at the sight of Wolf's uniform. "All the able-bodied men are at war, and the government is rationing food. What is she to do? Boil wallpaper and marry one of you?"

The girl – she could not have been more than 17 – flashed Wolf a grateful smile as she slipped away from the stunned youth brigade. He stood unmoving for a time, surprised at how his presence seemed to freeze the boys where they stood while the crowds in Marienplatz moved around them. There were six of them. He guessed they were 12 or 13 years old, although they seemed jaded beyond their years. He had heard that some of the youth brigades had been taken on field trips into Poland, where they practiced giving orders to political prisoners living in the ghettos. Show no pity, they were told. He was quite certain this bunch would have no trouble with that.

He dismissed them. They dispersed like a pack of puppies, moving to the other side of the square, where they would no doubt refocus their harassment on someone else. Wolf sighed in relief. If one of the little punks had so much as gripped his left shoulder, he would have been driven to his knees.

The Glockenspiel clock tower on the town hall was covered with a draping red swastika banner. Wolf walked under it, through the main archway and into the interior courtyard. He descended two sets of stairs and stood just above one of several Ratskellar dining rooms. As he had hoped, it was not busy. A few tables occupied by old men.

A maître d' in a smart suit approached. "Table for one?"

Wolf straightened his posture, working through the pain as he brought his shoulders into alignment. "I'm meeting someone. Take me somewhere private."

He was led through the first room, into a smaller secondary dining room, where there were fewer lights. Wolf sat at a corner table with his back to the wall. He pulled out a silver cigarette case and opened it, revealing several dozen food stamps. He presented them to a waiter and ordered two beers.

He didn't have to wait long. Leo Kruger arrived at the precise moment that the drinks were delivered to the table. Kruger sat down uneasily. The sullied blue shirt and dirty face told Wolf that he hadn't had time to stop home from work yet.

"Father Kruger," Wolf said. He gestured toward the second beer. "Please."

Kruger sat, but did not touch the mug. "Perhaps I wasn't clear at dinner," Kruger said. "I am no longer a priest."

Laughter swelled from the adjoining hall. Kruger turned to look.

"Don't worry about them," Wolf said. "It's good to see you. Of all the teachers, you were the best. Do you remember how you would sometimes let us stay after school? We could ask you about any subject, and you would talk for hours."

"Don't be delusional," Kruger snapped. "Everything has changed. What do you want from me?"

Wolf reached into his overcoat and removed a piece of paper. He set it on the table and unfolded it. On it he had written the foreign letters that he had watched Hoffman write with his own blood. "Do you recognize this?"

A waiter walked past on his way from the kitchen to the next room. Kruger turned and waited until he was out of earshot before speaking. "Where did you see this?"

Wolf hesitated. "France," he said, but thought better of providing more details.

"Odd," the priest said. "At the Louvre, perhaps?"

"No." Wolf sipped his beer, relishing the way the bubbles percolated on his tongue.

"The writing is an ancient form of Aramaic," Kruger said, his demeanor warming slightly. He slurped the foam from the top of his own mug. "And why is a Nazi asking me to translate a language that is most commonly associated with ancient Jews?"

"I'm not a Nazi," Wolf said in a voice that was at once defensive and yet barely audible. "At least not by choice."

"We all have a choice, Sebastian. I chose not to indoctrinate my students with propaganda. For that I spent three years in Dachau prison."

The bite in Kruger's tone was palpable. "I admire you for what you did."

"What good did it do? The result of my pride is sitting right in front of me."

Wolf felt suddenly small. "I was drafted," he explained. "Besides, the Ahnenerbe is a sort of research organization, full of academics."

"That description is generous, if not completely inaccurate. The Ahnenerbe generates politically convenient propaganda through the study of ancient Germanic cultures."

"Well, you could –"

"That's not up for debate. So I'll ask you again. Why is a Nazi asking me about a language spoken by ancient Jews?"

Wolf lowered his voice a notch. "I watched a man die while writing those letters in his own blood. He seemed to think they were important, and I'm trying to find out why. I owe him that much."

The ex-teacher took a long drink from his beer stein. He studied the writing once again. "The words are very simple and clear. *Yeshua bar Yehosef.* Jesus, son of Joseph."

The young soldier sat back in his chair, contemplating what he had just heard. The Holy Ossuary. Could it be true? Could it be the ossuary of Jesus? The Gospels and the apocryphal texts differed slightly on some points, but the primary narrative was well-established. Jesus had been crucified, and had died at some time before Longinus the Centurion had come with his famous spear. A wealthy man named Joseph of Arimethea, with the help of Nicodimus, had volunteered to take the body. They applied myrrh and aloes and placed the body in a tomb that Joseph had in fact created for himself. Three days later, Mary Magdalene had visited the tomb with two others and found it empty. The body had vanished. Soon afterwards, she had been the first to witness the resurrected messiah. Not as a ghost, but in the flesh. The existence of a Holy Ossuary would call into question the literal interpretation of the resurrection itself.

Wolf did not care what Himmler believed. He did not care what Dr. Seiler believed. They weren't even Christians. But the fact that the ossuary with Jesus' name on it had been kept in one of the world's great churches was another matter. Clearly, someone powerful within the church had believed it.

If only Kruger were still a priest, Wolf thought. Then I would confess what I saw. I would even confess what I have done.

"I learned Aramaic when I was a young apprentice," Kruger volunteered. "Back in the days when his Holiness Pope Pius XII was known as Nuncio Pacelli, I had the pleasure of serving him here in Munich. He knew of my fondness for languages. We would often speak Italian and of course, Latin. One summer he and his housekeeper, Sister Klara, arranged for me to apprentice in the Vatican Archives.

"I could not believe my luck," Kruger went on. "By day I worked long hours doing grunt labor. But the evenings were mine to explore. I gravitated towards the oldest works. The ancient codices. Fragments of cloth with ancient text printed on them. It was then that I encountered the languages that Christ had known. I was exhilarated."

The former priest drank more ale.

"Does the Vatican," Wolf said, pausing before he finished his sentence, "possess any alternate histories of the resurrection?"

Kruger's face was suddenly serious. "*Alternate* history? Everyone has doubts, Sebastian. It doesn't mean we can retell the stories as they suit us."

"That's not what I meant," Wolf said. "Is the manner of the resurrection ever debated behind closed doors? Is it possible that Jesus returned in spirit form only?"

Kruger shook his head. *"Handle me and see, for a spirit does not have flesh and bones, as you see that I have. Luke 24:39. Put your finger here, and see my hands; and put out your hand, and place it in my side; do not be faithless, but believing. John 20:27."*

Hearing scripture quenched something deep inside Wolf's soul. He had not been able to read the Bible, much less attend mass, since leaving for the Reich School years earlier. But the question remained unanswered.

"What of the other witnesses?" Wolf countered. "For example, Jesus is said to have told Mary specifically not to touch him. Paul also did not experience the flesh. He claims to have seen a light from heaven and heard Jesus' voice. Luke and Mark both related that Jesus appeared in a form other than his earthly self. Only later did they recognize him as Jesus, at which point he vanished like an apparition."

"As I have said repeatedly, I'm no longer qualified to give you spiritual advice. But I should warn you – interpret the story literally, but not the words themselves. After all, when Jesus spoke to crowds, he always spoke in parables."

"You did not answer the question."

"Christ returned from the dead. The salvation of believers was confirmed. The form in which he rose does not matter."

But it did matter. The truth was everything to Wolf. If Himmler sought the bones of Jesus Christ, then, for the sake of his mother, Wolf was content to play along so long as the bones did not really exist. But if they did exist, then everything he had ever believed would be called into question.

Wolf reached into his tunic and removed the octagon-shaped fabric Lang had purportedly found in Hoffman's mouth. It was stiff in his hands, crusted with a combination of Hoffman's saliva and blood. He placed it on the table.

Kruger bent to read the Latin inscription, but he did not touch it. Wolf thought he saw recognition in the old Jesuit's eyes. And fear.

"You've seen this before," Wolf said.

Kruger stood up and put on his weathered coat. "You are into something that you cannot possibly imagine," he warned.

"What is this?"

The former priest paused before leaving. "It's safer if you don't know. I urge you to find another path, Sebastian. May God keep and protect you."

Wewelsburg Castle

Wolf, Lang and nine other young Ahnenerbe paramilitary soldiers stood in a neat row atop the Wewelsburg Castle's North Tower. A light snow had dusted the castle and the surrounding forest the preceding night. Wolf's nose, which had been running earlier, had frozen solid. He rocked back and forth on the soles of his feet to avoid losing the feeling in his toes.

He peered through the notches between the tower battlements and saw the movements of the prison workers on the distant hillside. Had Nagel been truthful when he had said they could go free at any time, if only they would renounce their beliefs and fight in the army? If so, the conviction of their beliefs was remarkable. They were doing what millions of Germans did not have the courage to do.

The noisy stomp of Nagel's jackboots echoed up the stone staircase, then fell quiet as he reached the freshly powdered tower landing. All right arms stiffened in a salute. Nagel prowled behind them for several moments without speaking. He had not seen any of them since they had deployed to France, yet he did not offer them a general greeting.

"Wolf!" Nagel suddenly barked. "Step forward."

His mind exploded with possible infractions. Perhaps someone had seen him at the BMW plant, using his uniform to gain access to Father Kruger. Or with Father Kruger at Ratskellar. Or perhaps it had been the way he had chastised the Hitler Youth patrol as they harassed the girl in Marienplatz. First among the Reich's Ten Commandments would surely be Show No Pity.

He took one step, careful not to lose his footing on the icy flagstone. He felt Nagel pace behind him, and then saw him circle in front. His expression was grave.

"During the operation in Paris," Nagel announced, "Mr. Wolf showed extreme bravery. Even while wounded, he exacted lethal force to facilitate the reichsführer's escape from a hostile environment." Nagel opened his right fist, revealing an oval-shaped slice of black German steel. The design featured a swastika-emblazoned helmet with two swords crossed behind it. "It is with great pleasure that I now present him with the War Wound badge."

Wolf did not breathe as Nagel unbuttoned his coat and pinned the decoration to the left breast of his tunic. He watched as the commandant stepped backwards robotically and shouted "Heil Hitler!" The unit echoed the sentiment by repeating in unison.

He had only twitched when Nagel said, "Stay where you are."

Now he paced slowly in front of the unit. "But why was Wolf wounded at all?" he said, glowering at each of them. "Why were three of his fellow unit members killed in action? Why was the object we were to retrieve snatched out from under us?" Nagel looped behind them. "Lang? How about you? Can you tell us?"

"No sir," Lang responded with uncertainty in his voice.

"Because the enemy was waiting for us, my boys. They knew precisely when we would arrive."

The morning silence returned for an instant. A frozen wind blew, carrying the voices of the prison workers at the bottom of the castle. And then it was overshadowed by a light gurgling sound. A gasp. The irregular rhythm of shuffling feet.

The body of Matthias Ulrich fell out of line, collapsing face-first against the thinly dusted brickwork. The snow around him grew red and then began to melt as the hot blood rushed from Ulrich's jugular. Nagel stepped over his body. His dagger hung loosely from his left glove, shimmering with Ulrich's fluids.

The castle commandant turned and let the boys sweat for several moments. "Would Ulrich's partner in crime care to confess now? I promise to forgo summary execution, and recommend a fair trial."

There were no utterances from the ranks. Only the flapping of a swastika banner that hung from one of the battlements.

*

Matthias Ulrich was the only cadet to die atop the North Tower that morning. While the other eight surviving members of their unit were escorted downstairs, Wolf and Lang were quietly led inside the North Tower's upper room. It had been off-limits to the unit during their six-week training, and the shaken soldiers were surprised to find a lecture hall with modern amenities. A professor presented to an audience of civilian and military Ahnenerbe leadership.

Wolf and Lang stood in the back. Cold and traumatized as they were, they were captivated by a large projection screen showing the faces of two men, an adult woman and a baby. The woman had the letters OO typed beneath her face. The men were labeled A and AB. A question mark loomed below the baby's face.

Dr. Gustav Hahn, a plump, balding 63-year-old with a bushy, silver mustache, spoke at the podium. Wolf remembered Hahn from a conference his father had hosted at the University of Munich in 1937. He was the professor of Racial Studies at the University of Leipzig, and also headed the Society for Blood Group Research.

"In this case," he said as he pointed a fat finger at the screen, "a question of paternity between a Jewish male and an Aryan male left some question as to whether the child could be considered German.

"Three years ago, our former colleague, Karl Landsteiner, published a paper confirming the presence of the Rh factor in all known human blood. This past summer we were able to infuse Landsteiner's research with our own findings and determine paternity, confirming German citizenship for the child."

The audience clapped enthusiastically. But who was Karl Landsteiner? Wolf had never heard of him.

A man in a gray suit stood and began talking about the implications of the study on government legislation. As Hahn listened, smoke rolled off the Leitz Parvo 100, a slide projector like the one Wolf himself had operated at the Reich School. Professor Hahn quickly unplugged the projector, bent over it and blew. Hahn's breath hardly cooled the lamp – the shiny, heavy, black machine suddenly burst into flames. The audience roared with laughter as Hahn tore off his suit jacket and used it to smother the fire.

Heinrich Himmler stood, raising his arms above his head to restore order. Wolf had not noticed the reichsführer sitting in the front row. "Professor Hahn," he said, "The case study is almost as impressive as your firefighting."

The audience laughed again, which Himmler tolerated for a moment before renewing his call for silence. "Professor, does this mean that we can now conclusively determine racial identity through blood testing?"

Hahn removed a handkerchief from his pocket and used it to wipe sweat from his neck and forehead. "Herr Himmler, I can always count on you to get to the heart of the matter. Under the right conditions, we can now identify some genetic traits commonly associated with race at about 72 percent certainty."

"You seem very sure of your figures."

The professor nodded. "Last year we performed a double-blind study in which we exhumed the bodies of 200 deceased prisoners. Through an examination of the bodies and interviews with those who knew them, we documented hair color and eye color. At the same time, we gave a research team only dried blood samples from the prisoners for examination, keeping them ignorant of any other information. Using the techniques we developed, the team was able to properly identify nearly all the blue-eyed prisoners and most of the green-eyed prisoners. They also properly determined hair color in a minority of the prisoners."

The audience seemed to stop breathing as they awaited Himmler's response. Although it was quite cold in the building, large pools of perspiration-soaked fabric were growing under the arms of Hahn's shirt.

"While I am pleased to hear of progress," Himmler conceded finally, "We must do better. We must strive for 100 percent capability. I ask that you conceive of an accelerated plan and submit it to my office by the end of January."

"Yes, Reichsführer."

"And one other thing. We are never to speak of Karl Landsteiner in public again. Please make a note of it."

Wolf leaned to whisper in his friend's ear. "Who is Landsteiner?"

Lang shrugged. "Does it matter? We'll never hear his name mentioned again."

Attendants with white gloves pushed the room's massive double doors open. While Himmler was ushered away to more pressing business, Professor Hahn collected the burned Parvo 100 and carried it offstage. Non-Ahnenerbe personnel were summarily dismissed from the room, reducing the head count to Wolf, Lang, Nagel and a handful of academics who had worn their SS dress uniforms for the occasion.

"Mr. Wolf," a voice intoned. He turned and saw Dr. Seiler, whom he had last seen fleeing Notre Dame with the reliquary of the Holy Crown. He looked less impressive in his ill-fitting tunic. "Sebastian Wolf, isn't it?"

"Yes sir."

"I see congratulations are in order." He pointed to the Wound Badge pinned to Wolf's tunic. "Your mother will be proud."

"Indeed," Wolf said agreeably, although the truth was exactly the opposite. His mother had sacrificed everything – including her principles – to get him into the Reich School so that he might sit out the war within the safe confines of an Ahnenerbe research lab. He would have to hide the badge on his next trip home.

Waiters rolled in a pair of wheeled tables bearing hot coffee and an assortment of sausages and pastries. At the professor's urging, Wolf populated a plate with a few items, but could not force himself to eat. There had been far too much blood this morning – talk of it, and spilling of it – to whet his appetite.

"You are no doubt wondering about the fate of the so-called Holy Crown," Seiler began, speaking between bites. In his obsession with the Holy Ossuary, Wolf had nearly forgotten about the priceless relic that had been taken from Notre Dame. "It was immediately taken to the University of Leipzig for analysis. It has been determined that the thrushes were of the species known as Zizyphus Spine Christi, which is native to the Palestine region and is found in Jerusalem itself. The plant produces crooked branches, with thorns growing in pairs. The Zizyphus strain was actually mentioned in the second century references to the Crown, when it was purportedly kept at Mount Zion. Incidentally, this also matches the strain from a thorn that was retrieved from Trier Cathedral. From an anthropological perspective, the prospect of reuniting the Holy Crown with its original thorns is quite thrilling."

Wolf had to admit that there was something thrilling about this. The notion of using science to learn more knowledge about the life and death of Jesus was actually quite breathtaking. But he was equally distraught at the prospect of a spiritual object being analyzed in Seiler's laboratory. And he liked the thought of the crown ending up in Himmler's private museum even less.

*

Nagel ordered the staff to seal the doors. All chatter abruptly ended. The commandant climbed the steps to the stage, went to the wall and slid back a piece of wood paneling, revealing an enormous map of Western Europe. The occupied countries – Austria, Poland, France, Norway, Finland, Morocco, Tunisia, Romania, Belgium and many others – were colored with a swastika background.

"Please make yourself comfortable," Nagel announced. "First, we will start with introductions." He turned to his left and regarded a lanky, bearded SS officer with three silver pips on his collar. "Our esteemed colleague, *Hauptsturmführer* Bruno Fleischer."

Dr. Fleischer needed no introduction. He was the most famous racial anthropologist in Germany. He was an excellent marksman, and had filled half of Berlin's Ethnology Museum with taxidermy and pelts from his own gun. More recently, he had become a leading authority in the identification of ethnic groups through cranial examination.

Next, Nagel pointed to a rumpled-looking man in a brown bow tie. "And this is Paul Ritter, Dr. Hahn's colleague from the university. He is a partner in the Germany Society for Blood Group Research."

Nagel then gestured to Seiler, who was still grazing at a refreshment table, stuffing himself with Bavarian sausage. "I think we all know the Professor. Although the broadness of Dr. Seiler's expertise boggles the mind, he serves us here today as an expert in Christian antiquities and belief systems."

"And last but not least," Nagel said, nodding in the direction of the front row, "These two fresh-faced squad leaders are Wolf and Lang. They both participated in the liberation of the Holy Crown at Notre Dame. And despite their rank, they have witnessed firsthand what happens to those who do not keep state secrets in confidence. We can therefore speak freely in front of them. Professor Seiler, would you please frame our discussion?"

Dr. Seiler swallowed his last bite and emitted a small burp before straightening himself to address the others. "This concerns national security at the highest level. The genesis of this mission was four years ago, when my companion and I uncovered evidence of a possible rift in the ancient Roman Empire between the descendants of Romans of Nordic descent and local Semites."

"Let me guess," Fleischer laughed in a booming voice as he poured himself a cup of coffee. "This concerns the so-called Aryan Jesus?"

"Yes," Nagel confirmed. "Precisely."

"Another of Himmler's little fantasies," Fleischer snorted.

Wolf found Fleischer's insolence shocking. As if mocking Himmler wasn't enough, Nagel significantly outranked Fleischer. Perhaps, Wolf surmised, the academic nature of the Ahnenerbe allowed for more professional latitude. After all, the Ahnenerbe was powered by civilian brainpower. Although Fleischer and the others wore black SS uniforms, they were more professor than soldier.

"Please hold all comments," Nagel sniped. "Our time is extremely limited."

"As I was saying," Seiler continued, "My historical curiosity coincided with a practical need for the Fatherland to increase our oil supplies for the war effort. On this premise we were able to secure funding from the Ahnenerbe for an expedition to Iraq and Turkey, while *Reichsmarschall* Goring paid for the rest out of his own pocket."

"A true patriot," Nagel noted.

"Yes," Seiler agreed before continuing. "To summarize a very long adventure, our research provided some evidence that, due to the aforementioned conflict within the Roman Empire, the areas of Galilee and Nazareth had been dominated by the descendants of Nordic tribes at least two generations prior to the birth of Jesus Christ."

"And what proof do we have?" Ritter said in a tone that was only slightly less acerbic than Fleischer's had been.

"Clues within ancient literature that have recently been translated into German for the first time."

"And we're just to take your word for this?"

"We also discovered sites dating back centuries before Christ where Nordic runes were present. The findings were published in the Ahnenerbe Journal of Indo-Germanic Studies."

"Riveting I'm sure."

Seiler pushed his glasses higher on his nose. "In recent months we have realized the need to acquire and study Christian artifacts to validate these theories. For example, at the time of Christ, it was common to keep tokens from the body. Locks of hair, sponges used to wash the body and so forth."

"Would you agree," Nagel cut in, "that our recent military victories have helped this effort considerably?"

"Unquestionably. For example, we recently came into possession of a purported vial of Christ's blood from a cathedral in occupied Bruges. As legend has it, the blood was drawn from Jesus' body by Joseph of Arimethea and was later kept in Constantinople."

Now it was Professor Ritter's turn to show his impatience. "I fail to see how this is related to national security."

Nagel flashed red. "I would have thought the relationship would be obvious by now! The tide of war is turning, gentleman. It was previously thought that through invasion and diplomatic annexation, liberated populations would flock to our cause, and undesirable peoples would fuel the war effort by working in our labor camps."

Fleischer pulled a hand-rolled cigarette from a silver case. "I doubt anyone here was guilty of such irrational exuberance."

"I find your tone decidedly unpatriotic," Hahn said.

"Regardless," Nagel cut in, "the fact is that political indoctrination in the occupied countries has largely failed. It's also time that we all face the fact that Germany has been thrust into battles with armies that are much larger than our own."

The grim portrait of the national condition seemed to catch Hahn off guard. "How can this be? I am constantly hearing that we are liberating new Germanic populations with every new invasion. Poland. Austria. Norway. Czechoslovakia. I saw on the newsreel that even now Germans from Romania are protecting our flank in Stalingrad. How can we not have the largest army on Earth?"

The condescension in Nagel's glare could only come from someone who had already suffered the pain of commanding a humiliated army, as he had done in the First World War. "Just because these foreigners are Germanic does not mean that they want to fight for us. This is true even in Denmark, where, despite the shared ethnic heritage between Danes and Germans, Jews remain free, and military conscription numbers are far below expectations."

Ritter nodded in agreement. "I might add that the Japanese will only keep the Americans busy for so long. Once they are defeated, what's to stop the Americans from coming here?"

Nagel's voice held resignation. "Also true. We cannot win purely by military means. We *must* gain a psychological and political advantage."

Wolf felt the ground shift beneath his feet. It had been obvious that a great deal of focus had been shifted to the eastern front, and considering the news from Stalingrad, all signs pointed to a protracted war with the Russians. But it was the first he had heard anyone – let alone someone of Nagel's seniority – suggest that Germany could actually lose the war entirely.

He shuddered visibly, allowing himself, for the first time, to imagine the Russian flag flying from the Munich town hall building.

∗

After a brief respite, the group once again gathered in the sealed room. Bruno Fleischer lit his cigarette and drew from it. His blue eyes searched the faces of his Ahnenerbe counterparts, finally coming to rest on Dr. Seiler, whose expression of tight-lipped exasperation was directed at Fleischer.

"I still fail to see how the pursuit of religious relics will help the war effort," Fleischer said.

"What Mr. Nagel is suggesting," Dr. Seiler replied, "is that we look at the root cause of these troubles. Prior to the war, all of Europe was shocked by our technological superiority. They marveled at how our economy grew from the ashes of the Versailles Treaty to be the most robust in the world. Our achievements were without question. So why do they not embrace us with open arms?"

"The brutality of our armies," Fleischer stated. "We've all seen the news reels. The Wehrmacht celebrates openly while civilians lay dead around them."

"Fundamentally wrong," Seiler countered. "Brutality is not the problem. History tells us that civilizations are willing to accept cruelty and even mass murder during wartime, but only if it is framed within a religious context."

"And there lies the problem," Ritter said. "Today Germany is viewed as Godless."

Wolf found himself on his feet, unable to control himself. "The German people are not Godless," he spurted. "We're just made to believe that we should be."

Once the words had left his mouth, the group's attention left Wolf feeling empty and vulnerable. He shrunk back into his seat, filled with embarrassment.

The 32-year-old Fleischer was the first to come to his defense. "I have to agree. Hitler's views are out of step with society, but his views alone are what the world sees."

"And we must change those views," Seiler said. "We will use science to prove Christianity's relevance to the führer."

Wolf's mind tumbled back to Paris, when Himmler had alluded to such a strategy. *The war cannot last forever. Europe cannot sustain a protracted conflict. But imagine if the führer could be persuaded to turn to Christ?*

"And how would we do that?" Hahn challenged.

"By presenting a factual view of Christianity that is palatable to both the führer and Europe. One that the führer himself will administrate."

Fleischer snorted. "The führer will look grand in his papal tiara."

"You joke," Nagel said, "But imagine the implications on our allies. Take Italy, for example. We need a strong ally to protect our southern borders. Italy is a country of tribes that can only be managed and motivated through organized religion."

"They seem quite happy with the one they have," Fleischer noted.

"And yet they view Catholicism as totally disconnected from National Socialism. Therefore, their troops are not unskilled, but they are largely unmotivated."

"Germany may be increasingly secular," Ritter agreed, "but it's the Russians that are openly atheistic."

"As Himmler has noted many times," Dr. Seiler said. "From a propaganda perspective, there is an enormous opportunity for us to frame the Russians as the Godless enemy in the eyes of the world. Therefore our objective is to find additional scientific proof of an Aryan Jesus. If we can do this, then Hitler might be persuaded to embrace Christianity with the same passion with which he promotes his ethnic agenda."

Fleischer removed a silver flask from his pocket and poured several ounces of cognac into his coffee. "Haven't any of you read *Conversations with Hitler*?"

"Are you mad?" Nagel spat. "That book is filled with lies, and I find it highly suspect that you would be in possession of it!"

The book, which had also been published under the title *The Voice of Destruction*, had been written by Hermann Rauschning, the former president of the Danzig Senate. Rauschning was a politician who had infiltrated Hitler's social circle before fleeing the country in 1936. His book, which was officially banned in Germany, painted Hitler as a ruthless and conniving dictator who plotted the destruction of Catholicism even while negotiating a treaty with it.

"Relax," Fleischer said. "I don't own the book. On my last trip to Hamburg, I happened to find an excerpt dropped by British planes. My point is that Hitler is quoted in the book dismissing the Aryan Jesus concept as nonsense. He wants Germans to worship the swastika, not the cross."

"And you'd believe a traitor like Rauschning over Himmler?" Nagel said.

"I never said that."

Ritter stood, inserting himself in the middle of the battle. "Even if Rauschning's account is true," Ritter ventured, "Those conversations took place years ago. Who knows the führer's heart today better than Heinrich Himmler? If he says that Hitler can be persuaded, then we should trust him."

Ritter agreed. "Just imagine it. All of Europe united against Russia in a Holy War. Even the French Resistance might be persuaded to lay down their arms."

"And don't forget the Americans," Dr. Seiler added. "The Americans I have met in my expeditions seem to be largely inseparable from their religious beliefs. If Germany were to embrace Christianity, the Americans could never side with the atheist Russians."

"And let us not forget about the resettlement," Nagel pointed out, referencing the government's program of resettling Jews to the eastern territories. "There are still some very patriotic Germans who find these policies morally untenable because Jesus himself was thought to be Jewish. But if it could be proven otherwise, then this resistance might evaporate, would it not?"

Fleischer blew several rings of smoke. "Let's dispense with these fantasies and get back to the logic of this plan, shall we? Wewelsburg Castle is already full of Christian artifacts, and the Ahnenerbe journals are full of theories about Nordic people at the root of virtually every great civilization. How exactly will another expedition prove the ethnicity of Jesus?"

Dr. Seiler opened his brown leather attaché, removed several sheets of printed paper, and began distributing them. The first page contained a sketch of a chalk ossuary with dimensions of 51 centimeters by 28 centimeters by 31 centimeters. The estimated weight was between 15 and 25 kilos.

"The artifact we seek is none other than the ossuary of Jesus Christ," Seiler said.

Wolf's heart was a kick drum within his chest. He remembered Father Kruger's translation of the Aramaic that Hoffman had written in his own blood: *Yeshua bar Yehosef.* Jesus, son of Joseph.

Seiler continued with his explanation. "As you will read in this report, our spies have infiltrated the highest levels of the Holy See."

"The same spies that told us that the Holy Grail could be found in Spain?" Fleischer said.

"Our sources are sympathetic church officials from the Gnostic tradition," Seiler said. "Contrary to official Church doctrine, newly located Gnostic scripture tells us that early church leaders possessed the body of Christ. There is also substantial evidence that the Apostle Paul arrived in Rome with the remains as early as 46 AD. But once the extent of Nero's campaign to wipe out the religion was realized, an effort was made to conceal the ossuary for fear that it would be destroyed. The easiest way to do that was to deny the remains ever existed in the first place."

"Even if this fantastic tale is true," Fleischer politely objected, "the bones would not be in good condition today."

"As you will read, the remains were said to be carefully wrapped in clean burial shrouds, especially in regards to the skull. As our anthropologists have witnessed in Egyptian tombs, bone integrity can vary wildly in relation to storage variables."

Fleischer seemed bored, or at the very least, far from convinced of the evidence's authenticity. Wolf envied his skepticism. He wanted to believe that this was all a fairy tale, as Fleischer seemed to. But his heart could not let it go.

*

The sound of shuffling papers filled the room as the team eagerly devoured the intelligence brief. Dr. Hahn munched from another helping of cooling sausage, Ritter chewed his nails anxiously, and Fleischer continued to chain smoke.

Nagel checked his watch. "We must stay on schedule," he urged Dr. Seiler. "Please push on."

"As you will read," Seiler continued, "It seems that by the second century, the secret location of the ossuary – which had been buried in what is now the grotto underneath St. Peter's Basilica – was passed from one pope to another through a single apostolic messenger. The secret was apparently well-kept for nearly 1,800 years until the Napoleon invasion of Italy. Pope Pius VI was taken prisoner and, in the weeks after his removal to the Citadel of Valence, he grew ill. At some point in the weeks before he died, Napoleon learned of the ossuary, perhaps from the pontiff himself. And so he secretly moved the bones, along with much of the Vatican archives, to France."

Ritter sat up, in rapt attention. "Where, specifically?"

"As some of you may be aware, the relic of a saint was placed underneath an altar stone of every Roman Catholic church. These relics come in various degrees of importance, ranging from a tooth to a bone or a keepsake to an entire skeleton. Having come into possession of the ossuary of Jesus Christ, Napoleon could think of no better place with which to hide it than beneath the altar of Notre Dame Cathedral."

For the first time, Wolf observed the look of utter surprise on Nagel's face. "And this was the reason for the Paris operation?"

"Correct. It is Himmler's opinion, and mine, that the fierceness of the ambush on our anthropological team in defense of the ossuary only confirms its authenticity."

"And who was it that ambushed us? French Resistance?"

Dr. Seiler shook his head. "The assailants were a group known as the Black Order. They have ruthlessly protected both the ossuary and the pope for hundreds of years."

"I was under the impression that we had the pope under our control," Nagel said.

"The Black Order appears to be beyond the pontiff's reach. The Holy See seems to have even less knowledge of their operations than we do."

Nagel turned his gaze to Fleischer, whose aura of smug negativity seemed to be eroding. "What do you say now, Bruno?"

"I must admit that the historical significance of this ossuary is interesting. The war strategy is far-flung, but ingenious. I'm still not clear on how this proves anything in regards to ethnicity."

Seiler looked up at Fleischer. "You have no doubt examined thousands of living and dead skulls with conclusive results, have you not?"

Wolf remembered a photograph his father had taken of Fleischer in Tibet, which had eventually been published in the Ahnenerbe journal. He was using his skull calipers on natives and recording the measurements in a moleskin notebook.

"I have indeed," Fleischer confirmed.

"And through this work, you have discovered patterns in cranial structure that indicate Germanic ancestry."

"I have," Fleischer agreed as he imagined his calipers measuring the nearly 2,000-year-old cranium of Jesus Christ.

"Himmler believes," Seiler said, "That this evidence, taken together with our other research, would be all that would be needed to persuade the führer of its authenticity."

"And what if the bones are not in good condition?" Ritter asked. "What if they have crumbled?"

Dr. Hahn cleared his throat. "I spoke earlier about apparent breakthroughs in blood identification. I am told that our scientists in Switzerland are making equally exciting progress in the study of DNA. One emerging theory is that genetic identification may be achieved through bacteria that have remained intact within bone marrow."

"And barring that," Seiler continued, "it's possible that symbols on the ossuary itself might offer compelling evidence. The presence of runes, perhaps."

"Where is the ossuary now?" Fleischer queried.

Nagel stood and went to the map. "Our spies tell us that the relic has been taken to Italy," he said, his fingers tracing a rail line stretching between the Austrian and Italian Alps. "The Black Order intends to return the ossuary to its original resting place in the vast grottos beneath St. Peter's Basilica. But as they are well aware, the perimeter we have set up around Vatican City will make that difficult. Therefore the decision was made to place the ossuary in one of two temporary locations until the end of the war."

Dr. Seiler stood. "Any final questions?"

Fleischer finished the last of his whiskey-spiked-coffee. "Just one. Who's going after it?"

"You," Nagel responded.

The unflappable Fleischer looked fearful for the first time. "You must be joking. I'm an anthropologist."

"And an excellent marksman," Nagel countered. "We have no other options. The situation in Stalingrad is grim, gentlemen. All available reserve officers with combat experience have been deployed to the eastern front to stop the inevitable Russian advance. Your orders are simple: Bring the ossuary to Wewelsburg Castle by any means necessary. The outcome of the war depends on it."

✱

The double doors opened once more. Nagel's aide reappeared in the doorway. "Sir, the reichsführer requests your presence in the crypt."

"Very well," Nagel nodded. He took a flashlight as big as a police baton from the table and turned to the group. "Follow me."

Wolf, Lang, Ritter, Fleischer and Dr. Seiler followed Nagel out of the hall, into the corridor and to the southeast wing of the castle. There they descended a winding stone staircase until they found themselves in a vast wine cellar. At approximately 56 degrees Fahrenheit, it was substantially warmer than the castle's upper floors.

The aroma of mustiness, oak and fermenting wine was immediate and overpowering. The unit proceeded through row after row of barrels stacked nearly to the ceiling. Nagel seemed intent on reaching some predetermined destination, and yet there seemed to be no obvious path through the cavernous space. It was as if the barrels had been deliberately arranged in a sort of maze that twisted illogically through the room. Nevertheless, Nagel pressed on, following a path that he clearly knew by heart.

Fleischer dropped back until he was walking alongside Wolf. "I knew your father," Fleischer offered.

Wolf glanced up at Fleischer as they navigated the path through the room. He did not want to give the smug anthropologist the satisfaction of knowing that a photograph of him still hung in his father's empty study in Munich. "You worked together?" Wolf asked.

"Tibet," Fleischer nodded. "Your father was a good researcher. We all caught strange illnesses over there. I nearly died myself."

"Was it worth it?" Wolf pushed, earning a sideways glance from the older man. "I don't mean to be rude," Wolf explained. "I just want to know."

Fleischer shook his head. "I suppose not. There was no Aryan connection in Tibet. Just a lot of good hunting."

At last they came to a chain link gate fitted with a sign that read ATTENTION! DANGER! SALT MINE ENTRANCE!

Nagel unclipped a ring of keys from his belt, plucked a long jagged one from it, and unlocked the gate. Once the others had passed through, he shut the gate behind them, rattling it to ensure it was properly locked.

He switched on his flashlight and led them down a lightless hallway. Wolf's heart began beating hard in his chest. He began counting his steps in case he had to find his way back in the dark.

"Halt!" a voice shouted from farther down the second corridor. Wolf was temporarily blinded as a spotlight that seemed as bright as the sun itself swept across the group.

"Obergruppenführer Nagel," one of the voices said. "You may proceed."

The spotlight flashed off. Wolf, his eyes still blinded by spots, forced his feet forward, using the sound of Nagel's boots against the concrete as a guide. They turned a corner, where he saw a lift entrance with a guard sentry on either side. One of the guards presented Nagel with a clipboard. The castle commandant scrawled his name and date on the visitor form, and then passed it to each of the men in the group.

At last they boarded the lift, where the lighting was much easier on the eyes. The lift platform was roughly the size of a car, easily the largest Wolf had ever seen. As they began their descent, Wolf peered at the cut earth through the chicken wire surrounding the lift.

"The shaft is 800 meters deep," Nagel noted.

Wolf's mouth instinctively yawned open as a plugging sensation overtook his eardrums. Soon he could hear, over the whirring of the lift cables, the sound of metal on stone. A steady chipping that was rhythmic, if not perfectly syncopated.

"How many prisoners died digging this hole?" Fleischer asked.

"Not so many," Nagel replied. "Perhaps two thousand."

At last the walls flickered with shadows. The lift slowed and bounced gently at the shaft's bottom, sending Dr. Seiler wobbling against Lang for balance. The group stepped onto a floor of freshly poured concrete.

The room was lit with tunneling lights and filled with stone carvers in jumpers that were caked with white dust. The finished walls were carved with scenes from ancient Nordic myths. Against the far wall, a pair of enormous stone lions flanked the entrance into a second room. The sight reminded Wolf of photographs he had seen of the ancient tomb of the Egyptian king Tutankhamen.

Nagel led the men through the antechamber, between the lions, through the portal – which was easily 10 meters tall – and into a torch-lit crypt that was elaborately decorated with dozens of German noble flags. Hung high above was the Lucas Cranach painting of the Last Supper that Wolf had seen previously in Himmler's private museum. A lit cauldron burned in the center of the room, smoke drawing up through a ventilator that had been bored into the ceiling.

Heinrich Himmler stood in a corner, surrounded by three personal bodyguards. His shadow danced in the torchlight behind him, larger than life against the enormous rune-etched walls. He did not speak, but rather pointed to the eastern wall. Hahn, Ritter and Seiler led the way, followed by Wolf and Lang.

Cut out of the wall were five extravagantly decorated marble crypts. Wolf sensed an inner darkness grip him as he, along with the others, approached the first crypt. Despite an overwhelming sense of dread, curiosity propelled him forward until he was close enough to make out the engraving on the marker:

HEINRICH I - HENRY THE FOWLER
KING OF GERMANY
876– 936 AD

This defied all reason. It was common knowledge that the king had been buried at Quedlinburg Abbey for a millennium. Had Himmler actually disinterred the body from its ancient resting place to move it here? He quickly moved to the second crypt, where a large portrait of Frederick II hung. The nameplate read:

> FREDERICK THE GREAT
> KING OF PRUSSIA
> PRINCE-ELECTOR OF THE HOLY ROMAN EMPIRE
> 1712 – 1786 AD

He struggled to make sense of this spectacle. This crime. Had these bodies been moved for their own protection? Was a Russian invasion really so certain? Or was this just another manifestation of Himmler's sorcery?

The third sarcophagus was lavishly covered in medals and decorations from the Great War. A portrait of Paul von Hindenburg was suspended overhead, along with a bevy of rifles and swords.

> FIELD MARSHAL PAUL VON HINDENBURG
> PRESIDENT OF GERMANY
> 1847-1934 AD

The fourth sarcophagus was as yet undecorated and apparently empty. The nameplate read:

> FÜHRER ADOLF HITLER
> FIRST LEADER OF THE THIRD REICH
> 36th HOLY ROMAN EMPEROR
> 20, April 1889 AD -

Now the meaning of their visit here – 800 meters below Castle Wewelsburg – was perfectly clear. Should they be successful in their mission, this was where their prize would rest for all eternity.

Wolf's hunch was confirmed as soon as he caught sight of the fifth chamber, which had recently been cut into the stone wall. The nameplate read:

JESUS CHRIST
O – 38 AD

Venice
January 2, 1943

It had been a long time since Wolf had seen a city so boldly lit at nighttime. The wrath of British and American air raids had forced Munich, Berlin, Frankfurt and even Paris to observe nightly blackouts. And yet the good citizens of Venice seemed to have no fear. The orange-hued city flickered, dreamlike, through a layer of fog that rolled from the marshes across the lagoon.

The boat churned through the Grand Canal, its engine seeming to grumble more than hum. Wolf sat on a wooden bench in the aft alongside Lang and three other young soldiers – Adler, Bauer and Kalb. They had been entrusted with the task of finding the ossuary and bringing it to Germany.

Of these soldiers, Wolf was considered the least green, considering that he had both killed a man and also been wounded. And maybe they were right. He was no longer the same person that he was when he had left Munich for the fall semester at the Reich School. Not damaged, exactly, but certainly altered.

Bruno Fleischer stood at the stern, wearing a thick overcoat that, on such a cold evening, was the envy of every boy in the unit. Their leader had kept details of the mission to himself. The stern resolve he now possessed had come about gradually. They had traveled two days by train, coming south through Frankfurt, by way of Munich, through the Alps. Bolzano, Innsbruck, Verona. And finally, Venice. Throughout, the fantasy of holding the skull of Jesus Christ in his hands had grown on Fleischer. During the train ride to Italy Wolf had watched him fill the notebook in his pack with dozens of sketches. He talked excitedly of measuring the roundness of the cranium and presenting his findings to Hitler personally.

Fleischer was already the most famous racial researcher in Germany. Soon he would be the most famous anthropologist in the world. "When the new German Gospels are written," he told Wolf, "perhaps I will be credited as an author? Just imagine it. My name would be learned by German schoolchildren for the next thousand years."

With each passing hour, Wolf felt more certain that the ossuary must be kept out of Fleischer's reach. It had been Lang who had first broached the idea. Just after the train departed Bolzano Station, Lang had followed Wolf into the lavatory, jamming his foot into the door, wedging his way inside. Although they had been virtually inseparable at Wewelsburg Castle, the two old friends had not spoken privately since Christmas.

Lang had stood with his back against the train door, his face deadly serious, speaking just loudly enough to be heard over the sound of the track. "Do you believe it exists?"

A question with so many possible meanings. And yet no translation was needed. He spoke of the ossuary, obviously. The same thing that was on everyone's mind.

"I think it's possible," Wolf admitted. He was just as surprised to hear the words come out of his mouth as Lang was. "What if it happened the way Seiler described?"

Lang's eyes flashed in judgment. Looking back over the past months, it was obvious that Albert's death had formed the first wedge in their friendship, and Lang's cowardice in Paris had driven them further apart.

"You sound like a heretic," Lang whispered.

"If it's not real," Wolf retorted, "what were those monks in Paris fighting for?"

"I don't know."

"They must have believed. If they're right, and I am right, then you're the heretic."

Lang swallowed hard, his small eyes seeming to condemn his friend to eternal hellfire. "Either way, they can't be allowed to possess it."

At last someone else had said what Wolf had been thinking. Himmler's collection of stolen Christian art was simply repugnant. But the thought of the body of Christ taken to a crypt some 800 meters below the earth – where it would lay alongside Von Hindenburg and Adolf Hitler for all of eternity – was intolerable. Himmler was unworthy. The entire country was unworthy.

But there were other considerations. There were lives at stake. Potentially millions of lives. "Maybe they will really use it to end the war," Wolf said.

Lang shook his head. "If they believe they have found the Aryan Jesus, they will only use it as justification to kill more Russians. And more Jews."

There was no use denying it. Lang was right. "What should we do?" Fear prickled up Wolf's spine as he asked. He had the feeling neither of them would ever see their mothers again.

The boat passed under the Rialto Bridge, cutting through the patchwork of fog hovering over the canal. In the dim lamplight, Wolf caught his first glimpses of the crumbling city. Walls that looked as if they had not been painted in centuries. Cafés that seemed as if they had been there since the beginning of time. Figures in heavy coats and fur hats that could have been ghosts from any point in history.

But Wolf could not enjoy Venice's shadowy old world charm. His mind was cluttered with uncertainty. How was Lang going to keep the ossuary out of German hands? Was he going to sabotage the operation?

Now Fleischer turned and whistled, pointing at Wolf. The boy got to his feet, walked to the boat's stern, and stood next to the driver in the boat's open air cockpit. The captain held the wheel with his right hand and operated a spotlight – which only seemed to magnify the soupy fog in the canal – with his left. A hand-rolled cigarette hung from the corner of his mouth, burning unevenly.

"I need you to translate," Fleischer said. Wolf was more than eager. Like all the boys, he was starved for information. Fleischer had revealed no mission details whatsoever. Even their destination had been in doubt until they had changed trains in Verona. "Tell him we're looking for a place called Gritti Palace."

Wolf introduced himself to the driver, who, judging by his devil-may-care attitude, had obviously ferried his fair share of Nazis around the local waterways. He showed no fear of the black uniform. The middle-aged Venetian kept his eyes forward as he answered Wolf's questions, speaking as little as possible.

"He says the Gritti Palace is a hotel along the Grand Canal," Wolf told Fleischer. "Very close."

Fleischer nodded, seeming to be encouraged by the news. "Now ask him how close it is to the Basilica of San Marco."

Wolf had learned about San Marco from his history classes with the Jesuits. It was said to be an ancient Byzantine-style church built in 1071 AD. It had been there, some 500 years after its creation, that Pope Paul III had recognized the Jesuits as an official religious order.

The question seemed to puzzle the driver. "San Marco is only a few minutes' walk from Gritti Palace. But why would you go there? I thought you people did not believe in God."

You people. Millions of Catholics and Lutherans. Centuries of Christian tradition had been eclipsed by a mere decade of national socialism.

The driver glanced right, squinting at Wolf's face in the yellow luminosity radiating from the spotlight. "How old are you, anyhow?"

"Old enough."

The boatman shook his head. "At your age, you should be chasing girls."

"No," Wolf said. "I was meant to do this."

His own words surprised him, but he knew they were true. When he had been drafted into the Ahnenerbe two years ahead of schedule, he had felt victimized. They had promised him a life in academia, and he had instead been issued a rifle and marked with the tattoos of the SS. In Paris he had been thrust into a hidden conflict without any moral or practical compass. But now he was filled with the unmistakable sense of belonging. The future of Europe was at stake. The future of Christianity was at stake. And he had been placed in the center of the battle for the hearts and souls of Europe. He glanced skyward. Use me, he thought. Please. Use me.

*

A bellman in thigh-high waders stood waiting at the dock outside the Gritti Palace. He fastened a rope to one of the boat's anchors and offered Fleischer a hand as he stepped out of the watercraft and onto the wood planking. Wolf was next. His sore left shoulder ached as he locked hands with the bellman and pulled himself out of the watercraft. He gazed up at the faded frescoes adorning the hotel's 15th-century façade. The Palace, which was now a hotel, had been built in 1552 as the residence of Doge Andrea Gritti. It now flew the flag of Fascist Italy.

A concierge in a tuxedo greeted them at the entrance, which was tiled with black and white marble and adorned with large mirrors with gilded framing. Fleischer introduced himself. "Ah, Professor," the man exclaimed in perfectly enunciated German. "We expected you yesterday."

"Italian trains," Fleischer said dismissively. "My error was assuming they would run on schedule."

"No matter. We held your rooms."

The lobby was filled with German officers lounging in the smoky sitting area. They were surrounded by lavishly dressed prostitutes. Fleischer did not seem to notice them. "My men are hungry," he told the concierge.

"The *osteria* is open for another hour," the concierge replied. He led them down a hallway that was decorated with portraits of Renaissance noblemen. "Are you here to see the film?"

"What film?"

"*Munchausen*, of course," the man said. The boys had all heard of *Munchausen*. The film, sponsored by the Ministry of Propaganda, was rumored to be Germany's answer to America's *The Wizard of Oz*. A space fantasy set in Renaissance Venice. "Minister Goebbels has come personally to attend the Italian premiere. If you are very lucky, you might spot him."

What kind of secret mission was this? It was nothing like Wolf had expected. They ate openly in what was easily the most upscale restaurant Wolf had ever seen. A quartet played Vivaldi in a corner of the dining room. Wolf sat transfixed by the table's centerpiece. A bucking stallion, half a meter tall, constructed entirely of painted Murano glass.

Wolf ordered sardines. It did not take long before Lang caught his attention. His eyes were full of contempt, exuding hostility as he pretended to laugh at Fleischer's jokes.

Suddenly, Fleischer's eyes caught something across the room. He nodded, then nonchalantly put his napkin on the table and stood. "No drinking tonight," he instructed the boys. "Report out front at 2:00 a.m. sharp."

Wolf watched as Fleischer made his way across the room and shook hands with an Italian man in an elegant white tie and brown suit. A third man joined them. Dark suit, overcoat, holding a fedora. Wolf felt sure that he had seen him before. Paderborn? Paris? The Reich School, perhaps?

He excused himself to go to the lavatory. Lang followed him to the restroom outside the main dining area, locking the door behind them after entering. They found themselves in a luxurious restroom with marble floors and several toilets with floor-to-ceiling dividers. Lang raced along the stalls, ensuring that they were alone before approaching his old friend.

"What did Fleischer say to the boatman?" Lang demanded.

"Very little," Wolf frowned, taken aback by Lang's intensity.

"He must have said something."

"Nothing important. He wanted directions to this place. And he wanted to know how close it was to the Basilica of San Marco. "

"San Marco?" Lang repeated.

"How should I know?" He turned his back on Lang, stepped inside one of the stalls, unzipped, and began urinating into an open hole in the floor.

"That has to be it," Lang remarked. "San Marco is one of the most famous churches in Europe. It may be the only place in Venice that's worthy of the ossuary."

"Heinz," he ventured. "What are you going to do?"

The bathroom door swung open. Wolf zipped, then backed up and peered over his right shoulder as an old man with a cane entered. His friend was already gone.

✱

Wolf slid back his left coat sleeve and peered into the face of the black Doxa watch he had been issued at Wewelsburg Castle. It was 1:55 a.m. A stiff, cold breeze blew in from the canal, swinging the quartet of lanterns hung overhead. Even at this late hour, the hotel behind him was still lively. Guests returned in pairs from various taverns in the vicinity. Before him, several boats rocked like a row of restless horses.

Wolf was chilled to the core, and yet his face was damp with perspiration. The moisture in his shirt was nearly unbearable. He had worn it without relief for two days of travel, and his tunic only seemed to trap the perspiration inside. Had the fever he had felt after surgery in Paris returned? The old surgeon had said that a little bit was normal. The medic at Wewelsburg castle had changed the dressing and reported no signs of infection.

Maybe it was just nerves. His thoughts tumbled inside him now, gathering speed with each minute that passed without Lang's presence. By 2:02 a.m., the other three young soldiers – Adler, Bauer and Kalb – had all reported for duty. Both Lang and Fleischer were notably absent. Tardiness was out of character for either man. It was practically unpatriotic.

Would Lang resort to violence? What if he had decided to kill Fleischer? Wolf wished he had never given Lang his blessing. If discovered, they would all be questioned. The execution of Matthias Ulrich at Wewelsburg Castle was eminently fresh in his mind. The trembling he had felt at the report of Nagel's pistol still reverberated through his body. He still questioned whether Ulrich had done anything at all, or whether he had, as the least able of the new recruits, been selected as a sacrificial lamb to encourage obedience.

Two men emerged from the soupy haze. A third stumbled alongside them. As they drew closer, Wolf recognized the first as Fleischer. His face was locked into a grimace. The second man wore a long overcoat and fedora. He was one of the men who had met Fleischer in the hotel earlier tonight.

The third man walked with a limp. His nose, forehead and lips were so grotesquely swollen that Wolf did not recognize his friend until he was pulled close.

"Heil Hitler," Fleischer said. "Let me introduce *Kriminalinspektor* Zimmer. We have been in constant communication since the failure in Paris. Thanks to the inspector, we seem to have caught our mole."

The Gestapo inspector thrust Lang forward so that the four unit members could see his face. His hands were cuffed behind him. His left eye was swollen shut. He tilted his head upwards so that he might see out of his good one.

"Lang here was caught talking to one of the priests at San Marco," Fleischer said. "He was informing the father of our plans to come for the ossuary."

Fleischer found Wolf in the lineup and glared at him witheringly. "Am I correct in assuming that it was you who told Lang about our plans for San Marco?"

Shock coursed through Wolf's body. Recently he had become increasingly convinced that he had an important part to play in life. If he was destined to be killed by Fleischer here in Venice, why had God revealed so much to him in the past two months?

He thought of his mother. It had only been six days since Christmas. He knew in his heart that his brother would not return home. Hans had either been killed or captured in Stalingrad. After tonight, Gertrude would be the family's sole survivor.

"Wolf!" Fleischer demanded. "You will answer the question!"

"I was ignorant of any plans," Wolf said truthfully. "I told him only that you had asked about the location of San Marco."

Fleischer grinned and slapped Wolf on the shoulder. "Just as I had hoped."

Wolf winced, stunned by the camaraderie of the gesture. Maybe he wasn't going to die after all.

"I apologize for feeding you disinformation," Fleischer continued. "I wanted to ensure that our suspicions about Lang were correct."

"Shall I put him into the canal?" the inspector asked. He kneed Lang in the buttocks, sending him dangerously close to the dark water.

Fleischer lit a cigarette and considered his options. "No. You can't kill him. Himmler will want him interrogated."

Fleischer smiled, unfolded a map from his pocket and stepped under a lantern to survey it. After several seconds, he turned with a resolute face. "It's time for us to get what we came for. Inspector, if you would be so kind as to bring the prisoner?"

And so they began traversing a series of darkened medieval walkways. Fleischer led Wolf, Bauer, Kalb and Adler came next. The inspector and Lang brought up the rear.

The only sound was their boots against the cobblestones. With Lang in handcuffs, Wolf realized he was all that stood between Fleischer and the Holy Ossuary. Judging by the ease with which Lang had been apprehended, Wolf had to assume that his friend's attempts to warn the local priesthood had failed. He also assumed, by the deliberateness of Fleischer's march through the twisting streets, that the anthropologist had a solid idea of the ossuary's whereabouts.

He tried to separate himself from the others in his mind. They must not reach it, Wolf decided. Once they had the ossuary in their possession, sabotage would be out of the question. He could not destroy the relic. If it was indeed the body of Christ, then it must not be desecrated.

The question was, what he was willing to do? If needed, was he willing to kill to stop this? The ease with which he had killed at Notre Dame had surprised him. He had hesitated for only a fraction of a second after lining up the monk warrior in his iron sights. And after taking the shot, he had not lingered unnecessarily on his actions. He had simply rushed to Hoffman's side, riveted by the Aramaic message Hoffman had written with his own blood.

He began to rationalize what his mind seemed to propose. Five German lives in exchange for thousands saved. Millions, perhaps. Put in those terms, it was really not so bad. He had no love for Bauer, Adler or Kalb. Wolf reckoned that their minds had been programmed so completely by their training that they had no sense of identity at all. As for the inspector, it was assumed that anyone in the Gestapo was automatically a murderer. In that case, he also did not deserve Wolf's mercy.

Until now, Wolf had regarded Fleischer as just another good academic wasted by national socialism. Like his father, Fleischer's prime years were being squandered by the misguided fantasies of Heinrich Himmler. He actually liked Fleischer, whose only real sin seemed to be pride. Of all the men in the mission briefing at Wewelsburg Castle, only Fleischer had seemed to have any humanity. But it was his pride that would deliver the ossuary into the arms of Heinrich Himmler. Besides, how well did Wolf really know him? For all Fleischer's insolence at Wewelsburg, maybe he was just another sadistic Nazi on a quest for glory.

If Wolf did manage to kill them all, he had no idea how he would escape. He felt hopelessly lost by the labyrinth that was Venice. The further they went from the canal, the more desolate the streets became. A marine layer blocked out the stars. Navigation was hopeless.

Fleischer stopped and reexamined the map by the glow of his cigarette cherry. He pulled a flask from his pocket and sipped it, as if steeling himself for the darkened maze that lay ahead. "Are we lost?" Wolf asked, realizing only after he said it that he had sounded hopeful.

Fleischer frowned at him. He pointed down a dark passage with the cigarette. "That way. You first."

And with Wolf leading, the group pressed on with only the occasional glow of a lit window to guide them over the narrow footbridges. The MP-40 was slung over his right shoulder. The submachine had been designed for close combat. He needed only the right opportunity.

He began to walk faster now, testing his ability to distance himself from Fleischer and occupy the shadows. He began to imagine the rhythm of the ambush. Five paces ahead of Fleischer, ten paces ahead of Bauer, with Lang and the inspector in the middle and the others farther back. He would step into the darkness. Swing the rifle off his shoulder. Send the first burst into Fleischer's chest. Swing 30 degrees to his left, where Bauer would eat a burst of 9mm rounds. Perhaps Lang would protect himself by falling down? By that time the others would be falling to either side of the passageway. Spray a wide pattern on both sides, hoping to hit them before their own MP-40s were raised in firing position.

A nice fantasy, but too risky. He would chew through all 32 rounds in his magazine in only a few seconds. If he missed any of the men, there would be no time to reload before they returned fire. And then there was the inspector to consider. The Gestapo agent would surely use Lang as a human shield. Lang might or might not be ready to martyr himself to save the Holy Relic. Wolf wasn't prepared to make that choice for him. He would be patient for a bit longer.

When at last they came to the Rialto Bridge, which spanned the Grand Canal, Wolf finally knew where he was. Their boat had passed under this very bridge several hours earlier. Fleischer got in front and slowed the pace as they crossed. Then on the other side, he paused halfway down the steps and motioned for the unit to gather around him.

"Down these steps and through that passageway," he said pointing to a shadowy area beyond the bridge. "There should be a plaza. The market closed hours ago, so it is sure to be deserted now. On the southeastern corner is San Giacommo. Our contact tells us that the ossuary is there. It is said to be guarded by only a few priests."

Lang's smirk did not go unnoticed by Zimmer. He gripped Lang's cuffs and pulled back until the smile was gone. "What's so amusing, slave?" Lang said nothing, but Wolf knew what he was thinking. Notre Dame had also been guarded by but a few Black Order agents, but they had still managed to steal the ossuary and kill Hoffman and three others in the process.

"If I may," the Gestapo agent interjected, drawing closer to Fleischer. He eyed the man's coat. Seeing no bulges, he said, "Professor, I understand that on your Tibetan expedition, you singlehandedly rendered an entire species of yak extinct. And yet you are armed with nothing but a puny Luger."

Fleischer shrugged and gestured toward the unit. "Fighting is their job."

"Nevertheless," he said, "It would be foolish to assume that the ossuary is not well-protected."

The inspector disarmed Wolf and handed the rifle to Fleischer. Then he pushed Lang toward Wolf. "Secure the prisoner. One word out of your friend, and I'll cut out both your tongues."

The inspector tightened his lips and refocused his attention on the others. "You three," he pointed at Adler, Bauer and Kalb. "Make your way along the edge of the plaza until you have secured the far wall. We will cover the southeastern portion of the plaza. Only when we are confident that we are not walking into an ambush will we enter the church."

The five would-be combatants, plus Lang and Wolf, made their way down the bridge and walked the narrow access path through the darkness. As Fleischer had predicted, a shadowy plaza opened up before them. A series of archways on the far side that had only hours earlier been populated with vendors was completely dark, revealing nothing about their present contents.

On the near side, they found themselves under the wooden portico of a church. Consecrated in 421, San Giacometto was the oldest in Venice. Compared to every other church they had passed during their walk, its exterior was decidedly understated. There were no grand gargoyles, sculptures or ironworks to behold. The church's brickwork was heavily weathered, with no consistent color in any one piece of the facade. A tower with three modest bells opened over a clock that was only correct twice a day.

Several windows that had been added during the Victorian era were illuminated with a glint of candlelight. A shadow passed before the nearest window.

Zimmer drew his own Luger and guided Fleischer, Wolf and Lang deeper under the edge of the portico. The other three fanned out across the plaza. The black-uniformed soldiers virtually disappeared in the long shadows.

Wolf sensed that this was his moment. Yet without his rifle, how could he stop them? Should he cry out, alerting whatever rough priests may be inside the church? If he did so, Zimmer would make sure it was his last act on earth.

Sweat poured down his face. The palms of his hands itched. His eyes burned. Then something flickered underneath one of the black archways on the far side of the plaza. Zimmer tensed, having seen it as well. They all stopped breathing.

A sheet of white erupted from the far side of the plaza. The sound of rushing air was all around them. Someone screamed. A barrage of automatic gunfire broke out and sustained for several seconds. Zimmer retreated deeper into the shadows, dropping to a knee. Wolf steered his handcuffed friend behind a wooden beam as bullets ricocheted all over the plaza.

And suddenly there was laughter, every bit as alarming as the outbreak of white had been. Wolf recognized Fleischer's deep bellow. He looked up and saw what the anthropologist had found so hilarious. A pair of wounded birds fluttered on the bricks before them. Then there were three. And then a half-dozen. White feathers fell around them like snow.

"Pigeons!" the inspector spat.

Fleischer stood, holding the MP-40 at his side, and ventured out into the blizzard of white. "Adler?" he called out in a jovial, elevated whisper. "You got 10 of them at least. Too bad they don't give medals for pigeon hunting."

He stood for several moments, listening intently as wounded birds fluttered crazily around the square, as if drunk. Pieces of those that escaped continued to float around him until he was barely visible.

Wolf was the first to hear the approaching footsteps on the brickwork. Far too light for someone in jackboots.

A sickening crunch cut through the white noise. Wolf did not see what heavy object struck Fleischer, but he heard the man's blood spatter on the ground near him. Zimmer aimed his Luger and fired several shots where Fleischer had last stood. A swarm of shadows emerged from the archways on the far side of the plaza.

"Into the church," the Gestapo agent commanded with genuine fear in his voice. Wolf obeyed before he could think, pulling Lang with him toward the center of the portico, groping blindly for the oversized arched doorway. His right hand found the latch on the right-most door, and to his relief, it opened.

The three survivors found themselves inside a modest house of worship. Rows of lit prayer candles provided the only source of light. Several marble Greek-style columns flanked a handful of wooden pews. Rambling assortments of crucifixes were mounted on the walls. Bronze, silver, copper, wood. Wolf had never seen so many in one place.

Zimmer sealed the doors behind them, quickly locating the barricade plank and heaving it across a pair of enormous steel brackets. He turned, walking past the boys, reloading his Luger with a fresh clip. His eyes searched the far end of the sanctuary. "It's here," he said. "Hidden beneath the altar, probably. Tear the place apart."

Zimmer would not be content, it seemed, to escape with his life. He would deliver Himmler's prize at all costs.

The door groaned behind them as some outside force pushed against the barricade. Zimmer spun, firing two shots through the double doors. Lang, having narrowly missed being shot, lost his balance, falling backwards against the wall.

Wolf's chance was now. He unsheathed the dagger from his belt. The one that Nagel had awarded him upon his sudden graduation from the Reich School. The blade shimmered in the candlelight, as did the inscription.

The glint of steel flickered in the Gestapo agent's peripheral vision. Zimmer swayed left as Wolf lunged forward – fast, but not quite fast enough. A rush of warmth on his hand and wrists confirmed that the blade had found its mark. The inspector stumbled backwards.

Wolf turned and straightened himself, looking Zimmer in the eye. A flicker of hatred flashed in the Nazi's eyes. Zimmer exhaled unnaturally. His chin dropped, and Wolf watched as his chest ventilated for the last time.

The inspector dropped to the floor. A hooded figure stood behind his corpse, cradling a machine gun. A simple wooden cross hung from his neck. Others emerged from the sanctuary shadows.

Wolf had no fear. His core was filled with indescribable warmth. He unstrapped his helmet and let it fall to the floor. His mind was suddenly filled with light. He staggered, blinded, groping for a wooden pew with which to stabilize himself. His ears filled with a chorus of excited voices, although they sounded as if they were far away.

In the next moment he was somehow outside himself. He saw the top of his own head, white-blonde hair drenched with sweat. Arms outstretched at his sides, palms facing the altar, as if warming himself by some unseen fire. He went higher, hovering near the ceiling. He floated over the church's center aisle. He watched as the witnesses laid down their weapons and, one by one, removed their hoods in wonder.

And now he could see his own face. Streaks of red flowed from his eyes. Coin-sized wounds opened in the center of his palms. And he heard their cries. "*Stimmate!*" they cried out. "Stigmata!"

Vatican City
January 4, 1943

Sebastian Wolf woke in a room filled with canary-hued sunlight. The palms of his hands stung. A balding man stood over him, pressing a cool cloth against his forehead. He wore expensive-looking wire-frame glasses and a stethoscope around his neck.

"Good morning," he said in English. "Can you understand me?"

Wolf lifted his head. He was on a hospital bed, dressed in a white linen gown. The smell of the man's cologne made him woozy. He rested his head back on the pillow, noting the fine tailoring on the man's gray double-breasted suit.

Wolf cleared his throat and found his voice. "Where am I?" he asked, staying in English.

"Vatican City. I am Dr. Enzo Marchesi."

Vatican City? That was several hours southwest of Venice. The last thing Wolf remembered, he had been floating above himself in San Giacometto, the old market church.

A nurse appeared at his side, holding something that looked like a crop duster. She poked the tip under his gown and began pumping white powder that immediately went airborne, covering Wolf's torso, neck and face with white flakes.

"She spray you with DDT," the doctor explained as the woman blasted Wolf's scalp. "It's a...a *chimica*."

Wolf knew what it was. Farmers used it for pest control. He could only guess that this was some sort of routine delousing procedure for new hospital patients.

He drew his arms over his eyes, shielding himself with the white linen fabric until the powder had settled and the nurse had gone. As he uncrossed his arms, he took note of his hands. Scabs were forming in the center of his palms.

He remembered the hooded men in the old church. The Black Order? They had pointed at him and shouted, *stigmata*. It was like a dream.

He looked up at Dr. Enzo Marchesi. "Am I sick?"

The doctor shrugged. "Difficult to say. Every year I must travel to see people like you. The Holy See wants to know the reason for the bleeding. Sometimes they have skin disease. Sometimes they are fakers. So far, only one that I could not explain."

"Who was that?"

"Padre Pio. You have heard of him?"

Wolf shook his head wearily.

"Very famous priest. For 27 years Padre Pio has had the bleeding in his hands and eyes. And yet, I cannot find anything wrong with him. So they think it is a real stigmata. He is like a living saint. Maybe it is, maybe it isn't."

The doctor bent low, holding his stethoscope to Wolf's chest for several moments before rising up again. He turned, retrieving something from a nearby table.

"And then there is you," the doctor went on. "The bleeding comes in a very humble but very old church. In front of many credible witnesses. They drop guns, fall to their knees and pray. They spare your life. And the most horrible thing? You are a Nazi."

"My friend," Wolf said. "Where is he?"

"Shhh. Just rest." The doctor shook his head, took Wolf's right hand in his, and turned it so that the wounds faced the ceiling. "These I will treat with almond oil, just like in the time of Jesus." He held an oil dropper over the hand and squeezed two drops over the wound. A shock of pain went up Wolf's hand and wrist. He bolted up, straining against leather straps that bound him to the bed.

"Why am I restrained?" he demanded. "Germany and Italy are allies!"

The doctor shrugged. "They tell me nothing," he said as he seized Wolf's other hand and dropped oil onto it. "But you are not in Italy. You are in Vatican City. Inside Rome, yes, but Vatican City is a sovereign nation."

Wolf tried to protest, but the doctor seized the opportunity to slip a spoonful of foul, pulpy goop into his mouth. Wolf leaned to the side to spit it out. The doctor pressed one hand over Wolf's mouth, and the other behind his head. He was deceptively strong.

Wolf finally swallowed. The doctor released him, leaving Wolf gasping for breath.

"Opium poppy," the doctor explained. He picked up his medical bag and grinned as he headed for the door. "You will have good dreams now."

He was in a vast library, surrounded by overflowing bookshelves that spiraled upwards toward a massive domed ceiling. Sunlight streamed in from an oval oculus in the dome's center. Wind rushed in and out of the room every few seconds with regularity, its force gently rattling the bookshelves as if the structure itself were alive and breathing.

"Excuse me," someone said. Wolf looked up. The voice belonged to a raven-haired librarian standing behind a reference desk.

He straightened himself and puffed up his chest a little. He felt naked in the white linens. Where was his uniform?

"I remember you," she said.

Wolf could not place her. "Where did we meet?"

"Here, silly. You were outside burning books with your friends."

She was mistaken. Wolf was very young during the time of the book burnings, and his mother would not let him go. He blushed nevertheless. He surveyed the girl's straight teeth and thin, symmetrical eyebrows that had been plucked into gentle curves over her green eyes. He leaned over the desk so that he did not have to speak so loudly.

"Excuse me," he said. "I'm looking for something."

Gazing into her eyes made him forget why he had come. Girls were not allowed at the academy, and he had never even had a girlfriend.

"What do you want?"

"I'm looking for books by Karl Landsteiner," Wolf said in a quiet voice.

"The scientist?"

"You know him?"

"Everyone knows who Landsteiner is." The girl walked to a large set of files and opened the drawer marked "K." Ten seconds later, she shook her head. "I'm sorry. He's still on the list."

"List?"

"You know. The forbidden authors list."

"Are you positive? All the German researchers talk about Landsteiner."

"They're probably not supposed to."

"True. It's forbidden."

She shrugged. "One minute an author is on the shelf, and the next minute, they are on the list. A few minutes later, they are in the room."

"The room?"

"Where books go when their authors are on the list."

"Then I should be authorized to see the room."

"You should?"

"Yes. I'm with the Ahnenerbe."

She looked him up and down. "Then why aren't you in uniform?"

"I don't know."

"That's strange."

"Listen, you've got to help me. I've been assigned to research breakthroughs in the blood sciences. It's classified."

She smirked, as if amused by his lie. Her hand shook slightly as she grabbed a set of keys on a large brass ring.

Wolf followed her to the spiral staircase, watching the way she walked – painfully careful, highly aware of how every movement of her body might be interpreted.

"And where is your family from?" Wolf said. He had meant to simply make small talk and put her at ease, but he saw by her posture that the question had made her tense.

"Bavaria," she said. "Our family is one of the oldest and most famous in our village."

"Unquestionably German, then."

"Unquestionably."

They came to a set of double doors. The girl unlocked it and held the door for Wolf. He found himself amidst piles of books, some of them above eye level. "Most of the books on the list were burned," she assured him. "I was told that the books in this room have been preserved for archival purposes only."

Wolf looked around in wonder, daunted by the enormity of the mess. "How do you find anything?"

She let out a small laugh and led him to an area where books about science had been stacked into piles that resembled roman columns. She quickly located a book by Karl Landsteiner in the middle of a pile and began rifling through the books on top. Wolf pitched in to help, removing a large portion of the stack in one chunk. When he turned and bent down again, he head-butted her by accident, sending her to the ground with her hands covering her forehead.

"Are you all right?" He removed his cap and got down on one knee.

"I'm okay," she replied in an unconvincing voice.

Wolf took her by the wrists and pried her hands apart. A small bump was forming just above her right eyebrow.

He bent a little lower. He kissed the bump on her eyebrow. She did not move. She stopped breathing. But when he began to stand, she grabbed his face and pulled his lips to hers. He did not know how or why, but kissing came naturally to him.

And then suddenly he was high in the dome, sitting alone at a table on the observation platform. The girl was gone. The light shining in from the oculus was hotter and more intense now, much like the searchlights in the guard towers at Wewelsburg Castle. The sound of the building's ventilation was louder too. The wind rushed in, then out, in an endless pattern.

He picked up the book the librarian had found for him and unwrapped the brown covering she had protected it in. The book's title was written in English: *The Specificity of Serological Reactions*. Although Wolf's English was quite advanced, he had no idea what *serological* or *specificity* meant.

He flipped through the opening pages until he found the biography:

> Karl Landsteiner is a Nobel Laureate and considered one of the world's foremost pathologists, with specialties in anatomy, histology and immunology. He was born in Vienna in 1868, and graduated from the University of Vienna. He spent the next several years in the world's finest laboratories in Germany and Switzerland. Between 1901 and 1909, he revolutionized the medical world by developing a classification system for blood into types A, B, AB and O, paving the way for the first reliably successful blood transfusions. His work also led to resolving questions of

paternity. When he was 21, he converted from Judaism to Catholicism, later serving at a Catholic war hospital during World War I. In the 1920s, he left Europe to work at the Rockefeller Institute in New York. He cut ties with Europe by becoming an American Citizen in 1929. In 1930, he was awarded the Nobel Prize in Physiology or Medicine. In 1937, he discovered the Rh factor in blood.

Now Wolf understood Himmler's repugnance at the mere mention of Landsteiner's name. The world's foremost blood researcher had once brought glory to Germany, but now embodied everything Himmler hated: Landsteiner was a Jew, a Catholic and an American all at once. And Wolf admired Landsteiner all the more for it.

Goose pimples rose on the young stormtrooper's arms as he saw the photograph of Landsteiner in his laboratory. The big, inquisitive, forbidding eyes. The gray mustache, aerodynamic, like the wings of a diving bird.

"Read the first chapter," a man's voice said.

Wolf looked around. He saw no one. "Father?" he asked. No one answered.

He turned to the first chapter. The text was not what he expected. It did not appear to be a science book. There were no formulas or diagrams. It was scripture, and yet it was not the scripture that he had been taught as a boy. He began to read.

I. And the LORD said, I am God, and I have made you in my likeness.
II. And the LORD asked all people to apply their hearts to seek and to search out all the wisdom on Earth.

III.	For to know wisdom, said the LORD, is to bring truth to light, so that all people might know the essence of God.
IV.	And so there were many who sought wisdom, collecting and deciphering all of the languages and solving all of the mathematics in the world, and charting all of the stars in the sky, and dissecting and reassembling every living creature, so that all of the knowledge in Heaven might be distributed on Earth.
V.	And it came to pass that there were men who sought to keep knowledge for themselves. Would it not be better, they asked, if we alone had the means to communicate with Heaven? Would our communion with the Holy Spirit not be more pure if it were channeled through but a few learned men?
VI.	And these men created a new language, which they themselves spoke, forbidding all others to learn or translate it.
VII.	And it came to pass that these hoarders of knowledge let their hearts be filled with savagery, and they shamed all seekers of knowledge, and when they did not yield in pursuit of wisdom, slayed them without mercy.
VIII.	And LORD sent his only son, Jesus, to teach men to open their hearts and love one another and become a wise people, knowledgeable about all that God has created.
IX.	And many were touched in their hearts, including twelve Disciples. And the Disciples' names were John, Peter, James, Matthew, Thomas, Bartholomew, Thaddeus, James the

son of Alpheus, and Simon and Andrew and Phillip and Judas.

X. And as was his destiny, Judas betrayed Jesus.

XI. And Jesus let himself be captured so that he could sacrifice himself for the good of all people, and so that those who believed in the LORD might strengthen their beliefs.

XII. And the Roman soldiers did crucify him. And as Jesus died slowly upon the cross, He said to the most wicked, O you wretches; O you unfortunates; O you pretenders to the truth; O you sinners against the Spirit. Can you still bear to sleep, when you sleep on a bed of feathers, and the world lies upon rocks?

XIII. And as Jesus died slowly upon the cross, He said to his Disciples, guard the deposit entrusted to you. You will gather knowledge, and you will unravel the mysteries of the Earth, and also of the Kingdom of Heaven, and in doing so, you will be doing the work of the LORD.

XIV. And three days after Jesus died, he appeared first to Mary. And then to his tormentors. And then to his Disciples.

XV. According to His great mercy, He has caused us to be born again to a living hope through the resurrection of Jesus from the dead.

XVI. And a wise man said, if you confess with your mouth that Jesus is Lord and believe in your heart that God raised him from the dead, you will be saved.

XVII. And you will learn all that is knowable about every star in the sky, and so too will you learn all that is knowable about every drop of blood

	in the dirt and every hair upon the head of a child.
XVIII.	And you shall use your wisdom to feed the hungry, just as I have.
XIX.	And you shall use wisdom to care for the poor, just as I have.
XX.	And you shall learn wisdom to heal the sick, just as I have.
XXI.	And you shall use wisdom to create life, just as I have, for I have made you in my likeness.
XXII.	And you shall learn wisdom to unify all believers on Earth.
XXIII.	Go and make wisdom in all nations, baptizing them in the name of the Father and of the Son and of the Holy Spirit.
XXIV.	And I will give you a new heart, and a new spirit I will put within you. I will remove the heart of stone from your body and give you a heart of flesh.
XXV.	And there will be two great tyrants who will attempt to keep all that I have told you from the world.
XXVI.	And there will be a Shepherd who walks among you who has seen into the hearts of the tyrants, because he was born among them and has lived among them. And his name will be Sebastian.
XXVII.	And the Shepherd will devote himself to bringing all that is concealed into the light.
XXVIII.	And the world's great minds will join his flock in Fellowship.
XXIX.	And so too will the world's great leaders join the Shepherd in Fellowship, so that they may be in place when the time comes to usher in the new Rule of Light.

XXX. And when he has gathered all that is necessary to bring all that is dark into the light, you shall find a Virgin from the West, for all that has come to pass in the time of Jesus will come to pass again.

XXXI. And the One from the East will use her to make me anew, just as I have made you anew.

XXXII. And in turn, you will return my heart from stone to flesh, so that all men may share in the wisdom of the LORD. And the whole world shall rejoice.

XXXIII. And so it was in Bethlehem, it shall be again, through the prayer and toil and steadfastness of the learners of God's wisdom.

XXXIV. And those afraid of the Rule of Light will search the Earth for me. As it was in the time of Herod, it will be again. Many innocents will die, though they will be welcomed as angels into the Kingdom of Heaven.

XXXV. And when I am reborn to the world, the knowledge hoarders shall be exposed as bearers of false idols.

XXXVI. And as I grow and walk among you, the Fellowship will protect me from those who will lay great waste upon the Earth to prevent the Rule of Light.

XXXVII. And a wise man said, if you believe with your heart that the burden of the second coming of the LORD is upon the people of the Earth, then you will be saved.

*

When Wolf awoke, he found himself in another new location. Although sparsely furnished, the room was more like a guest room than an infirmary. The bed linens were made of fine Egyptian cotton and the walls were completely covered in tapestries depicting the repelling of the Goths from Vatican City in the sixth century. His bed had been placed on a 45-degree incline, with the head propped up under a stack of bricks and plywood.

He strained his neck slightly forward and took in a view of several adjacent buildings, red-tiled and elegant in the fading winter light. He raised his hands and regarded the raw crimson wounds that were starting to scab over. They were shiny with oil. His skin was wet with perspiration, but his mouth was dry. He thought he might choke on his own tongue. He began coughing.

Dr. Enzo Marchesi was suddenly at his bedside with a spoon. As he had last night, the doctor slipped the spoon into his mouth before Wolf could resist the foul-smelling liquid. "I give you ancient hyssop oil for the cough," he said. "Another something from biblical times. Bees like it."

The oil immediately squelched Wolf's cough, but the taste was unbearably powerful. A nurse was at his side now, holding a small white cup trimmed in gold. She raised it to Wolf's lips. "You are a lucky man," she said in a native Bavarian dialect. "This water has been blessed by His Holiness, Pope Pius XII."

Wolf drank it eagerly. Only a few moments later did he pause. "The pope? Really?"

"Yes. His Holiness developed a certain fondness for Germans during his time there."

He looked up, half-expecting to see the raven-haired librarian. The woman who had offered him holy water was not the librarian. She was not even a nurse. She was a nun in a broad, crisp habit that framed her face and shoulders. Golden eyebrows arched over blue eyes.

"You have an odd look in your eyes," she said.

"It's been a long time since I have seen a nun," Wolf said.

"I understand that many of the sisters in Germany have been forced into factory work."

"I think you mean the priests," Wolf said, thinking Father Kruger's job in the BMW aircraft factory. "I would be surprised if nuns worked in the factories. The Ministry of Propaganda has been quite clear that the role of women is to have children."

"That's just another kind of factory work."

He tried to guess the woman's age. Although she had beautiful bone structure, her habit hid every inch of hair, and her robes were formless, revealing nothing.

"Would you like to pray together?" she said.

"Not just now," he said. "May I have something to write with? I had a vision, and I want to write it all down."

"Careful how much trust you put in your dreams," she said. "The doctor gave you opium."

"It was not a dream," Wolf said. "It was God."

The woman retrieved a leather-bound notebook and pencil from another room and left him as he began to write. The library. The girl. The Karl Landsteiner book. The scriptures that were at once so familiar and yet so new. He recalled them word for word without effort, as if God himself were whispering them into his ear. *And the Shepherd will devote himself to bringing all that is concealed into the light.*

Wolf moved his arms, surprised to find that the restraints were removed. He sat up on his elbows and moved his legs to one side of the bed, gingerly moving them lower until the balls of his feet touched the floor. The notebook he had written in was on a wooden stool beside the bed.

The nun had returned. She sat in a chair at the foot of the bed, watching him.

"Am I free to leave?"

The nun went to the window, looking out. "That would be dangerous."

"Why?"

"See for yourself."

He stood and went to the window, feeling cold air ventilate the open-backed white linen gown. Just beyond the red-tiled rooftops of the Vatican museums stood a great wall, which he knew from photographs was the edge of Vatican City. A pair of Swiss Guards in flamboyant blue, red, orange and yellow striped uniforms stood guard at a gate. Just outside the walls, two Wehrmacht soldiers sat atop a Panzer II tank. Although they were several hundred meters in the distance, Wolf instinctively drew back from the window.

"Are they here for me?" he said.

"Not specifically," the nun said, crossing the room to sit in an armchair covered with purple fabric. "The soldiers have been outside the walls for weeks. Every week there are a few more."

"How did I…"

"You and your friend were brought in through the tunnels."

Wolf wheeled around. "But when I asked the doctor about Heinz –"

"Mr. Lang is quite safe," the nun said.

"Can you please summon a diplomat?" Wolf said. "I want to request asylum for both of us."

The nun returned to her chair. "I'm afraid I must deny your request."

Wolf was incredulous. "You cannot possibly be qualified to make that decision!"

The nun continued to sit quietly, deliberately controlling her voice. "We were not properly introduced. I am Klara Kohler, the pope's personal secretary."

The name was familiar to him. Father Kruger had mentioned a Sister Klara who had helped arrange for him to apprentice in the Vatican Archives. But he had said that she was the housekeeper for the pope when he lived in Germany and was still known as Nuncio Pacelli.

"You are surprised," she said.

"Yes," he admitted. In Germany there were virtually no women in positions of power.

"I am quite accustomed to being taken for domestic help. In fact I was head of a nunnery when the pope was known as Nuncio Pacelli, and I eventually oversaw his staff. Afterwards I was in Berlin, where I served him during his ambassadorship. Now I am His Holiness' voice on a number of diplomatic matters, including communications with the Holy See."

Wolf could not comprehend what he was hearing. "The Black Order took mercy on me. Why won't you?"

The nun flew out of her chair, pointing an accusatory finger at him. "You are hardly deserving of charity. You are only alive because they thought you were blessed with the stigmata." She paused, turning toward the window before resuming in a calmer voice. "There are those within the Vatican that may be distracted by such parlor tricks. I remain focused on the protection of the Church and the Holy Father through diplomatic means. The vultures at the gate are a reminder that the slightest change in public position will be our undoing."

"You can't protect the pope with talk," Wolf said, testing the waters. "Unless Germany loses the war, your new master will be Hitler himself."

He was not sure whether the nun heard him. She continued to pace, stopping occasionally to glare out the window at the German soldiers in the street. "His Holiness walks a fine diplomatic line," she said finally.

"You have no idea what you're dealing with."

"If they discover that we've been sheltering you, the diplomatic scandal will be the tipping point that will send tanks through our gates."

Impressed as Wolf was by the nun's bluster, he did not take it at face value. It stood to reason that someone with substantial influence had brought him to the Vatican. Had the Black Order intended to hand him back to Germany for the sake of diplomatic relations, it would have been far easier to leave him in Venice, or simply to kill him there in the church. But someone in their ranks had saved him and brought him to Vatican City.

He decided to test Sister Klara's limits a bit further. "I have heard rumors," he said. "They say that the Vatican is a safe haven for downed British pilots."

"Mere rumors."

"Others say there are American spies within these halls."

"Pointless conjecture."

"I served directly under Heinrich Himmler," Wolf said. He was stretching the truth, but not far. His mother had been wrong about the Reich School education keeping him from harm, but she had been right in thinking that it would provide him with elite access.

The nun turned to face him. "All the more reason for us to turn you back to the Fatherland."

"I have information the Americans can use. The locations of aircraft factories. Munitions factories. And I know the mind of Himmler. I know what he plans to do."

"No," she shot back. "That sort of information would only bring *more* bloodshed. Innocents would die. It would be immoral to knowingly cause so much death."

"Doing nothing would be worse. Besides, things are already going badly on the eastern front. And we all know what will happen if the Russians get here before the Americans."

The nun did not argue. Since the Soviet Union had declared Atheism its official doctrine, more than 25,000 churches had been closed. More than 100,000 priests were said to have been shot. Hundreds of thousands more had been sent to labor camps.

The nun turned toward the door. "I will pray on it."

*

He slept very little. He was too excited by the dream of the great library and the book and the scripture. When he did sleep, he dreamed about the ossuary. Was it real, or was it just another of Himmler's myths? He did not think it was a myth. Whatever the Black Order was, surely its soldiers would not kill Germans in Paris and in Venice to protect a false idol.

It was before sunrise when Wolf heard his door open. Dr. Enzo Marchesi was soon at his bedside. He set his lantern on the desk and took Wolf's left hand in his, checking his wounds. "Good morning. Your hands look improved. Any cough last night?"

Wolf sat up. "No."

"Good. You will need your strength today."

Wolf felt suddenly uneasy. What were they going to do to him? Had the nun really decided to hand him over to Himmler? He watched as the doctor once again listened to Wolf's heart and dropped almond oil onto his palms. It didn't sting as much now.

"Your conversation had an interesting effect on Sister Klara," the doctor said as he worked. "She spent most of the night praying in the Basilica."

"I didn't realize the pope's secretary could be a woman."

"Sister Klara may be the first," the doctor smiled as he poured some hyssop oil onto a spoon. "She rules the palace with an iron fist. They call her..." The doctor looked over his shoulder, checking to make sure that the door was still shut. "They call her *La Popessa*."

Wolf and the doctor shared a smile. He understood immediately that the term *La Popessa* was something of a backhanded compliment.

The doctor pointed to a blue garment folded on the dresser – a less flamboyant, standard duty Swiss Guard uniform. "Your disguise," the doctor said. "Get dressed. With luck, I will see you tonight."

Several minutes later, Wolf was led by two actual Swiss Guards down a staircase to the Curia's lower floor. They passed several priests in black robes and countless nuns that appeared to be employed in domestic capacities. On every wall, and down every hallway in the enormous palace, he was met with a new artistic masterwork. He did not pay them much mind. The only treasure he wished to see was the ossuary. What exactly had the church been hiding from its believers all these centuries?

He was finally led into an administrative room with no windows. Two men in black cassocks sat at a worktable with notepads and steaming cups of coffee before them. He was shown to a chair opposite them.

The priests did not introduce themselves, but when they began speaking American-accented English, he knew that they were also not what they seemed.

The Americans wasted no time on pleasantries. The olive-skinned American began asking the questions. An exhausting list that, at times, did not even seem organized into broad topics.

Where are the V-2 rocket factories? Where are the Messerschmitt factories? Where are the Stuka factories? Where are the Panzer tanks made? Did you see any Allied prisoners working in the factories? What foods are still available? How scarce was meat?

Wolf answered the inquiries as fast as they came at him, marking locations on elaborate topographical maps. *And the Shepherd will devote himself to bringing all that is concealed into the light.* Although he was confident in the righteousness of this work, he thought often about his mother. He knew that in collaborating with the Americans, he was putting her at risk too. But she was already at risk, he reasoned. Would she rather not die than live to see the plague of national socialism rule the entire earth?

The Americans chain-smoked cigarettes. They were neither friendly nor hostile. They simply listened and took notes, seeming to question nothing and be surprised by nothing. The interrogation continued throughout lunch and into the afternoon.

Wolf wasn't sure what time it was when the debriefing abruptly stopped. Two Swiss Guards appeared to escort Wolf back to his room.

In his room, a plate of bread and olives awaited him. Soon Dr. Enzo Marchesi visited him, checked on his wounds, and administered more herbal medicine. Wolf had so many questions of his own, but he was too tired to ask them. He fell asleep before the doctor had completed his examination.

Wolf saw the Americans for the next two days. Their questions were endless. How many Hitler Schools were there? What were their names and locations? What was the purpose of the Hitler Youth? How many divisions were there? What roles were the Hitler Youth expected to play in the event of an invasion? Were there any regular meetings where the top leadership gathered in a single place? What could he tell them about the labor camps in Poland? What could he tell them about the Jewish resettlement program?

He told them everything he knew, holding nothing back.

At night, the doctor tended to his wounds. Wolf asked about the Black Order, but the doctor didn't seem to know what he was talking about. And Sister Klara did not return.

On the third day, Wolf decided he had had enough.

"I have done my duty," he told the Americans. "Now I should like to be repaid in kind."

The olive skinned one lit a cigarette. He looked at his companion, who gave a nod of approval. "We've already made arrangements. You'll be taken overland through the Alps tomorrow. We have a contact there that will take you to Spain. From there, you'll be taken to Washington D.C. for further debriefing."

It was not what Wolf had expected. He felt suddenly winded. "I want asylum *here*," he said. "Not America."

He wanted to know about the ossuary. He wanted to see what was really in the Vatican archives. He wanted to know the truth. He deserved that much.

"Look kid," the American said, interpreting Wolf's silence as defiance. "If you don't want to cooperate in D.C., we can send you to a work camp in Alabama, but you're not gonna like it."

"I want to see Heinz Lang," he told them.

He could tell by the looks on their faces that they had either met Lang or knew of him. The olive-skinned one whistled for the Swiss Guard. Wolf was taken back to his room, where he sat detailing his thoughts in the notebook where he had documented the vision and the prophecy.

*

The cell door opened sometime after ten. Two Swiss Guards pushed a figure inside the room. Wolf took the candle from the bedside and raised it. It was Lang.

His friend's hands were cuffed before him. He was dressed in white linens identical to those Wolf had been wearing since his arrival. Wolf got up and embraced him. Lang's return touch was merely cordial.

"Are you hurt?" Wolf asked.

"No."

"Have you talked to the Americans?"

"As little as possible."

"We have to help them," Wolf said. "Better that the Americans drink themselves into a stupor at the *Haufbrauhaus* than the Godless Russians."

"I will keep that in mind."

"They want to send me to America, Heinz. I told Sister Klara that I want to learn about the Black Order and about the ossuary."

"You have to forget about that," Lang said. "The Black Order doesn't exist."

"What are you talking about? You saw them!"

"I saw nothing. One of the monsignors here said the Black Order was shut down centuries ago."

"And you believed him? Don't deny your own experience! They hit us in Paris and Venice. If they are real, then the ossuary has to be real."

"It was just the Resistance," Lang said. "A well-organized insurgency. That is all."

"Heinz, listen. I had a *vision*. God *spoke* to me."

Lang stood and headed for the door. Wolf sprung from his chair and grabbed Lang by the arm, toppling him over with his enthusiasm. Something metal clanged in the near-darkness. Lang scrambled to his knees, searching the dark floor for the object.

Wolf found it first. He stood, holding the shiny object up to the light. It was a long key inscribed with the papal crest.

"Heinz," Wolf said. "How did you get this?" Even with such limited visibility, he could make out the terror on Lang's face. "Why would you have a key like this?"

And suddenly Lang was screaming for the guard. Wolf moved in to silence his friend, and the two boys were soon wrestling on the floor. "Was it you, in Paris?" Wolf asked as the door flew open behind them. Wolf threw a punch, splitting Lang's lip. "Did you tell them we were coming? Did you help them murder Hoffman?"

The guards separated them. One of the guards held Wolf on the ground, and he looked on as Lang got up of his own free will and stood in the doorway. "*Blessed be the Lord, my rock,*" Lang said, "*Who trains my hands for war, and my fingers for battle. My loving kindness and my fortress. My stronghold and my deliverer. My shield and He in whom I take refuge.*"

"Do not hide behind scripture!" Wolf screamed. And then he began to feel the heat on his skin. His cheeks and palms were suddenly wet. But unlike Venice, he did not feel at peace. He felt as if all of Europe's rage was contained within him, bursting to get out.

And when his palms began to bleed once more, and the crimson tears fell from his eyes, he expected Lang and the guards drop to their knees and pray as the hooded ones had in San Giacometto. But they did not. Horrified, they groped for the door handle, found it, and escaped outside, locking it behind them.

PART III

UNITED STATES DEPARTMENT OF JUSTICE FEDERAL BUREAU OF INVESTIGATION

CLASSIFIED MEMORANDUM

TO: Deputy Director, FBI (100-428091)
FROM: SAC JC Wilson
SUBJECT: INTERNAL SECURITY

There are enclosed herewith to the Bureau three copies, and to the New York Division one copy, of a report received from CG 5724-S* on February 9, 1943. This report deals with the findings of a three-day debriefing of SS Unterscharführer Sebastian Wolf, who surrendered himself to American authorities at the Vatican in January 1943 after capture by an unidentified group (possibly Vatican Intelligence or an affiliated insurgent organization).

Debriefing began on Vatican premises on January 3, 1943. Post-debriefing, Subject was originally scheduled for transfer to POW farm labor camp in Murdoch, Nebraska. Request for transfer to Washington D.C. was granted on grounds that subject possessed unusually candid details about high-ranking Nazi government leaders and operations. Debrief continued in Washington D.C. on February 18 after Mr. Wolf was successfully evacuated to Spain en route to the United States. The following report includes relevant military details under consideration by the Office of Strategic Services (OSS) and Army Air Corps.

3 – **Bureau**
1 – **New York**
1 - **Chicago**

SYNOPSIS OF MILITARY INFORMATION HEREIN

Summary follows. Details copied to Army Air Corps for possible use in Strategic Operations.

Sebastian Wolf drafted at age 15 from the Reich School, a top Nazi political training academy in Feldafing, Germany. Subject detailed names and locations of instructors and locations of 12 additional "Hitler Schools."

Subject named 26 SS officers and 142 Ahnenerbe members, including highly detailed information regarding duties, ranks, and physical descriptions.

Subject reports food rationing in Germany to a greater degree than previously believed. Confirms reports of poor harvest previous year.

Subject reports Hitler Youth seen near anti-aircraft batteries in central Munich and various points in Brenner Pass (Alps) to protect key rail lines.

Subject denies knowledge of camps imprisoning ethnic minorities but claims to have known Catholic priest imprisoned at Dachau Camp near Munich and personally witnessed Jehovah's Witness labor camp inmates working near Wewelsburg.

Claims aircraft engine factory operational within old BMW plant (Munich) and detailed locations of six additional munitions plants near Frankfurt.

Confirmed existence of "breeding" programs to encourage population growth among ethnically desirable couples. Claims mother worked at one such camp (possible contact).

VALUE ANALYSIS

Opinion of intelligence value: HIGH/SUSPECT

Sebastian Wolf conveys an unusually high degree of potentially valuable internal SS/Ahnenerbe operational information. Subject appears both highly intelligent and highly charismatic, although given to occasional erratic behavior, perhaps as a symptom of battle fatigue. However, value of information is unusually detailed in relation to subject's seniority, calling into question validity of claims. Subject explained this by citing high casualty rate on multiple war fronts, apparently depleting draft pool, along with elite status of political institution attended.

In addition, subject's outlandish claims about occult rituals within the Nazi party are also suspect.

Subject repeatedly asked if meeting with Nobel Prize winner Karl Landsteiner could be arranged upon arrival in U.S. Wanted to discuss unnamed subjects relating to "blood sciences" and "D-N-A."

Subject left the Vatican under duress. Demanded access to unnamed "Holy Relic" before acquiescing to evacuation demands on January 8, 1943.

RECOMMENDATION

Wolf is only existing POW claiming to have personally worked with Heinrich Himmler since invasion of Poland in 1938. If sane, ongoing insight highly valuable for duration of war.

Recommend admit to federal facility in D.C. area for psychiatric evaluation. Further decision pending outcome of diagnosis.

62-43899-7789

MEMORANDUM TO
ASSISTANT DIRECTOR FBI

SUBJECT: Sebastian Wolf Escape

On March 17, 1943 POW Sebastian Wolf (see CG 5724-S*) escaped from St. Elizabeth's Hospital, Washington, D.C. where he had been under psychiatric evaluation after intelligence debriefing.

Agents surveilling suspected Nazi sympathizers and other subversive organizations in surrounding area were put on notice. There were no contact reports.

On March 23, Mr. Wolf was apprehended at the Rockefeller Institute laboratory in New York. Police report Mr. Wolf appeared at the Institute demanding to see Karl Landsteiner, a blood science specialist who won a Nobel Prize in 1930. Mr. Landsteiner is Professor Emeritus at the Rockefeller Institute and spoke with Mr. Wolf briefly before excusing himself to call police.

Landsteiner claims not to know Wolf. His statement that he left Europe prior to Wolf's birth checks out.

Landsteiner claimed Wolf alarmed him when he said that he had recently been in Wewelsburg, Germany with Dr. Gustav Hahn, who was one of Landsteiner's professional rivals in Germany. Hahn is a known anti-Semite whom Wolf had previously linked to a "Blood Science Research Group" that reports personally to Heinrich Himmler and other high-ranking Nazi figures.

Landsteiner said he then excused himself to phone the police. His assistant, John Hafner, said the following: "He told me that Dr.

Hahn and others had completed research demonstrating that ethnic identity could be identified by blood analysis and, in the near future, would be identifiable through DNA analysis. He said the purpose of his visit was to get Landsteiner's professional opinion on whether this science could be applied to other kinds of research. I told him that we were not interested in Nazi research, especially as it related to racial matters."

Wolf was returned to federal custody pending further investigation and psychiatric analysis.

It is requested that you advise me at your earliest convenience as to whether further investigation of this individual's knowledge of contemporary German medical theory, or Professor Landsteiner's, as it corresponds to the war effort, should be investigated by the Bureau.

C.E. Longsmith
Special Agent in Charge
Federal Bureau of Investigation, Department of Justice, New York

62-43899-7789

Office of Strategic Services
Official Memo

CLASSIFIED

DATE: April 2, 1945
TO: Office of the Secretary of War
SUBJECT: Operation Paperclip

This is a formal request on behalf of the OSS for the immediate and undivided services of POW Sebastian Wolf (see CG 5724-S*).

Given the American advance on the Rhineland, and the Russian advance in the east, the OSS has concluded that simultaneous occupation of German territory by both American and Soviet forces is inevitable. Of chief concern is the acquisition of German scientific and engineering knowledge, especially related to rocket science knowledge and hardware; jet aircraft design and hardware; nuclear fission science and materials; cryptography research and decoding devices; and certain medical and biological research and advancements, especially relating to genetics, breeding and biological weaponry.

The OSS's goal is to ensure that such knowledge is acquired and owned wholly by the United States. Therefore, the OSS is proceeding with Operation Paperclip immediately.

It is the belief of the OSS that Mr. Wolf's background could be leveraged to help establish relationships with members of the German scientific community. It is our understanding that Mr.

Wolf has been cleared psychologically and is not considered a security threat.

Please advise me immediately as to Mr. Wolf's whereabouts so that he can be activated and deployed.

Sincerely

James McAvoy Wyeth, Deputy Director
Office of Strategic Services

CENTRAL INTELLIGENCE GROUP
CLASSIFIED MEMORANDUM

February 06, 1946

SUBJECT: Consultancy for Sebastian Wolf
FROM: <identity withheld>

This is a formal request to grant political asylum for Sebastian Wolf (see CG 5724-S*) and install him as a temporary paid consultant to the newly formed Central Intelligence Group as agents monitor the Soviet Zone of occupied Germany.

As previously discussed, Mr. Wolf has repeatedly provided valuable intelligence information despite original fears that he suffered from delusions as a result of battle fatigue. The fact remains that the majority of Mr. Wolf's claims made upon capture have since been confirmed by the War Department/OSS.
    Mr. Wolf has been invaluable to efforts to import German scientific knowledge, including human resources, to the United States, in some cases acting as chief translator/liaison. Furthermore, since the occupation, Mr. Wolf has helped authorities find and recapture confiscated treasure from former Nazi Germany, including artwork and jewels. This includes several paintings now hanging in ▓▓▓▓▓▓▓▓▓▓▓▓▓▓▓▓

Given his cooperation with the United States since his capture, it is the opinion of this office that Mr. Wolf would be in mortal danger if repatriated to Germany.

If permitted to remain in the United States, Mr. Wolf intends to fulfill any request of service to the Central Intelligence Group before pursuing a career as an Episcopal priest.

Please advise at your earliest convenience.

THE FELLOWSHIP

UPDATE TO FILE 62-43899-7789

CLASSIFIED AUDIO TRANSCRIPT

Date: Friday, November 19, 1973 - 9:04am - 9:39am
Participants: Sebastian Wolf and █████████
Location: The White House

FIRST 3:12:35 RECORDING: BLANK

3:12:36 TRANSCRIPT FOLLOWS

██████████ They say you're a man of God *and* science. Do I have that right, Wolf?

Wolf: It's my personal belief that God has given us science so that we can better understand Him.

██████████ No kidding. Galileo could've used a guy like you around in his day, know what I mean?

Wolf: [laughs}

██████████ Says here you grew up Catholic and were later ordained Episcopalian. Say, did you know that something like 25 percent of all American presidents have been Episcopalian?

Wolf: I didn't realize that, sir.

██████████ Mmm-hmmm. Very savvy political move switching to the Episcopals. Right in the sweet spot. Goes all the way back to Washington. Roosevelt. Oh and Gerald [Ford] is one. Even the head of the ██████████ Committee – well you must know ██████. He's one too I think.

Wolf: You've done your homework.

▮▮▮▮▮▮▮▮▮▮ Do you think it would be a good move for me to convert?

Wolf: Not necessarily, sir. I believe religion can get in the way of following Jesus.

▮▮▮▮▮▮▮▮▮▮ Well that is an interesting thought. Good talk, this is. I like you. You impress me, Wolf. Look, you have a reputation as a man who is quite connected. I know ▮▮▮▮ ▮▮▮▮▮▮ is always over at Eden. You must have some great chow over there to get dinner guests like that.

Wolf: [laughs] I think the conversation is the main attraction, sir.

▮▮▮▮▮▮▮▮▮▮ Well I'll buy that for a dollar. Yes sir, you are one connected guy. You even brought all those sons of bitches over from Germany that are running NASA now, didn't you?

Wolf: I did what I could to help.

▮▮▮▮▮▮▮▮▮▮ Listen, Wolf, I was wondering if you could talk to ▮▮▮▮▮▮▮▮▮▮ for me. Used to be you could count on him. Up to a certain point, I mean. But he's blackmailing me, if you can believe that. Says he's going to blow the whole thing if I don't cooperate.

Wolf: What exactly is he threatening?

▮▮▮▮▮▮▮▮▮▮ [inaudible]

Wolf: I see. To answer your question, I can talk to him. I think I might be able to influence his process.

███████████████ Yeah. You call him. Good deal. Smooth it over, will you? Lord knows this is one tough job. You can't imagine. They're throwing the whole damned book at me but they don't understand that this job requires a different set of rules.

Wolf: Agreed. The rules that apply to most men don't apply to you. That is the nature of leadership.

███████████████ Damn right it is. [inaudible] What do you think God would say about this whole thing?

Wolf: That you were chosen to lead. You simply cannot be bound by the same rules as those who are destined to follow.

<u>NEXT 18 MINUTES RECORDING: BLANK</u>

UPDATE TO FILE 62-43899-7789

RE: Sebastian Wolf
BY: Special Agent Will Hollis

June 21, 2003

This document summarizes an inquiry into a private estate, owned by Sebastian Wolf (aka "The Shepherd"), commonly called Eden and located at 9012 River Rd, Rockville MD.

The inciting incident for the investigation was the publication of an article in Inside Washington magazine titled "The Country Club Cult that Rules Washington," written by Mr. Nathan Drucker.

BACKGROUND

Prev. file on Wolf closed in 1946, at which time domestic surveillance ceased. From 1946 to 1952 Mr. Wolf was granted amnesty in the United States and provided ad hoc consulting services to the War Department/OSS/CIG/CIA regarding postwar occupation in Germany. Wolf was instrumental in helping to establish several covert scientific research projects staffed with former German scientists, and served as the unofficial primary liaison between the Federal government and the community. The result of these initiatives was the widescale import of German knowledge and talent into select American agencies.

After this period Wolf became a U.S. citizen. He entered the Episcopalian priesthood and was thought to have gradually assimilated into mainstream life.

However, the aforementioned article written by Mr. Nathan Drucker of Silver Springs, Maryland, alleges that Wolf currently exerts undue influence over a number of prominent American politicians and resulting domestic & foreign policy, possibly extending to government funding of technology research in the private sector.

I conducted one in-person interview and one follow-up call with Drucker.

Drucker is a career journalist. He seemed highly agitated and exhibited paranoid behavior during both interviews. Claimed he had lost "editorial approval" over the article bearing his name but that it was "basically factual." Also indicated that he was conducting a personal investigation of Mr. Wolf's personal empire, which he claimed exerted influence over leaders in several foreign countries including China, the UK, Germany, Italy and various African nations.

Drucker alluded to threats to his personal safety as a result of the article's publication.

Drucker's vehicle smelled of marijuana. A subsequent examination of his Silver Springs residence revealed large quantities of anti-anxiety medication clozapine, which is used to treat a variety of disorders, including schizophrenia.

SUMMARY

Not a credible threat to domestic security.
No further action planned at this time.

PART IV

Palazzo Della Rovere
Rome

Blake Carver set the tablet computer aside and stood. The sun had set hours ago. He had finished Drucker's manuscript, as well as the associated classified documents Speers had sent him, in one long sitting. His feet were tingly. His eyes hurt. He was famished.

He went to the window, forcing himself to look at distant objects so as to retrain his vision. He focused his gaze on the dome of St Peter's Basilica, and then on the lights of the Royal Palace. At night, the palace was an arresting vision of power and majesty.

He tried to imagine how it would have looked in January 1943, when Sebastian Wolf had been imprisoned there. So much was unchanged. The architecture. The uniforms of the clergy and the Swiss Guard. But he would have also seen Italian police on horseback and plumes of steam rising from the animals' mouths. And although the official occupation of Rome would not begin until later that year, he would have seen plenty of German patrols in the streets. The Nazis must have thought it only a matter of time before the long red and black swastika banners hung from the palace façade. Given, how quickly every prior nation had bent to their will, how could they not have imagined coming and going from the Vatican gates as they pleased? How could they not have imagined decorating their homes with art looted from the Vatican museums?

A true monarchy operating for nearly two thousand uninterrupted years, with borderless influence over one billion followers worldwide. There had never been another earthly reign like it. And after reading a few chapters of Drucker's manuscript, Carver was convinced that Preston's killers meant to ensure it would endure for another two millennia.

He went to Nico's room, where his sidekick had fallen asleep with the lights on. "Wake up," he said twice, but Nico didn't stir. He picked up a glass of water on the nightstand and splashed it across Nico's face.

He shot up. "Dude, what is your problem?"

"We have new information," he said. "We need to regroup."

Nico flopped back down and pulled the covers over his head. "I need to sleep."

"The guy we got the information from died trying to give it to us."

Nico sat up. "Died? As in, he was murdered?"

"Yes." Carver didn't want to get into Nathan Drucker's life story, or how Ellis and Speers had managed to get their hands on his manuscript. There was no time for that.

"Fine. Consider me up."

Carver retreated to his room at the far end of the suite and sat on the edge of the bed to reflect further on what he had learned. While digesting Drucker's manuscript, he had grown increasingly suspicious of Father Thomas Callahan. It was now obvious that the priest's contact in Vatican Intelligence, and the one who had asked him to find Sebastian Wolf, was none other than Wolf's childhood frenemy, Heinz Lang.

In a professional sense, Lang's career arc was practically unrivaled. Like Pope Benedict himself, Lang had risen from the Hitler Youth and the ashes of a failed Thousand Year Reich to lead the Jesuits, one of the world's most influential and long-running religious orders, before stepping down to run Vatican Intelligence.

But just because Lang had headed up "God's Marines" didn't necessarily mean he was involved with a modern-day incarnation of the Black Order. But one thing was for sure. If he had asked Callahan to find Wolf, he was somehow connected.

The question was, was Lang's mission to seek and destroy, or to assist?

As important as finding the answer to that question was, Carver knew that he had to be careful in handling Callahan. It was too early to reveal that he knew about Wolf and Lang's association, and certainly premature to reveal anything further about Preston, Gish, Borst and the others.

But there was one burning question that had to be answered before all others. He picked up his phone and dialed Father Callahan.

The priest answered on the first ring. He heard the faint pitch of a teakettle simmering in the background.

"I was hoping you'd get in touch," Callahan began. "How's our fair city treating you?"

"Fine, thank you. But this isn't a personal call. I wanted to update you on that name you gave me. Sebastian Wolf?"

"Ah, yes. What'd you find out?"

"We checked out that address," Carver continued, knowing he had to give the priest something. "I can see why you're having trouble tracking the fellow down. The estate is completely deserted."

He heard the disappointment in Callahan's voice. "Surely you're not giving up, though. Anyone moving out of a place that big is sure to leave a few breadcrumbs."

"Don't worry. You know how tenacious I am. But in the meantime, I've got a question for you, Father. Was anything stolen from the Vatican recently?"

"Stolen?" the priest repeated. "You mean from the Vatican Museums?"

"No. Something from the red zones," Carver said, meaning non-public areas of Vatican City.

"Come to think of it, yes."

The kettle whistle grew louder. "Would you mind moving that off the burner?" Carver asked.

"Sorry." The racket faded before Callahan spoke again. "As to your question, as a matter of fact, a painting was stolen from the Royal Palace."

"What sort of painting?"

"An obscure work by…hold on a minute…" It sounded as if he was shuffling through newspapers. "Ah yes. Benvenuto Tisi."

"When?"

"September 21st. As it was explained to me, the pope was away for his last gasp of vacation at Castel Gandolfo, and of course most of the Swiss Guard was away with him, so security was relatively light at the palace. The working theory is that the thieves came and went through a laundry truck, but word is that they're not entirely sure. Obviously, security in the palace has been heightened massively ever since. Never seen it so high, as a matter of fact."

"I'll bet. I take it the investigators were not Italian police?"

"Indeed. Internal Vatican investigation. The Swiss Guard apartments are within the city walls, and the Rome police have no jurisdiction here."

Carver let forth a grunt of skepticism.

The priest sipped his tea audibly. "Something not sitting right with you?"

Even at face value, the story was implausible. Tisi, also known as Il Garofalo, had been among the most prolific Renaissance painters. According to historians, he had worked constantly, and had lived to be very old. During his lifetime, just about every church in Italy was said to have possessed at least one of his paintings.

But unlike the elite artists such as Rafael, Garofalo was without a signature piece. His work was often criticized for being frigid, both in expression and color. If the thieves had wanted a Garofalo, or several, they could have gotten them in hundreds of places where security was relatively light. Even with the pope away on summer retreat, the palace remained one of the most heavily fortified places in the world.

Carver did not doubt that there had been a robbery that had triggered such a massive increase in security. But he was willing to bet that what had been taken was far more valuable than a painting by a second-tier Renaissance artist. If his theory was right, Sebastian Wolf had finally completed the mission Heinrich Himmler had sent him on in 1943. He had found the ossuary.

Haborview Trauma Center Seattle

This time, Ellis woke. *Really* woke. She had been in and out of sleep for the past 36 hours. The back of her head was impossibly heavy and sore. She sat up, reached around and probed her skull gingerly. Based on the size of her headache, she expected to feel an appendage the size of a grapefruit. But her fingertips found only a cushioned bandage that was sore to the touch.

"The swelling's way down," a voice said. She looked up and saw a nurse at the foot of the bed. A Latino guy with a handsome face.

Her right side stung. She winced, shutting her eyes as the memory of the Taser prongs lancing her skin came flooding forth. The nurse was suddenly at her side, lifting the gown to take a look. The scabbed-over wounds resembled the bite marks of some enormous snake. "I can give you something for the pain," the nurse said.

Ellis started to turn and was immediately thwarted by crushing lower back pain. She now remembered being hit. And she remembered the man with the beard. The flaming beard. Had his face seriously been on fire? She didn't know. But he had hit her with something big. A plank, maybe. She couldn't remember what.

"Easy," the nurse said. "It might not feel like it right now, but you're lucky. Your mama must've fed you plenty of milk when you were a kid, cuz you've got no broken bones."

"I don't feel lucky," Ellis moaned.

"Shhh. Your boss is still sleeping."

"Boss?"

The nurse motioned to the second bed. "He's been snoozing over there for about an hour now, thank God. He's been asking us all kinds of questions, driving the staff crazy"

Ellis swiveled her neck slowly until she could see the second bed. The visitor was asleep on his back, snoring lightly. Wrinkled gray suit. Paunch-belly. Curly black head of hair. Salt-and-pepper goatee.

"Julian," she said in recognition.

Palazzo Della Rovere

The inbound call on Carver's phone appeared as IDENTITY BLOCKED for less than a second, then transformed as the DNI cloud database unscrambled it. The call was coming from SIS Headquarters in London.

Carver sighed. It had been days since he had heard anything from Legoland. Maybe they had finally found something useful.

He answered provisionally, requesting, as a security precaution, video chat prior to accepting audio. Carver was surprised when not one, but three faces popped up on the phone. The DNI's facial recognition software was slow to respond. It had to sync with its database of intelligence profiles, but it did, gradually, confirm the identity of each of the three faces onscreen: Sam Prichard, SIS Chief Brice Carlisle and the stunning Seven Mansfield.

"Is it my birthday?" Carver said. "I don't like surprise parties."

"Apologies for the gang bang," Carlisle replied dryly. "Unfortunately, I had no choice but to call Director Speers a short while ago to alert him about another sad chapter in this saga. He suggested we notify you straight away."

"I supposed I'll have to fly to London for the juicy details?"

The comment raised eyebrows, but Carver didn't regret it. He was still pissed about the waste – both in time and budget – incurred in flying to London because of Sir Brice's paranoia. There was nothing worse than abandoning an already cooling blood trail for the sake of bureaucracy.

Prichard and Seven held their breath until Carlisle spoke. "Now that you've got that bit off your chest, Agent Carver, would you mind turning on the BBC?"

Carver walked to the suite's master bedroom and switched on the television. He turned to BBC World and was immediately faced with a red ticker sliding across the bottom of the screen.

UN ENVOY SUK KENYATTA MURDERED IN GENEVA

Kenyatta was a former Kenyan prime minister and UN secretary general. He was not quite a household name in the States, but that was only because most Americans didn't follow international politics. Outside the U.S., Kenyatta had more name recognition than Sir Gish, Senator Preston and under-secretary-general Borst put together. He had been in the international news a great deal lately, as he had been appointed the UN envoy in charge of negotiating peace in central Africa.

Carver turned the TV volume down. "What happened?"

"We only learned about this 45 minutes ago," Carlisle replied. "All we know is that he was abducted from his car around lunchtime, and was found hanging, having been rope-tortured like the other victims, in his Geneva hotel. A piece of octagonal-shaped, striped fabric was stuffed into his mouth."

Sebastian Wolf had seen to it that his new religion was stocked to the rafters with influential scientists and politicians. *And so too will the world's great leaders join the Shepherd in Fellowship, so that they may be in place when the time comes to usher in the new Rule of Light.* And those leaders were now paying the ultimate price for membership.

"What was Kenyatta doing in Europe?" Carver asked.

"Geneva had been selected as neutral territory for negotiations. You can imagine how this will derail talks now. Each side will blame the other for his death."

A global war. Without state. Without end. Carver had seen Brother Melfi's handwritten proclamation in the evidence files Speers had uploaded from Seattle. The prophecy was coming true. Borst and Kenyatta did not even represent individual nations. They represented the United Nations.

"We're dispatching a unit to investigate the crime scene," Carlisle continued.

"Why bother?" Carver asked, although he was venting more than making a recommendation. "We know that Kenyatta was connected to Sebastian Wolf. They wouldn't have targeted him otherwise."

Judging by the puzzled faces onscreen, Carver realized the extent of the information gap that had been created in the past few days. There was so much to explain.

"I've got a lot of stuff to catch you up on," Carver continued. "For now, I feel confident in saying that the Black Order has returned, and that they are targeting senior members of the Fellowship World Initiative."

"Hold it," Prichard said. "In London, you said the Black Order had been dissolved centuries ago."

"Which was consistent with historical records," Carver agreed with appreciation in his voice. If he had been forced to fly to London to discuss something that could have been done remotely, at least Prichard had bothered to listen. "But we are witnessing the work of a highly organized, talented and sustained effort that is obviously well-funded and enjoys considerable reach. Only an organization with the maturity and impeccable intelligence of the Black Order could have known the secret relationship shared by Gish, Preston, Vera Borst and Suk Kenyatta."

Carlisle looked uncomfortable. "If I understand you correctly, you're saying the Vatican is behind this?"

Carver shook his head. "No. That would be like saying that the government of Saudi Arabia endorsed Al Qaeda because a few terrorists once lived there."

"Certain conspiracy theorists have said as much."

"And they were wrong about that. Did the Black Order once exist to defend and preserve the Catholic Church and the interests of the pope? Yes. But this level of extreme sadism and brutality would never be tolerated by the Holy See, at least not in its modern form. Odds are that the Black Order is today an autonomous order with no official ties to the Vatican."

Carlisle exhaled frustration. "Considering the escalation of violence, I suggested to Director Speers that our governments collaborate in earnest without further delay. He was in full agreement, and has already gathered the necessary approvals. The only question is where."

Carver was in no position to refuse. He needed the help. But this time, MI6 was going to have to come to him.

*

Carver spent the next hour bringing Nico up to speed. Until now, he had kept his asset at arm's length from the big picture. Carver had disclosed that some very important people had been killed in a very cruel manner, and that more killings were possible unless they were able to identify and locate the organization behind it. Now he provided background on why these things were taking place.

He paced the hardwood floor of their suite as he talked, stopping occasionally to hydrate and stretch. When at last he had laid out all that he had gleaned from Drucker's manuscript, the classified documents Speers had sent, and the crime scene details from Seattle, London and D.C., he noted something he hadn't yet seen in Nico's expression – panic.

"You okay?" Carver asked.

"How would anyone be okay after hearing all that?" Nico said. "This is epic! Who knows how high this goes? Is the

Chinese premier in the Fellowship? How about the Queen of England?"

Carver straightened up. "If Drucker's org chart is any indication, I think the answers to those questions are no and no."

The wiry hacker stood up, using both hands to pull absentmindedly at his hair. "But you said yourself that Drucker had been exiled from the organization for several years. His org chart is out of date."

"We can't worry about that now. The Black Order began killing the moment the ossuary was taken from the Vatican. We have no choice but to help them find it."

Nico's eyes grew wide. "Help the Black Order? They're terrorists!"

"They may be evil, but they're not terrorists."

"Oh come *on*! You said yourself that they killed a senator!"

"A terror group would have settled for any congressman. It would have also sought publicity. The Black Order's goals appear to be very defined. For now, they exist to repossess and safeguard the ossuary. If we can return it to the Vatican, then we have a chance at restoring security."

"I can't believe you're defending them."

Carver looked Nico directly in the eyes. "Believe me, Senator Preston's killers will be brought to justice. Leave that to me. But the Black Order could be further radicalized if we can't find the ossuary in time."

"In time for what?"

Carver pulled his tablet up off the table and tapped to open a document that Arunus Roth had sent him. "It's time that I shared this with you." He handed it to Nico, who was immediately lost in dozens of rows of financials.

"What am I looking at?"

"The old accounting books of LifeEmberz, Adrian Zhu's company. Early on, the company began experimenting with the extraction of mitochondrial DNA from exhumed bodies, some of which were hundreds or thousands of years old, then trying to clone offspring from it using stem cells. Highly controversial, obviously. A process that they were later rumored to have perfected after the company moved its offices to China."

"So?"

"Remember the two bodies we saw in the Rome morgue? They were Black Order operatives sent to kill Adrian Zhu."

"Because of something in the company financials?"

"No. Just listen. Until today, I believed Zhu might be working with Sebastian Wolf, but I had nothing to go on other than the octagon found on the gunmen and a strong hunch. Then I went back over the LifeEmberz files that the government seized after the company fled the U.S. Early on, LifeEmberz received a substantial seed investment, paid in cash. The company had originally told the IRS that it had been an anonymous gift. If you'll look at the initials on the balance sheet, however, the source is marked FWI, which they originally explained as standing for 'From Wise Investors'. After a second look, I think we know what FWI stands for."

"Fellowship…World…Initiative."

Carver nodded. "There was also a matching cash withdrawal from one of the Fellowship's accounts."

"Wait, Wolf was behind Zhu's research from the beginning?"

"That's right. And when the technology was perfected, he wanted to own it. That meant making Zhu a convert."

Nico collapsed in his chair at the realization. "He's trying to reincarnate Christ."

Carver took the tablet, pulled up the prophecy from Drucker's manuscript, and read. *"And when I am reborn to the world, the knowledge hoarders shall be exposed as bearers of false idols."* He looked at Nico. "Not reincarnated, Nico, but born."

"This is crazy. It's *worse* than crazy."

"People think Scientology is crazy too, but look how many powerful people are drawn to it?" He stood, looking down at the prophecy, then to Nico. "Well, now you understand the stakes."

"And what if we can't find the ossuary in time?"

Carver went to the window and rested his shoulder against the frame as he looked out. "Then the Black Order will be the least of our worries."

Somewhere Over The Northwest

The Cessna Citation X leveled off at 43,000 feet, flying at a speed just shy of Mach 1. At this rate they would be back in D.C. in less than two hours. Ellis did not feel the speed. At her request, Speers had ordered the cabin lights switched off for the duration of the trip. Her eyes were unnaturally sensitive to light. A normal symptom of the concussion, the doctor had explained as he had begged her to remain under his care for another night.

Half-circles, nearly dark as the bruises on her side and back, sat beneath her eyes. She was just as happy that Carver was still in Europe. The thought of facing him like this was humiliating. She hoped big sunglasses were in style this year, because she was going to be wearing them for at least a week.

She reached into her bag and retrieved an energy drink that she had purchased at the hospital gift shop. She could easily sleep, but she was sick of that. She wanted nothing more than to clear the cobwebs from her mind. To puzzle the pieces together.

She gingerly eased back into the cushy leather seat. The soreness wasn't diminishing, but she was getting used to it.

"Feel like talking?" Speers asked.

"Okay," she consented, although she could already tell that he was about to deliver some bad news.

He told her that he had sent the passports of the men who had assaulted her in Seattle to Arunus Roth, at DNI Headquarters in McLean, as well as to Blake Carver, who was following up with leads on the ground in Rome. Then he told her about Suk Kenyatta, the UN envoy who had been murdered in Geneva. He paused a moment, worrying that he had overwhelmed her with too much information.

"Nathan Drucker," she said. It was not immediately clear to either of them why she said it.

"What about him?" Speers said patiently.

Her eyes rolled upwards, left and then right as she strained to piece the memory together. The association came to her slowly. "The name S. Kenyatta was written in one of Drucker's notebooks. I'm sure of it."

Speers opened his attaché and began sifting through the stacks of loose notes. He couldn't see anything. "Do you mind?" he asked, as his finger grazed over the reading light button. He had sent copies of everything to McLean and Rome, but had yet to process all the loose pieces they had gathered from Drucker's house. Everything was happening so fast. In a perfect world, they would have weeks or months to piece together all the data points they had discovered over the past several days.

He soon found them among the stack. Six pages of hierarchies. Hand-drawn, barely legible, with entire sections scratched out. Notes and Bible verses written in the margins. And even the names, most of them, were simply surnames. Only occasionally did they contain a first initial.

Speers handed her the pages. The feel of the yellow notebook paper between her fingertips seemed to jog her memory.

"Drucker was trying to piece together a Fellowship org chart."

Ellis began telling him what she could remember. She sputtered, losing her train of thought frequently as she remembered what had led her to board the flight for Seattle in the first place. She found the name "V Borst" on one of the pages and pointed to it. It was near the top of Drucker's power list, near Gish and Preston.

"Okay," Speers said. "And you thought she was in danger?"

Her thoughts drifted for a moment. She felt weightless for a moment until the sound of Speers' voice brought her back. "No," she said. "How could I know that? I was hoping she could tell me who might have wanted Gish and Preston dead. I was hoping she could tell us where her daughter was."

"That would have been nice," Speers agreed. "Unfortunately, we have no clue what happened to Mary Borst after her plane touched down in Rome. It's like she vanished into thin air."

Speers switched on his phone and called McLean. Ellis listened as he told Arunus Roth that he wanted to match every name on the list to the identity of a public figure or scientist, and he wanted it by the time they touched down in Rome.

Ellis' head throbbed again. She shut her eyes. The vision of Borst's body hanging overhead returned to her. She was talking. She was trying to tell her something important. Ellis concentrated hard, trying to push away the white noise of her mind. She reached deep, trying to access the memory. It was like reaching into a deep, dark space. There was something down there, but it was too slippery to pick up.

Rome

Father Callahan was late. Carver sat on a park bench overlooking the Tiber River, drumming his fingers on his knee. The priest had messaged him an hour earlier, telling him that he had new information about the Vatican break in. The American had quickly agreed. Anything that could lead him to the whereabouts of the Holy Ossuary, or the zealots trying to protect it, could be the break he needed.

A cool breeze rustled the trees overhead. Carver eyed a couple holding hands on a park bench. Was it just him, or did they look a little old to be such enthusiastic lovebirds? When he watched them kiss, though, and saw the mutt-like mug on the guy, his doubts disappeared. They had to be in love. Not even the most dedicated spy could conjure up that much passion for a face like that.

He went over the details of his conversations with Callahan in his head. Although the priest had always been short on details, they had at least confirmed his instincts about the Vatican Intelligence's pecking order. The Vatican's philosophy when it came to choosing popes seemed to be the older, the better. That way there was less chance of any real change.

Apparently the same could be said for the Vatican's choice of Intelligence chief. The only person Callahan could have gotten the name Sebastian Wolf from was his nemesis, Heinz Lang. And he was as old as the hills. In his 80s, at least.

But he assumed that Callahan wouldn't have shared any critical details with Lang. He would have given him only what he needed to show value. Such was the way of double agents. Likewise, he had thrown Carver not a steak, but a bone, and he would no doubt be hoping to get a scrap in return.

He thought back to the morgue, when Detective Tesla had shown them the bodies of the gunmen. He remembered Nico's observation: *I thought it was curious that Father Callahan kept referring to the bodies as victims. Tesla never used that word to describe them.*

A black van cornered onto Villa Della Conciliazione, squealing its brakes as it accelerated.

A chilling thought hit Carver. If Lang had given Callahan orders to locate Sebastian Wolf, why would Lang wait to see whether Carver would share the intel with him?

He wouldn't. He would just take the asset who could find Wolf.

The priest was now nine minutes late. Suddenly concerned, Carver got up and began heading back toward the palazzo.

The priest had arranged their hotel reservations. Carver had performed a bug sweep, but only on their initial check in. And it would have been easy enough to eavesdrop from an adjoining room.

He pulled out his phone and dialed the palazzo. Nico answered on the third ring.

"Hey," Nico said, "Great news. I found the motherload on – "

"Not another word," Carver said. "Power down. We're checking out of the room."

"What?"

"I've got a bad feeling. Pack your things. We have to relocate."

"Hang on a sec. Someone's at the door."

He heard Nico's footsteps as he laid the room receiver down. Carver shouted into the phone. "Nico? Wait! Don't answer it!"

Carver quickened his pace as he passed two bronze-winged victories at the Ponte Vittorio Emanuele's north end. He now had a partial view of Villa Della Conciliazione, and its row of embassies, shops and the palazzo were on the other side.

Nico had still not returned to the phone. The street was illuminated with a soft yellow hue. It wasn't crowded like it had been in the morning, but there were still scattered groups of tourists, clergy and business people about. Carver pocketed his mobile and launched into a full-out sprint.

He quickly reached the Vatican Radio Building near the east end of Villa Della Conciliazione. At a distance of two city blocks, he spotted Nico's unmistakably lanky, pale frame as he was shoved into the black van. Carver ran at a blistering pace, focusing in vain on the license plate as the vehicle sped away.

Macabre visions flashed before Carver's eyes. Nico hung by his wrists. Blood pooling on the hardwood floor beneath him. Eyes bulging. Shoulders popping out of their sockets.

He pushed the dark ruminations away. That didn't fit the pattern. Nico was not in the Fellowship. He didn't even know Sebastian Wolf.

His senses heightened, it seemed as if he was suddenly aware of everything around him. A delegation of government types exiting the Brazilian consulate across the street. A group of clergy leaving the *Antico Caffe*. A monsignor stepping outside the Order of the Holy Sepulchre at the far end of the palazzo. A pair of Vatican policemen standing leisurely at the end of the street, smoking cigarettes. And just as it seemed that Carver was going to lose the vehicle for good, he spotted his saving grace – a large group of nuns crossing the Piazza Pio XII, the polygon-shaped arc directly in front of the massive oval of St. Peter's Square.

It was evident by both their zeal for their surroundings, and their pristine white habits, that they were not local nuns. They were pilgrims here on a trip of a lifetime. None of the roughly three dozen sisters paid any attention to the black vehicle careening their way. Only when it began to honk did any of them snap out of their wide-eyed wonder. Those that did see the vehicle froze in the crosswalk.

Only someone with Carver's conditioning could have heard the vehicle gearing down over the sound of his own breathing. Even if the driver was brazen enough to kidnap a felon in federal custody, they weren't stupid enough to take out a bunch of nuns.

As Carver gained ground on the SUV, he attracted the attention of the Vatican police. They stood upright, not quite understanding the situation, but clearly sensing the disturbance in their touristy atmosphere.

He was just 30 yards away now, close enough to the SUV to see that it had no rear license plate. As it cleared the throngs and began to pull away, Carver had a decision to make. If he pulled his weapon from the shoulder holster under his jacket, he might be able to shoot out a tire, and if he was very lucky, kill the driver. But besides possible civilian casualties, there would be a cost to rescuing Nico by force – full exposure to the Vatican police.

The policemen were armed, and there was a good chance that the armed policemen would take him for a madman, or a terrorist, and take him out. There was also a good chance he would be wounded and subsequently arrested. Speer's voice popped into his head: *Your status is completely deniable.* That had been made very clear. The American government would not claim him. Even if he told them that he was working for the Director of National Intelligence, Speers would have no choice but to deny it.

One thing was clear. He wasn't going to be able to find the Black Order from within a prison cell.

The van accelerated as the police stepped in to guide the remaining nuns out of the path of oncoming traffic. The windows were tinted too dark to get a last glimpse of Nico Gold.

*

There would be no going back to the palazzo. Although Carver rather liked the new suits he'd bought in Munich, retrieving them was hardly worth a bullet in the brain. Besides, everything he needed to find Nico Gold existed on the mission cloud.

He would have to ensure his freedom first. The Vatican police were moving across the square now, straining their necks to track Carver's movements over a swarm of tourists. Callahan had been right. After the burglary in the Apostolic Palace, they were on high alert.

Technically speaking, Carver had done nothing wrong. There was no crime in chasing a vehicle down the street. But if the police caught him, and chose to pat him down, they would quickly find an unregistered, concealed firearm under his jacket. By the time he talked his way out of the holding cell, Nico would be dead. And so would untold political leaders as the war between the Fellowship and the Black Order raged on.

One of the policeman tapped his earpiece and looked up, motioning to a Swiss Guard stationed high on the city walls. The guard's elevated position made him the perfect spotter. Carver had to get out of his line of sight, and fast.

He changed directions and walked into the middle of a tour group that was moving toward an exit in the Vatican walls. Stooping slightly to blend in among them, he went with the flow until they passed underneath a massive archway. Several meters above him was the *Passato,* the elevated walkway where popes throughout the ages had fled the Royal Palace for the relative safety of Castel Sant'Angelo. Before him was Via del Mascherino, a bustling thoroughfare lined with restaurants, shops and apartment buildings.

He looked at his watch. He was supposed to meet Prichard and Seven in an hour. It was a good thing that they had set their meeting place ahead of time. Even if he managed to escape, he was going to be unreachable for a bit.

When the group was free of the city walls, Carver bolted right into a corner gift shop, where he saw a black baseball cap with the papal keys imprinted on the front. He grabbed it from the rack, pulled it over his scalp, and laid a 20 Euro note on the counter without stopping for change. He exited a side street that was scarcely wide enough for a scooter and walked casually down the street with his hands in his pockets.

He sprinted until he came to the next big street. There he removed the SIM card from the phone Father Callahan had given him and crushed it under the heel of his shoe. Next he removed the battery and dropped the remaining hardware into a rubbish bin.

Now free of Vatican City, he walked north, looking for a communications store. He had to get in touch with Roth.

*

Carver knew that his freshly purchased prepaid phone would never meet agency security standards, but at least he knew that it hadn't been tampered with since leaving the factory. He headed toward Via Crescenzio, dialing Arunus' cell phone number from memory.

Roth answered. "Hello?"

"It's me," Carver said. "I need help."

The kid hesitated. "Sorry, bro, can you please authenticate?"

"Don't call me bro!"

"Okay, okay, Carver. What's up?"

"Listen carefully. I need you to do a remote data wipe of all classified documents on Nico's machine."

"Are you all right?"

Carver had no time for small talk. He had just 20 minutes until he was due to meet Carlisle, Seven and Prichard. "Repeat back to me what I just said."

"I need to completely wipe Nico's machine."

"No," Carver corrected. "Just sensitive information. Leave all non-classified docs, the OS and any software."

Nico had been taken, not killed. That implied that his captors wanted something from him. They wanted Wolf, and they wanted his help finding him. Carver had to be careful not to wipe the entire machine. If that happened, they might kill him.

"Just the classified data," Roth repeated. "Got it."

"First I need you to give me permission to access the mission cloud on this device."

"Okay. Hold on."

In less than a minute, Carver's new phone buzzed with the arrival of a text message that used a single-use link to the cloud location, where he would be able to access his credentials.

He spotted a cab slow to the curb in front of him. A pair of girls stepped out. Carver slipped into the back seat before the seat cooled, telling the driver to take him to the Trevi fountain, where he was to meet his MI6 counterparts.

By the time the cab stopped at the next traffic light, he was able to log into the mission cloud on his new phone. He clicked on the RFID icon that Arunus Roth had set up, which launched a global map. Carver watched as the map quickly localized to a satellite image of Rome.

A blinking dot showed the location of the tracking chip in Nico's arm. He was near the opera house, and he didn't appear to be moving. That could be bad, Carver realized. It could mean they were already interrogating him. Nico had never been trained for this sort of thing. If he was lucky, the Black Order would hold him while they waited for someone of authority to conduct the interrogation.

With the matter of Nico's tracking device solved, he looked in the mission cloud's upload folder, hopeful that Nico had been uploading his work continuously throughout the day.

The Deconsecrated Church
Rome

The goon touched the tip of the knife against Nico's ear. The pain was followed by a warm sensation that spread into his ear canal.

"I'm working, I'm working!" Nico began typing some java code into a notepad screen. The effort seemed to satisfy the goon, who retracted the knife, turned away and skulked back to the shadows.

He stood before a concrete slab, where his computer was jacked into an old-school Internet cable. His upper arms were swelling from the beating they had given him. His captors were surprisingly young. Barely out of high school, Nico guessed. The one in charge of minding him wore a black T-shirt and utility pants with the pixilated digital camouflage patterns that had been used, most ineffectively, by the U.S. military for a decade before being finally phased out. Nico had done his best to avoid looking directly at either man's face, so as not to give either another excuse to kill him. He knew only that his minder was clean-shaven, with muscle-bound arms and wire frame glasses. A plain wooden cross hung from his neck.

Even from the shadows, the goon was watching Nico's every move, ensuring that he didn't send a message to the outside world.

All Nico knew for sure was that they were in some sort of crypt that felt ghostly and unloved. Judging by what he could see from the battery-powered lanterns, the frescos had been pried from the walls long ago. On the far wall, a Chi-Ro – an ancient Christian symbol that fused a cross with letters –was all that was left of its former inhabitants.

There were two sarcophagus-size bays on the wall to his left. Bits of stone and marble were crumbled around the edges. Whoever had been buried there had been exhumed and taken elsewhere.

Behind him, a rope dangled from a pulley somewhere in the rafters. Anchors had been set up on a sort of concrete platform so that the ropes could be tied off. Nico wished he didn't know what those were for. Carver had shown him the crime scene photos from D.C. and Seattle as an incentive. Just knowing they were meant for him made it difficult to concentrate. He'd lived the last few years in fear of being extradited to Saudi Arabia, where they'd cut off his hands at the wrists. Now this.

Nico's first mistake had been answering the knock at the palazzo suite. He'd been expecting a piece of cheesecake from room service. His second mistake was pretending he didn't know Italian. For that, he had taken a beating, although the goons were careful not to damage his hands or face.

They said they knew he'd been cyberstalking Sebastian Wolf. They called Wolf *antichristo*. "Where did the *antichristo* go after Maryland?" one of them had asked. They spoke Italian, but they were an international duo, for sure. He had detected a Romanian accent in one, and he had heard the other muttering to himself in Russian.

Now they wanted Nico to find Wolf for them.

There was no question in Nico's mind about cooperating. He wanted to live. No way was he going to sacrifice himself to protect some cult leader.

But Carver was another story. That was the one person he didn't want to betray.

But even with Carver in his corner, there were no guarantees. He had already saved Carver once, during the Ulysses Coup, and what thanks did he get for that? Life as a fugitive in rural South Africa, only to be extracted into service against his will.

He knew that Carver would do whatever he could to make good on the promise for amnesty. But Carver wasn't the president, and neither was Speers. Eva Hudson was, and she was hardly a fan.

So he had already told his captors about the FBI files. He had told them about some of the scientific programs that had been funded by the Fellowship World Initiative. But the Black Order wasn't interested in any of that. They wanted to know where Wolf was right now.

He had to give them something soon. If he didn't, he was going to end up on the busy end of that rope.

According to Ellis' report, the old man and his entourage had inexplicably vanished from Eden days or weeks ago. He had already hacked into the flight registers for most of the major airlines flying out of Reagan National and Dulles for the past three weeks. He had checked JFK and LaGuardia just for kicks. Nothing. He'd checked AmTrak. Didn't check Greyhound. Wolf didn't seem like the type to ride a bus.

But that gave him an idea.

What if the Fellowship World Initiative had its own private plane? It would have to be registered. Even private airports kept flight records.

Trevi Fountain
Rome

Carver arrived a few minutes early. It was virtually impossible to find anyone among the throngs making their pilgrimage to the Trevi Fountain, which was precisely why he had suggested it as a meeting place. There was usually safety in numbers.

As if Nico's capture hadn't already put him on edge, he had made the arrangement to meet MI6 on the satphone Callahan had given him. He had to take every precaution now.

Seeking high ground, he climbed the steps of the Santi Vincenzo e Anastaio a Trevi, a 17th-century church with an exceptional view of the square. There he slid behind the 10 Corinthian columns out front, peering out from between them at the spectacle of art and utility.

He allowed himself a moment to feast his eyes upon the masterwork that was the square's focal point. While most tourists focused on the gleaming statue of Oceanus, appearing golden under the lights as he tamed the fountain's waters, Carver preferred function over form. The fact that turquoise-colored water, delivered via the *Acqua Vergine* and the 2000-year-old *Aqua Virgo*, could still be consumed here, in the middle of Rome, and without additional filtration, was doubly miraculous. Even at this late hour, locals and tourists alike drank from the spouts jutting out on the exterior walls.

He checked his wristwatch. It had been over an hour since Nico had been snatched at the palazzo. They had to get to him soon.

From his perch within the church's façade, he easily spotted his counterparts as they entered the sea of tourists. Sam Prichard's blue suit was reliably wrinkled, the tip of his collar brown and dingy. Seven Mansfield wore jeans, a white chunky sweater jacket, Superga sneakers and a blue cloche hat that framed her cheekbones perfectly.

As anxious as he was to get to make contact, Carver counted slowly to 10 as he scanned the rest of the crowd for suspicious activity. Aside from a couple of thuggy teenagers, it looked like a pretty clean crowd. Finally, he surveyed the windows on the surrounding buildings, any of which would have made for a perfect sniper's nest. At this, his level of confidence dropped significantly. Most of the windows were too dark to spot the business end of a rifle.

He couldn't risk meeting them out in the open.

Carver dialed the SIS number they had called him on earlier in the day. As he'd hoped, Seven answered.

"I see you," he said. "Meet me around the block on Arcione. I'll stay put for a moment to make sure you aren't followed."

Carver watched as they made their way back through the crowds and out of the square. Once they had disappeared from view, he counted to 10 once again. Still seeing nothing, he slipped down the stairs as quickly as he could before passing a series of restaurants and boutiques on his way out to the street.

A fly landed on Carver's neck. He immediately thought of the nanobot that had killed Nathan Drucker. He ducked and weaved the insect, swatting it away with exaggerated movements. A kid standing nearby laughed and pointed until his mom tugged him away. The fly was huge and black in the streetlight, hovering overhead for a moment before dive-bombing him again. This time Carver was ready, smashing it between the palms of his hands.

On a normal day he would have been disgusted by the fly guts streaked across his palms. Tonight he was just elated that it wasn't man-made.

The streets seemed almost busier now, after midnight, than they had by day. He joined Prichard and Seven and began leading them south, toward the last known location of the RFID chip in Nico's arm.

"I've located a Black Order cell," he announced, walking at a brisk pace. "We're heading there now."

"Now?" Prichard repeated, still absorbing the news Carver had just told him. "But there's only three of us."

"What do you suggest," Carver answered. "Calling in an airstrike? They've taken my asset to an abandoned church up on Via Agostino. If we don't get to him soon, they'll kill him, just as they killed Gish."

Seven picked up the pace to match Carver's. "How do you know he's still there?"

"There's a tracking device in his arm."

"Why would your asset have a tracking device in his arm?"

Carver pulled out his phone and pointed to the blinking dot on the city map. "That's a long story."

"Em, just how sure are we that the arm is still attached to his body?"

"Behave," Seven cut in, aghast at her partner's insensitivity.

The American pushed on, undaunted. "Valid question, actually. They probably want Nico to find Sebastian Wolf for them. And they know he'll be far more effective with both limbs attached to his body."

"How much farther?"

"15 minutes walking from here."

"Or three minutes with the right transport."

Seven suddenly broke left into a side street, where two old Piaggio scooters sat in the shadows outside a gelato shop. She had the front panels off both scooters within five seconds, and by the time Carver and Prichard realized what she was doing, had removed the white ignition wire caps.

She rolled one scooter forward until it had a little momentum, then jumped on and kickstarted the motor.

Carver couldn't help but smile as the bike purred. Seven peeled down the street before abruptly turning and speeding back to them. She screeched to a stop, motioning for Carver to sit behind her, while pointing Prichard toward the other parked scooter.

Carver climbed aboard, gripping the rear seat stabilizer with one hand and wrapping his other around her waist. He smelled Chanel No. 5 and minty shampoo. "Nice trick," he smiled, as his fingers tightened around abs that were far firmer than he had imagined.

Prichard took the second scooter by its grips and began rolling it forward, mimicking what Seven had done moments earlier. He got it going just as two kids came running out of the *gelateria*.

The kids sprinted nearly as fast as Prichard could get the bike going. As the scooters sped away, Carver looked back at them. Two guys, probably 15 years old. One was short and stocky, the other lanky and handsome. He saw something in their faces as they gave up the chase, stopping in the middle of the street with hands on their heads. Not just anger. Not just shock. More than that. It was closer to emotional devastation.

"Turn around," he told Seven.

"What?" Seven exclaimed. "Are you crazy?"

"Trust me. Just go really fast, and don't stop." She made a U-turn and gunned the motor. Prichard followed suit, nearly losing his balance in mid-turn. Carver reached into his inside jacket pocket, where he was carrying about 800 Euros pinched into a titanium money clip.

The boys suddenly looked scared. They split to either side of the street, giving wide berth as both bikes came blaring through. Carver tossed the neat bundle of cash into the shorter boy's hands.

"Softie," Seven shouted as they powered toward the Opera district.

*

They ditched the scooters a half-block from the church and proceeded up Via Agostino on foot. Carver spotted the church first. Of the 900 or so churches in Rome, it was easy to see why this one had been chosen for deconsecration nearly 150 years earlier. The rather inelegant building was built in the Baroque style, with a concave façade and a flat-roofed porch supported by a pair of columns that looked tacked on. Above the porch, two sculpted lions flanked the coat of arms of the House of Savoy.

The abandoned church was attached to a shuttered monastery. The front windows were all covered with iron mesh. Seeing no cameras, they approached the building and hopped the sidewall over an old sentry box. A black van with tinted windows was parked just inside the gated security entrance. Carver couldn't be sure, but it looked like the one he had seen outside the palazzo.

The three operatives jumped down to the other side and waited a moment before proceeding further into the church's concrete side yard. Carver put his left hand on the van's hood. It was still slightly warm. Seven crouched at one of the cellar windows and began testing the fragile-looking frame to see if it might peel away. The American whistled softly and pointed to the church's side door. It wasn't shut all the way.

"How many of those devils are in there?" Prichard whispered.

"I saw two in the van." Carver wished he knew for sure. And he wished that he had more resources at his disposal. A couple of throwable recon drones would have come in very handy.

Unfortunately, Father Callahan had been the Rome connection for gadgets and weaponry, and the priest wasn't exactly in the circle of trust at the moment. Besides, there was no time. If they didn't take a crack at this now, Nico might end up just like the others. Gutted at the end of a rope.

At least they had the element of surprise in their favor. The American pulled his SIG from his shoulder holster and chambered a round. Prichard and Seven both pulled out Walther P99s.

Prichard touched Carver's shoulder to get his attention. "What's the plan?"

"Nico Gold is the pale, skinny guy. Kill everyone except him."

Prichard looked to Seven, then back to Carver. "That's it?"

"Were you expecting Xs and Os? This church has been closed for 150 years. There's no floorplan. All we've got in the way of weapons is what you're holding. We're just going to have to fight our way in."

Carver gripped the handle of the heavy door. The hinges emitted a maddening, high-pitched squeal.

*

Nico's hands were trembling. A sound upstairs had made his captors all squirrelly. There were two wide staircases leading up from the basement from the north and south sides of the room. Each goon took a staircase and stood at the ready with their machine pistols.

Fearing a gunfight, Nico scrambled toward the safety of a far corner of the stone room. "No!" one of the goons yelled, switching to English. "You keep working or I kill you!"

Hopeful as he was about the possibility of rescue, the sensation of being under siege weighed upon him. What if it wasn't Carver up there? What if it was the guys from the Fellowship World Initiative? Weren't those crazy bastards just as bad, if not worse?

Suddenly both goons started firing up both staircases. And then they were taking rounds too. Rounds ricocheted off the stairs and whizzed by. Nico squatted with his hands over his head.

"Keep working!" the longhaired zealot screamed at him, looking back over his shoulder. "Or I shoot you!"

He straightened up and tried to focus on the screen. Concentrate, he told himself, willing himself to be braver than he really was. Nothing else matters. Just this.

Onscreen, he had the FAA flight record database for Washington Executive airport, AKA Hyde Field. The little airport was just 30 minutes from D.C., and about 45 minutes from the Eden compound. Earlier he had discovered the name and registration of Wolf's private plane, an eight-passenger Learjet he had picked up in the 1990s. Now he tried to run a simple query for the plane against the data set. His fingers and palms were slick with sweat. His arms ached, as if they would fall off at any moment. His hands seemed to move involuntarily. He had to keep retyping the simple command query again and again until he got it right.

Something exploded behind him, sending stone shards against his back. He turned in time to see the goon switching a new clip into his gun.

He heard a heavy object tumble down the stairs. He turned. The goon yelled "Got one!" in Russian.

Not Carver, Nico thought. Please, don't let it be Carver.

And now the other one shouted something in Romanian and kept firing at something or someone else. The output of gunfire going upstairs seemed heavy in proportion to what was coming down. He hadn't seen Carver with anything other than a handgun.

The database query he ran was impossibly slow. He hoped the connection would remain stable long enough to produce results. Another stray round, this time from the entrance at the other side of the room, bounced from the stairs to the ceiling, floor and back again.

"This is crazy!" he shouted.

"Shut up," the goon closest to him growled before resuming the gunfight.

The rope was behind him. Waiting for him. It was only a matter of time, Nico felt, before these cretins strung him up. He would experience the hopeless sensation of both shoulders dislocating from his body.

He looked right. Broken pieces of a stone slab were piled near the empty body bays cut into the wall. Nico suddenly found himself in motion. He picked up a piece of cut stone that had once been a piece of a burial tomb, heaved it over his shoulder, and rushed the goon.

As Nico swung the slab, his captor turned. Suddenly the bastard looked surprisingly human. Brown eyes. Pimples on the forehead. A look of stunned surprise.

As the stone connected with his skull, a mural of blood splattered across the archway. All Nico's adrenaline seemed to evaporate at once. His ears were ringing. He felt the urge to run, but there was nowhere to go.

*

From his position atop the first staircase to the crypt, Carver heard both machine pistols go silent. Seven and Prichard had been assaulting the other entrance. He was hoping one of them had breached the room. He had only come into this with two spare clips, and he was already two rounds away from empty.

Now gunfire resumed. It was coming from his side of the fight, but judging by the sound of the ricochet at the far end of the crypt below, it was aimed in the opposite direction. The shooter had been distracted by something behind him.

He had to make his move now.

Carver ripped a framed portrait of some long-dead archbishop from the wall beside him. It was approximately five feet in length, and three or so feet wide. Judging by the fact that it had been left behind in this gloomy place, he reckoned that it wouldn't be missed.

He placed the portrait at a 45-degree angle at the top of the staircase and leapt atop the makeshift sled. The edges of the stone steps had been worn down from centuries of use, making for a surprisingly fast descent toward the basement. He managed to hold his balance for approximately two seconds. Then he brought his legs under him and pushed off the sled from the ball of his right foot, exploding forward.

His shooting hand, head and shoulders were the first to enter the room. Time seemed to slow down. His form mimicked the *fleche* technique he had used to win countless fencing bouts over the years – pushing off from the ball of the front foot and flying forward unexpectedly in mid-air for a surprise attack. When facing lefties, Carver used the move to slip behind his opponents and score from behind.

Now in mid-flight, Carver's body cleared the threshold, floating not two feet from the assassin. He was a white, balding European who was obviously stunned by Carver's sudden presence.

Unlike Carver's expert swordplay, his midair shot did not find its mark. The round struck the wall over the man's shoulder. Carver braced his fall by tumbling into a lightweight wooden table. His gun skittered into the shadows.

A set of long blades fell from the table surface, clanging against the stone floor. The blades were sharp and shiny with precious-looking stones along the handles. Ritual blades, Carver noted. Could these have been the same knives used on the others?

Two shots hit the wooden table, splintering the thick wood and missing Carver's face by mere inches. Then Carver heard the chukka-chukka sound of an empty clip being discharged from the assailant's weapon.

He grabbed the longest blade of the bunch – about 18 inches – and rose up as the chrome-domed thug reloaded. Wielding the heavy blade, he sprung forward into a flunge – a combination of the fleche and the traditional lunge – that ended in a chop to the side of the head.

A section of the assailant's scalp flew overhead. He dropped his gun and tried to catch the severed flesh in mid-air. He then crawled toward the place where it landed, clutching it for a moment before the heavy loss of blood rendered him unconscious. Carver lingered over him for a moment, wielding the blood-drenched blade in a defensive stance, as the man's body worked out its final electrical impulses.

"Nico?" he called out.

"I'm all right!" a quivering voice called from the other side of the room.

With Nico safe, Carver refocused on the dead man's face. He couldn't be certain, but the wide flared nostrils, glasses and complexion bore a strong resemblance to the man on the security camera footage they had seen at Legoland.

He took a photograph of the dead man's face. *Are you the one who killed Sir Gish?* Carver wondered. *Did you kill Kenyatta? How many more are there like you?*

Now he heard Seven's voice. He turned and noted the blue glow of a computer screen flickering in the middle of the darkened crypt. He picked up an LED lantern and went to the other side of the room, where its florescent bulbs illuminated Seven and Nico.

Nico wore a dazed stare. His arms were bruised and lacerated in several places. Blood ran down one side of his face from the top of his ear. Carver felt a pang of responsibility. This wasn't what he'd had in mind when he'd extracted Nico from his home. Not even close.

He could tell by the look in Seven's moist eyes that something was very wrong.

"Where?" Carver said.

She pointed to the second staircase. At the bottom, the other Black Order assassin lay dead. His head had been bashed in by a blunt object.

A rivulet of blood snaked its way down the staircase. About halfway up, Prichard was sprawled face-down, his right arm twisted unnaturally behind him. He had been shot once in the chest.

A siren sounded in the distance.

Carver turned back toward Seven. "We have to get out of here."

"I'm not leaving Sam," Seven said.

He looked around. "This is going to be hard to explain to the police."

He went up the steps, removing Prichard's visa and other identification from his pockets. Nico collected both assailants' phones and began sweeping several other items that had spilled from the overturned table into a manila folder.

Seven was frozen in place.

"We're going," Carver said, taking her hand. "All of us."

Piazza di Spagna
Rome

Carver checked them into a luxury hotel near the Spanish Steps that was large enough to feel anonymous. To mask the powder burns and bloodstains on their clothes, they had bought three knockoff designer hoodies from a sidewalk vendor, zipping them as high as they would go. Nico tightened the hood around his head to mask the lacerations on his neck and ear.

Everyone managed to keep it together at the front desk. They did not speak in the elevator. There was a collective exhale as they finally reached the suite, which was larger than Carver's apartment back in D.C. He stood in the living room and watched as Seven went to the minibar and downed six tiny bottles of vodka. She also made fast work of the gin and rum samplers. As if it would help stop the ringing in her ears from the gunfire. As if it would help her stop thinking about Sam Prichard's body, which they had left in the old deconsecrated church crypt.

She went to the second bedroom and, without closing the door, stripped to her undergarments and fell into bed, weeping.

"Why don't you say something?" Nico said.

Carver turned. "Like what?"

"I don't know. Tell her it's going to be all right. Give her a hug. Something."

Carver shook his head. He knew better. His words of comfort would only seem hollow. He couldn't tell her it was going to be all right, because it wasn't going to be all right. At least not for Prichard.

A week ago, he had been sipping tea in his cushy MI6 office. He had never even heard of the Black Order. And tonight the Black Order had killed him.

Carver really knew nothing about him. Was he married? Were his parents alive? Did he have children? It was obvious that he wasn't battle tested, though. Carver had sensed that before launching the attack, and deemed it an acceptable risk.

Nico was their greatest asset right now. His life was simply more valuable than any of theirs. That was the cold, hard reality.

"You know what it's like to lose somebody," Nico reminded him.

The intensity of his glare startled Nico. "I told you," he said. "I don't discuss Agent O'Keefe with anyone."

"Meagan. Her name was Meagan. And you don't have to talk about her. Just tell Seven you understand."

He hated himself at times like this. He wanted to feel more. He didn't want to be so practical. But he could not force himself to think about O'Keefe. He couldn't say her name. If he did, then he would lose all focus. *He* would become the emotional one. Unable to think strategically. Unable to maintain his edge.

It was the downside of hyperthymesia. He did not relive painful memories with the same soft focus that others did. Time created no protective buffer for him. Every moment was relived in excruciating detail. He had learned to suppress effect over the years by denying such memories entry altogether. But once they were unleashed, it was difficult to bottle them up again.

Against his better judgment, he walked to the bedroom. He had not experienced fear during the gun battle tonight, but he felt afraid now. He found it remarkably difficult to put one foot in front of the other.

It wasn't just the fear of uncorking his own emotions, he knew, or the fear of confronting his own suppressed grief. It was a fear of attraction. Seven was witty and brave. She knew how to hotwire a scooter. He could imagine her London flat, white-walled and airy. An expensive bike parked near the front door, to which she owed her round, muscular haunches. A closet was half-filled with biking gear, and the other half with sensible evening wear, as she was often invited to events that required little black dresses and strands of pearls and good shoes.

He went to the bed where Seven was curled up in fetal position, clutching a pillow. Even as upset as she was, she was gorgeous. His eyes traced the contours of her athletic calves, which tapered into ankles that were strong but thin. It was wrong to want her at a time like this, but he did.

God, she smelled like a distillery.

She looked up at him. Waiting for Carver to speak.

"I lost a partner too." His own words surprised him.

Seven swallowed hard. "Really?"

He nodded. "About a year ago."

He sat down on the edge of the bed, keeping his back to her so she wouldn't see the manifestation of his desire in his pants. He put a hand on her calf. Patted it lightly. He felt her cozy up to him. Just close enough so that they were touching.

And he let himself think about Megan O'Keefe. They had been followed to a rendezvous at Arlington House, and they'd escaped into a section of ancient tunnel underneath it that had been built by Robert E. Lee, who had lived there before the civil war. He never should have let her walk point as the partially flooded tunnel led them under the Potomac. He had seen her green eyes bloodshot with fear and felt her tremble at the frenzied screech of the rats up the tunnel walls. It had smelled like burnt oranges down there. And there had been things in the water. Black snakes six feet long. Carp nearly as big around as his waist. She shouldn't have been there to begin with. It was his fault. She had been a NASA cryptologist when Speers had paired them up, and he had objected, at first, to working with an academic like O'Keefe on a mission that was likely to get hairy. He never should have demanded that she take weapons training. And he never should have pretended he hadn't fallen for her on that summer night in the train station. He should have done everything differently.

"Hey Blake," Seven murmured from behind him. He was transported back to the present.

"Yeah?"

"Would you just sit there while I go to sleep?"

The very thing that was hardest for him. Sitting still.

"Sure," he nodded without turning around. "Go ahead and get some shuteye. I'll be right here."

He would be true to his word. With one last task to do before getting some rest, Carver took his phone he had purchased earlier that day out of his pocket and prepared to upload evidence to the mission cloud. Before leaving the church crypt, he had snapped death portraits of the Black Order assassins. Then he had pressed the ends of their gunpowder-blackened fingers onto his phone screen to get their prints. Fortunately, he had an app for that.

Now he navigated to the mission cloud, which resided at a hellishly convoluted URL that only a security specialist could love. Once there, he entered the 23-digit passcode without hesitation.

He uploaded the death photos and the prints to the site with a simple message for Arunus Roth to ID the men. Then he put the phone away and waited for Seven to fall asleep.

The number of lacerations and bruises Nico had suffered kept his shower forcibly brief. He stepped out onto the marble tile, pausing to note the thinness of his white figure in the bathroom window before wrapping a towel around his waist. He opened the first aid kit he had found in the suite's kitchenette and began applying Neosporin to several wounds on his arms, neck and ear. Then he used all eight bandages.

Wearing only the towel, he ventured out into the darkened living room and looked to see if any alcohol had escaped Seven's thirst. He smiled as he found a Peroni beer. He cracked the lid and inhaled the fumes, savoring them before drinking.

Wow that was good. It wasn't like the Italians made the world's best beer. But any beer tonight was good. He was alive.

He walked back to the bedroom and opened the computer. He connected to the hotel wireless, and for the first time, saw the results of the search queries he had run at the church. Excitement pulsed through his veins. This was big.

He felt mildly astonished with himself. Where was the resentfulness he was accustomed to feeling? Where was the victimization? Why didn't he want to blame anyone for the fact that his left ear would need a plastic surgeon? He felt something he had not felt since he began committing cybercrimes for the thrill of it. Invincibility. He had been pulled back from the abyss tonight, and that in itself was proof of his power.

Now he understood why he didn't miss Madge. From the very first letter she had written him in prison, her goal had been to rehabilitate him. To *convert* him. To *own* him.

It was true that he had hurt people using his skills in the past. Madge had helped him understand that. But she had also wanted him to let go of those skills completely. And he had. Quit cold turkey. There hadn't been so much as a mobile device in the house at Kei Mouth. Given all that they had been through, and given the way the Feds had "repaid" him for his good deeds during the Ulysses Coup, leaving it all behind had made sense at the time.

But in the process he had allowed Madge to transform him into someone else. Someone *average*, in an anonymous place, with aspirations that nobody would ever care about. That wasn't who he was.

He closed his eyes, resolving to hold onto this feeling of renewal. His life was his again. There was only one piece missing. The control of his own destiny.

✱

Carver woke on the couch. He patted his chest, feeling for the shoulder holster to make sure he had not been disarmed during sleep. The weapon was still there. Then he glanced at his wristwatch. Good. It wasn't dawn yet.

He went to the balcony for some fresh air. A few street vendors were sleeping on the Spanish Steps in the very spots where, a few short hours from now, they would sell knockoff designer sunglasses, handbags and other wares. In the Piazza di Spagna he could see the illuminated Fountain of the *Barcaccia*, which had been created by Bernini's father, Pietro. The 400-year-old public artwork was such a kid magnet – they were always leaping on and off the thing, drinking from it, throwing stuff into it – that Carver had never seen it unobstructed. Here, stripped down to its core, it was shockingly plain. A partially submerged boat that seemed to be sinking fast.

He spun around, detecting movement behind him. It was Nico, dressed in a fuzzy white hotel robe. He opened the balcony door.

"Can't sleep?"

Nico shook his head. "I think Wolf is in Rome."

Excitement stirred within Carver. "Say more about that."

"A private Learjet owned by the World Fellowship Initiative landed at Ciampino Airport last week. There's a good chance that Wolf was on it."

Carver felt as if he had known it all along. Despite the killings in London, Washington, Seattle and Geneva, Wolf's past and present always seemed to point to the Eternal city.

He put his hands in his pockets and held Nico's gaze. "A lot of people would have given up after what you went through tonight."

Nico seemed stunned by the lack of irony in Carver's sentiment. "Well, out of the frying pan and into the fire, as they say."

"I won't let you down when this is over. I want you to know that."

Nico held his gaze for a moment before gathering himself. "This sincerity stuff is a little awkward coming from you."

"Yeah, I know."

"I was about to look at the stuff we took from the crypt. Care to join?"

Nico went to the little kitchenette and found the manila envelope next to the toaster. He dumped its contents out onto the Formica countertop. It was a hasty assembly of loose notes, receipts and documents.

The two men quickly rifled through the mess. It hit Carver that this collection of ordinary items could easily have been a collection from his own desk in D.C. Were they somehow tracking expenses for reimbursement, or was one of them simply fastidious about his own personal finances?

Among the many incidental receipts for fuel and food, were two punched airline tickets from Rome to London.

Nico examined the dates. "The arrival date at Heathrow was three days prior to Sir Gish's assassination."

Carver nodded. "Good. Upload them to the mission cloud."

"Will do. And one other thing. While you were sleeping, I managed to hack into one of the creep's phones. There were no messages stored on the device, but I did uncover these."

Carver took the phone and flipped through a series of candid photos of Sir Gish. In each he was dressed in a suit and was clearly on a subway car of some type.

"They were following him," Carver observed. "Look at this one. You can see a station ad for the London Eye behind him. That's right on Gish's daily routine to parliament."

Had they indeed gotten lucky and killed Gish's assassins last night? He hoped so. It would make Prichard's death a little easier to stomach.

Carver kept flipping. There were hundreds of pictures. Some looked as if they had been taken on a different device and simply downloaded to the phone.

One such image compelled him to pause. "The Council on Faith luncheon in Washington D.C.," he said, reading the image tag.

"Looks like it was taken on 35 mil," Nico added.

"For sure. It was taken in 2001. You couldn't get this kind of definition on digital back then."

Several young congressmen were pictured with a white-haired man whom, judging by the way they all deferred to him with their body language, they obviously regarded as a patriarch.

"This might be the last public snapshot of Sebastian Wolf," Carver said.

"Check out that hair. What's that gel he's using? Liquefied horse cartilage?"

"Tag it and upload to the mission cloud."

The final image was the one that really made Carver's heart race. The subject was thin, with neck-length black hair, an Anglo nose and Asian eyes behind black-framed Armani eyeglasses.

"Adrian Zhu."

It was all starting to add up. The Fellowship's investment in LifeEmberz. Zhu's disappearance in Rome. And now this confirmation that Zhu himself was on the Black Order hit list. There was no question about it. Zhu wasn't merely associated with Wolf's organization. He was critical to its success.

And if Wolf was in Rome, Carver was willing to bet everything that Zhu was still here too.

✱

Carver rubbed his eyes and yawned into his hand. Nico had finally gone to bed, but he had continued working. The sun was coming in through the balcony glass now, the light warming his back. In the last hour he had organized the items they had taken from the church crypt into three piles. One pile pointed at evidence that seemed to confirm that the Black Order operatives they had killed were likely responsible for the death of Sir Gish. Another pile pointed to a hunt for Adrian Zhu. And yet another contained the lone photograph of Sebastian Wolf. All were Black Order targets.

He called Dr. Charlotte Calipari, a molecular geneticist Speers had introduced him to at a State Department event the previous year. Although it had been some time since they had connected, and it was nearly 10 p.m. back in D.C., he took a chance. Calipari was the only person he had ever met who had supervised the creation of a paleo-DNA lab.

"If you had to build such a lab today," Carver asked, "and you wanted to also clone from dead tissue, where would you find the equipment?"

There was a long pause before her response. "Well that's not the sort of question I hear every day."

Carver was acutely aware of the strangeness of the question. The fact was that Calipari owed him no favors. The only tool at his disposal was flattery. "When we met, I was impressed by you. I thought if there was anyone in the world qualified to answer this, it would be you."

"You're too kind. Fortunately, the answer to your question is simple. Short of creating your own machines, there would be only a couple of places where you could turn to get what you needed. The community is very small. There are just two providers in the entire world that are really considered state-of-the-art right now."

Carver smiled. "And those would be?"

Psychiatric Office Washington D.C.

Ellis wore oversized sunglasses to mask the facial bruises she'd sustained in Seattle. She eased down on the couch, her demeanor cool and distant behind the big black lenses. The doctor had said she'd be a little foggy for the next few days. Her memories were coming back to her, but not quickly enough to be of much use.

The shrink was in her mid-40s, with long brown hair tied in a ponytail and expensive eyeglasses. She sat across from Ellis in an armchair that looked comfortable enough to nap in.

"So," she said after some cursory introductions. "You want to tell me what's on your mind?"

Ellis shook her head. "Honestly, I don't even know why I'm here. It's not my choice."

Speers had personally insisted that she come. Some agency rule about preventing post-traumatic stress.

The shrink nodded sympathetically. "I understand they gave you something out in Seattle to calm your nerves."

"Well I'm not taking it."

"And why is that?"

"My job requires that my thoughts be as clear as possible."

The shrink scanned the notes in her lap. "I was told you're not on active duty right now. That you'd been granted some recovery time."

True, she wasn't out in the field. But the weight of the investigation hadn't left her mind for one minute. She had spent every waking moment going over the case notes, including Drucker's manuscript. She was unable to stay awake for long periods, but even in sleep, the Living Scriptures were circling round and round in her foggy brain. She had trouble concentrating. She couldn't eat. And she dreamed in numbers. Some endless, unsolvable code.

The shrink leaned forward. "I specialize in trauma. I see a lot of military. It helps some people to start by telling me their experience in general terms. Even if your case was classified, telling me basic information is permissible within the privacy protections of our relationship. Believe me, I've heard everything."

Ellis doubted that anyone had told the shrink anything like what she had experienced. Nothing Ellis had seen in Iraq had even come close. What she saw in Seattle was straight out of a horror movie.

"You want to help?" Ellis said. "Okay. I need to remember something specific."

"What would that be?"

"A conversation. The night I was attacked, someone was dying right in front of me. She was telling me something. It might be important. A name, maybe."

The shrink was silent for a moment. "I'm not sure you're ready to remember that level of detail. It could do more harm than good."

Yeah, obviously. Part of Ellis was terrified of remembering any more. She might never sleep again. But her gut told her that she *had* to know.

"Haley?"

"There was a woman hanging over me," Ellis began, making a mental note not to mention Vera Borst by name.

"Hanging?" the shrink asked, trying unsuccessfully to mask the dread she felt inside. "Hanging how?"

"In mid-air." Her voice was suddenly tight with emotion. "She was bound at the wrists. Suspended by the wrists by a thick rope. Bleeding. She had been sliced up."

The shrink did her best not to show the revulsion that she felt. "Again, I'm worried that we may be going too fast."

"She knew she was dying. And I think she told me something important. A message of some sort. I need to remember what that was."

The shrink sipped her tea. An obvious stalling tactic. She was formulating what she wanted to say next.

"Can you do hypnosis?" Ellis asked.

"Sure, but in this case…"

"You want to help? Then I want you to hypnotize me."

Piazza di Spagna

Nico woke to slushing and splashing sounds. He looked at the clock next to the bed. He had slept four hours, which was more than Carver had allowed him since this little adventure had begun. His body complained as he turned, aching all over from the bruises he had taken during the previous evening's ordeal. There was a little blood on his pillow, too. He touched the ear that had been cut, not at all surprised to find that the scab had come off in the night.

He rose, shuffled into the bathroom and found Carver stripped down to his boxers, kneeling in front of the tub, rubbing a soaked garment with detergent.

"That shirt is dry-clean only," Nico said in a mock-scolding voice.

"Hilarious."

Carver stood, looking down at the tub full of submerged garments. He had been soaking them since daybreak with a bottle of stain remover and a packet of detergent that room service had brought up. Despite his scrubbing, those blood and powder stains hadn't faded much. It wasn't like they could just give them to the hotel laundry service. These clothes contained evidence that could put them in an Italian prison for a very long time.

"I'm ready to work," Nico said. "What's on the agenda?"

"I'm going to give you the names of two laboratory equipment manufacturers, along with the model numbers of some specialty items. Extremely expensive, completely custom, sold to a very limited number of customers. I want you to find out if either of them shipped equipment to Rome within the past two years. I don't care how you do it. Hack into their billing systems if you have to."

Nico leaned up against the doorframe and folded his arms across his chest. "Do I have to ask?"

"If my theory is right, a shipment from at least one of these companies should lead us to a lab here in Rome. And that is where we will find Adrian Zhu, Mary Borst and, if we are very lucky, Mr. Sebastian Wolf."

Psychiatric Office
Washington D.C.

"Haley?" Jack McClellan's voice startled Ellis as she emerged from the session. "You all right?"

"Yeah," she answered without thinking. And no, she wasn't all right. She had just been to a place in her memory that truly terrified her, and she didn't even know what time it was. She had forgotten that Jack was even here. It seemed like days since he had driven her here from the safehouse in McLean.

There were a couple of young girls in the waiting room. Both lowered their magazines slightly to sneak a peek. They were sizing her up. That was the way it worked in these places. You hoped to spot someone who looked more damaged than you. At least then you could feel a little better about yourself.

"Jill called when you were in there," McClellan said as he held the door open for her. "She wants to know if she could get lamb shawarma delivered. Said you know a good place. I told her nothing gets delivered to the safehouse, but we could get one of the guys to pick it up."

Shawarma? Screw shawarma. Couldn't he see her quaking? Couldn't he see what she had just been through?

Her forehead throbbed, and she remembered the big sunglasses. She'd slipped them back on just before standing up. To hide the bruises. It had been the shrink's suggestion. How had she put it? *You might be more comfortable with those on.*

A few seconds later they were outside, standing on 10th and G Street. St. Patrick's Cathedral was across the street. It had been her regular church a few years back when she had lived in Chinatown. She hadn't been there in a couple of years.

She darted between two cars and raced across the street.

"Where you going?" Jack called after her. "Haley? We have to get back."

When she entered the 18th-century church, she wasn't sure why she had come. The next mass didn't start for another hour. She sat in a back pew, unfurled her scarf and used the end of it to wipe the tear tracks from her cheeks.

"My job is to keep you safe," Jack said. He was standing in the aisle, looking down at her in a way that reminded her of her own father. "This kind of stunt stops now."

Ellis looked down at the piece of paper in her hands. A transcription of what she had recalled during her hypnosis. At the bottom of the sheet of paper, circled in pen, was a 32-digit alphanumeric sequence. Vera Borst had used her last moments to reveal it to her. Now that the hypnosis had finally been purged it from her subconscious, her relief was tempered by the fact that she still didn't know what the numbers meant.

"Haley, please."

"Just a little time. That's all I need."

Jack sighed. "Ten minutes. Then we're going, no arguments. Do we understand each other?"

A confessional booth came into focus along the western edge of the sanctuary. She recalled her first time in confession, as an eight-year-old child. She had been too shy to speak to the priest peering at her through the tiny veiled screen. After several unsuccessful attempts to start a conversation, he had simply laughed and given her a blessing. It was a good feeling that had stayed with her throughout her life.

Now she found herself on her feet, peering in through the open curtain.

"Have a seat." The priest's voice was more youthful than Ellis had expected. "Peace be with you."

Ellis drew the curtain behind her and sat, making the sign of the cross. The screen disguising the priest's face was closed. That was good. Ellis preferred it that way.

"Bless me Father," she said quietly, "For I have sinned. It has been 11 days since my last confession. These are my sins."

Her recap was automatic. Brief, lacking any real detail, and neatly categorized into several general areas: desire, envy, gluttony, greed and selfishness. As if the events of the past few days hadn't really happened at all.

The priest was silent for a few moments. Then he said, "Why don't you tell me what's really bothering you?"

The next sound from Ellis was somewhere between a cry and a laugh. She took her sunglasses off and held them in her lap. "Sorry."

"No need to be sorry," the priest said. "Would you like to do this face-to-face?"

"No offense, but no, I wouldn't."

"None taken. So what's up?"

She tried to gather herself. "I don't know why I'm here."

"Just start with one word. The rest will follow."

"What if someone asked you for protection? Someone with beliefs that were against everything you'd been taught?"

"Welcome to my world. Most of the people I help have no connection with our beliefs."

"I'm not talking about the weekly soup kitchen, Father. I mean *real* protection."

"As in mortal danger?"

Ellis nodded. "The person in danger is…someone that I don't know at all. And her child."

The priest hedged for a moment. "I would probably advise you to contact the authorities."

"I *am* the authorities."

"Oh. You're with the police?"

"I can't say more. But let me ask you another way. What if you knew that this child's very presence would cause violence and death? Would you still protect that child?"

"God doesn't ask us to make those types of decisions. For us, every life is precious."

"He's asking me, Father. What if the church itself was genuinely threatened?"

The youthful voice sounded weary now. "I have to ask…are you under the care of a doctor?"

"I'm not crazy. I'm asking for your spiritual opinion."

"All right. I'll tell you what the Catechism of the Catholic Church has to say on the matter. In short, those who hold authority have the right to use arms to repel aggressors against the community entrusted to their responsibility. And furthermore, the literature says that justice does not exclude the death penalty, if this is indeed the only possible way of defending human lives against the aggressor."

"That's helpful."

"To be clear, even within this context, it's never okay to use God's name to justify murder. We each take that responsibility upon ourselves, and throw ourselves upon the mercy of the Lord. If you are contemplating such actions, I would like to recommend several scriptural readings that may help you think as Jesus intended us to. Just a moment."

By the time the priest began reading, Ellis was gone.

Vatican District

"That's Father Callahan's building," Carver told Seven as he pointed at the elegant four-floor structure across the street. He had always guessed that with Callahan's income from the CIA, Vatican Intelligence and other sources, his digs were a cut above what most of the priests had in the Eternal City. This confirmed it. The apartment was on the third floor, with shutters that opened from both bedrooms. A small balcony jutted out from the living room with window boxes full of fresh flowers.

They had come in hopes of anything that would lead them to the remaining Black Order operatives.

It was broad daylight, but that didn't matter much. Carver didn't expect to find the priest at home. One way or the other, Callahan had been an accomplice to Nico's abduction. If he was working with the Black Order, he would be long gone by now. If he wasn't, he was likely dead.

"You do any climbing?" Seven asked.

Carver shrugged. "Not really. Just a couple of indoor climbing walls."

"It's just three floors up. Piece of cake. Just follow my lead."

He watched as Seven walked underneath the front canopy and jumped straight up, gripping the canopy frame. She swung her right foot into a crevice in the brickwork. Then she reached to the side, gripping a decorative flourish in the building's façade and, with spider-like movements, pawed her way up the building's face until she was high enough to grab the ironwork supporting the second floor balcony.

She paused to look down at Carver, who stood in awe on the sidewalk. "Coming?"

"No. Just buzz me in, will you?"

In less than a minute, Seven let him into the apartment. She was covering her nose with her sleeve, and Carver soon caught wind of the overwhelming stench.

"Somebody died," Seven whispered.

Carver didn't think so. He'd smelled plenty of decomposing bodies before. That was a stench you never forgot. This was something else.

The apartment was ransacked. Every drawer and cabinet in the place was open. The floor was strewn with clothing and documents. A suitcase that looked as if it had been carved up with a razor blade sat open on the couch.

The bathroom and lone bedroom were clear. Carver found the source of the smell in the kitchen. The refrigerator door had been left wide open. Carver slammed the door on a piece of raw fish and a few warm dairy products.

A shrill ringing sent Seven darting across the room. She spun so that her back was against the wall and her weapon was extended before her.

"Relax," Carver said, pointing to an old analog phone mounted on the kitchen wall. "You think I should answer it?"

Seven swallowed hard and nodded.

Carver picked up the yellow receiver and put his ear to it.

"I'd just about given up on you."

The voice belonged to Father Callahan. So he was alive. Carver slowly lowered himself into a chair, scanning the shelves and ceiling. Where was the camera?

"I suspect the line is bugged," the priest said, "so do be concise, if you please. You remember where I took you for dinner on your first trip to Rome?"

It would have been a ludicrous question for nearly anyone else. That had been years ago. The city was huge and contained thousands of restaurants that would seem similar to a foreigner. Nobody could have been expected to remember something like that.

And yet Carver did remember. He had arrived in town very late, arriving at the priest's apartment at 11:37 p.m. He had been famished. The priest had taken him to a *trattoria* called Osteria Dell'Angelo just a few blocks north of the apartment. The cross streets were Via Pietro and Via Simone. They had been served a fixed menu consisting of *tonnarelli cacio e pepe* and tripe and braised oxtail. The proprietor was an ex-rugby player who had chastised Carver for not touching his wine during dinner.

"Yes, I remember."

"I thought you might. Rendezvous in front in two hours."

The line went dead.

The White House

Speers sat on the couch opposite Chad Fordham. President Hudson was running a few minutes late, and Speers was grateful for the additional prep time. In the span of a week, he had gone from a broad, strategic integrator of the intelligence community to a hands-on doer who had to hyperfocus on a single massive threat and its ripple effect across borders, time zones and allegiances.

Carol Lam entered with a tray of her famous cappuccinos. On the edge of each small plate rested a small moist brownie.

"Fudge?" Speers inquired.

"Homemade," Carol said. Her smile faded when she saw Speers' swollen ankle elevated in an opposing chair. "May I ask what happened?"

"If I told you, Chad here would have to put you in the witness protection program."

"Well, enjoy the pick-me-up."

He intended to. The ankle was improved, but it still hurt like hell. Even a small gesture of compassion felt good. On the few occasions when he had come home over the past week, all he'd gotten was a cold glare and a garbage bag full of dirty diapers.

The president entered just as Carol left, wearing a black top with a white ruffled collar. "I have London on video conference," she said without preamble. She motioned for them to rise and follow her through the east door into her private study. There, Speers was astonished to see that the British Prime Minister had joined Sir Brice Carlisle onscreen.

The president quickly introduced Speers and Fordham. Sir Brice wasted no time on pleasantries. "I'm told that our joint operation in Rome last night eliminated Gish's killers in addition to the two others that were dispatched in Seattle. Where does that leave us? Are we out of the woods?"

Speers set his cappuccino on the table. "We are left with an unknown number of Black Order operatives still on the loose that may continue to target prominent world leaders. So no, we are not out of the woods. Our joint efforts in Rome continue as we try to locate the ossuary."

"The ossuary," Sir Brice said dismissively. "Surely you don't believe the myth. It's rubbish, right?"

Speers carefully measured the tone of his answer. "It really doesn't matter what we believe. The security situation deteriorated the moment it was taken from the Vatican."

"So according to you, people will continue to die until this relic is recovered. How many people are we talking about?"

"We have identified," Speers began, "with 95 percent confidence, 11 surviving senior members of The Fellowship World Initiative. This includes foreign ministers from Australia and New Zealand, several prominent Middle Eastern and European politicians, a congressman from Indiana, and the CEOs of two multinational companies. There are also hundreds of others that we suspect but have yet to verify."

Fordham cut in. "Until the ossuary is recovered, we strongly recommend alerting these individuals as to the threat they face, and if possible, extending security around them."

"And how would that help us?" Sir Carlisle probed.

"Isn't it obvious?" Speers said. "These are all people with significant power and influence. Until the ossuary is found, they've got targets on their back."

"Offering protection could be perceived as taking sides," the President said.

"No," Speers insisted. "This is peacekeeping."

The prime minister spoke for the first time. "Here's a mad idea. What would happen if we just let this play out?"

"You mean, just let them kill each other?"

"Precisely."

Speers chuckled, and then pulled it back, suddenly aware of how condescending he sounded. "Let me try to put this into perspective. Hundreds of years after the Crusades, we view the Sunni and Shi'a violence in the Muslim world as something that's so foreign, so unimaginable to us. That's just because we have short-term memories. It wasn't so long ago that Protestants and Catholics in Ireland were killing each other on a regular basis. And that was Europe for hundreds of years, by the way."

"I see your point."

"Do you? With all due respect, I'm telling you that this situation is a powder keg. If we're not proactive, we're going to experience global sectarian violence like the world has never seen."

The group sat in silence for several moments. The president looked up at the screen. "Gentlemen, I need just a few minutes alone with my staff, if you don't mind."

The screen faded to black before displaying the presidential seal. The President stood and went to the window. "Julian," she began while looking out at the south lawn, "you said it doesn't matter what we believe. What if our beliefs are the only thing that really matters?"

Rome

Carver and Seven sat picking at salads and San Pellegrino. The priest was already a half-hour late. They were taking a risk waiting here. Carver's trust in Callahan had waned considerably in the last two days. Still, his instincts told him that they needed to get to Lang, and that was going to be very difficult without the priest's help.

"I could down an entire bottle of grappa," Seven said, gesturing to a cabinet full of the stuff. "Every time I slow down, I see Sam's body on that staircase."

Carver nodded solemnly, not knowing what to say. Every comment that popped into his head seemed inane or insensitive. Finally, he said, "Were you two close?"

She thought about the question for a few moments before speaking. "Personally speaking, I didn't care for him. But he somehow managed to have a family, which is far more than I can say for most of us. There must've been something good about him."

"Right," Carver managed, even though he didn't agree. Even Charles Manson had a "family." That didn't mean there was anything good about him.

"What about you? Anyone waiting for you at home?"

"Just Marty."

"Let me guess. A dog?"

"A pipe organ cactus. He's very understanding about these long trips away from home."

Carver was relieved when his phone buzzed. His eyebrows arched as he read the text message.

"Callahan?" Seven said hopefully.

"Nico. He's got something."

He wasted no time in logging into the mission cloud. Nico had apparently infiltrated the booking systems for at least one of the lab equipment manufacturing companies.

Carver began perusing an air waybill from a company called Symplexicon Labs, and a detailed packing list containing virtually every piece of equipment that Dr. Calipari had mentioned. There was an additional set of shipments from 9002 River Road, in Rockville, Maryland. Eden.

Nico had linked the delivery address to a satellite map of Rome, along with a street view photograph. Carver was not surprised when he saw the Renaissance-era mansion near Piazza del Popolo. A man of Wolf's means was not going to downsize from Eden to a one-bedroom apartment.

A white Peugeot sedan pulled up slowly. It was obviously a rental. As for the driver, Carver would have recognized Callahan's bulbous head anywhere.

He laid 20 Euros on the table and ran out to the car with Seven. They got into the back seat and buckled themselves in as Callahan stepped on it.

"Where the hell have you been hiding?" the priest said, peering nervously into the rear view mirror. "I've been trying to call you."

"I had to ditch the satphone," Carver said, deliberately withholding the story about Nico's abduction. "When you didn't show for our meeting, I started feeling itchy."

The priest made a sharp turn into a parking garage, where Carver guessed he intended to leave the car.

"That makes two of us, my friend. My home security alerts went off about an hour before we were supposed to meet. I was finishing up a funeral at the time. Dust to dust, etcetera. You can imagine my shock when I logged into my living room camera feed and saw someone ransacking the place."

"Anyone you know?"

"Unfortunately, yes. Someone I've hired from time to time. And by the looks of the sound suppressor screwed onto his gun, he found a new employer."

The priest pulled into a parking spot and shut off the motor. A car came careening down the aisle. The priest, Carver and Seven unbuckled their seatbelts and dropped to the floorboards. The car's radio blasted Italian pop as it passed harmlessly.

"Kids," the priest sighed with relief. He popped the trunk and got out of the car. "I packed us some goodies."

The three went to the trunk and looked down upon a treasure trove of weaponry, ammunition, satphones and assorted devices.

"Time for a yard sale," Carver said. He reached in and plucked out one of many stun grenades that were still in the original factory box. "Could have used a couple of these last night."

"Was there some trouble?"

"You could say that."

"You remember Antonio Tesla?" Callahan said. "The detective from the city morgue?"

"Sure."

"He left several voicemails saying he was looking for you. He wants you to come down to the morgue to look at three more bodies."

Seven swore and broke away, stomping down the aisle of parked cars.

"What's with her?" the priest asked.

"One of those cadavers was her partner."

The priest shook his head. "Bloody shame. This thing's getting out of control fast."

Carver opened a rifle case containing a disassembled Heckler & Koch assault rifle. He picked up the butt stock and tested it against his shoulder. "It was nice of you to bring toys," he said, "but I was hoping for information."

"I did some snooping around, all right. You were right about Lang. I'm afraid he's gotten himself mixed up with the Black Order."

Carver nodded, having suspected all along. "I need you to take me to him."

Callahan laughed. "I'm afraid my access to the Apostolic Palace has been revoked."

"That won't be a problem. I found another way in."

"What in heavens are you talking about?"

"That little Vatican break-in you told me about? The one they spun as art theft? They didn't come for the Garofalo. And they sure as hell didn't come through the front door."

The White House
Washington D.C.

At Eva's request, Mary brought the rest of the fudge brownies into her private study. After wave upon wave of interns had hit the plate, just nine cut squares had survived.

Mary set the tray down on the table. "Rough day?"

"And about to get rougher," the president said. "Thanks."

She waited until Mary had left the room to pick up one of the decadently fudgy brownies. She forced herself to chew slowly. Lunch was usually a blur of quick micro snacks afforded by her caveman diet. A handful of nuts, a few berries, an olive or two.

"Madam President," Speers asked, "You ever regret declaring war on the vending machines?"

In an effort to boost the overall health of the staff, she had ordered vending machines removed from all White House areas. In their place, she had added refrigerators and shelves stocked with a variety of organic snacks. The move had inspired a variety of anonymous notes decrying the presence of items such as kale chips and unsweetened green tea, and demanding an immediate return of Cheetos and Diet Coke. To stave off complete mutiny, Eva had decided to pay for the new fare with her own money for one year.

"If the staff saw me eating like this, they'd hate me."

"I think you should have left just one machine," Speers said. "Chocolate only, with the prices jacked up so high that the staff would only use it in times of serious emotional crises."

"Like the one I'm having right now?"

"You don't seem emotional."

"The fact is, I have something difficult to share with you, and I wanted something sweet to kill the bad taste in my mouth."

The two intelligence directors set their treats down and braced themselves for bad news. Speers dabbed a napkin at the corner of his mouth.

"Given the misdirection tactics we employed in our public information efforts around the deaths of Senator Preston and Sir Gish," she said, "I asked you to give me clear options, but also to keep me ignorant from the details. It seems now that my directive wasn't so smart."

Speers folded his arms across his chest. "How so?"

"Today was the first time you've mentioned the name Sebastian Wolf in my presence," she said. "I have to disclose to you that Sebastian Wolf is an acquaintance of mine."

Speers swore, and then apologized for his language. His stomach felt as if he were freefalling. How could this happen? He knew the president was an Episcopalian. Was she also in the Fellowship?

Fordham slumped back in his chair, as if he had been slugged. "And how is it that you two know each other?"

Eva leaned back in her chair, looking up at the ceiling. "We were introduced by Senator Preston at the Council on Faith luncheon. He invited me to Eden for dinner. I began with my standard line about having someone look into my schedule, which means it'll never happen. Then the Senator told me that Wolf had helped create NASA, and that he was a major source of funding for genetic research, and that every president since LBJ had been a guest at his home at least once."

"Did Preston also tell you that he was a former Nazi?" Speers said.

"Julian, please shut up and let me finish."

"I'm sorry, Madam President."

"I suppose I felt unduly obligated. So I asked my scheduler to make it happen."

Speers was awestruck. "And?"

"And I enjoyed his company. After that, I invited him to the White House on two occasions."

Speers felt that his head would explode. The president of the United States had ties with a cult leader that had made himself the archenemy of the Catholic Church. And Senator Preston had facilitated the introduction.

"What was the nature of your conversations?" Speers asked.

"Truth be told, I found him to be an excellent sounding board on spiritual matters."

"Did you two discuss the Fellowship?" Fordham said. "Did you discuss anything related to these weird science projects he was funding?"

"No. Our conversations were very personal in nature. There was no business involved whatsoever. And he never mentioned this ossuary business. That is a complete shock to me, I swear to you."

Speers sighed. "We're going to need to ask you to fully document every conversation between the two of you."

Eva sipped her coffee slowly, and then set it down on the table. "No. That's not going to happen."

"Come again?"

"This will go no further than this room. I'm telling you this in complete confidence so that we can pivot our tactical situation as needed. I have no intention of having these details unearthed in a declassified document decades from now."

The two intelligence chiefs eyed each other. "Madam President," Speers said, "This has the potential to compromise our strategy."

"As I understand the situation," Eva said, "The outcome of the war between these two secret societies could adversely impact more than just national security. That's why I'm asking you to solve the situation in the shadows, without the need for us to retract our public statements or otherwise undermine our authority."

Speers leaned forward, lowering his voice. "I don't mean to be insensitive, Madam President, but the solution may require eliminating Mr. Wolf."

"Then I need to remind you that he's an American citizen who is permitted to practice freedom of religion."

"Yes ma'am. But – "

"Has Mr. Wolf been formally accused of a crime?"

"Not formally, Madam President. But we strongly suspect –"

"My understanding is that the Black Order, not the Fellowship, has been responsible for the violent aggression, as well as the crimes against Americans."

Speers wanted to tell her about the Nathan Drucker murder, but it was purely speculation at this point. They still had no leads on who had operated the nanobot that had killed him just blocks from the West Wing.

"That's largely true," Speers consented, "but there are dead on both sides of this. I can't tell you more without getting into a lot of detail."

Eva stood, signaling that the meeting was over. "Gentlemen, I want this matter brought to a quiet close. I want the satisfaction of knowing that those who killed Americans and our allies are avenged. I also want your assurances that the civil liberties of our citizens will be upheld, no matter how far away they may be."

The security chiefs thanked Eva for her time and exited through the dining room en route to the hallway. Speers removed his pocket square and dabbed the sweat from his face as they passed the cabinet room.

"Civil liberties upheld?" Fordham said, scratching his head. "What the hell was that all about?"

"It means she's not going to authorize lethal force against Wolf or the Fellowship."

"So where does that leave us?"

"In the same position we were an hour ago. Balance must be restored. And this is why you have a guy like Blake Carver. His status is deniable."

Castel Sant'Angelo

Carver, Seven Mansfield and Father Callahan stood at the south end of Ponte Sant'Angelo, the bridge connecting the Vatican district with old Rome. The bridge was studded with enormous white marble angels holding instruments of the Crucifixion. Whips. Nails. A lance. A cross. A crown of thorns. On the opposite side of the Tiber River, Castel Sant'Angelo, the Vatican's ancient fortress, seemed to bristle against the late afternoon skyline.

They stood on the sidewalk, all three wearing clerical robes, virtually indistinguishable from many of the other religious tourists along the river. A cold wind blew, threatening to blow back the hood Seven had pulled over her scalp.

"Don't make eye contact," Callahan warned her. Even without makeup, what showed of her face was unmistakably feminine. "God help me, if I survive this, I will flog myself mightily for giving you those costumes."

A hunch told Carver that Castel Sant'Angelo – which was rumored to have light security – was the entry point that the Fellowship had used to breach the wider Vatican complex. It was linked to the Apostolic Palace by the *passato borgo*, the 800-meter elevated walkway. It was the same route, in reverse, that popes over the centuries had used to flee danger. During the sack of Rome in 1526, Pope Clement VII had fled from the Vatican Palace to Castel Sant'Angelo while 147 Swiss Guard were said to have perished on the steps of St. Peter's Basilica.

Callahan had divulged an even more secretive way in, which made use of the underground tunnels linking Castel Sant'Angelo with the Apostolic Palace. Carver hoped he was right. Their lives depended on it.

Like so many truth-seeking pilgrims before them, they began their trek toward the Vatican by crossing the *Ponte*

Sant'Angelo. Much like the marble angels Bernini had sculpted, bearing the instruments of death, the bridge had been, for centuries, one of the Vatican's favorite execution sites. Enemies of the state had been hanged, burned, bludgeoned, beheaded and even quartered by the hundreds. If they failed to reach Lang tonight, a new wave of bloodshed would wash over Europe, and for that matter, the world.

They passed high over the Tiber River and neared the circular hulk of brick and limestone at the end of the bridge. Carver spotted Via della Conciliazione – where they had stayed until Nico's abduction – to the left. At the far end he could see the massive dome of St. Peter's Basilica, and the Vatican Palace, the seat of power for one billion Catholics worldwide.

Soon they stood directly in front of the imposing structure. At the top, a bronzed Archangel Michael drew his sword. Circular battlements were perfectly positioned to defend attacks from land or water.

A brown circular ditch stood where a moat had once encircled the structure. Carver imagined the carnage that had ensued when the Goths had come with an attack so fierce that the Roman soldiers had been forced, out of self-defense, to push priceless marble statues down upon them.

Castel Sant'Angelo had begun as a tomb for the Emperor Hadrian in 135 AD. Over the years it had morphed into a prison with an interior courtyard reserved for executing scientists and heretics. During World War II, Sebastian Wolf himself had been briefly imprisoned here.

No one bothered to search their packs as they entered. Callahan had been right. For a place holding so much priceless art, security was amazingly light. The palace, of course, would be another story.

Apostolic Palace

Heinz Lang's lip curled into a sneer as he entered his office. He paused at the door as he took in the vision of Father Callahan sitting behind his desk, surrounded by the portraits of Ignatius of Loyola, Francis Borgia and Everard Mercurian.

Carver stepped out from behind the door and shut it, caging the wizened Vatican Intelligence chief in his own office. Lang spun around at the speed of a much younger man, his black vestments swirling with his movements.

"Your Excellency," Callahan said, "allow me to introduce Blake Carver."

Lang did not appear to be intimidated. "Agent Carver," he said, "I had a feeling our paths would cross eventually."

Seven stepped out from a shadow at the other end of the room, where she held a loaded Beretta. The shapeless black cassock hid her feminine curves.

"And may I introduce my counterpart," Carver said. "Seven Mansfield."

She slid the hood back, revealing her face. Lang's face filled with disgust at the sight of a woman in clerical clothing.

"Your revulsion is nothing compared to the way I felt yesterday," Callahan said.

"Oh, Father!" Lang mocked. "Did you have an unwanted house guest?"

"Judging by the sound suppressor screwed onto the end of his gun, he didn't drop by to chat."

"You give me far too much credit," Lang objected. "When it comes to creating dangerous enemies, you are hardly in need of my help."

He went to a sitting area at the far end of the room with a billion-dollar view of St. Peter's Square at night. He rested his bones in a purple-upholstered chair, picked up a decanter emblazoned with the Society of Jesus emblem, and poured a crystal chalice full of Chianti.

"I would offer you one, Agent Carver, but I understand you always decline alcohol. An unfortunate result of your Mormon upbringing, no doubt. And on the other hand, puritanism is a habit Father Callahan would be wise to pick up, given his legendary weakness for drink."

Carver joined him, sitting in another of the purple chairs. "If wine is the secret to your longevity," he said, "Maybe I should reconsider."

"Oh, the Vatican is full of spritely old goats like me. The secret to a long life, as far as we are concerned, is plenty of walking, prayer, and yes, wine. Fortunately, the Vatican grounds offer plenty of opportunities for all three."

"Which makes your high-risk activities all the more perplexing."

"Must we play riddles? Out with it."

"From what I've seen, membership in the Black Order seems to diminish one's lifespan considerably."

The former Jesuit chief sipped his Chianti, focusing his eyes on Carver. "You need to get your history straight, Agent Carver. Pope Alexander VII dissolved the Black Order in 1655. He was a man of great reform. He sought to cleanse the empire of its brutality and prejudice, and by most accounts, he made remarkable progress."

"Until they were called to reform," Carver countered. "After Napoleon invaded Rome, he took the pope and the Vatican Archives to France. Their return two years later was said to have been brought about by relentless guerilla attacks by Black Order operatives."

"Friars."

"What?"

"The original operatives of the Holy Alliance and its more specialized units were Jesuits. Those who fought to return power to Rome in the time of Napoleon were friars, acting independently, ready to sacrifice their lives in Jesus' example for the glory of God."

"You're suggesting this was an organic movement, acting independently from the Vatican."

"Precisely."

"But even a rogue order must have a leader with connections. When did they recruit you? Was it that first trip to Paris, when German Intelligence had discovered that the ossuary had been right under their noses the whole time?"

The corners of Lang's mouth turned up slightly. "Impressive. Even if you don't quite have all the pieces figured out."

"Or maybe they recruited you even earlier. The Black Order was waiting for you in Notre Dame, weren't they? Someone had tipped them off."

Lang set the crystal glass on a wooden coaster. He went to a shelf, where he took up an angel figurine that looked, as evident by its imperfection, homemade.

"When I was 10 years old," he said, "Just before Christmas, my mother was decorating the house. One of her hobbies was making crafts out of clay, and she had recently finished making new figurines for the Christmas manger. She had spent several days perfecting them. In our tradition, the angels were the first to appear, and the baby Jesus and Mary and Joseph and animals were not typically put out until the days and weeks after Christmas, according to the biblical calendar. But that year she was so proud of what she had made that she put them out early. That night, a high-ranking party member from the Ministry of Propaganda, with whom my father did business, came over for dinner. The moment he saw the new clay pieces, he was outraged. Deeply put out by them, he was. My mother asked our guest whatever was the matter. He told her that the figurines did not look Aryan enough."

Lang turned, handing the clay angel to Carver. Apart from a chipped wing, the angel felt smooth in his hands.

"My father, of course, apologized," Lang continued. "He asked my mother to kindly put the manager away, but our guest was still not satisfied. He ordered her to smash the figurines into pieces. My father, who probably feared losing the man's business, quickly retrieved a mallet from the shed. My mother refused, and so he did it himself. The wise men, Joseph, the Virgin, the baby Jesus. All destroyed into a thousand broken bits. The angel you hold in your hands now is all that remains of the original set."

Father Callahan swung his feet up on Lang's desk. "Touching. I almost cried."

"The next day, a package was delivered from the Ministry. New Virgin, Joseph and baby Jesus figurines. They were all blonde. As a little boy who had worshipped both Jesus Christ and Adolf Hitler, I was devastated to realize that the two prominent forces in my life were at odds. I decided that I would have to be very careful from then on. But I knew that my loyalties rested with God. So I confided in one of my Jesuit teachers, Father Leo Kruger."

"And Kruger was Black Order," Carver said.

Lang nodded. "A descendent from the original line, apparently. And even then, he knew the Gestapo was watching him. He taught me the old ways."

Callahan rose from behind the desk. "You talk about service to God? You've ordered the assassinations of world leaders, potentially destabilizing entire regions. Is that how you demonstrate your faith?"

"The Kingdom of God must be defended at all costs. And unfortunately, our friend Mr. Wolf still holds onto the myth that Himmler programmed within his twisted heart. The legend of the so-called Holy Ossuary."

Carver leaned across the desk, his face only 12 inches from Lang's. "The blood trail leads to you. Give me one reason why I shouldn't kill you here where you sit."

"Here in Vatican City? I doubt this is the type of international incident the American government is prepared to explain."

Carver's answer came without hesitation. "My status is deniable. The White House won't be on the hook for your death. I will. And that's just fine by me."

"My death would not solve your problem, which, as you stated, is to eliminate the threat. My mission is merely to ensure the preservation of the Church and the righteous path of its believers."

The American straightened up. "And how is it that killing Senator Preston preserved the church?"

"Let me relate this to you in terms that an American can understand. In Texas, there are ranches where hunters pay top dollar to kill the dama gazelle. This is an animal that is nearly extinct in Africa, yet paradoxically, flourishes in Texas. On the surface, it is oxymoronic to kill an animal in order to save it. It is about as sensible as building nuclear stockpiles to achieve peace. And yet both tactics, while counterintuitive, are equally effective. In Africa, the animals were nearly hunted into oblivion. But the Texans are very smart. They understand that the game must be managed. The money paid by the hunters to kill only a few gazelles is used to save the entire species. And by doing this, they can restore balance to the ecosystem worldwide."

"You're not hunting game. You're hunting people."

"Even so, the parallels hold true. Our battle is also one of sustainability and spiritual balance. Good versus evil. God versus the devil. Do you have any idea what would happen if people stopped believing in the resurrection of the flesh? If they thought that the church had deceived them for two thousand years? The world would lose its moral compass. Fear of God, along with the promise of heaven, is a major deterrent to sin."

Carver leaned forward. "You say this whole thing is a myth. But you wouldn't risk instigating a worldwide holy war for just any old box of bones."

Lang checked his watch. "We are running out of time. Not just me, Agent Carver. All of us."

"Then tell me what this is all about."

"The knowledge you seek has been shared by only a handful of people over the past 2,000 years."

"You've got exactly one minute to give me the abridged version."

Senate Offices
Washington D.C.

A lone staffer was boxing up the last of the late Senator Preston's files when Hank Bowers arrived. The FBI section chief was bundled up in a heavy coat. A cold front had descended on Washington, complete with sleet and high winds. He slid his gloves off, pulled out his ID and held it out for the tall, thin kid to inspect.

"It's Mason, right?"

Mason Fielding nodded reluctantly. "Look, I already talked to the FBI. That was the day after the fire. I think my statement is on file, if you'd like to check."

There was no need. Bowers had already been through it countless times. The Bureau had dispatched a shadow team right after Mary Borst had disappeared. Although they had been kept in the dark from the Senator's true cause of death, they had still managed to collect a treasure trove of information about Mary.

Bowers took off his coat and sat down at one of several empty desks, indicating his intention to stay a while. The office was a ghost town, but it wouldn't stay that way for long. The governor of Texas had appointed a successor who was said to be en route to Washington.

He looked up at a UT Austin poster on the wall. "Hook 'em, Horns!"

"Did you and the senator go to school together?"

Bowers held his right hand out, using his thumb to point at his TKE ring. "Same fraternity.

"Ah."

"So you're the last man standing, huh?"

Fielding sat opposite, his arms folded across his chest. "Guess so. It's a little like digging a grave, to be honest."

"It was a terrible tragedy."

"I mean *my* grave, not the senator's. After I finish packing this place up, I'm out of a job."

"You ever consider a career in intelligence?" Bowers put two fingers into his jacket pocket, slid out a business card, and pushed it across the table. "We hire a new wave of recruits every year. Call me tomorrow. I might be able to put in a word."

Fielding picked up Bowers' card and examined it closely before sliding it into his front shirt pocket. A small spark of hope glimmered in his eyes. "How can I help?"

"I'm here about Mary Borst."

The staffer nodded. "I heard a rumor that she was killed in the fire. Then I heard maybe she was missing."

With all the collateral damage in recent days, Bowers had very little time to focus on the fire itself. There was no doubt in Bowers' mind that Borst had actually started it. But her motive was still a mystery to him.

Given the similar ways that Vera Borst and Preston had been butchered, it now seemed unlikely that Mary had started the fire to disrupt the investigation into the senator's killers. It was more likely that she feared something in the senator's home would lead them to the Fellowship and its activities.

"Have any thoughts since then?" Bowers asked.

Fielding shook his head. "I saw that story about her Mom in the news. None of us know what to think."

Bowers believed him. He had been personally monitoring Borst's mobile account since the night of the senator's death. Mason had texted her a few times and called. He truly seemed to have no idea where Mary was.

"Did Mary or the senator ever mention something called the Fellowship World Initiative?"

"Doesn't ring a bell."

"I understand you and Mary were involved," Bowers continued. Another fact he had drummed up by sifting through Borst's vast stores of personal communications. From what he could deduce, Mason and Mary had been more than coworkers for a period of weeks or months. "You sure she never mentioned the Fellowship?"

Fielding's face turned red. "I can't be absolutely sure, but I don't remember it."

"How long were you together?"

"Six months or so. The senator didn't like relationships among his staff, so we tried to keep it quiet."

"You're what, 27?"

"Yes."

"Did you and Mary ever talk about the future?"

"Yeah, but I eventually realized it wasn't going to work out long-term."

"What led you to that conclusion?"

Fielding got up and shut the office door, then returned to his seat. "There was nothing there physically. I kept expecting it to, but it didn't pan out."

"You mean sexually."

"Yes. At first, I thought maybe it was because she was really religious or something, but she never talked about that. After a while, I figured out that she was seeing someone on the side."

"And what led you to that conclusion?"

"At first she disappeared a lot. Never wanted to tell me where she was, or who she was with."

"And then?"

"One night I asked her, just hypothetically, if she wanted children. She said she was going to have one child. A boy. *One. Boy.*"

"She was that exact?"

"Yeah, it was weird. Usually, women just say they want children or they don't. She had the whole plan in place."

Bowers scribbled in his notebook. "What exactly did she say?"

"She said she was going to conceive in Rome, but the kid would be born in America."

"And did she say when this was going to happen?"

Fielding nodded. "She said she'd be a mother by the time she turned 26. That would be what, nine months from now?"

Apostolic Palace

Lang went to his desk and sat down. He slid open a drawer. "Slowly," Carver said as he took up a position behind him. The intelligence chief was old, but he was as unpredictable and dangerous a creature as Carver had ever met.

"Your assumptions about my personal beliefs are misguided," Lang said. He removed an electric cigarette from the desk, switched it on, and took a slow drag. Then he reached into the drawer for a second time, producing a transparent rectangular document display box. He set it on the desktop and gestured for Carver to come closer.

Carver remained where he was. "Your dagger," he said.

"Pardon?"

"Your dagger. The one you took from Wolf."

It had been a calculated guess. Something about Lang's gait – the way he carried his left leg, stiffer than the right – that had tipped him off. Sure enough, the old man bent down and raised the hem of his robes, revealing a sheath sewn into the inside of his left boot.

The steel glimmered as he pulled the blade from the sheath and laid it on the table. Carver picked it up and checked the inscription. *Mehr sein als scheinen*. Be more than you seem.

"Now then," Lang said. "If we're all feeling more secure, I think you'll find this artifact much more enlightening."

Carver rested on his elbows, studying the sketch that was pressed between glass. Judging by the color of the handmade parchment, it had been drawn a very long time ago. It depicted an ancient burial box in the Jewish or Greek style. Dimensions for the ossuary were neatly provided: 51 cm in length by 31 cm high by 28 cm deep. Weight: 20 kilograms.

Inscription: *Yeshua bar Yehosef.* Among the symbols engraved on the ossuary was the Chi-Ro, which was one of the earliest Christian symbols, layering the Greek X with the P. The monogram of Jesus Christ.

"This ossuary," Lang continued, "was discovered in the catacombs beneath what is now St. Peter's Basilica between 319 and 333 AD. All that is certain about the ossuary's origins is that Constantine's followers unearthed it when digging a well to serve the original church, which is now the site of St. Peter's Basilica."

"Wait," Seven said. "Wasn't the tomb of St. Peter also discovered underneath the church?"

"'*And I tell you that you are Peter'*," Father Callahan said, quoting Matthew, "'*And upon this rock I shall build my church.*'"

The intelligence czar confirmed with a nod. "To be exact, the bones of St. Peter were eventually discovered within 20 meters of the original ossuary resting place. Obviously, the concept of Christ's physical remains on Earth wasn't a completely unknown concept, but it was a contradiction of accepted scripture. Nevertheless, the presence of an old-fashioned burial box, entombed near the remains of Peter, and inscribed with Jesus' name, created doubt among the church establishment."

Father Callahan drew closer. "How much doubt, exactly?"

"We can only imagine the questions swirling in Constantine's mind. Among the papal archives, he had apparently seen a written legend. A rambling diary, in actuality, by an unknown author stating that after the crucifixion, the Roman governor Pontius Pilate had ordered the destruction of Jesus' body in order to keep the burial tomb from becoming a shrine for believers. According to the legend, it was this decision that led Peter to take Jesus' body, with the help of Joseph of Arimethea, and hide it from the Romans in Judea. Eventually, the diary claims, it was brought to Rome."

The priest's mouth hung open as he pondered the possibility. "Rome. Quite literally the last place on Earth Pilate's men would think of looking for it."

Seven ran her fingers through her closely cropped hair. "You described the legend as a rambling diary. How could that possibly stand up to scripture?"

"You have to understand the context of written history in the time of Constantine. There were very few written documents at that time. The oral tradition was strong, and belief in the core teachings of Christ was what mattered then, since there were thousands of variants between the Greek, Latin, Coptic and other versions of the Bible. Most, but not all of them, told of Christ's physical resurrection. And what was scripture but a series of stories handed down by eyewitnesses and apostles? It wasn't until approximately 50 years after Constantine's death that St. Jerome translated the old Latin into the authoritative Bible that we know today."

"Did Constantine believe the ossuary was legitimate?"

"Not especially," Lang said. "He was a firm believer in physical resurrection. But he was willing to consider the possibility that he would be proven wrong some day."

"So he decided to keep the ossuary safe, but secret."

Lang nodded. "He therefore mandated that the story of the mysterious ossuary be documented and passed on to each succeeding pope by the dead or dying pope's camerlengo. Eventually, the tradition was expanded to be shared with each new head of Vatican Intelligence, so that the secret could be protected in the event of foreign conquest. It also served to insulate the pope against any violence undertaken to protect it."

"And now?" Seven said.

"It goes without saying that the pontiff is innocent," Callahan cut in. "His Holiness would never agree to these atrocities in the name of God."

Lang crossed himself. "What we do, we do to serve God. It is my sincere hope that His Holiness remains naïve of the war we are waging to protect him."

"I'm not easily offended," Carver growled. "But I don't want to hear another word justifying these murders in the name of God."

Lang leaned back in his chair. "That's fine, Agent Carver, because I'm tired of talking. I've told you more than I should have in hopes that we might better understand each other. I suggest you get on with whatever business you have planned."

Now thoroughly satisfied that Lang was the leader they had been looking for, Carver sat in the chair opposite the desk and looked the old man in the eyes. "What if I could lead you to the ossuary, and allow you to return it to the Vatican?"

Lang folded his hands before him. "Then the secret would be restored. All hostilities would cease immediately."

Carver turned, suppressing a smile. He had Lang right where he wanted him. "I would need something else in return."

"Naturally. And what might that be?"

"The names and locations of the men who killed Rand Preston."

Subterranean Rome

It was Lars who first discovered that something was wrong. Just an unsettling feeling, quickly followed by butterflies in his stomach. Seconds later, the lights in the enormous home flickered, and then went out completely. The jumbo-size lift that operated 24 hours a day behind him – that which connected the palazzo to the subterranean chamber beneath Rome – ground to a halt. The darkness itself felt alive, like a dangerous organism that threatened to swallow him whole.

Magi's distant bark echoed up and down the elevator shaft. A husky growl that was unlike any sound the animal had made in the past.

Where the hell were the emergency lights? As soon as the thought had come to him, the battery-powered lights came to life. The peach-colored illumination felt strangely relaxing, as if he were in some upscale restaurant.

Then came the screeching. It took a moment before he recognized the terrible sound of the nightingale floors. It sounded more like bats than birds. Someone was running at full speed down the corridor. He forced himself to breathe as he crouched behind one of the climate-control appliances. He steadied the weapon before him, switched it off safety, and rested his index finger on the trigger.

It was just Mathieu. He raced toward Lars, his eyes impossibly huge. "They're here!" he yelled.

"Who's here?" a voice behind him shouted. Lars turned. It was Nicolas. He had just come from one of the interior chambers.

"Black Order!" Mathieu said, exasperated. "I don't know how many. I saw three, maybe four before the cameras went out."

Lars was furious. "Why didn't you call?"

"I tried! Communications are out!"

That figured. After having spent tens of millions acquiring and installing the lab into this ancient place, the communications equipment was comparably archaic. With wireless communications next to impossible from level to level, they had purchased a 1980s-era intercom system that had been salvaged from an abandoned Soviet missile bunker. As with everything down here, they had been too afraid of cave-ins to embed the wiring into the walls. It had worked great, but, as Lars had warned from the beginning, all it would take to cut off multi-floor communication was a pair of wire cutters.

Now he had no way to warn anyone else. "Let's go," he urged. Even if they made their stand there, the others could escort the Shepherd out the emergency hatch. It was time to release the bots.

Suddenly the nightingale floors were screaming one long, inharmonious note. God help us, Lars thought. The passageway was full of Black Order operatives.

*

Lang's international force of holy warriors advanced through the subterranean maze of catacombs, long-buried cobblestone streets and escape routes carved though the ages by the Roman Empire, various resistance movements and later, the Vatican itself. As they had agreed, Carver, Seven, Father Callahan and Heinz Lang trekked behind them.

To forge the unlikely alliance, Carver had provided Lang with the location of the ossuary. Per their agreement, Lang would be permitted to retrieve the ossuary and return it to the Vatican. In turn, Lang had agreed to reveal the identities of Senator Preston's killers. As a gesture of good faith, Lang had offered to hand them over before the assault even started. Carver, however, preferred to wait. He expected heavy security at the Roman villa where Sebastian Wolf was completing his life's work. They would need every gun they had.

The tunnels twisted this way and that. The porous walls seemed to have tear ducts, weeping water that was at times pure and at other times putrid. With only their headlamps for illumination, they trekked through passageways lined with the bones of long-dead Romans.

Time and again he flashed to the kill zone beneath Washington D.C. where he had lost Megan O'Keefe. The sight and sound of her stiff, waterlogged corpse had haunted his sleep endlessly. And now he relived the nightmare as they waded through three feet of water and the rats – hundreds of them – scurried up the walls around them. On his insistence, Seven walked behind him. As he turned to check on her, his heart skipped as he projected the face of his dead partner on hers.

Seven's voice broke through the quiet. "How far down are we?"

"About 60 meters and counting," Callahan replied. He had used the tunnels many times over the years. Dressed in olive green cargo pants, a black turtleneck and felt-bottom boots that would not slip on the wet earth below Rome, Father Callahan's preparation was admirable. Callahan carried a pack containing spare ammunition, guns, night vision goggles and other items that they had handpicked from the trunk of his car.

As he had told Blake, he was here not as an operative, but as a Christian. Callahan had been just a boy when his uncle had been killed in a torrid stretch of Protestant on Catholic violence in Belfast. The trouble over the ossuary would only bring more blood to the streets around the world. They had a chance to stop it tonight, once and for all.

"If we find Sebastian Wolf," the priest asked, "What exactly are we going to do with him?"

"That's for Lang to decide," Carver said. "We aren't allowed to touch him."

"And Adrian Zhu?"

"We have reasonable cause to apprehend him. That goes double for Mary Borst."

Finally they breached the immense reception room of the grandiose residence near Piazza del Popolo. It was to this stately address that Symplexicon Labs had shipped enough laboratory equipment to clone a herd of woolly mammoths. Lang's force quickly dispatched two armed guards in the Renaissance-era foyer, the blood spatter scarcely noticeable against the crimson-colored walls. Overhead, an enormous white glass chandelier swung back and forth. Portraits of long-dead Vatican royalty seemed to stare at them from all sides.

The high ceilings and ornate molding told of a structure that had been breathtaking before it had been prepared for siege. Looking up the mahogany staircase, Carver saw that the entrances to the second and third floors had been sealed off with razor wire, and the dining room was piled high with floorboards, dirt, nails and other debris that pointed to a sizable construction project that extended both above and below ground. The fact that the debris had been piled here, inside the palatial residence, only added further confirmation they had come to the right place. Someone had gone to great pains to hide the project from outsiders.

The ratatatat of automatic 9mm gunfire broke out from the fourth floor. Carver grabbed Seven and Lang and scurried to the far side of the cavernous room. Lang's fighters held nothing back as they returned fire.

Within seconds, they were already down a gun. A young, bearded Slovak had taken a round in the middle of his face, obliterating his nose and collapsing his airway. He fell sideways, narrowly missing Carver's lap. As he pushed the body away, Carver saw into the man's open pack. He had been carrying a double-braided polyester rope, eight-inch eyebolts and a heavy-duty portable hand winch.

They don't just want to eliminate Wolf, Carver thought. They want to punish him. Just like the others.

The Villa

Carver and Seven carried Heckler & Koch G36 assault rifles that they had taken from Callahan's stash of trunk treasure. Seven had used one while training with the Special Air Service, and spoke highly of the weapon's reflex sight, which used adjustable battery-powered illumination in low-level light situations. But for now, Lang's men would do the fighting. If all went according to plan, Carver wouldn't need to fire a shot until it was time to collect on his end of the deal with Lang.

Father Callahan carried all the explosives in his pack. He whistled at one of the Black Order mercenaries and tossed him a standard grenade. The priest pointed a finger up at the fourth floor.

The mercenary smiled, gave Callahan thumbs up, and hurled it to the top of the stairs with the expert accuracy of a center fielder.

"You idiot!" Callahan screamed. "You have to pull the pin first!"

The priest's words were gravely prophetic. Within seconds, the grenade flew back over the fourth floor balcony toward Callahan and the 10 surviving warriors.

Carver grabbed Seven and Lang and pushed them into an open coat closet. "Everyone down!"

The frag grenade exploded five feet above the surface of the chestnut marble floor. A burst of shrapnel hit the solid wood door protecting Carver, Seven and Lang. All was quiet for several seconds, during which Carver wondered whether they were the only remaining survivors.

Then two guns started up again, and he could tell by proximity – and by the sound of their weapons – that they were Black Order. The relief he felt at knowing there were survivors was an odd and unnerving sensation. *The enemy of my enemy is my friend*, he thought. No, that was bullshit. He and Lang were not friends. They were merely using each other.

He opened the closet and spotted Callahan unfurling himself from a cramped shelter position underneath a magnificently carved wooden chaise. All gunfire stopped, followed by a sickening thud. A body had fallen from the fourth floor landing, having been picked off by one of Lang's men.

Lang staggered out of the closet and surveyed the bodies of the 10 who had fallen in the span of just a few minutes.

"Well?" Carver asked.

Lang looked up, knowing exactly what Carver was asking. He shook his head. Senator Preston's killers were not among the dead. He nodded toward two survivors.

Carver regarded the two monsters that had travelled to Washington D.C. to kill the senator. Both were reloading. The elder of the two was in his mid-40s and had a crescent-shaped birthmark covering his left cheek. The other was in his 20s, with loose skin around his earlobes that Carver guessed were the effects of wearing gauge plug earrings.

Apprehending these thugs would solve nothing, for no trial was possible. Any criminal proceeding in the U.S. would expose the story the administration had released about Preston's death, and possibly, the shadow war over the ossuary.

He wished he could eliminate both of these scumbags right now. But that would solve little except avenging a single death. They would have to exercise patience. For the next hour, they were in this fight together.

✱

Sebastian Wolf sat cross-legged on the mattress, willing himself out of the meditative trance he had dwelled in for the past three days. He was unable to tell whether the explosions were coming from inside or outside, from above or below. The expansive maze of rooms and tunnels swallowed sound. The excavations down underneath the villa, into the lost catacombs and temples of Rome, had been ongoing for years preceding his arrival. So many entrances and exits. He had needed a chaperone to keep from getting lost.

A boom came from outside. From the hallway. He was sure of it. The sound of the nightingale floors was drowned out by Magi's incessant barking.

They were under attack now. And yet Wolf was calm. There was no reason to be anxious. It had been foretold.

The destiny of the Great Mission now rested with Adrian Zhu and the girl. They had just been here. Or had it been days since he had seen them? He did not know. He had lost track of time and space.

By his own insistence, he and Magi had remained undisturbed for some time. Such was his destiny. To be a pure conduit of light for the reincarnation of their savior.

But the time for prayer was over now. The nightingale floors sang like a flock of a hundred birds all at once. Intruders were in the house. He tried to call Lars, but all communications were down. Where were the guards?

He struggled to get to his feet, pulling at the black monogrammed pajamas as they slipped down his lean buttocks. As Lars had taught him during the drills, he went to his desk and punched a star pattern on the touchscreen monitor on his desk. The bookcase behind him hinged open, revealing a staircase.

He called for Magi. The dog was highly agitated, foaming at the mouth as the heavy bedroom doors bumped and flexed. The enemy was at the gates.

Wolf gripped the dog's lead and pulled him through the hidden doorway. Motion-triggered lanterns illuminated a coiling spiral staircase. Built within a hidden shaft in the villa's rear, it descended the home's four floors and continued underground to the laboratory.

He paused as he descended the first few steps. Had there been some way for him to seal the passageway? Surely there was, but he could not remember. Maybe he had never even known.

But now he recalled where the guards had gone. They were with Adrian Zhu and the girl. He had ordered it, despite Lars' protests. So be it, he had told Lars. We come into this world alone, and we leave it alone, he thought. And then we will finally feel the unconditional love of God.

But it would not happen yet. No. He wanted to be in the presence of the ossuary one last time. The lifegiver of the second coming.

And finally, on the first landing, he saw the two large black buttons that Lars had shown him. They were recessed in a steel casing and protected by a transparent cover so they could not be pushed accidentally. Yes, he remembered now. He was supposed to press them in sequential order, left to right. The first one would seal the stairway behind him. The second would release the swarm.

*

Lang's men blew open the doors to the home's master suite, releasing a wave of stale, putrid air. They held their weapons with one hand, using the other to cover their faces. The walls of the enormous room were adorned with crosses of every shape and size imaginable. Enormous books were strewn about the floor, many of them open and with pages ripped out, as if they too had been under attack.

"Nobody here," someone said.

The Vatican Intelligence chief slumped into an empty chair. Despite his rigorous regimen of long daily walks, the tunnels and four flights of stairs had taken their toll. He was running on pure adrenalin now.

"What died?" Callahan shouted as he entered the room.

Carver spotted the source of the rancid stench. It was not, as the priest suggested, rotting flesh. It was animal waste, evident by several heaping dog piles placed about the room and the yellow-stained baseboards.

The walls were painted with scripture. He also recognized several passages from Drucker's manuscript.

And when he has gathered all that is necessary to know to bring all that is dark into the light, the One from the East will use her to make me anew, just as I have made you anew.

And in turn, you will return my heart from stone to flesh, so that all men may share in the wisdom of the LORD.

And when I am raised, the knowledge hoarders shall be exposed as bearers of false idols.

"Over here," Father Callahan shouted. He pointed to an opening in the bookshelf. A secret passageway. He went out the door, and then popped back in.

"It leads to a coiling staircase. Emergency escape route, I'd guess."

"Or the entrance to the lab," Carver said hopefully.

A high-frequency hum entered Carver's consciousness. Like insect wings, but modulating evenly. He turned, scanning the dog piles for flies. He saw none.

He looked at Seven, who was keeping an eye on Lang. "You hear that?"

She nodded. "What is it?"

It was getting louder, and was soon joined by the sound of grinding gears. A thick steel door rolled down over the doorway they had come in through. Another slab of steel threatened to seal the secret passageway leading to the staircase.

Callahan acted quickly, pushing a trio of heavy, oversized books into the opening. It momentarily stalled the door's progress. Carver raced to help, grabbing a small bronze bust from one of the shelves. He shoved it in, risking his limbs as he got onto his back and kicked it into place.

He heard the gears within the walls slipping. Then came the smell of heat – like a hairdryer that had been on far too long. Next was the unmistakable burn of mechanical failure. The crushing steel halted with a loud metallic knock from within the wall.

He looked around the room at the others. With the entrance now sealed off, there was no way to go but down the passageway. Fortunately, the entire crew was slim enough to slide underneath the 16-inch gap. Except Callahan, he realized. He glanced at the priest's midsection and had his doubts.

"That sound," Seven said. She had her hands over both ears. Carver had been so preoccupied with securing their freedom that he hadn't noticed the incessant buzzing. It had grown louder.

Carver pointed up at the 20-foot ceiling and saw what he had failed to notice earlier – a shiny black orb, consisting of perhaps hundreds of tiny holes.

What he saw next truly terrified him. Emerging from the holes was a swarm of flies. Hundreds of them. Only they weren't flies, Carver knew. They were flying nanobots. Just like the one that killed Drucker.

*

Seven was the first to slide under the 16-inch gap to the relative safety of the passageway. Carver was right behind her, wriggling his muscular but lean build through the opening. He took Lang next, the old man's thin, long frame coming feet first as he scooted through on his back. His two henchmen were next.

And then there was Father Callahan. He pushed his backpack through first, and then his weapon. This was going to be tight.

Carver peered through the gap from the other side. The swarm had descended now perhaps five feet from the orb, and they were dispersing horizontally, a squadron of drones preparing for attack. "Hurry!" he implored Callahan.

Like Lang, the stocky priest came feet-first, perhaps anticipating that his midsection would prove to be the most challenging piece. His knees and thighs cleared, but sure enough, 16 vertical inches wasn't quite enough to get his potbelly through the space.

"Suck it in!" Carver yelled.

"I'm trying!"

The priest tried to make himself thin as Carver pulled from the other side. Within seconds Callahan was bleeding from broken skin at his waistline. He screamed for Carver to stop.

"It's no use!" he cried.

The American stuck his head under the space. The swarm had spread wide, and was now sweeping the room from above, as if they were a single collective.

"Lie still!" he commanded. "Those bots can't be individually controlled. Maybe they're motion-activated."

Callahan tried to quiet his body and minimize his breathing. No small task given that he was half inside, half outside the room, wedged underneath a steel door, with a threat of death hovering overhead.

Carver reached into Callahan's pack and pulled out two stun grenades. They were eight inches long with openings in the black matte metal casing designed to prevent defragmentation during the explosion. When Carver had pulled them from the priest's trunk, he had imagined using them on human beings. He wasn't sure whether they would effectively disrupt the nanobots, but he was out of both ideas and time.

"Everyone close your eyes and ears," he said, then tapped one of the priest's boots, "Except you. Just close your eyes, there Padre. Be very still."

Carver pulled both pins simultaneously and rolled the stun grenades into the center of the room. Carver used his index fingers to plug his ears. He felt a twinge of pity for the additional pain Callahan was about to endure. That was assuming he didn't die. Stun grenades weren't designed to be lethal, but they occasionally killed people all the same.

The blast came hard and fast. The shockwave belched a blast of hot air out the gap and into the staircase. Even kneeling just outside the room, Carver felt the fluid in his ears in flux, putting him slightly off balance.

He heard the priest screaming, which was a good sign. He peered under the gap. The swarm was gone.

"I'm blind," Callahan screamed.

"I told you to close your eyes," Carver chided him. The blinding light from the grenades caused all the light sensitive cells within the eye to activate at once. It would, however, pass.

"Agent Carver," Lang called from within the iron staircase. "We have to go."

Carver patted the priest on the leg. "Hang tight. We'll be back."

✷

They descended the iron helix that went ever deeper into the porous, spongy earth that had allowed Rome to be so easily tunneled in ancient times. A mechanical hum – gas generators, perhaps – droned somewhere in the distance. A series of construction lights strung along the walls provided adequate illumination.

Carver and Seven moved behind their unlikely assault partners warily, and always on guard. After all, this was merely an alliance of convenience. Carver had every expectation that they too planned on violently ending the partnership once they found what they had come for.

A series of ancient slabs, piles of broken pottery and pieces of sculpture were clustered near the far wall. Relics unearthed during the recent construction, Carver presumed. A bit further in, they approached a security post that looked much like the TSA stations at the airports in American megacities. Sheets of transparent blast-proof glass flanked a full-body scanner.

"Nobody here," one of Lang's soldiers said in wonderment.

A bad sign, Carver knew. By his count, they had killed only eight guards in the villa. Surely their numbers had been greater in recent days. Why had they already abandoned these underground security posts? Had the ossuary already been moved? Zhu would have had a week at most to work with the DNA samples.

At the end of the cavern, an open-air lift moved slowly up and down at regular intervals. There were no doors, no buttons. Getting on and off it appeared to be a matter of careful timing, much like a department store escalator.

He crossed to the other side, where a straight, smooth pole descended into another chamber where the facility's emergency lights glowed. The dog bark he thought he had heard earlier had not repeated. If their prize had escaped, there was no telling where they would go. Equipped with a map such as the one Callahan had, it was possible to walk from one end of Rome to the other using only the ancient tunnels.

"Wolf is here," Lang insisted. The old man was out of breath, but the thrill of the hunt propelled him forward. "I can feel him in my bones."

Lang's soldiers helped him onto the lift, which descended at an uneven pace. Carver and Seven joined them. The ride down to the bottom took approximately 10 seconds. Carver had lost all sense of depth. Were they a hundred yards below ground? Five hundred? The only thing he was sure of was that he didn't like this. The lighting had grown erratic, twittering on and off at irregular intervals. He hoped the generators weren't running low on fuel.

"The lab!" Seven said as they neared the bottom. She pointed at what appeared to be a decontamination chamber. Behind additional panes of transparent glass was the shining equipment that Nico had tracked to the villa.

Opposite the lab was an astonishing cavern. Vaulted ceilings. Spring-fed fountains. Walls decorated with faded frescoes of wildlife and chariots. And at the rear, a small throne room, perhaps 500 square feet.

Sebastian Wolf sat on an ancient throne that had been carved out of rock. It was easy to see why Wolf had built the lab here. Carver imagined him sitting there, observing Zhu's work through the transparent lab walls like some omniscient God supervising the creation of a new world.

The cult leader appeared to be unguarded, unarmed and unafraid. The Alsatian at his side barked ferociously. Wolf whistled one short, sharp tone that snapped the dog into quiet obedience.

The white chalk ossuary rested on a marble platform before him. Although Carver had seen the dimensions on Lang's illustration, it was still smaller than he had imagined, roughly the size of his nephew's toy chest.

Carver watched Lang carefully. He appeared to be almost as mesmerized by the sight of his old friend as he was by the ossuary. Lang had sworn a blood oath to protect this relic, and yet he himself had never actually laid eyes on it.

"Go on, Heinz," Wolf said. "See what your papal masters have hidden from the world for these two thousand years."

Lang walked forward, stretching his right hand out before him. He touched the chalk box, running his fingertips gingerly over the faded engravings on its side. And then he touched the inscription. *Yeshua bar Yehosef.* Jesus son of Joseph. Just as Wolf had claimed.

"Although we've had our differences," Wolf said, "We did the right thing in Venice, you and I. It would not have been right to let Himmler have this."

Wolf's Judas looked up at his former friend. "He would have had nothing. Just as you have nothing now."

Wolf chuckled. "My old friend. My Judas. If you did not believe this was the Holy Ossuary, then you would not be here."

"We'll have to cut the reunion short," Carver said. "Where's Zhu?"

Wolf smiled pityingly. "I'm afraid you are too late to catch Mr. Zhu. Our friend's time in Rome is already complete. He has left to complete his destiny."

Carver swore. It was just as he had feared. The speed of Zhu's work, even more than his innovations, was what had made him famous in the first place. And yet it was still astonishing. A world-class paleo-DNA lab had been created for a project that had lasted less than two weeks. And that was assuming that it was equipped with a staff that had set to work immediately after the ossuary had been stolen.

"I'll check the lab," Seven said.

"What are you waiting for?" Lang said, gesturing toward one of his men. "Go with her."

Wolf watched them go. "They will find nothing," he said. "But the empty feeling you have inside will no doubt pass, Heinz. Soon Mr. Zhu's role in the great story of our time will be evident for all people to see. And if you are still alive, then you too will join him in worshipping the return of our savior."

Lang held the cross he wore around his neck up to his lips and kissed it, as if protecting himself against Wolf's blasphemy. *"If a prophet or a dreamer of dreams arises among you, and if he says, 'Let us go after other gods,' which you have not known, 'and let us serve them,' you shall not listen to the words of that prophet or that dreamer of dreams."*

Wolf grinned. "Oh, I do love Deuteronomy. I really do. But I am not a false prophet, Heinz. And these bones before you are not those of a false idol. They are nothing less than evidence that Christ walked on this earth, and through the miracle of the knowledge God has endowed upon us, he shall walk again."

"May I kill him now?" one of Lang's soldiers called out. He appeared to be every bit as subservient to his master as Magi, the Alsatian, was to Wolf. "*Please* let me kill him."

Wolf spoke over the man's pleas. "This ossuary was, I am told, quite unusual from an anthropological perspective. In a typical Jewish or Greek ossuary, the bones would reside alone. In this case it appears that the disciples added personal effects to the box before it was brought to Rome. We found a stone vessel containing a lock of hair. In another vessel, a piece of sponge that could have been used by Joseph of Arimethea to wash the body. And there was a rusted nail, Heinz. From the true cross, no doubt."

"A clever rouse intended to deceive Pontius Pilate," Lang said.

Seven rejoined the group. "The lab is empty."

Lang's goon came up behind her now. He was breathing heavily, as if he were a child having a tantrum. "Can I rope him?" he pleaded.

"No," Lang said. He kissed his cross again. "We will not punish him. That will be left to God. But scripture does tell us that he must die. *That prophet or that dreamer of dreams shall be put to death, because he has taught rebellion against the Lord your God, who brought you out of the land of Egypt and redeemed you out of the house of slavery, to make you leave the way in which the Lord your God commanded you to walk. So you shall purge the evil from your midst.*"

Wolf rose from his throne, appearing to gaze over them. His face was content, as if he had finally arrived at his destination after a long journey. He held his arms out slightly to his sides. It was an invitation. He was ready to be martyred.

Lang reached under his cloak and produced the dagger. He ran his fingers down the shining blade. "I took this from you when you had your episode in Venice."

"Episode? That strikes me as quite clinical. Is that what you've called it all these years?"

"You don't actually believe you were blessed with the stigmata?" Lang said. "The gunshot you sustained in Paris had gradually become infected. You were ill with fever. Your visions were nothing more than a hallucination."

He drew closer to Wolf, offering him the dagger. Magi whined, alternating nervously between his master and Lang.

"I will save you the indignity of the rope," Lang said, drawing closer to the throne. "Take your own life now so that you can meet your maker and learn the error of your ways."

Wolf shook his head. "I left Catholicism long ago. But I must admit, I am still superstitious about suicide."

"Please. I will even hear your confession as you bleed to death. Perhaps then God would have mercy on your soul."

"I wouldn't give you the satisfaction," Wolf spat, his face suddenly full of hatred. "Now make me the martyr that I am destined to become!"

Lang lunged forward with the dagger. His aim was true, lodging the tip of the blade within Wolf's side. Magi jumped, clamping his jaws around the old Jesuit's wrist, shaking his head back and forth to tear the flesh.

One of the soldiers squeezed off three rounds, neutralizing the animal. The smell of gunpowder awakened Carver's senses. As Lang squirmed under the dead canine, and Wolf collapsed across the ancient throne, he knew the time to bring Preston's killers to justice was now. There would not be a better opportunity.

The four able-bodied survivors of the villa assault stood in a quadrangle of death, with the ossuary at the center. Both of Lang's henchmen stood on the other side of the marble platform. As Carver swung his rifle toward them, both soldiers were already in motion. Seven, too, had been at the ready, preparing to fire from the hip.

It was impossible to tell who fired next. The fusillade of automatic gunfire seemed to come all at once. The throne room was suddenly alive with chalk dust and smoke and blood spray.

Carver found himself lying in the dirt, winded. He had been hit. A coating of white chalk fell over him like snow. He felt his chest, where the pain was the worst. It was dry. The vest had held.

Somewhere to his right, he heard the unmistakable sound of a fresh magazine shoved into a weapon. He saw the silhouette of an armed man in the dissipating haze, moving toward him.

Carver rolled right and emptied the rest of his clip into the haze. He immediately rolled left in case there was return fire, but none came. All was quiet. All was still. He waited until the air cleared enough so that he could make out a boot, then a leg, and then another set of boots. Preston's killers were, at last, dead.

He got to his feet. Seven was slumped along the western wall of the throne room. The fabric of her hoodie was shredded in front, and the nanofibers of her protection vest were splayed, but not broken. Unconscious, but breathing. At best, she was going to have a few broken ribs. At worst, she could be bleeding internally. He had to get her to a doctor.

He stepped over her and pulled the dead dog off Lang. The Vatican Intelligence chief coughed and groaned. Still alive, but rapidly losing blood from deep bites in his wrist and throat. Carver tore a piece of fabric from his vestments and tied it around the man's wrist as a tourniquet. Before he could even tend to the man's throat, he saw the old man's chest grow still. There was no use trying to resuscitate him. Chest compressions would only expedite the flow of blood from his body. Heinz Lang's long journey was finally over.

He got to his feet and regarded the throne. Wolf was sprawled backwards across the imperfect stone furnishing, his arms splayed out to his sides. The tip of the dagger was still lodged within the ribs on his left torso. He had also been shot in the neck and chest. His white hair was tainted with crimson blood spatter and his eyes looked heavenward.

Carver gazed into the dead man's eyes, longing for the secrets they still held.

Safehouse
McLean, Virginia

Speers let himself into the unremarkable three-bedroom brick home near ODNI headquarters. The place smelled like bacon and eggs and coffee. The smell turned Speers' stomach. He had stayed at the office all night with Chad Fordham and Arunus Roth, monitoring the situation in Rome. To stay awake, the two of them had eaten an entire bag of leftover Halloween candy.

Jack McClellan stood from his post in the foyer. "Morning, director," McClellan said as Speers took his coat off and hung it on the rack behind the door.

"Evening, Jack. The girls up yet?"

McClellan nodded. "Jenna's always up. She's going stir crazy. Can't blame her, I guess. After Haley's little Mayflower stunt, we've really had this little place on lockdown. I've got people in the backyard, in the kitchen and in the hallway between their bedrooms. No closed doors allowed."

"You've been spooning them at night too?"

"Everything but," McClellan grinned.

"And Haley?"

McClellan furrowed his brow. "Quiet. Real quiet. She's up, though. I heard Jenna bring her some tea a little while ago."

Speers slapped McClellan on the shoulder. "Unless something changes, we can all go home in about 24 hours."

"Good. Haley's down the hall, second door."

As McClellan had indicated, Speers found the door to the bedroom ajar. Ellis was sitting in a rocking chair, sipping tea and gazing out into the backyard. She wore black leggings and a gray wool sweater that the secret service had brought from the apartment she shared with Jenna. A Bible and a pair of rosary beads rested on the table next to her.

Speers shut the door behind him. "How's your head?"

"Numb."

He sat down on the edge of the bed and looked around at the room furnishings. The bedspread, lamps and dresser had all been purchased decades ago, but they weren't what anyone would call classic. "Jeeze," he said. "You think this stuff would even sell at a yard sale?"

She sighed, but still did not look at him, and then took a long sip of tea. "What do you want, Julian?"

"To tell you that it's over. Wolf and Lang are dead."

Another long pause. She drew one leg up, resting the heel against the edge of the rocking chair. "And the ossuary?"

"En route to the Vatican as we speak."

Speers frowned. He wasn't expecting a high-five, but he resented the lack of any response. Maybe the concussion was worse than they had thought. Maybe he needed to have another neurologist check her out.

"Not that you asked, but Blake is all right, by the way. It's just a matter of getting him home now."

"I'm glad," she said after a pause. "Is that it?"

"We also got Preston's killers. You can thank Blake for that."

No smile. No reaction.

Ellis set her tea down. "You could have called to tell me all this. Why are you here?"

He pulled a grape lollipop from his pocket, unwrapped it and slid it between his cheek and gum. Screw his stomach ache. He needed a sugar fix.

"I need to know if you've remembered anything else about Seattle."

Her answer was quick. "No."

"How did it go with the shrink?"

Ellis turned to face him for the first time. "It's personal, Julian."

"Obviously, I want to respect your personal boundaries. But this is mission critical."

She returned her gaze back to the window. "Mission's over, Julian. You said as much."

"*Your* mission is over. You're right about that. But Operation Crossbow isn't. Adrian Zhu is still out there, and my people have to find him."

"Really? From what I can tell, your intel about him working on military projects was bogus. His passion is obviously elsewhere."

"The situation has evolved, I'll give you that. But we believe Zhu may be with Mary Borst. She's still missing. What if she's being held against her will? If you know anything, now's the time."

The hypnotism had indeed worked. The psychologist had been able to take Ellis back to that moment on Vashon Island. She had been on the ground, banged up and bloodied. Vera Borst had been swinging over her, hanging by a rope, suspended by her wrists, slowly bleeding to death from an array of small incisions to her torso. So much blood. But she had still been conscious. She knew she was dying. She had a message. *Mary,* she had said. The voice had been soft and earnest, as if whispered by a dying angel.

Mary. My daughter. The virgin. They know. It's her they're looking for.

Who knows?

The Black Order. And those afraid of the Rule of Light will search the Earth for me. As it was in the time of Herod, it will be again. Many innocents will die.

Herod? Who, King Herod? I don't understand.

Mary will carry the child. You must protect them. You must protect the child. The codeword. Shepherd with threes.

What followed next – a spoken 32-digit string of letters and numbers that Ellis had recounted under hypnosis –had been even more baffling. Eight sets of four characters. The shrink had copied the string onto a sheet of paper for her, but oddly, Ellis found that she had no need for it. She could recite the sequence from memory, as if she had known it all along. It was crazy. Ellis couldn't even memorize phone numbers.

And then last night, she had woken suddenly at 3 am with the realization. She knew what it was. *An IP address.*

She had switched on her computer and typed the sequence into a web browser. When a password prompt appeared, she had entered the codeword Vera Borst had given her. *Shepherd with threes*. When it didn't work, she tried a few variations. All caps, all lowercase, with and without spaces. Finally it hit her – *Sh3ph3rd*. Boom. She was in.

The resulting screen was all white except for the sign of the Chi-Rho and two lines of simple black webtext. *The Rule of Light Begins 6-28. Check back for further instructions.*

Now Speers' voice broke through. "You all right?" He was standing in front of her now. "You're not taking your meds, are you?"

"I'd like to be alone."

"Haley, I know this took a toll on you. And I'm very grateful for that. But if you remembered anything that might help us find her, no matter how painful…"

The words seemed to stick to the top of Ellis' mouth. "Mary Borst doesn't want to be found, Julian."

"You *do* know something, don't you?"

"What we all know is that she got on that plane to Rome by herself. We saw the security camera footage. I'd say that's proof she didn't go under duress. I think we should just pretend that she died in that fire, like we thought in the first place."

"Don't tell me you actually believe she's – "

"That doesn't matter. People are going to be gunning for her. They're going to be gunning for that child. If you bring her in, you're just making their job easier. You won't be able to protect them. Do you really want to be responsible for that?"

The hum of Speers' phone interrupted their conversation. It was a text message from Arunus Roth. He turned his back for a moment to read it: *Carver never showed at the extraction point. Please advise.*

Piazza di Spagna

The hotel elevator climbed past the second floor en route to the 10th. He had come in through the service entrance, avoiding the lobby altogether. Coming back here was insane, Carver knew. As a rule, he never returned to the roost after an operation was finished. Even when there didn't appear to be survivors, he assumed they were out there, like roaches after a nuclear winter. They always wanted their pound of flesh. They wanted any semblance of payback they could get.

His phone rang. It was Speers.

"You missed the rendezvous," he complained over the spotty connection. "The chopper pilot says he can't wait any longer. Are you close?"

"You should already know the answer to that."

Hadn't they triangulated his phone location to the hotel near the Spanish Steps? And as for Nico, hadn't they already checked the location of the RFID chip in his arm?

After all, Nico was the only reason he had returned.

He had not answered the room phone in nearly two hours. Nor was he answering either of the two stolen phones he had hacked into. Carver knew because he had tried them all endlessly. Fearing the worst, he had logged into the mission cloud to get a location on the chip. It was still here, within the hotel.

"Rome police is all over the villa," Speers said. "They're about to shut down all the train stations, the airport, you name it. We have to get you out of the city."

His tardiness could not be helped. Tidying up loose ends had taken more time than Carver had imagined. He had freed Callahan so that he could personally deliver the ossuary back to the Vatican. Then he had taken Seven to the British Embassy, where a consulate physician would patch her up before she would be whisked quietly out of the country.

The mission was over. Balance was restored. Except for Nico. What if he had made a mistake in leaving Nico unguarded again? He had been determined to get keep him alive and return him to the States to receive the pardon he deserved. Carver owed him that.

"You still there?" Speers demanded.

"Yeah."

"A local detective named Tesla showed up at the American consulate looking for you in connection with a double homicide. It's getting too hot. If you can't meet the chopper in 10 minutes, you're on your own."

Carver hung up as the elevator reached the 10th floor. Carver exited, stepping lightly as he moved down the unfamiliar hallway. He eased into the staircase, holding the door behind him to avoid any unnecessary noise. He remained motionless for several seconds, watching the shadows in the flights above him until he was confident that he was alone. Only then did he gingerly ascend to the 11th floor. As he approached the doorway leading to the corridor, he heard a group of revelers tramping noisily down the hall. Aussies, he figured by their accents. They were drunk.

He opened the door as the six loud drunkards passed. Just a group of tourists, he hoped. He fell into line behind them, scanning the hallway ahead for any signs of police. He saw nothing out of the ordinary. Still, he wasn't comfortable entering the room through the front door. Too dangerous.

A floor map was posted on the wall to his left. He stopped and studied it quickly, noting an alcove up ahead outfitted with a fire escape. He backtracked to the alcove, which was just large enough for two armchairs that enjoyed an unobstructed view of the piazza. He pried the window open.

An earsplitting fire alarm sounded. All the better, Carver thought as he climbed out onto the ironwork. If the cops were there with Nico, they would have no choice but to take him downstairs. If it was Black Order, the sensory overload might help distract them.

It was cool outside. A light mist was coming down, making footing difficult on the ironwork. Room balconies stretched out in a row on either side of him. If the floor map was correct, their suite was the third to his right.

He leapt up, gripping a metal rung in the landing above him, just the way Seven had showed him. He swung back and forth until he had enough momentum to propel himself over to the adjacent balcony.

His didn't stick the landing. His right foot slipped out from under him. Carver fell forward, crashing into a set of French doors. Fortunately, the glass didn't break. Looking through it, Carver saw an elderly couple scrambling about half-dressed, preparing to evacuate the building. They didn't seem to notice him. The alarm was simply too loud.

A waist-high wall was all that separated this deck from the next room. Carver scrambled to his feet and climbed over it. He was suddenly face-to-face with a little girl. She was inside, looking out the French doors, with her fingers stuck in her ears. Her parents were packing their bags, preparing to take every bit of luggage with them downstairs. Good thing this wasn't a real fire.

He smiled and waved at the girl, and then made his way over the final barrier and crouched behind a deck chair. The suite was well lit. Soccer was on the TV. Their dirty room-service plates and utensils were still on the main table and sitting area where they had left them yesterday, the result of leaving the don't disturb sign on the door. There were no signs of booby traps that he could see.

Holding his SIG out before him, he slipped his shoes off to be as quiet as possible, and opened the French doors. He quickly cleared the living room and kitchen. He went to the main bathroom. Wet towels were on the floor, just as they had left them. The closet was empty except for an unused ironing board and the room safe.

He moved on. The bed where Seven had slept was unmade and still held the faint smell of perspiration and Chanel No. 5.

The first signs of danger materialized on the carpet in front of the bedroom where Nico had worked and slept. Two small reddish-brown splotches. Carver dropped to a knee and grazed the spots with his fingertips. It was dried and hardened, scab-like.

Bad sign.

He entered the bedroom. Nico's bed was made. Neatly. Impeccably. No sign of his computer or the phones they had taken from the dead men in the deconsecrated church. He silently dropped to his knees and checked under the bed. Nothing but dust.

The blood trail – scant as it was – led to the bathroom, which was also fully lit. As Carver rounded the final corner, he braced himself for what he might find – Nico's body in the bathtub, or worse. He imagined the struggle. A whack to the head. Gloved hands holding his head below hot water.

He stepped sideways slowly, silently, until the bathroom was in full view. The shower curtain was pulled back. Save for some black body hair on the side of the tub, it was empty. The bathroom floor was also clear. There was no body. He was alone in the suite.

Carver let his shooting hand fall to his side. He stepped closer, noting a few more small splotches on the white rug.

"Not much blood," he said aloud, taking comfort in the notion. More blood than he would expect from a paper cut, but certainly less than from an execution.

The fire alarm ceased its ear-shattering clamor as he entered the bathroom. He was suddenly conscious of the sound of his own heart, his own breathing. He inhaled deeply once, then again, to calm his system.

The vanity was less tidy. Nobody had been killed here, but there was definitely enough dried blood in and around the sink to freak out the maids.

In the wastebasket, he spotted an emptied package of Band-Aids with a red travel sewing kit, no doubt delivered from room service. The handle and blade of the miniature scissors held bloody fingerprints. A tiny needle, with approximately two feet of attached thread, was coated with organic matter.

Then he saw it. Situated behind the 10-inch makeup mirror on the corner of the vanity, so that it was magnetized to several times its actual size. It had been placed there on purpose, he realized. So that he wouldn't miss it.

A tiny, clear capsule. No larger than a grain of rice. Smooth, except for four tiny extensions jutting out of either end. Like antennae.

The RFID chip. It looked a lot like the one he had injected into Nico's arm.

Carver holstered his gun and called Arunus Roth.

"I need a bio update on Nico Gold," Carver said.

Roth's tone was curt. "Aren't you supposed to be at the extraction point?"

"Just tell me what you see." All Carver could glean from the mission cloud was the chip's location. Roth would be able to see Nico's blood pressure and heart rate.

He waited a moment for Roth to return to the phone. "Judging by his pulse, I'd say he's sleeping. What's going on? Shouldn't he be with you?"

Carver laughed, but not joyously. He was at once devastated and perplexed and concerned and hurt and amazed. The crazy little bastard had actually dug the chip out of his arm and sewed it back up.

How had he managed to deactivate the tentacles? How had he managed to keep up the illusion that it was still in his body? The reading back in McLean was consistent with a still-embedded chip. In a sleeping man, no less.

"Agent Carver?" Roth brought him back to reality. "Is everything all right?"

"Fine."

"The pilot has left the extraction point. What are you going to do?"

Then Carver saw the note. It had been taped to the vanity mirror. It was handwritten. There was no salutation, and no signature. Just a few lines scrawled on hotel notepaper:

> This was fun, but I couldn't chance a trip
> back to the federal pen. I'm sure you'll
> understand. PS – tell yer geeks to fix the java
> in the admin panel. That's where I found the
> vulnerability.

Carver couldn't help but smile. Nico had freed himself the only way he knew how. He had *hacked* his way out of this. He had located a weakness in the mission cloud code, gotten in, and somehow deactivated the chip's tentacles. And at the same time, he had created a ghost chip signature that fooled them all.

Maybe that part shouldn't have surprised him. Nico was the best hacker he had ever seen. But digging it out of his arm? Even though it was tiny, and had been just below the skin, it wasn't exactly a splinter.

A voice crackled in his ear. "Agent Carver?"

"Yeah, Roth. I'm still here."

"Agent Carver, I've got a fix on your location. There's a helipad on the roof of the hotel. Should I see if the pilot can circle back and pick you guys up?"

His thoughts turned back to Nico. Carver couldn't blame him. Even if they could count on Speers' support, going back to the U.S. still had its risks.

He had no idea how Nico was planning on getting out of Rome. But he would find a way. That much was for sure. He was nothing if not resourceful. And a head start was the least Carver could give him. He owed him that much.

But the idea of heading home alone darkened his mood. Days of debriefings awaited him, to say nothing of the domestic intelligence committee. He shuddered at the thought of how pissed the committee chair would be if he knew that Nico had been here in Rome with him.

Roth was back in his ear. "Agent Carver? The helicopter – "

"Cut the pilot loose," Carver finally replied.

"What? Seriously?"

"Tell Julian I'll be in touch."

He hung up and popped the battery out of the phone. Then he entered the living room and sat on the white leather couch. His feet were blistered and his throat was scratchy. No telling how much dust he had inhaled in the tunnels. But he would have to ignore that. He had to stay focused. He had to save his strength.

If he could get down to the street without being spotted, he would be fine. The city was full of hideouts. Its underground was as porous as Swiss cheese. He could lay low until things cooled down. Then he would go to Geneva. He had a safe deposit box there with a fake passport and a little emergency money. He figured he had earned a little time, and he was going to spend it. Not much. Ten days, maybe. Just enough time to get off the grid and recharge. He went out to the balcony, relishing the thought as he began his descent.

Epilogue

Maternity Ward
Olympia, Washington
9 Months Later

Carver stood at the front desk, waiting for the station nurse to get off the phone. He caught sight of himself in the reflection of a glass cabinet. He was in need of a shave. His suit stank of Chinese food, and the shower he had taken this morning hadn't helped.

He had been on the road for 17 days straight without a break. All the leads had been weak, but he was in no position to ignore them. They were all he had now. He had rarely seen anyone disappear so completely.

Somewhere down the hall, some guy was yelling. "*Go hard, honey, go hard!*" The woman's rhythmic grunting reminded him of all the female tennis players on TV.

The station nurse hung up and looked up at him. The weariness in her eyes told him she'd been working a long shift. "I'll need to see ID first."

He handed it to her. She took it and laid it on the photocopy machine, closed the lid and pressed the SCAN button. Her fingernails were two inches long. He hoped she didn't touch any patients with those claws.

"Now what can I do for you?" She said as she handed his identification back to him.

Carver placed both photographs on the counter.

"Looking for a fugitive," he said. "The man's name is Adrian Zhu, but he could be going by another name. He may be with a woman. Her name is Mary Borst. And again, probably using an alias."

The station nurse hovered over the two photographs, putting her finger on Mary Borst's face. "When was she due?"

"Could be anytime. If the baby was premature, she could have been here weeks ago."

The nurse shook her head. "I'll tell you the same thing as I told the last guy. I haven't seen them."

Carver felt his face flush. "Last guy?"

"You're the second person this week to ask about these two. The last guy showed me the same pictures, except he said nothing about the one guy being a fugitive. Said some bad people were looking for them. Said they were in danger."

And those afraid of the Rule of Light will search the Earth for me. As it was in the time of Herod, it will be again. Many innocents will die.

Carver swallowed hard. His mind was tap dancing. "I'll need to report this. What was the guy's name?"

"If you don't know already, maybe you're not supposed to know."

"Was he a fed, like me?"

She hedged, drumming her nails on the counter. Click-click-click-click-click.

"Please." He glanced at her name tag. "Wanda? I have to find the scheduler who made this mistake. You don't really want two or three more people like me coming in and wasting your time, do you?"

She shrugged. "I guess it'd be all right." She went to the file cabinet and opened it. She was back in a minute with a folder full of photocopied identification cards. She flipped through the paper, talking to herself as she tried to remember the exact date.

"Ah-hah," she finally said. "Here is your mystery man."

She placed the paper flat and turned it so Carver could see. He bent down. The name on the ID was Sean O'Rourke. His badge was FBI.

Only he wasn't O'Rourke. He wasn't FBI. And he was no longer assigned to Operation Crossbow.

The man in the photo was Father Thomas Callahan.

AUTHOR'S NOTES

Now for a bit of historical housekeeping. You might be surprised to learn that a number of the shadowy organizations in this book, and more than a few of the events, are based on reality.

For example, the Nazi obsession with Christian antiquities and the occult was not something dreamed up for the *Indiana Jones* movies, nor for the sake of this book. Seven decades have passed since my grandfather, serving with the 70th armored infantry battalion, marched into Germany to end the nightmare of Nazism. And yet one of the lingering mysteries of this dark era in human history is why Himmler, who devoted considerable time to destroying the church despite being raised Catholic, poured so many wartime resources into the pursuit of religious relics.

Nothing I've written in *The Fellowship* will answer that question, as it is a work of fiction. But during my research, I discovered that the truth about many of the people and objects mentioned in this book are far stranger than anything I could have imagined.

In the book, Sebastian Wolf is enrolled at the Reich School, which is where the real children of the Nazi super elite such as Martin Bormann Jr., son of Hitler's private secretary, were groomed for leadership. Incidentally, although Bormann Jr. became a priest and outspoken critic of the Nazi regime until his death in 2013, I want to make clear that none of the characters in the book are actually based on him. For those interested in learning more, I found the documentary series *Hitler's Children* to be an excellent source of interviews with former students.

The organization that Wolf is recruited into, the *Ahnenerbe*, was also real. While routinely publishing an academic journal, anthropological expeditions to Tibet, Antarctica and the Middle East sought to find evidence that virtually all great civilizations were somehow the result of ancient Nordic or Germanic influence. The collection of artifacts was seen as critical to this effort.

Now here's where it gets really weird. In 1940, Heinrich Himmler led a delegation to Spain's Montserrat Abbey in hopes that he would find the Holy Grail that Jesus Christ used during the last supper. Himmler believed that he had found a clue to the relic's whereabouts from the Richard Wagner opera *Parsifal*, which hinted at the grail's location in a castle in the Pyrenees, and had first been performed in nearby Barcelona. According to interviews of a German-speaking monk in *The Desecrated Abbey*, by Montserrat Rico Góngora, Himmler believed that the Grail would give the German army supernatural powers that would win the war.

While Himmler never found the Holy Grail, he had already managed to get his hands on another mystical object – the so-called Spear of Destiny. Also known as the Holy Lance, the spear was believed to have been used by Longinus, the partially blind centurion, to pierce Jesus' side at the crucifixion. Centuries later, Roman Emporer Constantine believed that carrying this lance into battle rendered his army invincible. As legend has it, the spear was subsequently possessed by the Holy Roman Empire during its reign in what is now Germany and used in coronation ceremonies. Although it was moved to Vienna in 1796, Germany eventually reclaimed the prize, along with the crown jewels, during its annexation of Austria in 1938. As we all know, possessing the lance didn't win the war for Germany. The relic remained in the Bavarian town of Nuremburg until it was found by the invading American army in 1945 and returned to Vienna, where it can be seen today.

In *The Fellowship*, Himmler travels to occupied Paris in search of the Holy Ossuary. A shootout ensues inside Notre

Dame Cathedral, which purports to hold many holy relics, including reeds from the Crown of Thorns and nails from the True Cross.

Anyone visiting Notre Dame today might be shocked to learn that an actual gun battle occurred there in 1944, and was even caught on film. The incident started when French General De Gaulle led his men and thousands of civilians to reclaim Notre Dame from German hands. The shocking footage shows sniper fire raining down on the general and his freedom fighters in the square right in front of the cathedral. According to BBC accounts, the assault raged inside Notre Dame as well. Although the general escaped unharmed, many others weren't so lucky. For the curious, you won't find anything on this in the church's little gift shop, so you'll have to find the footage online or in a library.

So did the Nazis really believe that possessing these mystical antiquities and others would lead to a German victory? After a great deal of research, my feeling is that Himmler, for one, really did believe it. His belief in mysticism, the occult and reincarnation is well-documented. His personal masseuse, Felix Kersten, wrote in his memoirs that Himmler believed himself to be the reincarnation of a dead German king.

The Fellowship chapter in which Wolf is taken to the secret crypt containing the relocated bodies of ancient and contemporary German rulers, is closely based on fact. Among the most curious of the occupying American army's finds was a Nazi crypt located deep within a salt mine. The crypt contained priceless Christian art, Germanic antiquities and most shocking of all – the relocated bodies of several nobles, including Frederick the Great and Frederick Wilhelm I. Among these was an empty coffin bearing Hitler's name. A thoroughly creepy eyewitness account of this find can be found in the March, 1950 issue of *Life Magazine*.

Perhaps more disturbingly, Himmler also hoped to find evidence that Jesus was of Aryan descent. The mythology he attempted to create around this idea was convenient to say the least, in that it helped justify the regime's extreme social views, including the persecution of the Jews and the destruction of the church. The first account of this concept being discussed within the Nazi inner circle can be found in *The Voice of Destruction,* written by former cabinet member Hermann Rauschning prior to the start of the war.

In *The Fellowship*, Rauschning's book is mentioned as contraband because it really was. In it, all sorts of explosive private conversations among senior German leadership are revealed. For example, Hitler ominously says that the clergy will be made to dig their own graves, which they were, both literally and figuratively. But when someone suggests the idea of the Aryan Jesus, he is dismissive, saying, "Do you really believe the masses will ever be Christian again? Nonsense! That tale is finished…They will replace the cross with our swastika."

Still, Himmler continued to pursue this idea for years afterward, even throughout the war years. According to Góngora, the belief that both Jacob and Jesus were Aryan drove him to search for the grail in Spain. Obviously, it was utter nonsense.

Moving on, it seems that the Vatican has never publicly acknowledged the existence of its intelligence agency. And yet, we have centuries of books in multiple languages detailing its activities in juicy detail. The Black Order is one of the more well-documented Vatican espionage organizations. Olimpia Maidalchini (1591-1657), the sister-in-law of Pope Innocent X, is reported to have not only secretly controlled the pontiff, but also created The Black Order, a unit of assassins that ruthlessly destroyed the Vatican's enemies.

Let me say for the record that modern Jesuits do all sorts of good deeds and come from all walks of life. Many are incredible teachers. However, many early Jesuits were soldiers. And although the order was originally recognized in Venice, they did not endear themselves to the city, making the Piazza San Marco the notorious epicenter of the brutal *strappado*, or rope torture.

Have I taken great liberties with all these factual nuggets? Definitely. Such is the power of myth, and such is the nature of entertainment.

Interested in learning more about what really happened? In addition to the films, books and magazines I've already noted, I also strongly recommend that those interested in learning more about these subjects read *La Popessa: The Controversial Biography of Sister Pascalina, the Most Powerful Woman in Vatican History*. Also, *Jesus and the Ossuaries*, by Craig E. Evans, is a great anthropological perspective on the Holy Land. Also, the *Gnostic Gospels*, by Elaine Pagels is a terrific explainer of evolving views on resurrection throughout the ages.

Characters

Blake Carver, intelligence operative.
Haley Ellis, intelligence operative.
Sebastian Wolf, CEO, Fellowship World Initiative.
Heinz Lang, Head of Vatican Intelligence.
Adrian Zhu, CEO, LifeEmberz.
Father Thomas Callahan, double agent.
Nico Gold, fugitive cybercriminal.
Nathan Drucker, journalist.

THE FEDS

Eva Hudson, President of the United States.
Julian Speers, Director of National Intelligence.
Claire Shipmont, Deputy Director, ODNI.
Arunus Roth, associate project coordinator.
Rand Preston, senator.
Mary Borst, assistant to Senator Preston.
Chad Fordham, FBI Director.
Hank Bowers, FBI section chief.
Will Hollis, FBI special agent.

INTERNATIONAL

Seven Mansfield, MI6 operative.
Sam Prichard, MI6 operative.
Lord Nils Gish, MP, Labour Party leader.
Lars, security specialist.
Dr. Dane Mitchell, life partner to Vera Borst.
Vera Borst, mother of Mary, UN Undersecretary General.
Suk Kenyatta, UN envoy.
Antonio Tesla, detective, Rome Police.

Characters from the 1940s

Sebastian Wolf, Reich School cadet.
Heinz Lang, Reich School cadet.
Mrs. Lang, mother of Heinz.
Gertrude Wolf, mother of Sebastian.
Hans Wolf, brother of Sebastian.

THE AHNENERBE ELITE

Nagel, Commandant of Wewelsburg Castle.
Dr. Rudolph Seiler, authority on ancient Nordic society.
Bruno Fleischer, racial anthropologist.
Dr. Paul Ritter, blood researcher.
Dr. Gustav Hahn, professor of racial studies.

THE CLERGY

Father LeFevre, priest, Notre Dame Cathedral.
Father Leo Kruger, priest.
Dr. Enzo Marchesi, personal physician to Pope Pius XII.
Sister Klara Kohler, secretary to Pope Pius XII.

THE SOLDIERS

Albert Hoppe, Reich School cadet.
Beck, Reich School drill instructor.
Hoffman, Himmler's chauffeur.
Zimmer, Gestapo detective.
Adler/Bauer/Kalb/Matthias – Ahnenerbe assault unit.

THE MISSION PLAYLIST

 William listened to these songs while writing *The Fellowship*. To see the entire list, follow William's playlist, "The Mission," on Spotify!

1. Tripwire, by Brand New Heavies
2. Black Venom, by the Budos Band
3. Genesis, by Justice
4. If They Move, Kill 'Em, by Primal Scream
5. Uzi, by El Michaels Affair
6. Lights Out, by Menaham Street Band
7. Starfighter, by Hypnotic Brass Ensemble
8. The National Anthem, by Radiohead
9. Eurocrime! by Calibro 35
10. Web of Deception, by Thievery Corporation

William adds new songs regularly. To be notified when he makes changes to the list, follow William and subscribe to "The Mission" on Spotify.

READ BOOK 1 IN THE BLAKE CARVER SERIES

LINE OF SUCCESSION

The nation is rocked by a series of high-level assassinations so devastating that the magnitude is hidden from public view. As the Pentagon begins retaliating against suspected radicals abroad, Blake Carver soon realizes that his job isn't as easy as hunting down a group of foreign extremists. **This war** isn't about religion, foreign policy or oil. It's up to Carver to stop a powerful adversary seizing control of the planet's most precious resource: water.

- FOR MORE INFORMATION -

WILLIAMTYREEBOOKS.COM

Made in the USA
Lexington, KY
22 March 2017